PRAISE FOR
J. R. WARD AND HER
BLACK DAGGER
BROTHERHOOD SERIES

"J. R. Ward's urban fantasy romance series is so popular, I don't think there's a reader today who hasn't at least heard of the Black Dagger Brotherhood."

—*USA Today*

"Impressive."

—*The New York Times Book Review*

"Frighteningly addictive."

—*Publishers Weekly*

"J. R. Ward is the undisputed queen of her genre. Bar none. Long live the queen."

—Steve Berry, *New York Times* bestselling author

"Sharp, sexy, and funny."

—*The New York Review of Books*

"J. R. Ward's unique band of brothers is to die for. I love this series!"

—Suzanne Brockmann, *New York Times* bestselling author

"J. R. Ward is one of the finest writers out there—in any genre. She's in a league of her own."

—Sarah J. Maas, #1 *New York Times* bestselling author

"Ward is a master of her craft."

—*New York Journal of Books*

"Tautly written, wickedly sexy, and just plain fun."

—Lisa Gardner, #1 *New York Times* bestselling author

J.R. WARD

LASSITER

• THE BLACK DAGGER •
BROTHERHOOD SERIES

POCKET BOOKS
New York   London   Toronto   Sydney   New Delhi

Pocket Books
An Imprint of Simon & Schuster, Inc.
1230 Avenue of the Americas
New York, NY 10020

This book is a work of fiction. Any references to historical events, real people, or real places are used fictitiously. Other names, characters, places, and events are products of the author's imagination, and any resemblance to actual events or places or persons, living or dead, is entirely coincidental.

First Pocket Books paperback edition November 2023

POCKET BOOKS and colophon are registered trademarks of Simon & Schuster, Inc.

For information about special discounts for bulk purchases, please contact Simon & Schuster Special Sales at 1-866-506-1949 or business@simonandschuster.com.

The Simon & Schuster Speakers Bureau can bring authors to your live event. For more information or to book an event, contact the Simon & Schuster Speakers Bureau at 1-866-248-3049 or visit our website at www.simonspeakers.com.

Interior design by Davina Mock-Maniscalco

Manufactured in the United States of America

10 9 8 7 6 5 4 3 2 1

ISBN 978-1-9821-8004-1
ISBN 978-1-9821-8006-5 (ebook)

Dedicated to:
Wrath, who almost twenty years ago came
and showed me his world.
Lassiter's story, just like all the ones that have
been or will ever be . . .
. . . starts and finishes with you.

GLOSSARY OF TERMS AND PROPER NOUNS

ahstrux nohtrum (n.) Private guard with license to kill who is granted his or her position by the King.

ahvenge (v.) Act of mortal retribution, carried out typically by a male loved one.

Black Dagger Brotherhood (pr. n.) Highly trained vampire warriors who protect their species against the Lessening Society. As a result of selective breedings within the race, Brothers possess immense physical and mental strength, as well as rapid healing capabilities. They are not siblings for the most part, and are inducted into the Brotherhood upon nomination by the Brothers. Aggressive, self-reliant, and secretive by nature, they are the subjects of legend and objects of reverence within the vampire world. They may be killed only by the most serious of wounds, e.g., a gunshot or stab to the heart, etc.

blood slave (n.) Male or female vampire who has been subjugated to serve the blood needs of another. The practice of keeping blood slaves has been outlawed.

the Chosen (pr. n.) Female vampires who had been bred to serve the Scribe Virgin. In the past, they were spiritually rather than temporally focused, but that changed with the ascendance of the final Primale, who freed them from the Sanctuary. With the Scribe Virgin removing herself from her role, they are completely autonomous and learning to live on earth. They do continue to meet the blood needs of unmated members of the Brotherhood, as well as Brothers who cannot feed from their *shellans* or injured fighters.

chrih (n.) Symbol of honorable death in the Old Language.

cohntehst (n.) Conflict between two males competing for the right to be a female's mate.

Dhunhd (pr. n.) Hell.

doggen (n.) Member of the servant class within the vampire world. *Doggen* have old, conservative traditions about service to their superiors, following a formal code of dress and behavior. They are able to go out during the day, but they age relatively quickly. Life expectancy is approximately five hundred years.

ehros (n.) A Chosen trained in the matter of sexual arts.

exhile dhoble (n.) The evil or cursed twin, the one born second.

the Fade (pr. n.) Non-temporal realm where the dead reunite with their loved ones and pass eternity.

First Family (pr. n.) The King and Queen of the vampires, and any children they may have.

ghardian (n.) Custodian of an individual. There are varying degrees of *ghardians*, with the most powerful being that of a *sehcluded* female.

glymera (n.) The social core of the aristocracy, roughly equivalent to Regency England's *ton*.

hellren (n.) Male vampire who has been mated to a female. Males may take more than one female as mate.

hyslop (n. or v.) Term referring to a lapse in judgment, typically resulting in the compromise of the mechanical operations of a vehicle or otherwise motorized conveyance of some kind. For example, leaving one's keys in one's car as it is parked outside the family home overnight, whereupon said vehicle is stolen.

leahdyre (n.) A person of power and influence.

leelan (adj. or n.) A term of endearment loosely translated as "dearest one."

Lessening Society (pr. n.) Order of slayers convened by the Omega for the purpose of eradicating the vampire species. Ruled by his resurrected son, Lash.

lesser (n.) De-souled human who targets vampires for extermination as a member of the Lessening Society.

Lessers must be stabbed through the chest in order to be killed; otherwise they are ageless. They do not eat or drink and are impotent. Over time, their hair, skin, and irises lose pigmentation until they are blond, blushless, and pale eyed. They smell like baby powder. Inducted into the society by the Omega, or now, his son.

lewlhen (n.) Gift.

lheage (n.) A term of respect used by a sexual submissive to refer to their dominant.

Lhenihan (pr. n.) A mythic beast renowned for its sexual prowess. In modern slang, refers to a male of preternatural size and sexual stamina.

lys (n.) Torture tool used to remove the eyes.

mahmen (n.) Mother. Used both as an identifier and a term of affection.

mhis (n.) The masking of a given physical environment; the creation of a field of illusion.

nalla (n., f.) or *nallum* (n., m.) Beloved.

needing period (n.) Female vampire's time of fertility, generally lasting for two days and accompanied by intense sexual cravings. Occurs approximately five years after a female's transition and then once a decade thereafter. All males respond to some degree if they are around a female in her need. It can be a dangerous time, with conflicts and fights breaking out between competing males, particularly if the female is not mated.

newling (n.) A virgin.

the Omega (pr. n.) Malevolent, mystical figure who targeted the vampires for extinction out of resentment directed toward the Scribe Virgin. Existed in a non-temporal realm and had extensive powers, though not the power of creation. Now eradicated.

phearsom (adj.) Term referring to the potency of a male's sexual organs. Literal translation something close to "worthy of entering a female."

Princeps (pr. n.) Highest level of the vampire aristocracy, second only to members of the First Family or the Scribe Virgin's Chosen. Must be born to the title; it may not be conferred.

pyrocant (n.) Refers to a critical weakness in an individual. The weakness can be internal, such as an addiction, or external, such as a lover.

rahlman (n.) Savior.

rythe (n.) Ritual manner of asserting honor granted by one who has offended another. If accepted, the offended chooses a weapon and strikes the offender, who presents him- or herself without defenses.

the Scribe Virgin (pr. n.) Mystical force who previously was counselor to the King as well as the keeper of vampire archives and the dispenser of privileges. Existed in a non-temporal realm and had extensive powers, but has recently stepped down and given her station to another. Capable of a single act of creation, which she expended to bring the vampires into existence.

sehclusion (n.) Status conferred by the King upon a female of the aristocracy as a result of a petition by the female's family. Places the female under the sole direction of her *ghardian*, typically the eldest male in her household. Her *ghardian* then has the legal right to determine all manner of her life, restricting at will any and all interactions she has with the world.

shellan (n.) Female vampire who has been mated to a male. Females generally do not take more than one mate due to the highly territorial nature of bonded males.

symphath (n.) Subspecies within the vampire race characterized by the ability and desire to manipulate emotions in others (for the purposes of an energy exchange), among other traits. Historically, they have been discriminated against and, during certain eras, hunted by vampires. They are near extinction.

talhman (n.) The evil side of an individual. A dark stain on the soul that requires expression if it is not properly expunged.

the Tomb (pr. n.) Sacred vault of the Black Dagger Brotherhood. Used as a ceremonial site as well as a storage facility for the jars of *lessers*. Ceremonies performed there include inductions, funerals, and disciplinary actions against Brothers. No one may enter except for members of the Brotherhood, the Scribe Virgin, or candidates for induction.

trahyner (n.) Word used between males of mutual respect and affection. Translated loosely as "beloved friend."

transition (n.) Critical moment in a vampire's life when he or she transforms into an adult. Thereafter, he or she must drink the blood of the opposite sex to survive and is unable to withstand sunlight. Occurs generally in the mid-twenties. Some vampires do not survive their transitions, males in particular. Prior to their transitions, vampires are physically weak, sexually unaware and unresponsive, and unable to dematerialize.

vampire (n.) Member of a species separate from that of *Homo sapiens*. Vampires must drink the blood of the opposite sex to survive. Human blood will keep them alive, though the strength does not last long. Following their transitions, which occur in their mid-twenties, they are unable to go out into sunlight and must feed from the vein regularly. Vampires cannot "convert" humans through a bite or transfer of blood, though they are in rare cases able to breed with the other species. Vampires can dematerialize at will, though they must be able to calm themselves and concentrate to do so and may not carry anything heavy with them. They are able to strip the memories of humans, provided such memories are short-term. Some vampires are able to read minds. Life expectancy is upward of a thousand years, or in some cases, even longer.

wahlker (n.) An individual who has died and returned to the living from the Fade. They are accorded great respect and are revered for their travails.

whard (n.) Equivalent of a godfather or godmother to an individual.

CHAPTER ONE

11287 Gordon Memorial Parkway
Caldwell, New York

Does this make my ass look big?"

As the question was tossed out all casual, like it made any damned sense, Eddie Blackhawk opened his mouth to answer. Then he shook his head. "I'm not sure how to respond to that."

"Come on." His best friend, Adrian Vogel, motioned through the window of the gray-and-black Mini Cooper. "Be honest."

For a split second, an image of the guy looking up with expectation caught and held in Eddie's mind, a fishhook memory that was unnecessary after the centuries they'd spent together: Ad was a hard-core handsome type, all the Hugh Jackman anyone could want in the tall and dark department, just paired up with a Claire's boutique's worth of silver piercings on the trailheads of his nose, his lower lip, his outer ears. He'd shaved his head recently—because he'd bought a Manscaped trimmer on account of the Pete Davidson ad and he didn't have anything else to shave—and his hair was already growing back in, a shadow over his skull. His clothes were black and so was his jacket. So were his weapons, although like his naughty bits, they were covered.

"Hello?" the other fallen angel prompted. "What do you think of me and the car?"

"I'm amazed you can fit your posterior region in it." Eddie glanced around the wilted dealership. "Why are we here again?"

"Ass." Adrian got out, his heavily muscled body expanding to its customary height and width like it was reinflating after a vacuum-packing. "You can curse, you know. It's not going to kill you."

Considering they were both immortals, the subject of what could unalive them was moot—as was any practical opinion about this shoebox-sized toy that was being marketed as roadworthy. And while Eddie glanced around for what felt like the hundredth time, he would have appreciated an answer to his own question: What the hell were they doing in this place? Between the fake wood paneling, the faded pictures of eighties-era cars going all airborne around tight turns, and the for-sale stock that looked like candidates for parts harvesting, he felt like they'd been sucked back four decades and Kate Bush should be piped in as a new release, not as a throwback soundtrack on Netflix.

Then again, they'd made their deal with God, hadn't they. And with all the progress they hadn't been making over the last three years on their mission, why *not* end up here? It was no more directed or random than any other place in Caldwell.

"Hi," a quiet voice said, "can I answer some questions about the Mini for you?"

Eddie's eyes shifted over and then had to move down, way down. The brunette woman who had approached was barely over five feet tall, and given her air of exhaustion, he guessed her age was anywhere between twenty-five and forty. Like the other salespeople, she was wearing a gold plaid suit jacket over her slacks, but the thing was a tent on her, to the point where she'd rolled up the sleeves.

"I think we're good," Eddie murmured. "Thanks, though."

She reached up and tapped the safety pin that was holding the right side of her glasses together—as if she were worried that like the screw it replaced, the thing was going to fail on her.

"Well, if you need anything, I'm—"

"I got this, Steph."

A man with a porn mustache, a full plaid suit—not just the jacket—and a hockey-player elbow pushed her out of the way. "Bud James, how we doing? I'm the owner, you've seen me on TV."

A proud finger swung around to a life-sized cutout of himself. Which had clearly been slimmed down with filters. "That's me, your buddy in the car business. Nice suit, right? Great car, right? Let's take it for a test drive."

Eddie tilted to the side. The woman who'd been moved out of the way was backing off, her soft-soled shoes squeaking on the scuffed blue and white floor tile. As she tugged at her jacket, she took a deep breath and faced away across the showroom's collection of buffed-up beaters. Another couple was coming through the door and she hitched her shoulders before intercepting them.

"How we doin'?" Bud James put his face in Eddie's. "So how about a test drive."

Ad, who'd been circling the Mini like he wanted to date it, came over, and for a split second, you had to wonder whether Bud was going to have a problem with all the Goth.

Naaah. Bud didn't seem to mind. Then again, the guy would probably sell cars to a demon if they had the cash or credit.

"No reason to test-drive, I'll take it."

Bud smiled like a billboard and called over his shoulder, "Ring the bell, Mabel!"

As an elderly woman with bright blue eye shadow creaked to her feet at the front desk and started clanging like her life depended on it, two other plaid-clad, Bud-club salesmen pumped their fists.

"Let's go do your paperwork," Bud said as he smacked a hand on Ad's shoulder. "Have to say, when I saw ya coming, I figured you'd be going for the Charger over there."

Eddie glanced over at the blacked-out, block-fronted fist's worth of steel, glass, and tires. "That's a nice car."

"We'll sell it to you, how 'bout that?"

When Bud went to pull the clap crap on Eddie, the fallen angel narrowed his eyes—and the man froze in the half-slap position and backed off. "I see you're a reserved man. I respect that, I totally respect that, yup? C'mon."

Ad went jazz hands in excitement. Then he hopped and skipped into Bud's office, looking like the Grim Reaper on a sugar high.

As a ripple of warning tickled Eddie's instincts for no good reason, he looked across at the saleswoman. She had a fragile hope on her face as she took the couple over to a minivan.

"C'mon," Ad called out. "Let's do this."

Bud's office was a smaller version of the showroom, same decor, same worn-out time warp. On the wall behind the desk, a banner read "YOU'VE GOT A BUDDY IN THE CAR BUSINESS," the slogan spelled out on a blue-and-white background, with two bobblehead images of Bud anchoring the announcement.

"—loan application, why don't we." Bud sat at his desk, a plaid king on a paper throne. "I'll just do a credit check—"

"Cash," Ad said as he parked it as well. "I'll give you fifteen."

Well, if that didn't shut Bud up. But he recovered quickly, jacking the waistband of his Rodney Dangerfields up over his paunch. "Well, now. You're a good customer, I can tell. But I don't think I can go that low. I gotta keep my lights on—"

"Fifteen thousand." Ad outed a wad from the pocket of his leather jacket. "And you'll take care of the tax."

As the counting began, orderly piles of ten hundred-dollar bills lined up in front of Bud and the man got really quiet. When the last dole-out finished, and Ad sat back and smiled, it was clear that the asking price was going to be adjusted downward. Nothing like a little liquidity to tilt the course of negotiations.

"It's Stephanie Kowalski's deal," Eddie said in a low voice. "She sold us the car."

Bud's eyes shot over. "I'm sorry?"

"You're giving her the credit for the sale."

"Are we redoing history, son?" When Eddie just stared at the man, Bud cleared his throat. "I don't like people telling me my business."

Eddie stepped up to the desk and swept the money into his hand. "Come on, Adrian. CarMax has fifty of these online—"

"Now, hold on there." Bud jumped to his feet. "Let's not be rash."

"Call Stephanie in. Tell her the good news and I'll give you the cash."

When Bud looked at Ad, as if he expected some backup, the fallen angel just shrugged. "What my boy says."

Bud muttered under his breath as he went to the open door and leaned around the jamb. "Steph. Get in here."

◆ ◆ ◆

Twenty minutes later, Adrian was having his picture taken standing between Real Bud and Cutout Bud, the Mini Cooper was out front in the open air, and Eddie was holding the key while petting the Charger's hood. As he tried on for size what it would be like to get behind the muscle car's wheel and drive off, he eyed the plate glass window that ran down the facade of the showroom. He imagined that the shower of shards would fall like diamonds, gleaming and sparkling as they hit the checkerboard floor and scattered in their liberation.

"Well, you get your friend to c'mon back for that Charger!" Bud exclaimed as he clapped his hands. "Mabel over there needs her exercise, doncha, Mabel."

Over at her desk, Mabel nodded and pumped an elderly grip like she was honking the horn of a mobility scooter.

Bud leaned in and lowered his voice. "She's an important member of the team."

"For sure," Ad said as he stuck his palm out. "Thanks, Bud."

"No, thank *you*."

Adrian started for the door like he was a politician, raising a wave to the plaid salesmen, nodding at Mabel, pounding his pec and flashing the peace sign to an oil-smudged mechanic in the corner. Eddie just walked out the side door and shook his head at the Mini Cooper. The thing had tires the size of bagels and a back hatch with all the room of a carry-on bag—

"Thank you so much."

Eddie glanced over his shoulder. Stephanie Anne Kowalski—thirty-four, married, two kids, husband up on drunk driving charges, mother in a nursing home after a stroke, primary residence teetering on the verge of foreclosure—had come out of the dealership, and as she approached him, her hands came together at her sternum, as if she were praying.

"I just wanted to tell you how much I appreciate . . ." Her words trailed off as her brown eyes focused on something just over his head. As her stare grew wondrous, she made the sign of the cross over her heart. "You're an angel."

He smiled at her gently and ignored the adoration. "You were the one who approached us. It's only fair—"

"You have a halo."

Eddie frowned. "No, I don't."

Her head slowly turned to Adrian, who had paused with one leg in the Mini. With a shaking forefinger, she pointed in his direction.

"He's an angel, too," she breathed, an expression of awe rejuvenating her.

Eddie glanced in the direction of his best friend. Nothing was showing anywhere around the guy—but in any event, a human shouldn't have sensed it even if Ad wasn't camo'ing his essence.

Time to get out of here. "Goodbye, Stephanie, you take care now—"

The grip on his forearm wasn't strong, but the contact arrested him, a strange sizzle shooting into his bones and coursing throughout his body.

As he looked at the woman ... the features of her face disappeared, the broken glasses, the eyes, nose, and mouth, smudging out, nothing but a flesh-colored, oval void left where they had been. And then came the voice.

It was nothing that Eddie had ever heard before, a sweet singing soprano as well as a deep resonant alto, the syllables weaving in and out of a harmony that struck him in the chest.

Great Bear Mountain.

As soon as the words registered in his mind, the spell was broken by a clap of thunder so loud that all of the salesmen inside the dealership ducked and covered their heads, and even Ad dove into the Mini for safety.

The woman's body stiffened with such force that her arms and legs shot straight out from her torso and she fell back, flat as a pancake. On reflex, Eddie grabbed her before she hit the sidewalk, and lowered her carefully onto the ground—and he had a sixth sense about what was coming next. Sure enough, the seizure that struck her was so violent, it was as if she were a tap dancer, every part of her in movement, things slapping, clapping, flapping on the concrete.

Over at the Mini, Ad reemerged, his body surging forward as he started to run over—

Eddie's palm stopped him in mid-rush, and when

he was certain his favorite firebrand wasn't going to continue to come on strong, he rubbed his palms together, and hovered his hands over the woman's chest—

Energy sizzled up, called into Eddie's corporeal form, the licking, sparking charge entering him and making his eyes roll back. Distant voices chattered around him, swirling in a spin that his brain told him was about his perception, not any physical rotation, and yet suddenly he was the earth and they were the sun and—

"I got you."

From out of the chaos, Adrian was a constant, their roles briefly reversed, the wild child becoming the calm in the center of the storm. Strong arms gathered Eddie up and broke the connection before he, too, fell onto the concrete.

Flickering lights now, and he wondered why the sky had a short in it. Except no, it was just his lids going haywire.

Man, there was a lot of plaid around him all of a sudden.

Before he could do the math on that one, Ad's face appeared right above his own, the angel's piercings seeming to sparkle with all the blinking. "It's okay, just breathe with me. Eddie, I need you to breathe—my guy, you're not breathing. Do it with me."

As his best friend held him tight, Eddie followed the instruction because he didn't have a B plan, and with his mind shorting out, he wasn't going to come up with one anytime soon. Part of his problem was that it wasn't just about the energy he'd taken into himself. It was that he knew what the message meant.

Great Bear Mountain.

Three years. They had been searching in vain for so long, their mission a failure, their target eluding them. And now a direction had been served, likely because the Creator had lost any faith they could do the job He'd given them.

They had to go to . . . Great Bear.

Next to him, Stephanie Anne Kowalski sat up and looked around at the plaid-clads who'd come out of the dealership.

"You're all right," Ad murmured as Eddie likewise hauled his torso off the sidewalk. "Yup, you're okay—"

"I know where Lassiter is."

The other fallen angel grew perfectly still.

Then Ad glanced back at the Mini with resignation. "Well, at least I know why I brought us here. And, hey, now we have wheels."

CHAPTER TWO

10.8 miles north of Great Bear Mountain
Adirondack Park, Upstate New York

In the gathering dusk, the mountain air smelled of pine and kindling buds, the scents carried on a lazy, cold draft that trickled down the elevation, weaving around and over boulders and branches, weeds and wildlife, the frigidity of space encroaching upon the earth. Across the valley, the sun's very last rays created a hearth in a juncture of peaks, the intersection of surging topographies a cup of palms in which the light was nestling for a brief, dying time, only embers now, no warmth to speak of.

As Lassiter, the fallen angel, emerged from the cave, he thought of McDonald's.

Drawn by the finality of the peach glow, he walked

out to a keyhole view of the splendor, tossing a small satchel back and forth between his hands. Like the golden arches memory that was suddenly dogging him, the sight before his eyes was a distillation of experience rather than something currently sensed, a refraction of the world as opposed to that which was in-the-moment sensed and seen.

In his current frame of mind, the present was as the past brought to mind, a memory that was subject to faulty interpretation and accuracy.

Had it been a Big Mac and fries? he wondered idly. *Or a Quarter Pounder?*

Those specifics were gone now, but he had most of the rest of the details of what had started him on the path that led here, to this night, this view. Three years ago he had been sent by the Creator to rescue the Black Dagger Brother Tohrment, son of Hharm, from grief. The mission had been an oxymoron combination of promotion and punishment. Lassiter hadn't been looking for the former, and had had too much of the latter, but in any event, his opinion about it all was as irrelevant as where the assignment took him. The Creator had had a plan for him and, like destiny, hadn't cared about what he thought.

He'd had free will, however, so he'd gone to the golden arches first, in a little thumb-of-the-nose at the Big Guy. Yeah, but then he'd realized food was probably the best place to start anyway. Tohr had been AWOL in the Adirondacks, living off the blood of forest animals—and Jesus, who didn't need a hamburger on a good day, much less after going *Naked and Afraid* for how long?

Unfortunately, he'd eaten most of the fries on the way in to the brother.

Hey, he was an angel, not a saint. And that had always been his problem. But his rescue had worked. After a time, the fighter had emerged from the mourning of his murdered *shellan* and found a new life, solidly back in his old role as the King's second-in-command. The calmest and most level-headed of the Black Dagger Brotherhood remained scarred at the soul level, but he had carried on, as survivors had to, as the living must do.

With the job done and dusted, Lassiter had figured he'd be called back home, but not all that long thereafter, a second promotion had been offered by a third party that Lassiter sure as hell hadn't seen coming. As with the Tohr thing, he hadn't had any interest in the job, but when the Scribe Virgin told you she was turning the vampire species over to you, and good luck with all those souls and their bright ideas? Well, there you had it. Your time card was punched . . . for infinity, or whenever you gave up the job, whichever came first.

Lassiter stared out over the valley below. He'd assumed he'd last a little longer than this. Like, at least five years. Ten. Fifty. A century.

Except here was the problem. When he'd arrived on the scene in Caldwell, he hadn't particularly cared about the people, and that had made things really easy because the outcomes hadn't mattered as much. Besides, the TV had been good, and he'd enjoyed a non-lucrative but highly satisfying side hustle of irritating the ever-living shit out of Vishous, son of the Bloodletter.

Smooth sailing. Until then, sure as a case of the flu, the feelings had crept up on him, a contagion caught from the courage and the loyalty around him. Before he knew it, he'd started to worry about the vampires in that old stone mansion. Worry had led to motivation. Motivation had led to him blurring lines, bending rules . . . breaking the non-interference contract the Creator held all angels to.

Destiny, after all, was—or should be—a game of solitaire. Each individual had their spread to play, their own choices to make, and nobody else was supposed to be slipping them extra cards so that they could get un-stuck when that pesky three of hearts just wouldn't come up in the stock.

At first, it had been little things, but like all bad hab-its, he'd gotten more and more comfortable with violat-ing his principles.

And now he was here.

Kind of ironic, really, that doing what he was explicitly not supposed to had culminated in him breaking himself.

Memories of the demon Devina barged in, and as he shriveled in his own skin, the irony wasn't lost. Way back when, he'd gotten in trouble in the first place for dabbling with sexual expression. His higher order of angels were not supposed to bang, and even though he'd been careful to never, ever let things get to actual pene-tration, his I-did-not-have-sex-with-that-woman had ultimately failed to get him off the hook.

Who knew he'd end up saving his virginity for a demon.

To save the soul of a male of worth, he'd given his body over to Devina. And now he was here, standing alone in front of a dying sunset, trying to remember details about a McDonald's order that was three years old so he could avoid thinking about all the people he was letting down . . . as well as the one vampire he missed with a yearning and sadness that was worse than all the humiliation and disgust he was carrying around from his time with the demon.

A different image came to him, of a female with hair that had the gleam of polished sterling silver, and eyes that were the same shimmering color, and a face that tilted up at him . . . as all around at her feet, wild flowers bloomed in a swirl even though it was not the season.

Why bring your girl a bouquet when you could give her a meadow full of blooms? he'd thought at the time. Especially if you were saying goodbye.

He could still picture his Rahvyn's delight as she had twirled about, and in this, he had every single detail with pristine clarity, her hair shining as it spooled out into the moonlight, her body lithe in her civilian clothes, her smile not shy but a revelation of feminine beauty and mystery. She had been in his heart before that moment. Seeing her that night? She had entered his immortal soul.

Then again, maybe that had been less about his gift and her reaction to it . . . and more that he had known they were parting. Forever. 'Cuz even if they were in the same room after that evening? He was still going to be farther than the outer bounds of the heavens from her.

And yup, in the aftermath of the demon's treatment, he'd traded places with Tohr. Now he was the one out in the woods alone, mourning a female he'd bonded with because he couldn't have her. The fact that his female was still alive didn't mean anything.

There was no way he could be with her now. For one, he needed to protect Rahvyn from the demon. The farther he stayed away from her, the better, so he didn't make a target out of his female. For another . . . he was not who he had once been.

Lassiter glanced down at his corporeal form and wondered how something that didn't really exist could affect him so much. This image of a body, which he chose to inhabit when it suited his purposes, was not *him*. He was an entity, rather than anything mortal. Yet what had been done to him lingered, the violence and the contamination transmitted through that which was an illusion into that which was real.

All he wanted was to return to the great ether, just disappear into a flush of energy that had no consciousness whatsoever. And the only reason he hadn't followed through on the immolation?

He thought of the Black Dagger Brotherhood, the King . . . their families and *doggen*. The civilians. The Chosen who had been liberated.

His Rahvyn.

For the species' benefit, he needed to rally. He needed to get in gear. He needed to pull up his bootstraps, get motivated, get back into the game, address the ball, find his stance, assume the position.

The pep talk didn't work. It hadn't worked.

He was beginning to worry it wasn't going to.

Crossing his arms over his chest, his eyes refocused on the sliver of glow at the horizon. There was almost none of the sunset's illumination left, and he found the parallel apt. There was not much of him left, either.

On that note, he looked down at the satchel he'd brought out with him. Opening the neck, he poured some of the contents into his palm. The tangle of golden links glowed, even in the gathering darkness, and he moved the weight around. He'd worn the necklaces, bracelets, and earrings for years because there was something of the sun in gold, and when he hadn't been able to get outside to bathe in the solar stuff directly, he'd liked to have the warmth against his skin. Plus, given that his wedding jesses had been stolen some time ago, maybe there had been a little making up for that on his part.

More than a little.

He'd taken all his gold off before he'd turned his body over to the demon. Now? He wasn't putting it back on. Ever. The shit would probably turn black.

Funneling the links back into the little bag and cinching the tie, he wound up a pitch and sent the satchel flying into the view's anonymity. Just as it was silhouetted against that faint hearth of a sunset, he blew it to hell and gone with a burst of energy, the sparkling explosion like a fall of stars.

Enough, he thought. No one was coming to save him. Saviors did not get rescued.

He needed to go back to the Brotherhood, to Caldwell, to the species that he had agreed to oversee. Enough of this self-imposed purgatory—

That image of Rahvyn's enchanting face intruded once again, sandblasting his best intentions away.

He'd only held her once. When he'd told her goodbye.

Something hit his hand, and he glanced down. The silver droplet glistened and the heat that registered was the first sensation he had felt since . . .

Well, since he'd come here to this mountain, at any rate.

Shaking the tear off, he pulled a swipe under his eyes and then regarded the pads of his fingers. What came out of him when he was in pain was like mercury, the reflective liquid smooth and clingy, preferring to find a stasis point that was perfectly round if it could gather enough of itself.

Turning away, he walked back to the entrance of the cave.

He had known true love when he'd seen it, when he'd scented it in his nose, when he'd felt it in his body. Then he'd done a terrible thing to himself for the right reason, and there was no going back.

Better to have loved and lost?

"Bullshit," he muttered as he ducked his head and disappeared once more into the hideout.

CHAPTER THREE

Non-temporal Plane of Existence
Somewhere in Time and Space

O f course I like you."

As Rahvyn lowered herself to the hot-pink grass, she crossed her legs under her seat and put her elbows on her knees. Overhead, the psychedelic sky was a brilliant orange, clouds of red and yellow drifting by, the pseudo-sun a brilliant, glowing blue. Fluffy trees of ostrich plumes and golden branches undulated in a soft breeze that smelled of lilies, and birds made of heat waves and shimmers flittered by. Off to the side, a lavender lake was still, its surface a mirror that reflected back the world that had been created as both a sanctuary . . . and a vault.

When there was a ruffle, she shook her head. "No, it is not your fault. And I am very sorry I am not terribly good company."

The Book was open before her, its ancient parchment folios undulating gently in their spine as if it were breathing. Bound in human flesh—or perhaps vampire?—the entity was no more about words and pages than this metaphysical plane she was hiding them in was about reality. The Book was a conduit for energy in the universe, neither bad nor good, its possessors and their inner worlds determining the course of the spells and incantations held between its covers.

Which meant the thing was capable of great goodness . . . and unfathomable evil.

There was another ruffle.

"Oh, thank you," she murmured. "I appreciate your concern. But I shall endure."

The dismissive sound that came back at her could have meant the Book was doubting her endurance or mayhap her course, but either way, there was no unkindness. With her, it had only ever been full of grace. Then again, unlike so many others, she had never had any interest in harnessing its power—and further, she believed it felt as though a debt was owed because she had rescued it from an untenable, abusive situation: Safety had been requested, and safety had been provided, without questions or expectation of recourse.

Knowing how the poor thing had been used, she could understand why removal from the demon Devina's sphere of influence had been sought—

Fast flipping now, as if the pages were a spinning wheel that went round and round, no beginning, no end.

"Please don't," she whispered in defeat.

Yet it would not listen to her.

Closing her eyes, tension taloned up her spine and dug into the nape of her neck, and on reflex, she tugged at the sweater that clothed her and switched the arrangement of her legs in the jeans she wore. Neither eased the tension.

And when things stilled, she did not want to look because she knew what she would see.

She opened her lids anyway.

And there he was. As if the Book had become a window, she saw through the interior of its contours a male who was never far from her thoughts: Lassiter, the fallen angel, was iridescent-eyed and blond-and-black-haired, his face constructed of powerful angles and balanced by an intelligence that, having watched him in a crowd once, she believed he kept well hidden under a drape of humor.

"Oh, Lassiter . . ." Then she cleared her throat. "Whyever do you keep showing him unto me?"

The pages fluttered, as if it were attempting to point at something.

"Yes, I know he's the one. Therein lies my sadness."

More fluttering and then a couple of slaps.

"I wish I spoke folio, I truly do." There was a heave of pages, a sigh of paper—as if she were being deliberately obtuse. "And if your commiseration with my mourning is the way you're trying to repay me—"

Much flipping the now, the sound like it was applauding.

"It is? Well, that is very sweet." She brushed its pages with a soft touch. "And I understand that you are grateful for this respite here, but I am happy to be of service to you. I know what it is like to be used for one's gifts and in ways that harm. My own commiseration with your situation is the purpose for the security I offer."

A wedge of pages puckered up and blew a kiss.

Rahvyn smiled. "Yes, we are kin, are we not."

Looking out over the landscape, she toyed with changing it once again, shifting the colors and the arrangement of flora, mayhap turning the lake into a waterfall, perhaps creating an unnecessary, but attractive, shelter.

"Lassiter bid me farewell, however," she heard herself say. "Even if I went to seek him out, he wouldnae hear me in that fashion. He departed from me—and he is probably correct. What would I have to offer him?"

Flipping again, as if in disagreement.

And then the wheel started up once more, an infinite number of folios flashing by—until there was an abrupt stop and the Book bumped itself closer to her. Words she could not translate choked both of the pages, the text in orderly lines—

All at once, the letters began to quiver within their alignment, the vibration intensifying until they broke free and jumbled across the page, scattering like marbles and running into each other's paths. Waves began to form, rushing forth and receding, only to coalesce and fly away once again.

And then they froze and held their position.

"I am afraid I am unable to read . . ." She let the statement drift into silence.

With a frown, she tilted her head. It was not text of a strange and unfamiliar derivation. It was not writing.

Portraits.

The letters and symbols had pulled together to reveal two faces, one on each side of the open folio. They were males, and the longer she stared at them in an attempt at recognition, the clearer the depictions became, until they were as pencil drawings attended to with leaded tip over and over, the shadows darkening and bringing out a three-dimensional nature that was positively sculptural.

The Book clapped again, the emphatic sound an obvious attempt to focus her—except she was already locked upon what it was showing her.

It clapped again.

"You want me to go find them?" she asked. When there was a third smack of the folio, she shook her head. "I am sorry, but however important they are to you, I am not going to go look for these two males—"

A sharp clap interrupted her.

"But you need me, too. This landscape is in my mind, so if I am here I know you're safe. No one can get to you—"

The faces broke apart, the letters bursting into action as they whirled around once again, the features dissolving . . . only to re-form in a different alignment of eyes and nose and mouth.

"My cousin, Sahvage," she whispered.

Another scrambling, another face, this time a female. "His *shellan*, Mae."

In a relentless procession, more portraits created by the letters cycled through, and she knew them all: They were the males and females from her time in the present down below, the people at Luchas House, where she had taken shelter. Nate, the male she had saved. Shuli, his best friend . . .

Her sadness at the gallery was such that Rahvyn lifted a hand to her sternum and rubbed at the physical pain. Nate's face was especially difficult to see, given all they had gone through after he had been shot . . . all she had done unto him.

The letters continued to shift, and currently, the visages alarmed her. No civilian males were these. One by one, the Black Dagger Brotherhood appeared. She knew not all their names, yet they were not the kind of thing that was easily forgotten.

And now . . . the last portrait.

Her heart stopped. The male had long black hair falling from a widow's peak, and a visage that was both aristocratic and cruel. Dark lenses—which she had learned were referred to as wraparounds—covered his unseeing eyes and added to the menace he presented, a threat that was alleviated not in the slightest by the deep, ferocious furrow between his brows.

Wrath, son of Wrath, sire of Wrath, the great Blind King—

Those glasses were slowly removed by a steady hand . . . and then those strange, nearly pupilless, eyes stared straight out upon her.

With a hiss, Rahvyn jerked back. Yet they could not see her surely? This was but a rendering, and in any event, the male had no sight upon which to call.

The lips began to move, as if he were trying to tell her something—and then from the four corners of the open folio, a black tide rushed into him, the roiling letters overtaking him as he began to scream. The tight swirl of utter darkness consumed him . . . and then an explosion wiped all of it away, leaving only blank pages.

In horror, Rahvyn sat back and covered her face with her hands. When she finally collected her wits enough to look once again, she saw that single letters were falling from the top of the open pages to the bottom, like rain.

No, it was snow. It had to be because the flurrying symbols collected at the base of the book's display, the level growing higher and higher.

"I am not a savior," she whispered. "I cannot—"

A portion of the Book's pages curled up and then blew out one side, like a tongue: Pfffffffffffffffffft.

A sense of impending doom tightened her throat. "What happens if I leave here? I do not know if it compromises you in some way—"

The Book closed itself abruptly. After which its gnarled, ugly cover pulsated, as if it were flexing.

"You can take care of yourself," she murmured.

The sharp clap was an affirmative if she'd ever heard one.

"But I should rather stay here with you—"

The Book flopped itself open and the windowpane reappeared, Lassiter's face not as something created by an artist's hand, but as a photographic representation of the fallen angel, a flickering light playing over his grim features.

He was before a fire, she guessed, and as she tracked the way the golden illumination made his eyes shimmer, she realized that the wall behind him seemed to be some sort of rock. Had he taken shelter in a cave for some reason? She had overheard someone saying that he lived with the First Family and the Brotherhood.

Why would he be alone in the wilderness? Was he in danger?

"The angel is wrong," she said roughly. "I am not the Gift of Light."

The Book clapped again and did not stop, the urgency of the two sides impacting and falling back like a military drummer's beat.

She thought of the portrait of the King, consumed by evil.

And the two males she did not recognize.

Then Lassiter.

"Their destinies are all connected." When there was no reply, she looked over with even more dread. "Tell me."

Before there was a reply, Rahvyn was already getting to her feet. "Where do I find—"

The collection of letters flooded forth and made another drawing out of the scramble. But what was shown to her . . . made no sense at all.

"The golden arches?" she said with confusion.

CHAPTER FOUR

Caldwell Insurance Building
13th and Trade Streets
Downtown Caldwell

The demon Devina shot up off her satin pillows with a scream trapped in her throat. As she panted in the dim glow of her lair, she put her hand to her heart. Behind her sternum, the pounding was so heavy, she felt like a fifties cartoon who was in love. *Thumpa-thumpa-thumpa.*

Where the fuck was he—

Instantly, she was calmed.

Against the backdrop of her racks of haute couture clothes, standing tall, proud, and incredibly naked, her one true love was facing away from her and focused on the display of her Birkin collection. As usual, the ass view of him was every bit as delicious as the full frontal, his blond hair gleaming under the subdued ceiling lights, his shoulders marked with bright red claw marks from her nails, his tight little tuchus a perfect set of buns fresh out of the oven.

And just as delicious.

Which explained her teeth marks on the golden globe to the left.

Just a dream. It had only been a dream, she thought as she eased back against the headboard and pulled the covers off her bare breasts. Her nipples were red and swollen from him working on them and her sex was a low-level throb between her legs.

She had black-and-blue marks in so many places.

From when he'd held her down.

He was a demon lover, for sure, and not just in descriptive title. The male was everything she had ever wanted, all but custom designed to her specifications, and for a moment, she glanced down her racks of blouses, skirts, dresses, and trousers . . . to the far corner, where a municipal trash bin sat, lonely and out of place.

She had put the Book on top of the thing because that collection of incantations had been insolent and unresponsive and had needed a reminder that but for her pulling it out of the remains of that house fire, it would have ended up in a landfill. Goddamn, that entity had been a pain in the ass.

But she'd needed it.

And hey, the spell had worked, hadn't it. To get her

true love, she'd had to project how she wanted herself to be adored and then she'd had to go out into the world and ruin someone else's love. Both parts had been really simple, as it turned out. And the fact that Lassiter had been the one that she'd fucked while fucking him? A very satisfying BOGO.

Who knew that taking someone's virginity could rob him of—

"Why the hell are you keeping this one?"

As her lover spoke up, Devina was not feeling the tone. But then her male twisted around on his hips, and the top half of him put in an appearance. His shoulders and pecs were Michelangelo-molded, and his six-pack was right out of *Men's Health*. His face, though, was what really captured her attention. He was model-beautiful, with high cheekbones and a square jaw, his lips molded with a sensuous curl to the top and a prominent plumpness on the bottom, his brows arching in arrogance, his pale hair waving back from a broad, intelligent forehead.

His eyes were his most epic feature, however. Deeply set and heavily lashed, his pupils were an all-wrong, resonant blue, and what should have been a colored iris was a jet-black rim that seemed to crowd into the center.

They were unlike anything she'd ever seen.

Then again, so was the rest of him. And it wasn't just the physical components.

It was the aura of evil that emanated from him.

"The purse is destroyed," he said impatiently. Like she was stupid. "Why are you keeping it."

Devina narrowed her eyes and curbed her enthusiasm.

No, the Himalayan Birkin 35 with the diamond hardware was *not* destroyed. Yes, it had been subjected to fire, its toasted crocodile skin still releasing a whiff of barbecue, its white, gray, and brown pattern mottled with ash, its handles no longer in a perfect set of arches. But the bag remained at the top of her collection of Hermès's most exclusive purses.

"You should be more respectful," she said in a tight voice. "That is what brought you to me."

The Book's spell had started with her having to choose something of great personal importance and stare at it with all the love she wanted herself to be regarded with—and she'd picked the ruined masterpiece not only because it was the holy grail of all purses, but because she was ugly, too. Marred. Nasty. How had T. Swift put it in the good ol' days? A nightmare dressed like a daydream.

And all of the other men and males she'd ever wanted had known it.

So yes, the Birkin had been her object, and she'd trained her eyes on everything that was ruined—and let her heart fly with the soul-defining emotion she'd been cheated of.

"You should throw this out."

As a flicker of fury tickled her urge to murder, she had to smile. Of course her one true love would have to have a set of balls, and not just anatomically. Spice was the antidote to boredom, and conflict kept her interested.

Up to a fucking point.

"Do you even know what that bag is?" she drawled. Like *he* was stupid.

Those unusual eyes shot over to her. "My *mahmen* had a collection of them. Even before Sarah Jessica Parker carried a Birkin on HBO in two thousand two."

Utterly stunned, Devina could only blurt, "According to a *Vogue* article, that blue one was a fake."

"My *mahmen*'s weren't. She was on the list."

A bloom went through Devina's entire body, and it was sexual, even though he wasn't touching her or talking about body parts and what he wanted to do to them or with them. That he knew about *the list?* From back when there was one?

And *Sex and the City?*

Dear God, he really was the perfect male.

"I will never throw that bag away." She ran a hand through her luxurious brunette hair. "There is more value to it than its blemishes suggest."

"How did it get burned?"

"I had a prisoner here. She tried to break out by lighting it on fire and triggering the building's alarm."

He glanced up at the ceiling. "I would have thought humans were no match for you."

"The bitch's plan didn't work," she lied.

His head turned back to her and his eyes narrowed. Something about the way he stared at her made her nervous, so she threw the covers completely off herself and rubbed her thighs together.

"Come here," she commanded.

Her lover pivoted toward her, but he didn't move. Well, didn't come over to the bedding platform. His cock moved, for sure, the length hardening as he stared at her.

"I want to watch you touch yourself," he said.

"And I want you to do all the work."

As she arched back, her body slid slowly down the slick sheets until her head was on the pillow again. Looking over her taut breasts, she put her fingers in her mouth and started sucking the lengths in and out, the rhythm lazy, the intent anything but. With her legs sawing back and forth, and her nipples going even tighter, she stared across the distance between them.

He was trying so hard not to come over to her. She could tell.

And when his hand reached down to his hips and he palmed the enormous erection that had made such a spectacular appearance, she realized she had everything she had ever wanted. Her collection of designer clothing and accessories, all of it cherry-picked over time from the best of the best . . . her lair with its safety provisions that kept her insulated from the world at large . . . and this male who was never going to leave her—and would always love her even though she was only beautiful on the outside.

As her lover began to stroke himself in sync with the penetrations of her fingers breaching her lips and re-emerging, a cresting pleasure shot through her with such force that her eyes rolled back and her body exploded with an orgasm so great, she felt as though surely she might shatter.

And he wasn't even touching her.

When the demon Devina's release faded, she sighed and floated inside her skin, enjoying the way the air moved gently across her nipples and her plump lips—and also her fingers, which cooled like ice as she allowed her hand to flop onto the sheets. In between her legs, she was swollen and slick, ready for him even as she remained sore.

She could will the pain away if she chose. She did not.

Lying there with her eyes closed, she imagined her male's stare on her glorious nakedness as he continued to pump himself off. He hadn't come, and she was touched by his forbearance. That he was willing to forgo his own pleasure so that he could enter her and fill her up? What a gentlemale—and no doubt his molars were gritted and his fangs distended as he fought against his urges, torturing himself in the best possible way.

To make shit harder on him, she curled her hips to the side so she flashed him her ass. Then she deliberately moved one leg up at the knee so that he could see exactly what he was missing.

Maybe she'd deny him some, just because she could.

And there was such security in knowing he was always going to be by her side.

A prisoner of love who never wanted to get out of jail, free or otherwise.

She smiled to herself.

Smiled some more.

Smiled . . .

. . . and waited . . .

Devina frowned and popped her lids. Her lover was still hard as a fucking rock, and his fist was still riding up and down that thick shaft, and his mouth was open as he breathed in a pant.

Except instead of looking at her, his eyes were searching her lair, passing by the open kitchen area, the bath section with its claw-foot Victorian tub, the acres of clothes hanging on those department store racks. When his gaze settled on the door out, her veins flushed with a cold rush.

It wasn't like he was waiting for a knock from Uber Eats.

And there was no reason for him to care about the exit from this plane of existence, no call for him to be contemplating, in any way, what was going on in the outside world. She was his universe, and wherever she said they were, he was going to fucking stay.

They were in love, goddamn it, and this was an infinite motherfucking honeymoon.

"What are you looking at," she demanded sharply.

Once again, he took his own sweet time meeting her eyes—and what do you know, the defiance was not sexy.

"Nothing," he murmured.

Fuck.

For all her infinite days and nights of existence, going back to the split second of her summoning out of the ether by the Creator, she had been a conduit of unfathomable destruction, carnage, and suffering.

And if somebody were to bundle every one of her evil deeds, culminate all of the pain she had caused all of the living things she had destroyed, toyed with, or exploited . . .

It wouldn't come close to what it would do to her if he left.

"You're going nowhere," she growled. "You're mine."

"Did I say I wanted to leave?" he drawled.

Devina sat up and pulled the sheet back over to cover her breasts. "It doesn't matter if you do." She pointed across to the door with her red-polished forefinger. "That is forever closed, and what's more, you love me with all that you are. So you aren't going to *want* to leave."

The silence between them was the kind of thing that turned thin air into solid wall. And with each passing moment, the coil of fear deep in her gut cranked tighter and tighter. Even though she knew of the Book's power, and had seen what it could affect, she became paralyzed that for some reason, in her case, that which had been conjured at its direction, all settled and set in stone, would fly, fly away—

Her male took a step forward. And another. And . . . another.

And then he was prowling up the foot of the bed, his arms bowed out, his malevolent stare lit like fire, his long fangs dropping even farther down.

His erect sex hanging and bobbing, ready to fuck her.

When he got within range, he locked a hard grip on both her knees—then he wrenched her legs wide and jerked her down to him. Splaying her as if he were going to field-dress her like a deer, he angled his head down and stared at her glistening core.

The blast of heat she felt as he palmed his arousal again and started jerking himself off replaced the bitter cold of her terror that he would leave.

And that was when she smiled again.

A simp would never do it for her, not long-term, no matter how physically beautiful. She was going to need to ride the knife edge of her fear of abandonment from time to time or she would grow complacent and lethargic. Happy home had never been her thing.

She was a creature of chaos—

As Lash started to come, he angled the hot jets right at her core, the slashing, splashing impacts, the way he reared back and grimaced, the sounds of his harsh breathing and creaking of the bed, the kind of thing that tossed her over the edge again.

She orgasmed as he did.

And then he wasn't done with her.

Like an incubus, he swooped down onto her, sealing his lips on the folds that he had just slicked up, eating her sex . . .

. . . owning her body in the same way he owned her soul.

Fuuuuuuuuuuuuuuuuuuuck, he kept this up? She wasn't going to need to ever use that goddamn door again, either.

CHAPTER FIVE

Rumble in the jungle.

In the end, Lassiter decided to leave his hideout because his empty stomach was turning his south of the equator into a site of unrest. But as he dematerialized and traveled through the cool spring night in a scatter of molecules, he had no real thought of where he was going to get some food.

Well, he knew one place he was *not* going. Even though Fritz, the Brotherhood's butler, rode herd on an amazing bunch of *doggen* chefs, and he missed the crêpes suzette like they were a family member, he wasn't showing up for First Meal at the mansion. He couldn't face those people.

But he couldn't ignore them, either. Or maybe that was more . . . *shouldn't*.

It wasn't until he re-formed and got a case of the woozy-wobbles that he did the math and realized he hadn't been out in the sun for days now. That, more than any transient "hungry," was the bigger issue for his cravings. He needed to absorb sunlight, that immortal energy source, to be at his strongest—

Lassiter tilted his head and looked up. But not to the sky.

The golden arches in front of him were glowing like a false sun, and for a split second, he wondered if maybe he could try to grab some of that yellow light. It seemed more appetizing than the Big Mac he was going to try to choke down—

Beeeeeeeeeeeeep.

"What the *hell* are you doing, waiting for your brain to show up?"

At the ripping horn and the shooting scorn, he jumped out of the way of a truck entering the drive-thru lane. The big-as-a-house F-150 had been murdered, everything blacked out from the windows to the rims to the bumpers and the body paint, and the guy behind the wheel was as midnight-icured as his ride, his black hair and goatee paired with black clothes, his dark, nasty attitude like an anti-social projection so that everything was badass-uniform.

"Sorry," Lassiter murmured.

"Yeah, whatever."

With an engine roar, the truck sped off to crush the order window, and Lassiter watched it go with a feeling of nostalgia.

He missed Vishous. Even though the brother never had a nice word to say.

Actually, that was the most endearing part of the guy, his constant parboil of irritation a low barrier to achievement: That twitchy sonofabitch was easier to tee up than a golf ball.

As another car went by, this time a Volvo station wagon, he looked through the restaurant's windows. Inside the well-lit interior, there were all kinds of humans milling around, the place kind of busy given the late hour and the remote location—

Holy crap.

This was the McDonald's where he'd gotten Tohr's food three years ago. Then again, his little *Land of the Lost* cave was right around the corner from where he'd found the guy, relatively speaking.

Feeling like full circle was the name of the game tonight, whether he liked it or not, he went over and pulled open the door, catching a whiff of hot oil. As he once again took a shot at remembering what he'd bought Tohr, he looked around and didn't approve of the renovations or the change in business practices. A bank of self-serve soda machines took up the wall next to the opposite exit, and gone was the lineup of open-air cash registers, with their uniformed attendants and trays. Now there were ATM-like order stations with people touch-screening their meals in, and the folks working with the food were fewer and farther between.

It all seemed so digital and impersonal, although if he was looking for companionship as he ordered his Happy Meal, that was pretty pathetic.

Making his choices and manifesting a Visa card to pay for them, he turned to the pickup monitor mounted at the ceiling to check where he was in the queue—

· A handsome blond man the size of a house was pivoting away from receiving his meal, and talk about a calorie load. The amount of hamburgers and fries and sundaes on that tray suggested he was feeding a family of four—except he went off alone to the drink fill station. Given the size of him, that pro wrestler's body was clearly used to processing that kind of binge. Or maybe it was just a little snack on the way home . . . whereupon he was going to eat his own garage out of starvation.

Riiiight, because he was an absolute beast *when he was hangry,* Lassiter tacked on as he thinned his lips.

It was when a guy with a mane of long, streaked blond hair sauntered in with a buddy who had a skull trim that the angel sent a glare up to the ceiling.

"If the ghost of Peter frickin' Steele walks through that door next, I'm leaving."

Of course, the Creator wasn't going to hear him, and even if He did, the ya-gotta-be-kidding wasn't going to make any impression. But come on, obvious much?

"And Vishous would never drive a truck," he muttered as his number popped up in the come-n-get-it screen's pole position.

After he grabbed his Big Mac and his fries, he went over and stared at the drink choices with his cup. He picked Coke because he felt like death and surely caffeine and sugar would perk him up.

There were plenty of seats to choose from, and he

headed for a table with a pair of benches in the front windows because it was far away from Not Real Rhage—who was unwrapping and woofing back his chicken sandwiches and his Quarter Pounders like he was chasing after high cholesterol and a heart attack.

Outside, cars went in and out of the drive-thrus of the Wendy's and the Arby's across the street—and that's when he remembered this side-of-the-highway conglomeration of fast-food joints and gas stations was crammed in tight to the exits on either side of an overpass. Which explained all the people at the late hour— well, the ones not force-fed to him, at any rate. If he remembered correctly, this was one of the last stop-offs before the Northway started hauling it through the big mountains toward Canada, so people needed to get their grub and their fuel or hold their peace for fifty miles.

What the hell *had* he bought Tohr when he'd been here?

The food tasted really pretty good, and the Coke did juice him up, and as he sat by his little lonesome, he watched the folks come and go: An old man in a black suit with his white hair precisely tended to and his eyes bright in spite of his age. A woman with a long black braid down her back and a body that suggested she could meet a full-grown male more than halfway in a ground-game fight.

An English-looking gentleman in tweed and a cravat on the heavy arm of a Bounty-worthy lumberjack.

A pair of guys, one with dark hair and a Goth vibe, the other a redhead who was dressed like James Spader ca. *Pretty in Pink.*

"Where's the Duallie baby carriage," he said under his breath. "You're slacking."

As a couple consisting of a dark-haired man in a very nice jacket and tie and a blond woman who was dressed like she was going to the opera waltzed in, he tossed his napkin and crossed his arms over his chest. Given that the Creator was capable of great and grandiose things, why in the hell was He wasting His time corralling all these doppelgangers to a Mickey D's at the side of the Northway in upstate New York on a random . . .

What day of the week was it?

He couldn't immediately remember, and as part of his brain churned over the calendar, he shook his head at the vastness of hours ahead of and behind him—and then extrapolated the same for the eight billion people on the earth. So many lives being lived minute-by-minute, all of the cycles of birth and death churning in a constant consumption and release of energy on a rock ball hurtling through space. Reduced to its granular details, existence really was just a bunch of biology in a fruit salad of physics calculations, wasn't it?

Utterly pointless in the grand scheme of things.

Except then there was love. Love was life to the dead, and make no mistake about it, a person could be a corpse even if they had a heartbeat.

Even if they were immortal.

When a fine-fellow-well-met with a Mohawk and an amethyst silk suit pimped into McDagger-con, Lassiter pulled a fuck-it and got to his feet. And the reason for the leavin' was as ridiculous as this display of almost-theres.

Then again, he should be glad a nearly-Rahvyn wasn't opening any doors and ordering a McFlurry.

He was liable to break in half—

"It was a Big Mac. Just what you're eating the now."

Lassiter froze in a crouch of bench evacuation. That voice. That . . . unforgettable voice.

Closing his eyes, he breathed in and smelled meadow flowers. And as he braced himself to look over, he couldn't decide whether the Creator was merely being cruel or if destiny's ultimate navigator was just going to make it fucking impossible for him to go black-hole on the job he'd taken from the Scribe Virgin.

"How do you know what I ordered him," he asked roughly.

"Perhaps I should not have come," she whispered in response.

Feeling like he was moving through quicksand, Lassiter twisted around—and lost the ability to speak. The female who was never far from his mind was really in front of him, no doppelganger this. No almost-there. No nearly-her.

As their eyes met over the single hamburger and empty cup on her tray, their connection snapped into place, no gaps in any seams, no rough edges, no bad angles.

Even though he knew they could never truly be together.

And God, if she'd been exquisite in his memory, she was heart-stopping in her actuality, her silver eyes wide as she stared up at him, her delicate face glowing, her platinum hair down over her shoulders in a waterfall of waves.

She made the world go away for him, and he was struck by an urge to speak his truth.

"Would you like fries with that," he blurted as he stared down at his one and only love.

+ + +

Wake up.

Lash's eyes flipped open, and he threw a hand out— not toward the female who was sleeping next to him, but down the side of the bed, to the seam between the mattress and the box spring. For his gun. A knife. A baseball bat.

It was a reflexive move, the kind of thing he had done countless times. Back when he'd . . . been alive.

Retracting his arm, he scanned the open area. Nothing was out of place in and among the racks of couture . . . and there were no intruders popping from behind the privacy screen in the bathroom area or the white leather sofa in the center of the space . . . also no sounds or scents from out in the hall beyond.

Then again, the voice had sounded like his own.

He rotated his head on the satin pillow. The female next to him was in a deep sleep, one breast exposed by the ripple of sheets, her naturally red lips parted, her brunette hair glowing with copper highlights across her own pillow. She was a fucking smokeshow, a total dime. But all you needed were hair extensions and a good plastic surgeon and you could replicate her looks.

So what the hell had she done to him?

That was the question he'd been asking himself ever

since he'd been called out of his father's *Dhunhd*, brought back to Caldwell, and delivered to *her*. Like he'd been conjured out of thin air by the female, dial-a-date style.

And he was beginning to suspect that was what had happened. She wasn't a vampire, and she certainly wasn't human—and sometimes, when he deliberately refused her, the way her eyes narrowed and turned into pits of murder, he was pretty fucking sure he knew what he was fucking.

She was a demon.

As the word reoccurred in his brain, he focused on her breast. She wore a suit of skin, just like he did—and what do you know, he was in no hurry to find out what she really looked like underneath the window dressing.

Yes, his lover was a demon, and she was compelling him to be with her. That had to be it—because lurking behind this made-no-sense obsession he had for her, he remained his true self: The hunter, the killer, the destroyer, all the essentials of who he was were still there, he just couldn't seem to access his motivations or power—

Go. You're free.

Lash snapped his head back toward the lair's steel-reinforced door. As his upper lip peeled off his fangs, he waited for the voice to come again. But that was stupid.

It was his own—

Go NOW. You're free.

Lash sat up slowly, rising from the hips like an OG vampire coming off the tufted quilt of his coffin. After checking to make sure the demon was still asleep, he shifted his legs out of the satin sheets. Under his bare feet, the floor was cold through the plush rug, and when he stood up, the air seemed to swirl around him—to the point where he looked down at himself.

A fine mist had formed around his ankles, and as it made like a tiny hurricane, it doubled and redoubled in size, the fog ascending up his calves, his knees . . . his pelvis.

Go now, you're free. HURRY.

He didn't intend on fighting the order, but as his free will surged, a flood of intention and planning momentarily blinded him—and he didn't realize he was in movement.

In fact, he was floating toward the door on a wave of that mist, sure as if it were a conveyor belt.

As he reached the steel barrier of the lair, his fangs tingled and his body throbbed with aggression. Just as he began to penetrate through the door's molecules, he glanced back at the bed. The female was still asleep, but she was twitching, her long, smooth legs kicking underneath the sheeting, her hand clawing at the pillow— then her head flipped over and she looked right at him.

Or would have looked at him, if she could have. Her eyes were closed, her beautiful face twisted into a grimace.

As he remembered what she tasted like, a stir of sexual instinct made him pause.

She'll be here, he thought. Anytime he wanted.

Turning back to the door, he passed through and hated the acidic, clingy sensation—but compared to the tortures of *Dhunhd*, it was nothing he couldn't endure.

And then he was on the other side.

The basement corridor was a straight shot of concrete in both directions, all kinds of closed doors with corporate logos offering nothing of interest. He chose left for no particular reason because either way would take him to the outside world—

The security guard came sauntering around the corner down at the far end, his cell phone up in his hands, the soft squawk suggesting he was listening to a game. Uniformed, dark-haired, in his early twenties—and out to fucking lunch: The whistled tune that percolated up from him, a little ditty that was discordant and disorganized with an unreliable beat, suggested he was lax about more than just doing his rounds properly.

The dumbshit was about to walk right into an intruder.

As the mist that had carried Lash through the door dissipated from his naked body, the scent of the human became very apparent, and with proximity also came an assessment of the potential for a good fight. There was none. The kid was fit in the manner of youth rather than activity—no paunch yet, but the shoulders were unremarkable and so were the pecs.

Not that that would matter.

When Lash was done with him.

CHAPTER SIX

"W hat the hell."

As the words on Eddie's mind were spoken out loud, he himself leaned in closer to the windshield. Which was not hard to do. The Mini had all of the vertical loft of a Converse All Star, and forget about legroom. He was wearing his knees as earrings and bent into a crouch. If the airbag ever went off? His nose was going to get punched through the back of his skull.

"Are you seeing that?" Adrian demanded as he took his foot off the gas—and then, like it wasn't perfectly clear what he was talking about, the other angel jabbed his forefinger forward. "*That.*"

"Yeah, I do."

The glowing line going down the out-in-the-boonies

road ahead of them was the kind of thing you couldn't miss—and no, it didn't have anything to do with the yellow stuff painted in the middle. This stripe was on their side of the divider, the phosphorescent trail continuing into the distance until it appeared to make the upcoming corner and keep going.

Eddie looked back at the Northway exit they'd just gotten off. The direction of "Great Bear Mountain" had been all well and good, but as it turned out, it was like telling someone to go find a guy named Mike in Minnesota. The mountain's footprint covered a massive territory, and for the last however many hours, they'd just been driving around aimlessly, poking into trailheads and pit stops, diners, drive-ins, and dives, straightaways and stop signs.

No Lassiter. Nothing even vaguely Lassiter-like.

Which, considering the guy was a mushroom cloud waiting to happen, was a good thing from a public safety standpoint. Given their mission? It was just more frustration.

"I guess we follow it," Eddie said as he tried to see around the bend. "Maybe this is the compass we need."

Ad rocked the gearshift back and forth in neutral. Then he flipped things into first, released the clutch, and eased in the gas. The Mini crept forward, as if the car were hesitant.

"Or maybe we just quit this shit." Ad glanced over with annoyance. "Lassiter isn't anywhere around here."

"And you know this how?"

"You think you're going to get cable or Internet this

far out in the fucking boondocks? No way he's going without TV."

"What else do we have to do? We might as well see where it takes us."

"This is a wild goose chase—"

"The last three years have been a f—" Eddie stopped himself before he *-ucked* after the *fff*. "This whole frickin' thing's a goose chase. So why not bloodhound after whatever this glow is."

"It's *fuck*." Ad gave them some more speed. "And I don't get this clean-living act with your vocabulary."

As they puttered around the turn in the lane, a thicket of roadside emporiums appeared, stars in the pavement's Milky Way.

"Do you need gas?" Eddie asked as they approached a Shell station.

"We're doin' okay—oh, hey, it's a McDonald's, you want to eat?"

"No, just keep going. In case the stuff has a half-life."

"The fries?"

"No, dummy. The glow."

As they went by the golden arches, Ad looked across the seats with a yearning that suggested his sodium nitrate levels were low. But he continued on—and so did the weird illumination.

"Taco Bell?" the other angel said with optimism. "Come on, I need a chalupa and so do you."

"No way. I'm immortal, but there are limits to what my digestive tract will handle."

"Plop-plop, fizz-fizz—"

"That is *not* your slogan."

Ad laughed even though they were passing the purple bell logo. "I love Carter Anderson."

A quarter of a mile later and the brief conglomeration of fast food was over. After that, all they had was more forest, the thick tree line an arbored fence like Mother Nature didn't want any trespassers killing her vibe. And the phosphorescent strip was still going strong—what dimmed were Eddie's convictions. Maybe Ad was right, and what he'd thought was a sign was just like the Great Bear thing, a nothing burger—

The glow disappeared.

And not just as in ended. As in extinguished completely, nothing more ahead, nothing at all behind them.

"Well," Ad announced, "this was *really* great—"

"Stop!" As the angel hit the brakes, they both jerked into their seatbelts, and Eddie pointed to the right. "There's a dirt lane. See? Let's go in there."

His best friend looked through the side window, his seat groaning from the shift of position.

"I've always wondered whether Bigfoot is real," the angel muttered as he spun the wheel and punched the gas. "Maybe tonight's the night I find out."

"You wear a size fourteen. I'd say that's prima facie evidence right there."

"You're no fun."

As the headlights swung around, the nearly imperceptible break in the lineup of trunks and branches became more visible, but only marginally so. And as they bumped off the road onto a pair of dirt grooves, the trees seemed to crowd in.

There was something else, too. About ten yards in, the forest started to not look right, the landscape indistinct in a way that wasn't tied to fog or weather. He didn't know what the hell the buffering was.

Ad rubbed the heel of his hand in a circle on the windshield. "I can't see a damn thing."

They'd gone another fifty yards or so when a cock-eyed cattle gate appeared and Ad slowed them down again. The old thing connected a busted-up chain link fence that had a curlicue of rusted barbed wire as a toupee.

"Look at those video cameras."

"Keep going," Eddie murmured as he squinted over the little hood and willed the barrier open.

The visual blurring continued to weave through the environs as they ascended the mountain's flank, the details of the pines and other trees smudging to the point where they just disappeared into the darkness, the headlights not penetrating very far, the lane appearing up ahead as if it were being built foot by foot as they went along.

What was clear? The series of gates—and they got progressively newer and more sturdy. Eddie opened each in succession, all the while wondering who the hell would go to this kind of trouble to keep trespassers off their property.

"I got a bad feeling about this," he muttered.

"Aw, come on. It's an adventure, right?"

"Not the kind we're going to enjoy."

The angle of ascent grew stiffer, and the disorientation permeated the car, a fuzzy wave going into Eddie's body and messing with his mind as nausea turned his stomach.

Finally, they came to the last barrier. Twenty-five feet tall, with signs warning it was electrified, the gate linked up a twenty-inch-thick concrete wall that seemed to go to the ends of the earth in both directions.

As they passed through, the conviction that they had to turn around struck him hard—no really, they needed to *never* come here again, *ever*—and Ad coughed into his fist like he also had bile rising in his throat, and the car itself sputtered . . .

And there it was.

The drive made a turn and revealed a great gray stone mansion and a courtyard with a winterized fountain.

"He's here," Eddie breathed. "Lassiter is *here*."

Ad hit the brakes and peered upward. "Because he took Bram-damn-Stoker for a roommate—oh, cool, they got gargoyles."

The grand house had a variable roofline that suggested its layout extended deep into the property to the rear, and it was not hard to picture a *Game of Thrones* dragon coming around its spire. Off to one side, there was an attached garage that was bigger than most municipal facilities, and on the other, a freestanding miniature version of the larger whole that was clearly some kind of caretaker's cottage. All around, diamond-paned windows glowed with yellow light—but suddenly, shutters started to come down in a coordinated descent, as if the mansion had taken an Ambien and the stuff was kicking in.

"Make sure you have your halo on," Eddie muttered as he popped the handle on his tiny door. "I don't think we're going to have to knock."

"My disco ball is like my American Express. I don't leave home without it."

As Eddie got out, he assessed the front entrance of the palace. A set of carved double doors was anchored by a set of stone steps that belonged on a cathedral.

With the shutters locking into place at the base of all the windows, Eddie murmured, "They know we're here—"

Instantly, warriors in black leather appeared from out of thin air, guns up and targeted, their massive bodies blocking the entrance in a clear message that if you wanted inside, you were going to have to go through them.

Vampires, Eddie thought. That Stoker crack was no joke.

"Well, if this isn't the best welcome wagon I've ever seen," Ad said in a cheery voice. "I feel right at home!"

Eddie shot over a glare that was studiously ignored. Then he focused on who he guessed was in charge: One of the fighters was standing at the head of the steps, his military haircut and grim, dark blue eyes suggesting that he was very comfortable with killing things—yet the fact that neither he nor his troops had immediately pulled a trigger was a clear indicator that he had a brain.

Lifting his palms up, Eddie said, "We mean no harm. We're just looking for—"

Behind the fighters, the cathedral doors blew open by some tremendous force, the carved panels slamming back against the stone jambs. What appeared was the stuff of nightmares: A tremendous male, his eyes hidden behind black wraparounds, his powerful body clad in black leather, his waist-length black hair, which fell from a widow's peak, draping his powerful shoulders.

With the illumination streaming out from the interior, it was as if he were supernatural.

Except he was not. He was mortal. And his presence made the others uncomfortable—though no one broke ranks, their expressions tightened, and Eddie couldn't understand why. The guy looked like he could will death if he wanted.

But enough with the size-up.

"We're looking for Lassiter," Eddie said in a loud, clear voice before things escalated. "We've come for the angel."

CHAPTER SEVEN

Rahvyn could not believe she had found Lassiter. She had not understood the golden arches that she had been shown by the Book, and this eatery, wherever it was, had not been her intended destination. Yet when she had re-formed? She had found herself before the very landmark that had been illustrated—so clearly, this was the ancient tome's doing, this coming here.

"Would you like fries with that," Lassiter said unto her.

Staring up into the male's eyes, she briefly lost her voice. Such extraordinary eyes he had, all the colors at once ringing round his pupils, the hues swirling and iridescent—and his gaze was not the only thing that arrested her. Though her memory of him had been keen, it was nothing compared to his actual physical presence, his blond-and-black hair gleaming in the dull lighting, his shoulders so broad under his black pullover, his lower body filling out loose black pants she recalled being referred to as joggers.

Breathing through her nose, she scented earth and pine upon him, and she remembered what the Book had shown her . . . firelight on a stone wall. Mayhap he had sequestered himself away on a mountain somewhere—

Something was off. Something was . . . wrong about him.

Shaking herself to attention, she nodded down at the crinkled napkin and the empty burger box on his tray. "Are you leaving the now, then?"

Please do not go, she thought.

"I can wait while you eat." He slid back into the bench. "Join me?"

Putting her tray down, she sat across from him and recalled the words he had spoken to her. "Forgive me, but I do not know whether I want fries." She tilted her cup toward herself, even though she knew there was nothing in it to inspect. "And it appears as though I have forgotten my drink."

Verily, she had forgotten everything when she had seen him sitting alone and staring out the windows. But she had been worried that he would send her away if she had no food.

"Here, have my Coke." He put his cup on her tray. "Or what's left of it."

As she focused on the straw sticking out of the plastic top, all she could think of was that his lips had been on the thing.

"Wait," he said, "I'll just go fill your own—"

"No." Her voice was sharp. "I would prefer—this is rather fine."

With a flush, she picked up his drink. Cupping her palms around its base, the cold transferred through her skin and into her bones, and it felt like a warning. But she brushed that off by staring at the face that had haunted her.

"You have lost weight." As one of his brows twitched, she feared she had offended him. "You look well, though. Very . . . well."

He closed his eyes and sat back in the bench. Then he let his head fall loose as if he were staring through his lids at the ceiling.

"How did you know I was here?" He leveled himself and smiled, though the expression did not change the heaviness in his eyes. "Or do you come here often."

"I have never been here before."

He focused down at the fake wood table between them, and as the silence grew deep as a well, she glanced around at the humans who milled to and fro, gathering their sustenance, carrying it out or sitting down to eat. She envied them their easy lives.

"Would you prefer me to leave," she asked as she tightened her hold on his cup.

"I already said goodbye to you," he murmured. Like he was speaking to himself.

"Yes, you did. I was there."

When he turned to stare out into the night, at the

golden arches, she studied his profile. He had a fine nose, straight and true. And a jaw that was flexing and relaxing as if he were grinding his molars.

Tck-tck.

She looked toward the sound. Over at the bank of self-serve soda machines, a man was putting his cup under a green tab that read "Sprite." Nothing was coming out, but he kept trying the little lever, the *tck-tck* released anew each time.

"If you've never been here before, how did you know where to find me? Or was this just a McDonald's lottery you happened to enter."

"I should not have come."

Rahvyn went to put his cup back on his tray, but it caught the lip and started to fall—

Lassiter snatched the drink before it tipped over, but the force of his grip popped the top and Coke went everywhere in slow motion, the explosion shooting up a cascade of brownish liquid. Except suddenly, between one blink and the next—it was not soda. It was blood in the air, red as a ruby and thick as syrup—

The smell of burned flesh and chemical smoke flooded her nose, spearing into her, as she saw the portrait of the King in the Book, a black tide rushing in toward him from all four corners.

Death.

Rahvyn screamed and jumped up in the bench, her legs getting caught under the table, her arms paddling and flipping her tray, the burger, still tightly wrapped in its paper, going the way of the soda. The blood.

Abruptly, she was lurching as well, off-balance and falling, too. As her vision swung in a wild arc, she saw the ceiling Lassiter had not stared at, and next came the hard landing as she hit the floor. With her breath kicked out of her, her head rang like a bell, confusion and panic tangling her thoughts—

The one grounding she needed, indeed, that she had been searching for, appeared right above her, Lassiter's face taking up her entire field of vision, blocking out the places to sit and eat, the humans who were gathering about her, the drinks machines.

All she saw was him.

The angel was talking to her, his lips moving, his strange and beautiful eyes boring into her own as though he were trying to will her into coming around.

She deciphered nothing of what he was saying. Part of that was the paralysis in her mind from the impact . . . but most of it was because of what she saw.

Or what she did not see.

Lassiter's aura was gone. There was no longer a shimmer around his head.

◆ ◆ ◆

It was the smell that woke the demon up.

As Devina's lashes fluttered, her nose wrinkled and she fought a sneeze. What the hell was that *stench*? It was like rotten meat . . . and baby powder?

"What are you cooking?" she muttered into her pillow.

She was lying facedown on their bed, and she was so relaxed, so languorously satisfied, that the energy required to roll over and focus on whatever her lover was doing in the kitchen was more than she could be bothered with. Her body had been so perfectly used, so ridden and owned, so contorted and penetrated, that she just wanted to enjoy the float for a little longer.

It felt like she had waited an eternity for—

The demon whipped her face up off the pillow for long enough to spit out, "Will you *please* take whatever that is off my stove?"

The fact that she sprinkled a p-word in there was evidence of her tremendous personal growth. As recently as a couple of days ago, she would have gone with the fuck'ing, and not in a good way. Hell, she might have even led with some lead. But true love had changed her for the better.

Maybe they needed to go for a vacation. Fiji? Yes, something tropical. They could even pretend to be humans. Go to a travel agent. Book first class—because if you flew private, not as many people could envy you during the flight. And when they landed, they could go stay in one of those luxurious huts that were staked over the aquamarine water.

Waiters would bring them fresh fruit and gourmet meals. They would get couples massages and swim in the ocean—

"Okay, this is bullshit."

With a violent twist, she jacked herself up and over—

No one was at her stove. Nothing was burning. And nobody had spilled a thing of baby powder in her bathroom area because, hello, she wasn't an old biddy who used the stuff.

For no good reason, she swung her eyes to the toasted Birkin. But like it was suddenly going to start smelling—

"Where are you?" she demanded. "Lash. Where the *fuck* are you."

Jumping to her feet, she looked around and thought about the dream that had woken her up before. Tendrils of it reattached and clawed into the center of her chest as she spun on the ball of her foot, searching, searching . . .

Her lover was gone. She didn't need to cast aside the screen around the tub to know he wasn't behind the silk panels. How the *fuck* had he left?

As her anxiety threatened to get totally out of hand, she told herself that the spell was still in force. Lassiter's true love was ruined, she had her male, all was good. Her taking a quick crash-nap after a marathon sexfest was not going to change any of that. So . . . this was part of the dance. The push and pull. Maybe he'd gone out to buy her something—

She glared at the door. *How the* fuck *had he gotten out?*

Prowling over to the steel panel, she clothed herself, wrapping her body in a second skin of black leather, popping her arches tall with a pair of stilettos, sweeping her hair up in a twist. When she arrived at the exit, she put her hand on the cool metal.

He should not have been able to leave, and not because of any physical lock.

Glancing over her shoulder, she eyed the rows of clothing racks, some of which were six feet tall, all of which were stuffed with hanging clothes. But what was the likelihood he was playing hide-and-seek in her Chanel? No, she'd sense him if he were here.

Back to the door. She'd worry about how he got out of the damn thing later. Right now, she had to find him, and as she stepped through the portal and reentered the physical world of Caldwell, she felt the shimmy of the transition—

"Oh, *God*."

The stench was so bad, she put the crook of her elbow up to her mouth and nose. She had always hated baby powder to begin with; the shit was right up there on the no-go list with vanilla-infused perfumes. But add in a whiff of roadkill?

Gagging, she almost stepped back into her lair for a couple of clean breaths—because conjuring a World War II–era gas mask onto her face would ruin her hair and makeup. But then something caught her eye, way down to the left.

A glossy . . . puddle, on the pale concrete floor.

She'd recognize that color red anywhere. It was one of her wardrobe staples.

With a wave of her hand, she lined the corridor with Jo Malone scented candles, the Velvet Rose & Oud fragrance crowding into the air, thank fuck. As she walked along the hallway in the flickering light, it was like proceeding down an aisle, and for a split second, she pictured her blond lover at the end waiting for her in a tuxedo, one of her shadows standing in for the preacher because, duh.

The curdling dread she was trying to hold off with rational thinking returned to her the closer she got to the carnage, but not because she was worried something violent had happened to her male.

Quite the contrary.

She stopped at the pool of blood, and smelled the copper.

It was definitely a human who had done the leaking. But there was something else . . . black streaks and smudges. On the concrete wall, on the floor by the sanguine pool.

Lowering herself onto her haunches, she swiped her forefinger through some of the strange inky substance— and she didn't need to make it all the way to her nose. That was the source of the stink.

Wrinkling her nose, she manifested a damask napkin out of thin air, and then decided she needed something stronger. A restaurant-type wet wipe appeared on cue and opened its foiled packet for her, the damp square just what she needed.

As she wiped the nasty off her finger, she reminded herself again that if Lash were just a doormat, they would never last. This, though, was more than a little defiance.

She thought back to the word that had appeared on her wall, when the Book had been engineering this result with the spell it created for her.

OMEGA.

Her eyes focused on the human blood. There was so much of it. Quarts of the stuff.

"Jimmy? Where you at, my man?"

Looking up, she got a stiff-angled view of a security guard stopping dead as he saw the candles lining the corridor. Then he glanced down at her, focused on what she was kneeling by, and went straight-up horror movie drop-jaw. As he sputtered and flapped one of his arms like he'd gotten a bee sting on his wrist, she recognized him. He was one of the younger ones she fucked with when she was bored, making disembodied footstep noises around him and sending drafts his way just to freak him out.

When he started to fumble with the communicator on his shoulder, she rolled her eyes, willed him into some amnesia, and sent him away. She'd have preferred peeling his skin off and leaving him all anatomy-chart on the floor next to what was no doubt his buddy Bobby's hemorrhage, but right now she didn't need the hassle of a bunch of cops showing up and going Karen on this situation.

Humans were *so* reactive to dead bodies.

Just as she was trying not to come to a conclusion that seemed unavoidable, a glint of silver caught her eye. In the midst of the blood puddle, a metal wedge nearly the size of her palm caught the candlelight, and she had to stretch her arm out to reach it.

It was the security company's shield, torn off a uniform.

As she wiped the blood off with her thumb, she shook her head; and then she tossed the thing over her shoulder. The Lessening Society had never interested her. That shit had been between the Omega and the vampires, the war that had waged for centuries having nothing to do with her shit. Still, from time to time, she had run across the undead, soulless soldiers who had been initiated into the order.

That was the sickly sweet smell. She just hadn't recognized it at first.

And this was where one had been inducted.

Devina rose to her full height. Then she closed her eyes and put out her hand. When a tickle registered on her palm, she popped her lids. The lock of blond hair was tied with a tiny black satin bow.

She'd cut it from her lover's head when he'd been sleeping, and as she'd done the snip-snip, she'd had a flare of conscience—not because she'd arguably violated his privacy, but because the spirit of the spell was being tainted by her insecurity.

After all, if this was her true love, why would he ever leave her.

Now she felt like a fucking genius.

Pinching the fibers between her forefinger and thumb, she held the bundle to the dull ceiling light, the strands like spun gold.

They would show her where Lash was.

And when she found him?

They were going to have one hell of a marital moment. A little push-and-pull was fine, but taking off on her? Unacceptable.

Unless he was buying her a present, of course.

That human he just turned better be carrying a fuckload of shopping bags.

CHAPTER EIGHT

Wrath, son of Wrath, sire of Wrath, stood at the entrance of his fucking home with his shitkickers planted and the wind coming up the mountain blowing his hair back like he was Cindy-goddamn-Crawford from the eighties. In a ring in front of him, the Brotherhood was lined up and ready to fight, the scents of their aggression thick in his nose.

Along with their rank-and-stank disapproval that he'd crashed this party.

Like he cared.

What *was* tickling his whole asshole, to borrow the phrase from Hova, was the arrival of the two males who'd triggered V's monitoring system way down at the bottom of the mountain. The security sensors had picked them up immediately, and Wrath had overheard all kinds of chatter describing their Mini, their slow ascent up the drive, their disembarkation from that stupid pocket rocket of a toy car.

They shouldn't have been able to navigate through the *mhis*.

So yeah, he was coming out to join the fun, too, and he didn't care if it got the brothers' diapers in a wad.

"We're looking for Lassiter. We've come for the angel."

As one of the pair spoke up, Wrath flared his nostrils. The scents that weaved through the familiars of his warriors were a variant of clean salt water.

"Names," Wrath demanded.

"Eddie," came the response. "And this is Adrian. We mean you no harm, we come in peace."

Wrath bared his fangs as they fully descended from the roof of his mouth. "Does it look like we're worried about you doing shit on my property?"

"Ah . . . no, sir. It doesn't."

"And what do you want with Lassiter."

"No offense, that's our business."

"No offense, but fuck off with that. What do you want with him."

He sensed the pair glancing at each other. Maybe they actually turned their heads, maybe they didn't, but they were definitely checking in without speaking. And what do you know. He had the time and inclination to wait things the fuck out to see what they came up with.

"We are family," the other one, Adrian, said in a cheery voice. "Sister Sledge. You know."

"Hey, I like that song—"

As somebody *shhhh*'d Rhage, Wrath closed his eyes behind his wraparounds and focused on the energy coming at him. Neither was evil or playing a subterfuge game by lying, but that didn't mean they could be trusted. You could sucker-punch a lot of people while acting in your own self-interest.

"We've been sent here to collect him," the Eddie one said. "And bring him home."

"You can have him," V muttered.

Wrath sent a glare in the brother's direction. "Who sent you."

"So Lassiter has been here?" Eddie pressed.

"What are you," Wrath demanded.

"I'm an Aries, he's a Virgo," the other guy said. "He drives me nuts. He alphabetizes the spices. Like, why?"

For a moment, everyone seemed to focus on the commentator. Like they couldn't believe—

"You are totally related to that fallen angel," Wrath felt compelled to comment.

"Cousins, you might say," came the happy answer. "And we've been looking for him for about three years. Our boss wants him back—oh, hey, kitty-kitty. C'mere, little guy."

A meow lit off next to Wrath, and then his keen hearing picked up the nearly imperceptible padding of four cat paws toe-beaning their way by him and proceeding down the steps. There was a second feline vocalization, and then the kind of cooing that was more typically associated with grandmas and babies.

"What do they call you, my man?"

"His name is Boo," Wrath said dryly. "And he doesn't like people."

Well, other than Beth and iAm.

"Good thing I'm an angel, huh," the Adrian one explained. "Isn't that right, Boo-boo."

"Look," the first guy spoke up again. "We don't want trouble. We just need to—"

"And what if Lassiter doesn't want to leave." Wrath cocked a brow. "What're you going to do then."

"He doesn't have a choice, and he knows this."

"You come with handcuffs?" V grumbled. "Because I am not that lucky and there's a *Golden Girls* marathon next weekend."

Wrath took a moment to retreat to his happy place—where he imagined wrapping Vishous's entire head with duct tape and leaving no gaps for the lip-flapping or the breathing.

Then he forced himself to refocus. "Lassiter is not here."

"Do you know where he is?" the Eddie guy asked.

"No, I don't. I can't help you with that."

"But he's been here." When Wrath nodded, the angel muttered something that sounded like a curse. "Can we leave you a number where he can reach us?"

"I'm not playing secretary for you."

"It would be a decent thing to do."

"We're not into being decent for trespassers, sorry. I will say that your door prize, for leaving now under your own steam, is that we won't break any of your legs showing you the way back down the mountain."

"You know," Adrian said over the purring, "I'm going to go out on a limb here and suggest you do not have a future in the cruise ship industry. Or any hospitality field, really."

Wrath blinked. And then laughed a little. "I'm not interested in a career change outside of Caldwell, thanks. Especially not with Devina's new boyfriend—"

"*Devina?*" the Eddie one said sharply. "No."

"You know her?"

There was a clearing of the throat. "That's a name I didn't think I'd have to worry about anymore."

"She is a bitch. For real."

"Do you—how do you know her?"

V spoke up. "We did some rounds with her just the other night. And got to check out her new male. Things are going *so* great."

"I'm sorry—she's *here?* Now? That's not possible."

"I wouldn't gate-keep my boys," Wrath drawled, "on shit they've actually seen."

"And fought," someone cut in.

The trespasser's words got tight and fast: "You don't understand. Her mirror was destroyed. She's trapped in the Well of Souls again."

Wrath waved off the whining. "Whatever, I don't argue with reality or convince others of it, so you can fuck around and find out. Now hop back in your little Matchbox car and get the fuck off my property. If you ever come here again, I will regard it as a declaration of aggression and you will be dealt with as such. You may be angels, but we have weapons at our disposal that can put holes even in immortals. Am I clear."

It was time to get the males off the mountain. Even though all of the *shellans*, young, and *doggen* of the household, along with Sahvage, Murhder, and Payne as guards, were safely down in the training center, the trespassers were still too close for comfort. And then next up on the to-do list was figuring out why the *mhis* had failed to protect the landscape.

Maybe it was an angel thing.

"Let me leave a number," the Eddie guy said. "Please."

"If you are what you say you are, I'm sure you have ways of reaching out to Lassiter. And if he's shutting you down, that's your problem, not ours." Wrath started to smile again, and this time, it wasn't about a fangs flash. "But yeah, before you ask, a couple of my boys will take you to where Devina was last seen."

He imagined some flavor of male recoiling in surprise: "So you read minds?"

"Lil bit. Consider that demon a consolation prize for the lack of Lassiter you're leaving with. Although good luck with her. You're going to need it."

"I'm pretty sure you're wrong."

"See for yourself. Either way, don't come here again." Wrath pivoted on his shitkicker and started for the vestibule. "Oh, and give me my fucking cat back."

◆ ◆ ◆

"Are you feeling better now that we're outside?"

As Lassiter asked the question, he already knew the answer. Rahvyn was perking up as she strolled down the restaurant's sidewalk next to him, the color returning to her cheeks, her balance good, her breathing nice and even. Though they were side by side, she was the one leading them, and when she stopped in front of the golden arches and looked up, he just kept staring at her.

In the artificial yellow glow, it was as if she were in the sunlight, and how lovely was that.

Yet she was troubled. He could tell by the way she crossed her arms over her chest. And when a breeze came in and blew strands of silver hair into her eyes, she lifted a hand and swept things away with impatience.

"What happened back there?" he asked.

"I do not know."

Yes, you do, he thought to himself.

"What did you see," he said grimly. "In your mind."

Somehow, he wasn't surprised as she slowly shook her head, and did he really need to know the details? She had been terrified as she had shot out of that bench seat, sure as if the Grim Reaper had rushed up to their table with his scythe and a Diet Coke.

"Why did you leave me back in that meadow full of flowers," she asked in a low voice.

When he didn't reply, because he had no intention of telling her a goddamn thing about his time with Devina, she lifted her chin. "'Tis all right, you can keep your privacy. Just tell me that is why you say nothing the now. That is all I ask. No lies between us. Ever."

As her eyes shifted over and met his own, he blocked all of his thoughts. "I have no privacy to protect."

A sadness crossed her expression. "Lassiter."

He put his hands up and backed away. "I'm sorry. We can't . . . do this."

"Why? There's no harm in talking."

But that was the problem, wasn't it. As he stared at her, he didn't want to talk. He wanted to pull her in close and hold her. He wanted to stroke her silken hair. He wanted to breathe in the scent of her arousal, and ease her head back . . . and stare into her eyes as he dropped his mouth to hers and—

An image of Devina rammed into his brain. He saw the demon straddling him, her breasts bobbing as she fucked him, her eyes boring into his with the kind of evil glee that came when a person enjoyed cruelty.

Why was it that even though that female had been the thief, he felt the guilt of having stolen something? It was as if the void created by her lack of conscience had been filled with his shame.

Helluva way to maintain the essential balance of things.

"Lassiter, say something."

As he tried to figure out what kind of syllable salad he could toss her, a little car went by out on the road and his eyes shifted over to it because he couldn't bear the tension—except then they stayed on the Mini: Just as the pocket-sized pod passed by the streetlamp at the McDonald's entrance, the illumination penetrated the driver's side window.

It was just a flash, a mere instant where the profile registered, but the identity was concrete and conclusive.

Adrian?

What the hell was that fallen angel doing back on the planet? And this far upstate?

As implications started to swirl, Lassiter wanted to groan. Like his life couldn't get any more complicated?

Reaching up to the nape of his neck, he tried to massage some of his WTF away. "Ah, Rahvyn . . . look, I'm sorry. I have to go now."

Instantly, her face became a mask of composure and she bowed a little. "But of course, do what you will."

He glanced at the golden arches. "How did you know I was here? Just tell me."

"I merely had a feeling."

In the silence that followed, Lassiter reached out to brush her cheek—but dropped his arm before he made contact. "Who's lying now."

Before she could argue, he put his palm up. "If you want only the truth between us, it's a two-way street. And please, don't come looking for me again. You *have* to stay away from me."

"Why." Defiance carved into her features. "If that is what you want, you will have to tell me why."

"It's not safe." He searched her face. "You can't be around me. I'm contaminated, and you're the one thing that I care most about. I can live with just about any hell except for hurting you."

Her eyes, those lovely silver eyes, widened, and her mouth fell open a little.

"Take care of yourself," he whispered. "And by extension, my heart."

Closing his eyes, he dematerialized away—and

although he left the female, he took her with him somehow, too. And as for the question about how she'd found him, he supposed the particulars didn't matter. Maybe it really had been a whim, but he doubted it. He'd never told her about coming up here to help Tohr, and even if he had, why would she think he'd been chilling at this particular McDonald's on this specific night at this exact time.

She was holding something back.

And as he pictured her lips parting, the only thing he knew for sure was that she wasn't safe around him.

For a whole host of reasons.

CHAPTER NINE

ahvyn followed the angel.

After Lassiter departed from the restaurant, she stood in the false glow of the golden arches for a few heartbeats. And then she up and traveled in his wake.

He was not hard to track. While he flew through the night, seeming to follow a small, boxy vehicle that proceeded off the winding country road and onto the way of speeding vehicles, he left a sparkling trail behind him, a ghostly marker that she had never seen before. And as she went along, she was forced to re-form at regular intervals to check her trajectory—and each time, she worried that she would lose him.

She did not. His shimmering trail continued down the way of the fast cars and trucks, and presently, she inferred that whate'er destination awaited them all, it was somewhere within the city proper, with its towering glass constructions and its right-angled streets. Soon enough, the gray-and-black buggy departed onto the puzzle work of asphalt lanes, and now she had to be of additional care, lest he would see or sense her in the closer quarters.

Meanwhile, the car moved without confidence along the one-ways, as if the driver were searching for the correct route, perhaps because he or she were being given incompetent directions—or because they could not properly translate the dictates of whatever navigational device or program was being utilized.

It was hard to pinpoint when the ringing recognition hit her.

She was very much distracted by not losing sight of Lassiter's trail, yet as they penetrated the density of buildings, an awareness prickled upon her, traveling down all her nerve endings until she was painfully alert—and she had a thought that it was better to remain of the air as much as she could.

Danger was upon them all.

Just as she re-formed at the corner of an older building, the little car slowed, blinked one of its taillights . . . and turned in out of sight, the glowing trail following like a flag.

Rahvyn looked about. There were no humans close by, either on foot or in vehicle, and she jogged silently forth, having to fight a choking sense of doom. Slowing as she reached the lane that had been utilized, she cautiously leaned around the building's cold, mortared foundation.

A broad swath of pavement was marked by a pattern of many yellow lines, and the little car crossed the vacant expanse as Lassiter discreetly re-formed himself. He was very careful in choosing his spot, staying downwind and tucking his sizable body in the eaves of a neighboring building's roofline.

And then the true character of the sojourn became apparent.

Members of the Black Dagger Brotherhood stepped free of the shadows at ground level: Zsadist with his scarred face. Rhage with his preternatural fair beauty. Vishous with his goatee. The trio were dressed in black leather, and she was well aware that they were fully armed, their open jackets revealing the black blades strapped, handles down, to their powerful chests.

Her heart began to pound. This was what the Book had showed her in portrait form.

This was why it had sent her away, not just for Lassiter . . . but for these brave, strong males.

And Wrath.

Further confirmation came with what emerged from the diminutive vehicle: Two tall males straightened unto their full heights, one with a long dark braid down his back, the other with a shaved head and piercings in his ears.

These were the pair of males the Book had shown her, the ones she had not known.

And they were not vampires, she thought. They were something else . . .

They had halos, just as Lassiter had once had. They were of his kind, and yet he did not reveal himself unto them.

He recognized them, however. From his perch, he stared at them as if their appearance was a shock, and not in a good way. But would not he greet them? Especially if they were with the Brothers?

Double-checking on him once again, she took a deep breath and heard his voice in her head.

Take care of yourself, and by extension, my heart.

She needed to leave. She had no business being even on the periphery of what was clearly a military exercise of infiltration. Instead, she closed her eyes and concentrated on the texture, color, and arrangement of the stones that formed the six-foot-high decorative frieze around the base of the building that sheltered her presence. When nothing altered of her body, she worried her pounding heart was going to prevent the shifting— but then she felt the orientation of her molecules ripple themselves into a new alignment, what was her physical form now assuming the appearance of the creamy stone and pale gray mortar.

When she was certain the transmutation was complete, she reopened her lids and moved her position, progressing down the building so she could close in on the clutch of males.

"We go in this way," the Brother Vishous announced. "Through the mailroom."

The Brother turned to a series of broad doors that were lined up at waist height off the ground. They were the kind of thing she had seen located off to the side of houses, and she remembered Nate working on the ones out at Luchas House. He had explained the ancillary structure was a "garage," but how would they get a car inside these? There was no ramp?

This was the least of her concerns.

Evil.

The building the warriors were going to enter was steeped in darkness, stained with it, though there was nothing showing upon its exterior. Surely the Brothers sensed the threat, too? And Lassiter? It could not only be her.

With a lithe shift, Vishous jumped up to the lip of one of the garage doors, and after manipulating something down at the base, he hoisted the metal panels up on tracks, rolling them into the ceiling above. Dim lights glowed in some kind of barren interior, and she glanced back at Lassiter's position. He was still up there on the roof next door, watching everything.

But he was not going to stay where he was: In the ambient glow of the city, his face was drawn in tight, grim lines, as if he were in a kind of intense inner debate, and she was certain he was going to follow at a careful distance.

Knowing this, Rahvyn ghosted into the building herself, flying over the heads of the other Brothers and the angels as they propelled themselves off the pavement with powerful lunges and landed in the open area in near silence. Unsure what they were going to do next, she chose a temporary perch hovering in the far corner by a reinforced panel she assumed opened into the structure at large—and indeed, after Vishous shut them all in, he focused on that door, which opened on its own, as if he had willed it so. Rahvyn wafted herself in front of the group, weaving her essence over the polished concrete floor, continuing along with them as they proceeded down the corridor. At another steel door, which Vishous also opened, she was the first to descend a set of stairs.

As she emerged upon the lowest level, the foreboding she felt was so intense, she nearly lost the concentration necessary to keep herself camouflaged against the environment—

"Does anybody else smell that?" one of the angels hissed.

She could sense nothing olfactorily in her current incarnation, but as the Brothers traded glances and promptly unsheathed their daggers, she knew exactly what they were going to say. And she hated being right.

"Yup, that's a *lesser*," one of them replied grimly. "Fucking hell . . . the war is back on."

✦ ✦ ✦

Of course Eddie and Adrian were back.

As Lassiter watched the fallen angels disappear into the loading dock of the older skyscraper, the confluences of the night were wearing him the fuck out. First, all those humans cosplaying the people he lived with. Then Rahvyn showing up. Now the Creator's Frick &

Frack henchmen. And what the hell were they doing here with the brothers—

Devina.

Oh, shit. Maybe they'd come for the demon and not him? Because this was the seat of her lair—assuming they could penetrate her metaphysical camouflage.

As the implications of it all fell on his head, he had a momentary paralysis.

Off in the distance, he heard the thumping bass of a club's sound system. Some tires screeching. A cop car's siren. All around, the downtown was doing its night thing, festering addictions and law violations, humans racking up stupid score points and winning stupid prizes.

Meanwhile, his past and present were colliding over the airfield of a sadistic bitch who was capable of everything. And the solution for him? Go up to the Sanctuary and sit around like a house cat.

Yeah, 'cuz that was going to help this situation.

Looking down at the pavement, he measured the five-story drop and then let his weight free fall. The landing sent shock waves of pain through his feet and up into his knees, and he sucked the sensations deep into him because it was easier than feeling his anger and sadness. Seeing Rahvyn had been like getting clocked in the head, and he was not over the injury to his already wounded thought patterns—but he wasn't going to let his personal tragedy get in the way of his ability to do good hair.

Thank you, Miss Dupuis.

As he started for the loading dock, he didn't even bother fronting like all he was going to do was observe. Although he was going to stay hidden for as long as he could—

"Come back for more?"

At the intrusion of the female voice, Lassiter closed his eyes as every inch of his skin tightened like he'd been lashed. For a split second, he imagined picking up the gray-and-black clown car Eddie and Adrian had gotten out of—and throwing it broadside at the demon who had shown up behind him.

Instead, he pivoted around calmly. And made sure his thoughts were locked down tighter than a vise.

Fucking hell, she was so ugly. From her long, luxurious brunette hair, to her full red lips, to the cleavage and the rest of her won't-quit body, she was trash-pile vile, that Dior's Poison she insisted on wearing a grape-based stench in his nose. Bracing himself for an up-and-down by those pit-black eyes of hers, he made sure his focus was on her and only her.

Nothing else.

No one else.

Especially not the five males who had infiltrated the building.

As the wind hit his back, the demon leaned in, her nostrils flaring. "What . . . the *fuck*."

Shit, he'd slipped—

"You saw her." Devina looked around the empty parking lot. "Where did you see her? You were with her—I can smell that female on you."

"There is no female—"

The palm that came swinging at him was a high-flyer well landed, the stinging impact on his cheek and the clapping echo a wake-up that he didn't need: His adrenal glands were doing just fine, thank you, ma'am.

Although he would have taken some satisfaction in getting under her skin in different circumstances.

"That's why he left." Those black eyes gleamed with menace. "It's your fucking fault, you were just with your female."

Lassiter shook his head. "I ate alone at a McDonald's in the fucking boonies. Sorry, guess you're confused."

As she brought her arm up for another round of pickleball for the puss, he caught her wrist and jerked her back.

"Yeah, enough of that—"

"You know it's never going to work out with her, right?" The demon leaned in, even though he was exerting enough pressure on her bones to powder them. "I fucked you and I took your virginity and you don't have anything to give that stupid cunt. Every time you're with her, you're going to see me, and that's what gets me mine. You're ruined and I get mine!"

Her words were like a freight train coming fast and faster, and the culmination was a burst of energy that exploded out of her. The force was so great, he was blown off his feet, sent bottle-rocket high into the cold night air, his body crumpling into a ball like she'd wadded him up. Disorientated, he was aware of gravity pulling him back down, but his fall was a tumble, lights spinning around him.

Just before he hit the asphalt, he caught the total non sequitur of a neon palm tree glowing green and brown on a stretch of golden beach.

What the—

"Fuck!" he blasted, as the impact knocked all the oxygen from his lungs and carried the word in his head out to the rest of the world.

The pain was paralyzing. Then again, even though he was immortal in a corporeal illusion, bones were bones, and he was subject to the laws of compound fractures when he was in his body.

Compromised as he was, he was defenseless.

And the demon knew it. Devina took her own damn time coming over to him, and on the approach, her hair fanned out around her head, even though there was not enough wind hitting her to get that effect. Jesus, she looked like there were flames emanating from her.

Maybe the shit wasn't her hair after all.

"He left me because of you," she growled. "For me to have my love, you can never have yours."

Lifting her hand over her shoulder, she summoned from the darkness a shadow that was shaped like a spear, the harnessed evil so tangible the muscles in her arms flexed as she held it aloft.

"This is all your fault. You took him from me—"

From out of nowhere, something tackled the demon, hitting her at waist-level like a linebacker and driving her back with such force, her body's contours blasted through the solid wall of the building he'd been on the roof of. The hole that was left behind was classic Warner Bros. cartoon, busted mortar rising as dust as her arm-raised position made the cutout look like it was cheering a score in a game.

With a groan, Lassiter tried to lift his head, and when his vision went wonky and he felt a strange rush of cool air, he reached behind and touched a wet spot just above his nape.

Oh . . . crap, he thought as he inspected the silver blood on his fingers.

It was quite possible that the bone he'd broken most was his goddamn skull.

And to think he'd assumed his coccyx was the worst of it.

"You're bleeding bad," somebody said. "And I think part of your brains are on the pavement. Take a deep breath, this is gonna hurt."

As he was lifted up, he screamed and lost his sight completely—and shit got even worse as he was stuffed into a suitcase, his legs and arms, all of which seemed snapped in half, bending at wrong angles.

"Put your seatbelt—actually, never mind. Like a car accident can hurt you now?"

There was a jolt forward, and it was so violent, his face smashed into something that smelled like vinyl, cheap perfume, and old curry. Then there was a lurch to the side.

After that: "Hold on to your butts."

Squealing tires now, and as another round of fire

pokers went after every square inch of his body, Lassiter blinked his eyes clear and got a close-up of his own knee: The thing was pressed up against his nose.

Just as he was about to pass out, Adrian, the fallen angel he had been avoiding for three years, twisted around from the driver's side. The big idiot smiled like this was a reunion to be savored.

"There are no snakes back there. Don't worry."

"Stop making Samuel L. Jackson refs and just fucking drive."

Ad turned back to the job at hand. "You used to be more fun, you know that."

Yeah, actually . . . he did.

CHAPTER TEN

After Eddie played bulldozer with the demon, taking her through not just an exterior wall but two interior ones, he rolled on top of her and tried to keep her pinned. He knew it wasn't going to last, but the dominance didn't have to. He just needed enough time for Adrian to evac Lassiter in the Mini.

Straddling Devina's hips, he put his elbow to the front of her throat and grabbed his own wrist so he could lean in and apply even more pressure. The choking sounds were satisfying, and so was the gaping maw of the demon as she tried to drag air down into her lungs—and to get herself free, she clawed at his face, her nails ripping into his skin, the scent of his blood blooming.

Red drops fell from the scratches onto her cheeks, and for a moment, she was so beautiful in her straining hatred, he nearly lost his concentration. Even messed up from the tackle, her physical perfection was undeniable, but that wasn't the attraction: He hated her with a passion that sometimes confused him, because on occasion, when they were face to face like this, the wires got crossed and he wanted her.

Not because he loved her, though.

Fuck no—

You snooze, you lose.

As she rallied without warning and sent him flying, that was what went through his mind—and hey, check it. They were in an open-air office, the two desks he sailed over messy with paperwork and colorful brochures. The far wall caught his momentum, his shoulder shattering the glass on a poster of a Carnival cruise, his body landing on a Xerox machine the size of a small refrigerator.

No more fucking around.

Swiping the blood off his face and spitting out a shard from the picture mount, he quick-footed his balance, sank down into his thighs, but left his guns where they were, holstered under his light jacket. No use throwing bullets into this mix. She'd be just as likely to send them back at him.

Across the travel agency's layout, Devina was looking like she'd been in a collision with—well, a building. Her hair was matted with gray blood, her bustier and skintight black leathers smudged with dust, one heel missing from her stilettos. Yet she stood there with her hands on her hips, all Wonder Woman, like she was ready to cat walk.

"Is that how you greet an old friend?" the demon said before coughing and then spitting off to the side. "Fuck, Blackhawk. You could have just called me a cunt."

"Cunt."

With a roll of her eyes, Devina cleaned herself up, all the dust and debris—including the paper clip hanging off one lock of hair—disappearing, her leathers no longer scuffed, that heel back where it needed to be.

"Look, I'm not interested in your interference," she announced. "Whatever is going on between that angel and me is none of your business—"

"The Creator sent us for Lassiter. You want to get in the middle of that? You're welcome to. I'll just grab a chair and my popcorn and watch the floor show."

Those black eyes narrowed. "So you're taking him away? From the earth?"

Eddie was not an angel who ordinarily shared intel with the enemy, but something about the way she'd gone suddenly still made him inclined to chat.

"Yup. We're here to collect him."

Crossing her arms over her breasts, she seemed to get lost in thought. "Fair enough. Have him, he's yours—but just so we're clear, when you leave with him, he'll be gone. Like out of commission forever."

"The end result's not up to me. I'm just the messenger with the summons."

"Lucky you," she murmured. "I'll let you live then."

At that, she blew him a kiss and dematerialized like she

had an appointment somewhere. Maybe to get her nails done. Or have some poor bastard drawn and quartered.

Gritting his molars, Eddie hated when she did the whole last-word thing. Goddamn it, now he was going to spend the rest of the night trying out retorts and wishing he could feed them to her—

"What the fuck happened here—"

"Why the fuck did you run off—"

Two of the Brothers arrived on scene in midsentence, the male with the goatee in the lead—Vishous was his name—and the blond Ken doll right on his heels. And it went without saying that they didn't use the locked glass doors, but stepped through the cutout in the brick wall. More efficient that way, and it didn't trigger the alarm.

The fact that there was a hole in the side of the building but the security system was silent seemed like a fine commentary on the way the night was going.

"It was the demon, wasn't it," Vishous said. "And that's Lassiter's blood on the pavement out there, isn't it."

"I didn't have time to explain back in the basement," Eddie shot back as he brushed dust off his jeans. "But yeah, she just took off."

The blond Brother, the one with the bright blue eyes, lowered his black dagger as he looked around. "You know, I like the way you redecorate. It's whimsical, with just a hint of wrecking ball."

"I was inspired," Eddie muttered. "What can I say."

"You're bleeding."

"I'm fine."

Over at the hole in the outer wall, the scarred

Brother stepped in and announced, loudly and clearly, "Your friend drove off with Lassiter, and you're going to take us to them now."

"Says who."

"So you're kidnapping the angel, then."

Eddie tilted his head. "Are we going to have a problem here?"

"Yeah, I think we are." The Brother's yellow stare flipped to black, those eyes narrowing. "But it's not going to be a big one. You've lost a shit ton of blood, so you're not going to be a lot of trouble, and we can prisoner swap you for our angel if we have to."

"Or the other guy can really just keep him," Vishous intoned. "I mean, let's look at all the options, shall we?"

As Eddie opened his mouth to respond, the world went for a little spinny-spin-spin, and he threw out a hand, hoping to save himself from another Xerox-related recline. The copier was saved, however. The big blond one swooped in, and like the lead in a dance pair, did a waist-and-nape grab that made Eddie the girl in the dip.

The Brother smiled as he looked down, flashing bright white fangs. "Tootsie Pop?"

"Whhha . . . ?" Eddie mumbled.

Something in a purple wrapper appeared in his face. "I think your blood sugar's low."

A whiff of grape was the last thing Eddie was aware of before he went library book . . . and checked the hell out.

◆ ◆ ◆

Behind the wheel of the Mini, Adrian was ten-and-two'ing it, his body curled around the steering column, his right leg straight out into the wheel well like someone was goosing him in the ass. The smell of Lassiter's blood was thick in his nose, the sweet perfume like fresh-cut flowers—none of that copper human crap.

Funny how eau d'artery motivated a guy to screw the traffic laws.

Not that Ad was really bound by anything human.

He had no real idea where he was going as he barreled along, blowing through red lights and stop signs, the buildings that flanked the one-way crowding up close to the sidewalks like they wanted to try traveling themselves. The direction he was heading in didn't matter. The only thing he cared about was getting some distance between him and Lassiter and that demon. Well, that and having Eddie somehow show up unhurt after he'd—

The ghostly apparition appeared right in front of the car, and Ad barely got a glimpse of the spooling white hair and the shockingly pedestrian clothes before he stomped on the brakes and wrenched the wheel.

The Mini veered off course like a jumping bean, popping the curb and catching some air. Fortunately, the thing wasn't much wider than a shopping cart, so as it hit the sidewalk, he was mostly able to course correct and keep it from ending up in the display window of a boutique. But then a municipal trash bin jumped into his path and he had to hit the brakes again. Somehow, the paper-clip-sized calipers and what was left of the donut-sized radial tires did the job.

As he bumped against his seat belt and caught his breath, he thought, *Wow, just in time*: He was staring into the plate glass frontage of a bagel shop, the headlights piercing inside and picking out the tables with their chairs upside down and off the floor.

"What the hell was that?" he asked no one in particular. "And I wonder how good the lox is."

Then the back door was wrenched open.

Snapping a hold on his gun, he swung the muzzle into the seat behind him—

It was the apparition.

"Let me help him, please," a soft voice said. "I beg of you."

Ad lowered his weapon. The female was not of the world, but nor was she an angel. He didn't know what the fuck she was. What he was clear on, though, was the heartbroken way she was looking at Lassiter.

"G'head," Ad heard himself say.

She couldn't kill him, after all. At least . . . she shouldn't be able to.

And Lassiter did need help. He was crumpled in the rear, crammed in, creamed from the careening—and there was silver blood all over the black seat. Just as Ad was about to offer to get the angel out—or shit, he didn't know what—the female extended her hands and closed her eyes. As cold night air weaved through the Mini's interior, ushering out the bouquet of an immortal's blood spilled, she started to hum.

No, that wasn't her. That was . . . what was coming out of her.

Glowing light pooled all around Lassiter, its vibrational waves creating the sound, and Ad knew without any doubt that the energy was from the font of the Creator: Instantly, the injured angel's body eased, a shuddering exhale released as pain clearly drained out of him.

"Who are you?" Ad whispered.

He didn't get a reply. The female was concentrating solely on the summoning and delivery of salvation, her delicate face fierce in her endeavor—

As the theme from *Star Wars* lit off, Ad jumped—and wondered what the hell John Williams was doing conducting an orchestra in the middle of downtown Caldwell. Except then he realized that it was his phone.

Fumbling around in the pocket of his leather jacket, he answered without checking the screen. Then again, there was only one person who had the number.

"Where are you? I have Lassiter."

"Well, that's just great. We have your boy Eddie."

Ad closed his eyes. "I'd ask how a vampire got this number—"

"You're Eddie's only favorite in the phone log thingy. This is Rhage, by the way."

"Rhage, how're you."

"Good, fine, yup. Oh, hey, good news, Eddie's alive." There was a pause, and then the Brother said, in a wry way, "I mean, I don't think he can be dead, can he? It looks like he's having a little nap? Anywho, you have our fallen angel, we have your buddy. How about turning this into a one-for-one tradesy situation."

Ad refocused on whatever was happening in the back seat. "Lassiter's a little busy right now."

"Why, because you have a TV?"

"No, I think a female with silver hair is playing auto mechanic with his proverbial engine."

"Rahvyn?"

Ad shifted the phone away from his mouth and said to the female, "Is that your name, Rahvyn?" When he didn't get an answer, he said into his cell, "Is that her name?"

"Where the hell are you?"

Ad turned back around so he could check the navigation map that was glowing on the dash. "Market and Fifteenth. And I'm not going anywhere, trust me."

It had been a pretty good plan, driving off with the angel they'd come to find. Of course, the head wound had been a wrinkle, but nothing that he hadn't intended to solve, provided Eddie handled the business with that demon.

How the hell had Devina managed to escape from the Well of Souls?

"We're coming now," the vampire said.

As Ad ended the call, he wondered where the demon was now. Wondered what would have happened if this female hadn't shown up. Wondered how the night had come to all this.

When he'd bought the Mini, it had been as a joke. Now the thing was an ambulance without the bubble lights and the sirens.

Proof, he supposed, that on any given night in Caldwell, New York . . . any fucking thing could happen.

CHAPTER ELEVEN

Well, wasn't this cozy.

As Lassiter opened his eyes, he recognized that he was lying down comfortably on something soft, and Eddie and Adrian were standing next to a bunch of brothers. The fact that he recognized all of the males was probably a good indicator that he hadn't suffered any ill effects after cracking his head open like an egg on the pavement. And hey, he could remember how it had happened, too: After Devina had gone nuclear on him, he'd hit the—

"Rahvyn," he croaked.

This brought all kinds of heads in his direction, and to avoid meeting the eyes of his peanut gallery, he glanced at the monitoring machine he was hooked up to. Oh, look. He had a heart rate, his lungs were working, and he had blood pressure.

And he knew where he was: The Black Dagger Brotherhood's subterranean training center. Which had, among its many attributes—including a very nice break room with a good television and a lot of free food, a weight room that he avoided like the plague, and a swimming pool that was as big as a lake—a hospital-grade clinic with its own OR, examination rooms, and recovery suites.

And what do you know, they'd put him in one of their medical beds.

"Where's Rahvyn . . ." he mumbled.

"She's just down the hall," somebody said. "She's fine."

He wasn't sure who was speaking—which suggested that though his memory was fine, his faculties were maybe not as a-okay as he was hoping.

"Can I see her?" No, that wasn't forceful enough. "I will see her now."

Someone stepped forward out of the gathered fighters.

It was Vishous, and of course, the guy was a wet frickin' blanket: "Not yet. You've got some talking to do."

For a split second, Lassiter thought of all of those doctor soaps he'd watched in the seventies and eighties. *Marcus Welby, M.D. St. Elsewhere. ER.* Fine, *ER* was in the nineties. Inevitably, there had always been some poor schlub in a hospital bed, people surrounding them, a dire prognosis saved by the brilliance of the medical staff—except when the show had needed a bad outcome so it could seem real.

And on the staff, there'd always been one brilliant, cynical sonofabitch everyone loved to hate.

As Lassiter's vision sharpened a little further, he thought, *Annnnnnd here we are, Caldie style.*

V was like Hugh Laurie in *House*. Except smarter, and better-looking. And for once, the brother wasn't smoking a Turkish hand-rolled. The rest of him was right, however. The goatee, the tats on the side of the face, the black hair, the black leather all over the body. And the expression of irritation and hauteur.

Like a Nobel Prize winner who'd been asked to read a grocery list.

"Where the *hell* have you been," came the demand.

Lassiter glanced at the other brothers, and then the fallen angels. All of them were also waiting for an answer, just being less judgy about it, as if they might have recognized that sometimes, people had a right to take a couple of nights off—

"You have *no* right to flake out on us," V snapped. "You don't want my *mahmen's* goddamn job, fine. But don't take up space if you're not going to do shit—"

"Fuck you," Lassiter cut in. And then he went on a roll, rising off the bed as his voice rose in volume. "I fucked that demon so Balthazar could have his female, and I kept Devina occupied tonight while you all went into her lair—and I've done a dozen other stupid fucking things I shouldn't have, to make sure none of you get hurt or disappointed as you live your lives. So excuse me if I need a goddamn *break* every once in a while!"

By the end of it, he was yelling, and when he

finished, he flopped back down—and hit the back of his tender head again.

"Fuck!" he barked as he put a hand up there.

As he felt around and got no sense of wetness, he thought, well, at least he wasn't leaking anymore.

Abruptly, Rhage leaned out of the group. "You want a Tootsie Pop? Eddie rudely turned me down back at the travel agency he assaulted, so I have an extra one."

"To be fair, I passed out," the angel muttered. "That's not rude—"

"Yes, fuck, I want one," Lassiter bitched as he put his hand out. "And can you unwrap it."

Rhage played an excellent Fritz the butler, just without the wrinkles and the penguin suit: Split second later, there was a purple globe on a white stick front and center, and you know what? It tasted fan-fucking-tastic.

Man, thank God he wasn't human. Or a mortal. He'd be dead or hooked up to a ventilator while they debated on when to pull the plug. Instead, he was going to be all right in another hour or two. Tops.

All because in the back of that Mini, Rahvyn had helped the healing process along immensely.

She'd followed him. The sneak.

He thought of her standing in front of him in the lee of that golden glow at the Mickey D's, so resplendently beautiful, more lovely than he remembered, her eyes on his as she leaned forward as if—

He left me because of you! For me to have my love, you can never have yours!

As Devina's voice barged in, Lassiter bolted up again,

and immediately, the brothers and the angels leaned away, like they expected him to *Exorcist*-it and start golf-sprinkling pea soup.

He looked at Vishous, because, hey, if anyone could figure out anything, it was him. "Devina . . . is in love, right?"

V took out a hand-rolled. As he put it to his lips, somebody pointed out, "There's oxygen in here."

"Yeah, there is, unless you think we're breathing water?" The male lit up, exhaled, and motioned to the far side of Lassiter's bed. "That cylinder over there isn't hooked up, relax. And as for the demon, it's true. She's got herself a little boyfriend and we've got problems. Lash is back, and fully functional. We found evidence that he inducted a *lesser* outside her crib, and the two of them shacking up is bad news for us."

The cursing behind the guy was low and ominous— and peppered with f-bombs.

"She conjured him," Lassiter heard himself say. "From the Book."

"Excuse me—"

"Huh—"

"Wait, what?"

Gesturing with his lollipop, which was already dwindling in diameter, he said, "The Omega is gone."

"Far as we know." V nodded with deference at his roommate, Butch. "The *Dhestroyer* Prophecy was lived and breathed thanks to the cop."

"And the son was dead."

"Yeah. Donzo. In *Dhunhd*."

Rhage lifted up his forefinger. "Which would make it *Dhunhdzo*, actually."

As V glared at the brother, Lassiter remembered the details. In a bid to finally end the war on vampires, the Omega had gone back in time and planted a Trojan offspring in Caldwell, one that had been absorbed into an aristocratic family. The truth about the sire being evil hadn't even been known by the male himself, and the young had matured unaware of his lineage. After entering the Black Dagger Brotherhood training program, Lash had survived his transition—and then had come the big reveal.

The male had taken the news soooooo well. He'd slaughtered the family he'd thought was his own, and then taken a squadron of *lessers* around to all the grand estates he'd been to as a member of the *glymera*, killing those bloodlines also. Following the raids, which had been the single greatest success for the Lessening Society, Lash had set about enjoying his *Fore-lesser* status, in classic nepo baby fashion. It hadn't lasted. Like all the others before him, his favor had faded and the Omega had chosen someone else to lead.

The son had been given no more slack than the strangers. Then again, loyalty had never been one of his daddy's attributes.

"The demon brought Lash back." Lassiter talked the logic out slowly as he put it together. "Devina was desperate for a male and used the Book, which was in her possession at the time. She must have found some kind of spell in there . . . and got herself the love of her life, which explains how Lash must have been liberated from *Dhunhd*—God, it all makes so much sense."

"Um . . . does it?" Rhage asked. "I'm not following. I think someone should get this angel a whiteboard and a marker."

One of the other brothers chimed in. "So he can write PENIS on it with a Sharpie like you did and give himself a heart attack when it doesn't erase?"

"Hey, that was supposed to be a good joke."

"Yeah, just not one you could rub off."

"Well, it was a piss-poor penis, what can I say—"

"Can we *not* do this right now," V snapped at the pair.

In the pause that followed, Eddie cut in. "I still want to know how Devina ended up free from the Well of Souls."

Lassiter waved his hands to get everybody's attention again. "'For me to have my love, you can never have yours.' That's what she said to me. Clearly, there are conditions on Lash being with her—so how else could you explain it all? She must have conjured him." He pictured that demon with the wind in her face, her hair moving like black vipers. "And if Lash is starting to rebuild the Lessening Society, we need to make sure they stay broken up. Nothing is going to make her more psychotic than being denied what she wants, and she'll go after him. Hound him and get in his way. She's done it before, right?"

Butch nodded. "I've been on the receiving end of that routine. It's intense. She will not take no for an answer."

"Good, that's what we want. The pair of them must be kept apart, and I can make sure that happens."

He looked over at Eddie and Adrian. They may have

helped out back when he'd been attacked, but he was under no illusions that he'd been stuffed into that Mini just because of his injuries. They'd intended to take him to the Creator.

Still did.

Abruptly, Vishous tilted forward on his hips and moved his lit stick back and forth between them. "I'm sorry, you're gonna need to back this up for me a little. You're in *love?*"

+ + +

Whilst Rahvyn sat in the training center's break room, she was hungry, and yet the displays of fresh fruit, snacks, and drinks held no appeal. She felt as though she was in the non-temporal realm with the Book, suspended outside the entropy that was the rule when one was upon the earth.

As she looked around at the vacant tables, empty chairs, and lonely couch, she thought about the last time she had been down here in the Brotherhood's clinic. Not unlike this evening, things had started out on an unexceptional note . . . and proceeded into territories of fraught emotion and danger.

As with tonight, it had been a male of worth who had been injured. Unlike tonight, it had been a mortal, and Nate had died of a gunshot wound directly before her. The mourning of his parents, and the pleading of her cousin, Sahvage, had been a call to action that she had ultimately heeded, though she had known what she was doing was against the laws of the Creator's universe: She had used powers she could marshal, but had never understood, and pulled the young male out of the continuum of life and death, setting him aside on a protected shelf that insulated him from the grasp of the grave, fore'ermore.

An unholy outcome for a righteous reason.

The short-term effect had been positive, with only her—and perhaps Sahvage, the first and only other she had saved thusly—knowing the grim reality that eternal life was merely the cessation of physical mortality. All other aspects of the soul, the heart, the mind, remained subject to the battering and erosion of experience.

Such endurance was a curse. Especially when you were going to watch others around you, those whom you valued, whom you loved and relied upon . . . leave you behind.

Closing her eyes, she covered her face with her hands, as if she could shield herself from the assault of her conscience. But it was too late for that, and what was worse? She had deserted Nate to his fate. Saving the Book and securing it in her mental netherworld had been an excuse to remove herself from the departure of Lassiter and the ramifications of her being a savior when she should not have been. It had not been the right thing to do with regard to the young male.

"I think you saved him."

She dropped her hands. The fallen angel with the braid down his back nearly had to duck his head as he came through the doorway, and he paused to look around at the vending and soda machines, as well as the hot buffet, which was currently closed down except for bowls of apples, oranges, and bananas.

Rahvyn was not fooled. He had come for her, not sustenance.

"He would have recovered," she said roughly. "I merely endeavored to ease his pain."

The angel went over to the machine where bags of chips and pretzels were lined up in rows and separated by corkscrews. "Hey, these are free? The dollar bill slot is blocked."

She recalled sitting here with Nate, at this very table, conversating with him about weighty matters—but also lighter ones, which had included him explaining the names of the dispensing facilities and their operations.

"Yes, they are free."

"Sweet."

The angel began pushing all kinds of buttons, little parcels dropping down into the well, his selection as he punched into the number pad seemingly random. And when he bent to retrieve what he'd chosen, he had a quiet joy on his face, as if the fact that this was not costing him a dime was a lottery win.

Proof that even immortals could be enchanted by simple pleasures.

Yet she was not fooled by the surface gloss upon his mood. Darkness abounded within him.

"Mind if I join you?" he asked on the way over.

He set his parcels of calories down on the table without waiting for her reply, and then paused and looked at her with eyes the color of red wine viewed through candlelight.

"Please do," she said remotely.

"Not feeling company, huh."

Dropping into a seat, the heft of him dwarfed the table that had seemed quite appropriately sized with her upon it, and she watched his large hands rifle through the colorful bags. He chose Cheetos, a snack she remembered the staff at Luchas House eating from time to time.

"I don't blame you," he said in a casual fashion. "For taking a breather. I needed a break, too. Lot of Brothers in your boy's room."

"He is not mine."

"Oh, right." He tilted the open neck of the bag to her. "Want some?"

"Ah, no. Thank you."

She looked away, her eyes going over the other tables with their empty chairs. So many alternate places he could have been sitting—and she began to construct excuses for her departure as she turned in her seat and focused on the TV that was mounted up on the far wall.

The local news was doing a story on the damage to the "travel agency" building next to where Lassiter had been attacked by the demon, a reporter standing as close as he could to a police barricade, the flashing lights strobing him as well as the uniformed officers who milled around.

"You are the one who saved him," she said stiffly. "When the demon attacked."

"So you were watching us. I thought I sensed some-thing."

She did not look away from the images upon the television. The idea that a square of glass could project a moving picture all the way up here on the mountain from downtown was incredible. Indeed, she had been told it was all over the world.

"You don't belong here, do you," the angel said.

"Neither do you," she countered.

"Touché." He was opening another, different bag now, the crinkling loud in her ears in the silence. "Mind if I ask you how long you've known Lassiter?"

"If you'll excuse me"—she rose—"I think I'm going to—"

He caught her wrist. "Sit. Down."

In the tense pause, she wondered what he would do if she resisted.

"I'm here to take him away," came the grim voice. "So if you want him to have a chance at staying, you're going to have to explain to me why you care about where he's at, one way or another."

Now she met the burgundy stare of the angel. So this was why Lassiter had told her goodbye, the cause of his leaving. And she wasn't fooled. How she felt about him would not matter one bit with regard to his destiny.

"Let go of me," she said in a low growl. "I do not do well with males who seek to confine me, and I would hate my wrath to be expressed in this place of peace."

Instantly, the hand released. "You don't belong here."

"You said that before and I have not denied it."

"You are . . . young and old by turns." The male eased back in the chair and peered into the bag, as if hunting for the most perfectly formed, triangle-shaped, orange-dusted Doritos. "It's quite curious."

He was right, of course. She was nine and twenty years . . . and also nearly two centuries old.

"Why are you taking Lassiter and where to?" she asked.

"Sit down and I'll tell you. Or you can leave, and I'll follow you. FYI, the first choice is your better outcome."

Rahvyn slowly lowered herself back into the molded plastic chair. "Answer my question."

"Where are you from?" The angel popped another chip in his mouth and the crunch as he chewed it was muffled. "And if you say the Old Country, I'm going to conveniently forget all the details about what my mission is, and wouldn't that be a loss to you. Given how curious you are about the Lassiter situation."

"I do not believe I care for you."

Those eyes flashed to hers. "The feeling is mutual."

At that, he shook the bag, leaned back, and poured whatever was left of the contents directly into his mouth. When he righted his head, the way he cocked his brow in expectation was as grating as his line of inquiry.

"I am from the year eighteen hundred thirty-three," she snapped. "If we're using the human calendar."

There was a split second of assessment. Then he nodded. "That explains it."

"Now, where are you taking him."

"Out of this time. You must know all about that kind of thing, huh."

Next up on his menu list was a bag of chocolate M&M's, and he opened the little pouch with a quick rip.

His stare narrowed on her. "Speaking of time, in about five minutes, one of the Brothers is going to come down here to get you. They're going to take you to Lassiter."

"So you arrived here wanting to vet me in some fashion, is that it?"

"You bet your bippy it is. 'Scuse my French."

"You are . . . a friend of his then?"

He laughed in a short rush and poured some of the colorful confections out in his palm. As he shook his head ruefully, he muttered, "I just don't get the new colors. Like blue? And now purple? 'Course, they still taste the same."

"Are you? A friend?"

"I don't know if that's quite the term I'd use. I am not his enemy, for sure, and I care about his well-being. Let's face it, he's . . . very important in the scheme of things. And that's why I'm curious about you, a female throwing around healing energy like that? Kind of miraculous. Kind of dangerous. It goes either way with you, doesn't it."

As his eyes locked on her in a knowing fashion, Rahvyn looked back at the TV. The reporting had switched to a broad swath of linked-up purveyors of goods, a mall, she had been told it was called. A woman in a red coat was in focus and gesturing theatrically, next to a glass entrance that was shattered.

It appeared to be a night for things getting broken: Brick walls, store windows. Lassiter's skull.

"Is that why you endangered yourself to protect him from Devina?" she said. "Because he is important?"

"Yes."

"Well, he is important to me as well, and that is why I was there."

A slow smile eased the tension in the bold features of the male's face. "For two people who don't like each other, I guess we have him in common."

"It appears as though that is true—"

The door to the break room opened, and in its jambs, Vishous, son of the Bloodletter, stood without apology.

"You were right," she murmured as she got to her feet. "They have come for me. It is as if you can see into the future."

"Not really. Which is why I'll be watching you."

Rahvyn glanced at the angel. He was not looking at her, focused instead on the colorful disks of covered chocolate in his palm. She wasn't fooled.

Somehow, he knew what she had done . . . at that castle back in the Old Country. To that *Princeps*, and all his guards. Other unholy acts for a righteous reason.

"Rahvyn?" Vishous said. "You want to see your—"

"He is *not* mine," she cut in.

But if he would have me? she thought to herself as she weeded in and out of the chairs and tables. She would be more than willing to belong to him.

CHAPTER TWELVE

And there she was.

As Rahvyn came into the recovery room, Lassiter felt a flush go through his body, and while the brothers and Adrian silenced their chatter, it was like they disappeared—and took the rest of the universe with them.

She was so hesitant, although whether that was because she wasn't sure of her reception or because there were so many warriors crammed into the shoebox-sized room, he didn't know. At least there was an easy solution to the latter.

"Leave us," he commanded as he pushed himself up higher on the hospital bed.

There wasn't a lot of discussion, and thank God. His energy was low and what he had was for Rahvyn.

As the door eased shut behind the peanut gallery, he motioned with his hand. "Can you come here? You're very far away."

She seemed to float over to him, although she was walking—yes, her feet were on the floor. When she stopped at the base of the bed, he motioned for her to get even closer.

All he got was one more step forward.

Her hair gleamed in the dull fluorescent ceiling lights, the platinum fall split over her shoulders. She seemed pale, her lips blending into her face, and her eyes stayed lowered from his own.

"Are you leaving tonight—"

"I'm glad you're here—"

They both fell silent. For a split second, he was back in the cave, resolved to rot out there on the mountain, caught in the limbo between annihilation and existence. But now Eddie and Adrian had showed up, and he'd figured out Devina's angle.

So the question posed by the Clash was answered.

He did not want to go. Not now.

His purpose was this female. Maybe it always had been and he'd just been too terrified by that, especially after the shit with the demon.

"I'm sorry," he blurted. "I know I've been walking away from you. My reasons were what they were, but now . . ."

"You are not leaving?"

Not if he could help it. "No, I'm not."

"What has changed," she whispered.

He thought of the big reasons he had been determined to keep away from her: The danger of Devina. His shame over what he had let happen to his body. His sense that Rahvyn needed someone less complicated. If he was honest with himself, he knew he would not be able to overcome any of the deficits alone, much less as a trio. But now he had a motivation that gave him . . . permission? Maybe that was the word. To get the fuck over himself.

He would be with Rahvyn, in spite of his unworthiness. Because he had to.

If he had his true love, Devina would not have hers—and that would keep her and Lash apart and the demon busy. And if the bitch decided to come after him to try to split him and Rahvyn up? Then he was going to take care of business while the Brotherhood took care of Rahvyn.

How fucking ironic that duty was getting him what he ultimately wanted. Which was this female.

Aware Rahvyn was waiting for a response, he didn't know what to say. The last thing she needed was to get tangled in the ugliness, and he was going to have to protect her on a lot of levels.

"Thank you for your help tonight," he hedged.

Her long exhale told him his dodge disappointed her. "I'm sorry I followed you."

"I'm sorry I put you in a position of having to." He smiled a little. "Look at us, apologizing left and right."

"Are you well?" She motioned over her head. "Your injury was quite severe."

Lassiter banged on his skull with a fist. "Right as rain—"

She put her hands out. "Do not hurt yourself further!"

"You know, you might have a point." He rubbed the spot as his head pounded a little. "Seriously, though. I'm okay."

Rahvyn finally came all the way up to him. And when he reached out his palm, she hesitated—but then took what he offered in a firm grip.

"I am . . . very sorry," he whispered.

As the words came out of his mouth, he was aware that only he knew their full significance. Only he knew he was apologizing for being a coward. For being ashamed. For . . . needing an external impetus to act on his heart's desire.

"For what do you apologize," she said.

"Running from you." And himself. "I don't . . . I'd like to stop running. That's why I'm not going anywhere. That's what's changed."

Funny, that demon had robbed him of so much, but she'd given him a kind of gift as well. If allowing himself to fully fall for Rahvyn got them all where they needed to be with Devina? Then yes, he did feel as though he had *permission* to be selfish and express his emotions, let himself go.

Kind of a fucked-up way to heal, wasn't it.

Rahvyn leaned her hip against the mattress. "What about the others."

"You mean Eddie and Adrian?" As her face tightened, he switched his grip and stroked the inside of her wrist. "I'm not worried about them and neither should you. I'll take care of it."

"All right," she said as she nodded.

A strange sensation uncoiled in his chest, warm and loose, and he went with it. "I think it's time for me to get out of this bed."

With a groan, he sat all the way up and started shifting his legs out from under the thin sheets. Things were going great—until his bare feet hit the floor and he realized he was naked.

"Ah . . ." He glanced around. "Clothes."

"Oh."

The flush that hit Rahvyn's face put color back in her cheeks, and he had to fight not to reach up and touch her hair—and then his eyes lingered on her lips. He wanted to kiss her. He always wanted to kiss her.

Except even as an anticipation thickened his blood, memories of Devina came between them, sure as if the images and echoed sensations were bricks that were tangible, his revulsion the mortar that made solid that which was all in his mind.

Fuck you, Devina, he thought.

"Can I take you somewhere beautiful?" he said hoarsely.

Squaring her shoulders, Rahvyn cleared her throat. "You do not have to be nice to me just because I tried to help."

"That's not why I'm being nice to you."

Rahvyn opened her mouth. Then closed it again. When she crossed her arms over her chest, he could feel the distance return.

"Indeed, I am more accustomed to your departures than your presence," she said roughly. "Therefore you will understand my hesitation. The only thing more painful than your leaving is the prospect of getting further attached only to have you disappear once more."

"Further?" he prompted.

"I have made no secret of my . . ."

When she shook her head sharply, he hung on, hoping to hear the words he wanted her to speak. That was such bullshit, though. She was right. He had been more reliable for his absences than a male who deserved her inner thoughts.

"I haven't stopped thinking of you," he said. "I might have been gone, but I took you with me."

She looked up. "For true?"

He nodded slowly. "On my soul, for true. And I just want to take you to a place that's peaceful. There's been too much drama tonight. Too much . . . pain, for too long."

And that was the God's honest on so many levels.

Rahvyn tensed her shoulders, as if she were leaping off into waters that might prove to be too shallow. "I would like that."

Lassiter started to smile. "After I get some pants on, of course."

◆ ◆ ◆

This place was a fetid mess.

Back in downtown Caldwell's seedier zip code,

where most of the structures were abandoned and humans with good sense didn't venture out after dark, Lash regarded the entryway of a filthy, four-level walk-up with all the enthusiasm he'd have greeted an outhouse in the wilderness. The building was Victorian in derivation, with bays on each floor that extended forward, and ornamentation at the eaves, but the shithole showed every bit of its age, city sludge striping down its facade, chips out of its stone steps, slates missing from its roof.

As a cold breeze weaved around his legs, a woman screamed an obscenity somewhere behind him and there was a crash. Then the wind changed direction and he caught a whiff of human urine and rotten food.

Imagining that stench in August, he reflected on how he had grown up, in a mansion full of *doggen*, every need anticipated and tended to, the decor gleaming of generational wealth, the voices in the grand rooms soft and accented with the proper lilt that only came with distilled knowledge and privilege—

A blaring horn cut through his replay of things long past, and then a vehicle barreled around a corner a couple of blocks down and headed in their direction.

"I want that SUV," he ordered his subordinate. "Get it."

"What?"

For a split second, he nearly slapped the dumb bastard security guard he'd turned outside Devina's version of Bergdorf's. But both his hands were busy with his duffle bags of stolen weapons and gear. The Dick's

Sporting Goods they'd broken into and five-finger-discounted had dressed them both properly and given them some basic armaments. It hadn't done shit for the raw material that was *not* in the dipshit beside him.

"Get. That. SUV—"

"How do I—"

"Oh, for *fuck's* sake. Drop your haul and stop the fucking thing."

The command was followed with all the gumption of a teenager, a muted metal clanging chiming on both sides of the moron, after which Lash's one and only inductee into the Lessening Society loafed out into the middle of the road. As the slayer put both hands up and winced, like he was trying to bring a baby buggy to a standstill and worried about his fucking shins, Lash wondered how, in a city of two-million-plus humans, he'd managed to recruit such a total waste of space.

But the lame-ass got the job done.

The blacked-out Suburban hit its brakes, and there was no moment of confusion for its driver and passenger. Without missing a beat, two men put down their windows, stuck their guns out—and opened fire, the *pop-pop-pop* echoing around the decrepit Grand Canyon of the street.

Now that is more like it, Lash thought.

His slayer was hit in the chest too many times to count, a three-D torso target getting practiced on by a pair of experts. And talk about cinematic. Spotlit by the headlights, the security-guard-now-*lesser*'s arms raised up as he jerked to the rhythm of the impacts, the assault salsa driving him back until he fell over onto the pavement.

As the stinging aroma of gunpowder and weed replaced the neighborhood's piss scent, laughter bubbled out of those open windows.

When Lash dropped his duffles, the driver looked over at the clanking, and a pair of dark eyes narrowed in a way that suggested a new target had been isolated and identified. It was not possible to assess the man's height, but the shoulders were thick and so was the tattooed neck. More than that, the cunning stare and the way the guy was so comfortable using his firearm affirmed value.

"You owe me," Lash said.

The human shifted the muzzle of his autoloader over so that it was pointed toward Lash's torso. "You want some?"

"Yes," Lash drawled, "I do."

There was a moment of pause, as if the response was a surprise. And then the human began to empty what was left in his clip.

Walking forward, Lash put out his palm and collected the slugs one by one, their trajectories shifting as they were called home by the center of his hand, the jingling sweet and soft as the projectiles collected in a little lead puppy pile.

The trigger finger that had been so busy eased off, and as a swill of gaseous emissions curled up from the tip of the gun, Lash closed a grip around the payload.

"What the fuck . . ." the human breathed.

On the far side of the driver, the passenger was pulling a pole-axe, too, his stare wide in the glow of the dash.

"Do you want to live forever," Lash said in a low voice.

"Get the fuck back, man—"

"I asked you a question." Lash stopped at point-blank range, and to help things along, he positioned the human's arm so that the muzzle of the gun was precisely in the center of his own chest. "What is your answer. Do you want to live forever."

When the driver tried to yank the weapon away, Lash put his thumb on the forefinger that was wrapped around the trigger—and forced the discharge of the last bullet in the magazine.

The sound was loud at such close range, the impact such that Lash's entire body jerked. Ah, yes, .45s packed quite a punch.

He held those dark eyes the entire time, not even blinking.

On the far side of the center console, the guy riding shotgun decided he was done: "I'm out!"

As the man fumbled for the door release, Lash glanced over and willed the lock to hold tight. Meanwhile, out in front of the grille, the *lesser* who'd played Smith & Wesson pincushion sat up on the pavement and pulled open the hunting jacket that draped his soft body. Looking down at his sternum, he probed the black ooze that was staining the front of his camouflage t-shirt.

"What . . . the fuck is . . ." The driver did not finish. Could not finish.

Prepared to settle the debate, Lash worked his shoulders, rolling them back and forth; then he swallowed, over and over again. Finally, he coughed into his hand.

"Would you like this back," he said as he offered the man's bullet to him.

The guy made the sign of the cross over his sternum. "*Madre de Dios*. What are you."

Over the flapping of the passenger, who was pumping the door handle like he was performing CPR on that side of the SUV, Lash said, "You don't need to worry about that. All you have to answer is one simple question."

"Wh . . . wha . . . what?"

"*Do you want to live forever.*"

CHAPTER THIRTEEN

I t was around ten a.m. the following morning that Beth, née Randall, mated of Wrath, son of Wrath, sire of Wrath, rushed down the subterranean tunnel to the back entrance into the training center. When she got to the reinforced steel door, she shifted her son onto her other hip so she could punch in a passcode. As the copper lock retracted, she glanced over her shoulder with a sickening feeling.

"We're here," she said to Wrath. Even though he would already know that by the shifting sounds.

Opening the heavy panel and revealing the supply closet, she propped the weight with her whole body and tried to get herself out of the way.

Wrath was big under any circumstances. Carrying his beloved golden in his arms, he required even more space—but just like the announcement of their arrival, any commentary on how he was going to have to duck and curl around the dog to squeeze past the reams of papers and the stacks of folders, pen boxes, and printer cartridges was unnecessary. Though his eyes did not function anymore, his senses always fired on all cylinders, and sure enough, he navigated through the jambs with no problem, turning to the side, lowering his stance, shuffling George into the cramped space.

Now it was Wrath's turn to play wallflower, and he was less successful than she'd been at shrinking. As he pressed back against the shelving, she wedged by with L.W. and opened the way into the office.

On the far side of Tohr's administrative space, she did her duty for the last time with a glass panel, and the second they stepped into the concrete tunnel that ran the length of the facility, Doc Jane leaned out of one of the clinic's doorways.

"Down here," V's mate urged.

Wrath led the way now, and Beth checked on how their son was doing because there was nothing she could do about any of this and sometimes you needed to feel like you could help something, someone. Her son was rock-solid. Even though they'd woken L.W. up and disturbed his sleep, he wasn't crying and cranky. He was staring forward at his father and the dog with those grave, now-green eyes of his, his expression that of an adult who recognized that something was very wrong with the dog—and if anything happened to George, his father, the King, was never going to get over—

Stop it, she told herself.

George was fine. The animal was young, only what, five years old? Six, tops? It just felt like he and Wrath had been a pair for a lifetime, the two of them so symbiotic in their movements and silent communication it was as if they were one person.

Grath. Weorge.

Whatever.

The golden was probably just suffering from an upset stomach. No doubt he'd been slipped something at Last Meal by Fritz. The household's elderly butler had a thing for him, but who didn't? Heck, maybe Rhage had given him a gallon of ice cream under the table.

"Thanks for this," Wrath said in a grave voice as he came up to Doc Jane.

"No problem. I just hope I can help."

Wrath did another duck and shuffle, and then they were all in the exam room together. To locate the table, he moved more slowly now, shifting his hold on the blond-furred bundle of paws and tail, putting one arm out, his hand at waist level. When his fingertips came in contact with the examination bed, he explored the contours, got a bead on its dimensions, and gently laid the dog on the padded cushion.

"So what have we got," Jane said as she unlooped her stethoscope and went to stroke George's head. "We're not feeling so hot?"

The golden offered her a lackadaisical nudge with his muzzle and a half-hearted wag.

"There's something wrong with him, but I don't know what it is," Wrath said. "He sleeps next to us on his bed. About twenty minutes ago, I woke up because I heard him whimper and I found him sitting in this really weird position, all braced forward, his mouth open though he wasn't panting. He kept whimpering, like . . . he was trying to tell me something was wrong."

Beth went over and sat in one of the chairs against the long wall. Settling L.W. on her lap, she made sure he was facing outward so he could see what was happening. He'd never been a kid to cuddle into a chest, seek comfort on a shoulder, nuzzle into the neck. He wanted to be confronting whatever was before him.

Not exploring. Confronting.

"Well, I'm not a vet," Jane murmured as she plugged her ears with her instrument. "But let's take a look at our breathing and our heart rate."

As Wrath went to stand at his head, George licked his master's hand, as if he were trying to be brave—and when Wrath murmured to him, the golden laid his head back down, his mouth going slack, his breathing slow and irregular.

"He's going to be okay," Beth murmured in her son's ear.

L.W. didn't pay any attention to her. He just stared at his father as Wrath stayed right by his dog, his dagger hand on George's head.

"I'm just going to take a listen, good boy," Jane murmured as she pressed the metal disk around the area right behind George's elbow.

When she frowned and kept moving the stethoscope around, Beth's stomach did another bottom-out, like she was on a rollercoaster that was flying over a dip in its rails.

"What is it?" Wrath asked, like he'd caught the shift in the doctor's energy.

Jane didn't answer him. She lifted George's jowl and peered at his gums.

They were gray.

Oh, God, Beth thought.

This wasn't indigestion. The dog was dying.

+ + +

Mortals, particularly of the human variety, existed in such a narrow bandwidth of understanding.

This was a good thing, Devina reflected as she re-formed at a secluded exterior corner of the Galleria Mall's T-rex footprint. Such ignorance and all its blinded bliss kept nonessentials out of the way, and if things had to be done in their midst, camo and cover-up was much, much easier than dealing with supernaturals.

On that note, she brushed at her black leather pants and rearranged the form-fitting black cashmere sweater she'd changed into. Even though it was April, there was a nip in the air this morning, and besides, wearing a bustier for this investigation felt too close to the desperation that was squeezing her tits.

Squeezing not in a good way.

Glancing up, she noted the skies were laden with clouds, the sun's warmth nowhere to be felt, the churning weather promising a cold, bracing rain.

So the vibe was right, according to her mood.

Stepping out of the shadows, she proceeded down the sidewalk, measuring the acres of empty parking lot. The *Jurassic Park* metaphor was apt on another level. These dying shopping centers were dinosaurs in retail fact as well as scale, their anchor stores lifting up off of the plains of concrete and rebar, floating off, some to the ether of the web, others into the purgatory of bankruptcy, many into liquidation and nonexistence.

Proof that the habit patterns of discretionary income spending could cause extinction events for whole sectors of the economy.

As she rounded the corner, she was very aware that she was attempting to distract herself with inane thoughts, and hey, that was fucking self-care, thank you very much. Just like the two guys she had gone out and fucked last night. And the eleven pints of Häagen-Dazs she had woofed back over the course of the last few hours. And the $119,863.95 she had put on her American Express black card at NeimanMarcus.com.

Not that any of that shit had helped any more than the mental chatter was. Her little lock of hair bullshit had failed as a locator.

Oh, and *Love Is Blind* 3 had *really* not helped. She'd made it through the first happy coupling-up and exploded her TV in a fit. Which had caused her to have to conjure another. Which had appeared on cue, obligingly turned itself on to cable instead of Netflix . . . and ultimately, thanks to a breaking news update, led her here to the mall.

Devina slowed down and regarded the busted front entrance of a Dick's Sporting Goods store. Barricades, yellow police tape, and uniformed CPD officers had turned the crime scene into a tourist attraction, what few shoppers were coming and going stopping to stare.

Time to go to work.

Sauntering over, she caught the eyes of all of the cops, and given the way things were going for her, the fact that they clustered up against the tape to talk to her made her feel like maybe she wasn't complete dogshit.

"Can we help—"

"—you, miss?"

"Can—"

"—we help you—"

"—miss?"

They talked over each other, each tossing out the same sentence as if it were a job requirement. Up close, they were interchangeable, all of them on the young side, like guarding stores that had already been burglarized was relegated to their relatively low level of competence and experience.

"I work here," she said as she deliberately twirled her hair.

The Betty Boop, help-me-big-daddy bullshit was boring, but usually got the job done without her messing with men's brains. Sifting through all their memories right now? No offense, but she didn't need to see their wives and girlfriends giving them head while she flipped switches to get herself inside the goddamn store. And with so many of them? She'd have had to brainwash them as a group.

But hey, the male attention was definitely a balm.

"When I left last night," she continued, "I forgot my

phone in my locker. My manager told me to come down here and ask if one of you could escort me in to get it? I mean, I saw the news, I heard about the break-in."

"We can't let civilians in," the one on the far left said as he jacked up his gun belt. "This is a crime scene."

No, really? And here she thought it was a cock convention.

"Oh, lighten up, Jer," someone said from the back.

As "Jer" got fluffy at the slap-down, an older cop with a been-there-done-that face and a six-beer-a-night gut pushed the young-buck others out of the way.

"C'mon, honey." He lifted the tape. "I'll take ya in."

"Oh, thank you."

Ducking down, Devina was sure to give Jer a batted eye while she breached the barrier that was flimsy in substance, ironclad in boundary. On the far side, she followed the older cop, content to model walk in his wake over to one of the side doors that was still intact.

Whoever had broken into the store had had a chip on their shoulder. They'd smashed the revolving glass entry both coming and going, shards on the ground outside on the left and shards on the inside of the store on the right.

It had to have been Lash, she thought. Assuming the reports about what had been taken were accurate.

And clearly, he was stealing instead of conjuring to conserve energy after his first induction.

"Lot of these new guys," the cop said as they walked into a cathedral of merchandise and equipment, "just gotta—what do they call it? Flex? Jesus Christ, what a waste of time."

"I'm really grateful." She smiled at the officer. "You're my hero."

He didn't seem affected one way or another by her charm, and she respected that: "Just tryin' to help you get your phone. Let's get to the back of the house."

Once again falling in behind him, she looked around. In this part of the store, everything was orderly and non-ransacked, the exercise apparel hanging, slim and colorful, on round racks, the hints of what could be found deeper into the Dick's showing on the fringes: camping and sports equipment, a canoe hanging from the rafters, stand-up displays of dehydrated food that could last for years.

"So what happened here," she asked as she surged ahead so they were side by side. "Do you know who did this?"

"Can't comment on an ongoing investigation. Sorry."

The officer didn't sound sorry. So she didn't feel apologetic as she barged into his mind—oh, who was she kidding, she wouldn't have cared anyway . . .

Okay, talk about your backfires. When she accessed the part of his memories that had to do with the investigation, what she was shown was like scratching a poison ivy rash. You thought it was a good idea, but in the end, you did yourself more harm than good.

The cops had security footage of a tall, powerfully built—NAKED—blond man, with an equally naked, but not at all powerfully built, guy, pulling up to the front of the store at just after midnight, in a navy blue Toyota Camry that had a front bumper that was falling off and sparks flashing behind one of its blown-out tires. The pair had disembarked and walked over to the entrance, and the blond man had broken the glass on the right side of the revolving door just by putting up his palm.

The cops were real confused about that part. As well as the way the alarm had instantly been silenced as the pair had progressed into and through the store. After that, things had gotten much more conventional, at least as stealing went. The two "men" had clothed themselves in the hunting department, taken some duffle bags—and then made like shit was for free in the section where guns were sold.

The older cop had watched the security feed himself, so she took a moment, while he was standing there, frozen and staring up at her like his brains had funneled out his doughy ass, to replay the black-and-white video a couple of times. The sight of Lash moving around with that powerful body of his, even distilled as it was through the recollection of the cop, was enough to make her—

"Why you cryin', hon?"

As the words registered, she shook her head and said roughly, "I'm sorry, what?"

The cop motioned around her face. "You're cryin'."

Devina brushed her cheeks. "I'm not."

"Here." The guy leaned to the side and took out a cloth handkerchief that was starched and folded into a precise white square. "Can't have a pretty face doin' like that."

She took what he held out, and as she stared at the thing on her palm, she imagined that his wife probably ironed them for him with curlers in her hair, a little TV on the counter in the laundry room keeping her company, a soap opera burbling like visual soup in the background.

Devina sniffled and blotted under her eyes carefully. "How long have you been married? 'Cuz I know you didn't iron this yourself."

"We made it thirty-six years. She died this past February, on the seventh." He nodded at the handkerchief. "Don't have many of those left that she washed and tended for me. I think that's the last one, actually."

The words were spoken in the same laconic tone as the man had told good ol' Jer to pipe-down-sonny. But behind the syllables? There was a loss so deep that the guy was hollowed out on the inside.

She knew how that felt.

"I'm sorry," Devina said.

He shrugged. "What are you going to do."

The officer turned away, but she stopped him. "Is it true? That you'd rather be dead."

He blinked like he had no idea what she was talking about. But that was a lie. His inner thoughts were bared before her, and she knew that underneath the daily duties he distracted himself with, he was yearning for a get-out-of-jail.

"Is it true," she whispered.

"Yeah." He cleared his throat. "I miss her that much. Kids are grown and busy. She was the one who kept them around. I sit at home alone at night . . . what is there for me, you know? It wasn't supposed to be like this. I'm supposed to retire next month. We were going to travel. I was going to buy her an RV and we were going to . . . travel."

The bleakness in him touched her in a way that seemed as shocking as her wasting any time at all on some human who was nothing in the grand scheme of things.

"And you believe she's waiting for you," Devina prompted.

As he glanced around, she looked at the silver shield that was on his chest. The name on it was "Massarini" and the number was 216.

"I don't know," he said. "Maybe she's in heaven or maybe we're all worm food. Either way, I'm good because I'm not feeling like this anymore, or else I'm with her. Better'n where I'm at."

Funny, how sadness could age someone. Though his features did not change, the folds that ran from the sides of his nose to the edges of his mouth seemed to gouge farther into his face, and the wrinkles by his eyes and across his forehead likewise deepened. The color seemed to fade out as well, everything draining, draining, draining. Until he looked like he was eighty.

"You've been praying," she told him. "You want out."

"Yeah, I do. It'll be a relief—goddamn, why am I talking to you like this? I don't tell anybody this." He laughed awkwardly, the forced smile not lasting. "I don't talk to nobody."

"Are you sure," she said quietly. "That what you prayed for is what you want. There's no going back."

"Yeah." His eyes returned to hers, and there was

nothing in them. No emotion, not even sadness. "I am sure."

Devina extended the handkerchief to him. "Here, take this back. You don't want to lose it."

As voices percolated down from the second floor where the ransacked gun department was being processed for prints, he reached forward—

Closing her hand around his own, Devina stared deeply into the man's watery brown eyes and gave things a squeeze.

The officer gasped, his brows flaring, his shoulders jerking back. Then he retracted his arm and grabbed the front of his chest. Weaving on his feet, he stumbled a little, fell against a display of water bottles, lost his balance completely. As all kinds of Yeti bounced around him on the hard floor, he slumped into a crumble and fought for breath.

Devina held the handkerchief to her own heart for a moment. Then she bent down and tucked it into his clenched fist. "You'll see Nancy. Give it about a minute."

Turning away from him, she blinked her eyes and looked up so that no more tears fell. "Help," she cried out calmly. "Help. Something's wrong with him."

As her voice echoed around, other law enforcement people came to the balcony above, and when they saw the cop sprawled on the floor with the traveler mugs, they started racing for the open staircase.

Leaving them to it, not that there was any resuscitating the widower from his widow-maker, Devina decided she didn't need to see the break-in's aftermath, not now that she'd witnessed the theft itself thanks to the old cop's rock-solid memory of the security footage.

Out in the gray daylight, she squinted and took her phone from her ass pocket. Flashing it at the officers, she said, "Got it. Thank you."

A couple of them pride-bustled in their unis, kicking their chins up like they had done shit. But at least good ol' Jer did the duty and lifted the yellow stripe for her.

"Glad we could help," he said, all Mr. Man.

"Nancy's husband took care of me, not you."

As she tilted under the tape, he looked at her ass like he could have motorboated her butt cheeks, if he'd wanted to—and just as she was about to make sure the bean burrito he'd had for breakfast carved a fire path out of his body and took half his colon with it . . . he gave her a little intel nugget that solved her now-what.

Or rather, his communicator did.

His little shoulder-mounted speaker went off with a squawk, and as he reached over to silence it, an update came in about another scene. One that was downtown in a rough neighborhood.

One that the CPD was dismissing as unconnected to this highly alarming and dangerous theft of shotguns and hunting clothes.

One that had a weird, eerie feel to it—and a bunch of black stains.

As she headed off to see if Lash had had anything to do with whatever had happened there, she sent that burrito on its final mission.

At least she was smiling a little as she dematerialized.

CHAPTER FOURTEEN

"How magical this realm is."

As Rahvyn spoke up, her eyes did another circle around the serene landscape, with its lush grass and brightly colored tulips, its elegant temples and arching trees. Indeed, the mystical plane Lassiter had brought her to was somewhat similar to where she had stashed the Book, safe and insulated from invasion, thanks to a forest ring that she instinctively knew was a metaphysical boundary.

"It is nice, isn't it?"

Lassiter walked forward, and though he was big and tall, his footfalls left no marks in the springy bed of the lawn. Likewise, she had the sense that nothing grew out of alignment in the foliage, everything forever cresting the apex of its growth cycle, the odd, milky sky feeding whatever energy needs were required.

"Things weren't always like this." He stopped and looked toward a temple with an open-air facade and what appeared to be living spaces inside. "When the Scribe Virgin was active and the Chosen were here, everything was just white. And I gather the layout and architecture were changed a little, too, after Phury took over."

She attempted to imagine a monochromatic wash over the verdant, the rainbow-bright, the vivid. "This is much better."

"I agree. So does Phury." Lassiter resumed his slow-go wander. "When he took over as the Primale, he freed the Chosen of their lives of service, and then redecorated the place. *Boom!* Crayola all over everything."

"Truly, I cannot believe I am here," she murmured. "The Scribe Virgin's Sanctuary . . ."

Raised in a traditional family, she had been brought up to revere and pray unto the creator of the vampire race, that figure in black robes who, on occasion, someone would say they had seen, and no one would believe they had. She had known, too, of the Chosen, the sacred order of females who served the Scribe Virgin in worship and as recorders of the lives of the vampire race—every event, of every soul's journey on earth.

And now she was here . . . with an angel who refused to acknowledge his own true power or role in it all. Lassiter merely ambled along at her side as they had explored a pool that shimmered with water so pure it was as liquid glass, and shrines with columned loggias, and the Treasury with its wealth of gems and precious items.

She would never forget pushing her hands into the hip-high baskets of sapphires, emeralds, and rubies.

"And now this is all yours?" Rahvyn asked as they approached the largest temple complex.

She mostly kept the awe out of her voice. Or perhaps . . . not.

"I don't think anyone owns the Sanctuary." He stopped at the foot of the grand entrance. "I think we all just pass through here for a while, mortal and immortal, sometimes for a short time, sometimes a long one, only the stories recorded in the volumes of lives left behind. And speaking of recording, here we are at the Temple of the Sequestered Scribes. Come on, I'll show you the inside."

As he walked up the steps to the formal, columned entry, it was with no particular regard—like the stones he placed his feet upon were just incremental pavers, the purpose of which was to secure an ascent to an entryway of no particular import. And then he opened the ornate door with no pomp, no flourish.

Just a portal into a building.

For a moment, all she could do was stare up at him—and she had the strangest revelation as she did.

Now she knew how the villagers had felt about her.

Back in her timeline, in the Old Country, she could remember people regarding her with wonder and a bit of fear. After word had gotten out in her little village that she had resuscitated a prized horse, and then located a missing young who had become lost in the wood, the males and females she had grown up around had started to hold her in some reverence. At first, it had made her anxious. Over time, it had begun to irritate her.

In truth, she had no greater understanding of the origins of her abilities or her purpose in possessing them than they had, and their elevation of her had made her own lack of foundational knowledge all the more resonant. Surely, if someone had been "gifted" as she was, the Scribe Virgin would have provided some tutelage into, if not the hows, at least the whys, of it all.

"Rahvyn?"

As the angel said her name, she took in the whole of him, from the fall of his blond-and-black hair, to the boxy, blue, loose top and pants he'd put on—"scrubs" as he'd referred to the set of clothing. He was beautiful, in a masculine manner . . . and different in a way she could sense clear as the physical presence of his.

"Sooner or later," she heard herself say, "you are going to have to tell me what changed within you."

"What do you mean?"

"Where is your halo."

He blanched and reached up above his head. "I didn't know it was gone."

"But you are not surprised, are you." When he did not respond, she knew she was correct. "You are going to have to tell me the why of it."

There was a pause. "All right, but not today. We have time."

"Do we? What of Eddie and Adrian. The former told me they have come for you."

The angel's iridescent eyes narrowed. "I'll take care of all that. I promise."

With a nod—because what else could she do other than trust him on both accounts—she ascended to join him at the decorative doorway. The fact that he assiduously stepped aside so there would be no contact of their bodies as she passed by stung a little.

But the room they entered was so astounding, she let the minor rejection go.

Under a soaring ceiling, set across an ancient stone floor, a series of desks were arranged in rows, and each of the stations was kitted out in identical fashion. Upon the hand-hewn tables rested a pot of sanguine ink, a feathered quill, and rolls of parchment tied with ribbons—as well as a crystal bowl that was so beautifully made, so finely blown, that the basin was as clear as the still water it contained.

"The scribing stations," she murmured in awe. "For truth, I did not believe they actually existed."

Walking forward, her hand lifted, as if she would touch any part of it, either the backless stools, the feathers, or the ink—and yet of course she would ne'er dare. This was the sacred space of the recorders of history, the chosen among the Chosen, the most important deed performed in service to the *mahmen* of the species.

Rahvyn glanced over her shoulder. "I cannot believe . . . I am here."

Her words drifted as their eyes met. Lassiter was staring at her with an undisguised, naked yearning, his arms crossed over his chest as if he sought to confine himself and his emotions, his feet planted solidly as if he had ordered them to hold his body in place, his torso set in the stiff tension of self-control.

Perhaps he had not desired the contact between them a moment ago . . . because he desired such too much.

"Come check out the library," he said in a brisk voice.

As if he were trying to divert himself.

This time, as he stepped around her in a wide berth, she was not hurt. The scent of his arousal told her what his lips could not.

The body, after all, never lied.

✦ ✦ ✦

Maybe he shouldn't have brought her here.

As Rahvyn looked around the Temple of the Sequestered Scribes with wonder and reverence, Lassiter couldn't see anything but her—and he thought of the way things had been when the Scribe Virgin had been in charge, all those sacred females teeming around the Sanctuary, recording the history of her race and performing devotionals, and reproducing with the Primale to spawn new members of the Black Dagger Brotherhood as well as more Chosen.

There had been people everywhere up here in the past. Not anymore.

He and Rahvyn were very, very alone.

And that was making things difficult for him, in ways that his self-control should have had no problem with. Instead, his thoughts had their own agendas, and they kept going to things like . . . full contact . . . of mouths . . . of bodies . . .

It was as if, having decided he wouldn't be stopped by what had been done to him by Devina, he had given free rein to the attraction that had always simmered under his surface for Rahvyn—and the lust was taking over everything.

To get a little more air, he went down all the rows of desks to a set of double doors, and after opening them, he walked into the vast library that housed the chronology of the entire race in orderly lineups of tall shelves.

Well, the chronology at least up until Phury had let the Chosen go free.

"All of these books . . ." Rahvyn said with wonder as she joined him. "These are lives? Every one?"

"All of the vampire souls that ever went before and came after."

Just like with the scribing stations, as she went exploring, she stopped short of touching anything, her hands hovering in the air. And as he focused on those fingertips of hers, his libido suggested he had plenty of things she could make contact with if she wanted to—

Shut up.

Rahvyn turned around on a spin, her silver hair fanning out. "I'm sorry?"

Lassiter coulda-hadda-V8'd himself, knocking his forehead with the heel of his palm. "That wasn't directed to you." And he wasn't about to explain he was talking to his cock. "The volumes are pretty impressive, aren't they. Not that I've read any."

He went over to one of the shelving stacks and pulled out a random tome. Flipping it open, he didn't allow his eyes to focus on the orderly symbols of the Old Language. Even though it was now his right, he felt no need to intrude on the privacy of someone else.

He was having enough trouble with his own privacy at the moment.

"What's in this vault?"

Lassiter glanced over to where she'd wandered. The reinforced panels were taller than she was and wide enough to accommodate three of her standing shoulder to shoulder, the steel glowing in the odd, diffused light.

"That's where the histories of the Black Dagger Brotherhood and all the First Families are kept. Phury told me he reinforced it a little. And by 'a little,' I think he meant a ton."

"Indeed," she breathed.

Now she touched something, her fingertips descending the contours of the molding that surrounded the vault's entry—and for a moment, he replaced his abdominal muscles with the carpentry's undulations. His breath caught.

"Do you get a volume?" she asked as she glanced over her shoulder at him.

"No, I don't."

Her eyes flashed with surprise. "Why not?"

"I'm not a vampire."

"But you're in charge."

"Am I? I think that's the Creator." He mostly kept the bitterness out of his voice. "We're all under Him and his whims."

Lowering his eyes, Lassiter focused on the book in

his palms and fanned the pages all the way to the end—
except then he stopped and frowned. The blank sheets
of parchment were marked with shadowy etchings that
were not legible, and when he backtracked to the last of
the ink that was properly, vividly, present, he saw that
the lines of symbols were filling themselves in, the
shapes darkening on their own.

He looked around at all the volumes, the thousands
of volumes.

Jesus, he thought. *The histories are writing themselves now.*

And clearly, free will was not the bill of goods it had
been sold as.

"But no one is writing anything down anymore."

"I don't think that's a problem." He clapped the book
shut and shoved it back into its slot. "Anyway . . ."

Rahvyn came over. "Are you all right?"

"Of course I am."

"Talk to me, Lassiter. You must tell me what is on
your mind."

As he stared down into her eyes, he felt a fucking
maelstrom rise inside him, conflicts twisting and turning in his gut. And for all the reasons he should stay
quiet, he found that he wanted to be truthful with her.
Even if only in one way.

"I want to kiss you." That stare of hers flared and he
nodded. "It's a truth I've been trying to deny. For your sake."

As he heard his words hit the airwaves, he pictured
Eddie and Adrian dragging him off to the Creator.

"Lassiter?"

"Yes."

"Why are you so afraid of kissing me?"

Even though he knew it was Rahvyn in front of him, somehow Devina took her place, the brunette-haired demon a barrier that was as tangible as that vault Rahvyn had just put her hand on.

"I do need to tell you something," he said in a halting voice.

"What," she whispered.

And yet the words didn't come. Not direct ones, at any rate.

"When I came here to Caldwell," he hedged, "and then when I started . . . here, after the Scribe Virgin left . . . I didn't think I was going to get involved. But I learned that I couldn't help myself."

"Forgive me, I do not understand?"

He moved his hand around, and then focused on the vault. "All of these souls, I'm responsible for them. They are my reason for being, these vampires. Their destinies . . . ? Are my own now."

Unable to stay still, he broke off from her and stalked among the shelves. And as if she recognized he needed his freedom, she waited silently—until he was back standing before her.

"I will do anything to help them. So I have done . . . things I shouldn't have . . . to help them. Do you understand what I'm saying?"

"What kinds of things," she whispered.

"Oh, Rahvyn. Bad things."

Crossing her arms over her chest, she shivered. "Like what."

Reaching out, he brushed her cheek, and thought of how different this moment would have been if he hadn't willingly put himself in Devina's cross hairs: It would have been uncomplicated by the disgust that was clogging his throat, the self-loathing getting even worse as he focused on Rahvyn's sweet mouth.

"I shouldn't have gotten involved as deeply as I am," he mumbled. "Losing objectivity makes you do things you wouldn't ordinarily think of. Things that you couldn't ordinarily contemplate . . . things that you didn't want to do, would never do. But feel as though you have to."

"Wrong deeds for the right reasons," she intoned.

"Yes."

"I know what that is." She put her hand on his arm. "Your heart is pure, though. Your intentions noble. Forgive yourself, that is what you must do."

He thought of Devina and Lash, and then how much he loved the female in front of him. "Even if I'm still doing it?"

"Perhaps you should stop."

Shaking his head, he said, "I can't. At least not right now."

"Then my wish for you is that you make peace with your choices." Abruptly, her face tightened, as if she were in pain, deep pain. "I know how you feel, and I do not relish your responsibility. But those under your care are very fortunate."

He recalled what she had done to save Nate's life the night the kid had been shot.

This was why she was the one, he thought. Nobody else could truly understand the situation he was in.

"Lassiter," she said tightly. "I must confess something."

"About what?"

Her silver eyes drifted down to his mouth. "I want to be saved. By you."

A bracing electrical charge bolted through his body. "Oh, God, Rahvyn. Are you sure."

"Yes," came her rock-solid reply. "Please . . . save me."

As if he could tell her, among all mortals, no? Still, his reply was in slow motion, him taking one final step into her, her putting her small hands on his chest, the stillness of anticipation closing in on them, locking in on them.

Slipping his hand under her platinum hair, he stroked the nape of her neck. "I'm sorry."

"Why do you keep saying that—"

He cut her off by covering her lips with his own, the kiss gentle, the feeling in his blood volcanic. He told himself to stop as soon as the seal was made. He didn't. Tilting his head to the side, he deepened the contact, stroking her mouth, plying her.

When he brought her up against his body, he made himself promise . . .

. . . he would stop.

Before things got to the point of no return.

Wasn't that where he needed to take them both, though?

CHAPTER FIFTEEN

It was just a dog.

As Wrath was caged in the exam room, that refrain was what was going around and around in his head, circulating like a vulture. He wanted to pace. He wasn't leaving George's side.

Because this wasn't just a dog.

Running his hand down George's flank, over and over again, he felt like this was not what was supposed to be happening. Nope, not now. Not today. George had been fine yesterday, and he was far too young for this. Goldens lived to be twelve, right—

His hand slipped onto the patch of fur on the belly that had been shaved to do the ultrasound. As that rib cage expanded and then shuddered on the exhale, he bent to the golden's soft ear.

"It's okay, buddy. I've got you."

When he stroked George's ruff, the dog nuzzled into his palm, and there was a lick, as if even though the animal suffered, his love for his master was untempered by his pain; he was just less able to demonstrate his loyalty.

Then everything went limp, and for a split second, Wrath thought it had happened. It was over—

A hitched breath made a whistle in the jowls. And after that, George coughed.

"I'm not getting another fucking dog," he said bitterly. "I am *not* going through this shit ever again."

"Wrath, we don't know what's going on—"

"Do you *really* think he's walking away from this?"

The door opened, and Wrath's hypersensitive nose picked up Doc Jane's scent—and it had changed. She was scared now.

"What is it," he snapped.

The female waited until the door closed on its own, his ears picking up the whisper-silent bump as the thing hit its jambs.

"We've, ah, we've found something on the ultrasound. On his spleen."

As Beth gasped, Wrath gripped the fur under his hand—and had to force himself to relax his fist. "And it is?"

"I'm not a vet and neither is Manny. The mass should be biopsied for proper diagnosis, except we're not qualified or equipped to do that. We don't have what we need to safely put him under, and we really wouldn't be able to understand his vitals—"

"You operate on humans and vampires. You're surgeons, that's what you do."

"It's not appropriate—"

"Well, make it appropriate!"

As he got loud, he sensed Beth flinch over on the chair, and as she went *shhh*, he knew she was calming L.W. Or calming herself by soothing the young whether or not he needed it.

Doc Jane adopted a professionally calm routine that somehow was more dreadful than if she'd gotten emotional. "We are not going to operate on this dog. We've found a good vet, however—"

"Fine. Send Fritz to go get him or her. Bring them here, now—"

"What do you think it could be?" Beth asked roughly. "The mass."

"I can't really say for sure—"

"Tell me," Wrath cut in. When there was a stretch of silence, he figured the females were exchanging glances. "It's my fucking dog. You're going to tell me what you think it is—"

"Hemangiosarcoma."

The word landed like a grenade that had been tossed at him and he'd caught in his bare hands. "He's too young. It has to be something else."

"That's why we need a vet."

Wrath angled his head down to George, as if his piece-of-shit eyes still worked, as if he could actually see what he could only create from memories of other golden retrievers that he'd encountered when he'd still had a little vision. Meanwhile, out in the hall, the inevitable gathering of brothers was muted. Goddamn, he didn't want to face them. He didn't want to talk about this because he didn't want to be living it in the first place, and though the fuckers meant well, he didn't have the energy to share his pain with them—

"Give us a minute," Beth murmured to Doc Jane. "Will you?"

"Yes, of course. Take all the time you need. We'll make arrangements for the vet."

That door opened and then re-shut, the fighters' voices flaring and cutting off sharply, as if the assembled expected some sort of report about how he was handling the bad news—because they'd know the grim update already. They'd have read all the no-doubt grim on Jane's face as she'd entered the room.

Wrath dragged a hand through his long hair. "They won't be able to do anything for him."

"I'm sorry?"

"If that's what it is. Hemangiosarcoma isn't treatable. Like, chemo doesn't work. They can remove the spleen, but it's a blood cancer. In the endothelial cells and the vessel walls. He might well have a tumor on his heart, too. It goes there."

"Wait, what—how do you know all that?"

"You think I haven't been preparing myself for this? I researched the most common causes of death in goldens about a month after he came into our lives. I just never thought it would be this soon. It's too soon. It's not right. It's too—"

When his words got choked off, he thought, *Nope. Not doing this again, ever.*

Even if he spent the rest of his nights banging into walls and tripping over ottomans? Even if he fell on his goddamn face and knocked every shin he ever had, it was better than this. Anything was better than this.

"Maybe you're wrong." Beth cleared her throat. "Like Jane said, we need a vet, a good one. And then we'll see what they can tell us."

"He has been logy. For the last week, come to think of it. He didn't want to play ball the other night at the Audience House. And Fritz said he didn't like his dinner—"

"Let's not get ahead of ourselves."

Wrath nodded, but not because he found any merit in the sensible advice; he nodded because he didn't want to be a total prick.

"I'll apologize to Jane," he muttered under his breath. "For talking to her like that."

"You're upset. She'll understand."

Bending back down, he put his mouth right next to George's ear. "Papa loves you," he said softly.

As George lifted his head and nuzzled Wrath's cheek, he thought maybe Beth was right. Just because he'd voice-commanded a load of shit into Google and listened to a bunch of things that killed golden retrievers didn't mean he'd manifested this—they had found something, though. Hadn't they. On the spleen.

Silent killer. The kind of thing you didn't know about until the dog bled into its heart and collapsed into lethargy without a lot of warning.

"What about Payne?" Beth asked quietly. "She's been known to heal."

"I already thought of that." Wrath shook his head. "Her gift comes at too high a cost. She used it on some human up in Leczo Falls a couple of months ago. She cured him of Alzheimer's and was flat on her back for eight weeks. Even the Sanctuary didn't help her. We need her up on her feet and able to fight if Lash is back in town."

There was no reason to turn his tragedy into a burden for the whole household.

"Talk to me," Beth said.

He looked in his *shellan*'s direction, but couldn't bear it even in his blindness, so he refocused on George. Feeling the animal's ribs expand and contract under his dagger hand in a shallow pump, he choked out, "I just wish I'd had him as a puppy. If I was only going to get a couple of years with him . . . that time was too precious to waste."

◆ ◆ ◆

In downtown Caldwell, in a neighborhood where more than half of the walk-ups were uninhabited and the others uninhabitable, Devina stood in the middle of a potholed street, her stilettos planted on the rim of an oily black stain that smelled like baby powder and dead animal. The substance had sunk into the cracks of the asphalt as if it were a sealer, the gloss reflecting the cloudy sky.

Her lover had been here.

And where had he gone next, she thought as she

looked outside of the yellow crime scene tape. The flimsy length had been strung in a square around the trunks of four dead trees set into cutouts in the parallel sidewalks, a highlighter pen drawing attention to nothing that had been focused on for very long. Yes, the police had responded to a shooting here, at least from what Jer's squawking communicator had informed her. But unlike in the suburban part of town with that retail break-in, the CPD wasn't sparing much of their workforce on this decrepit block.

No doubt shootings were a dime a dozen down here, and the surprise was that the disturbance had been called in at all.

Assessing the busted-out, rotting apartments that ran the street filled her with disgust—although not for Lash and the fact that maybe he was in one of them right this very moment, hiding from the daylight. Shit, she wished she could feel that kind of haughty disdain for him. No, she hated the humans who had built this up, and the ones who had let it fail, even though none of that cast of characters had any bearing on the fact that her one true love had been in this shitty zip code, for a time.

And had gone.

She needed to hate *somebody* in all this, though.

Glancing down at her Louboutins, she planted one in the mess and moved the toe of her stiletto back and forth in the viscous puddle, watching as the *lesser* blood gleamed like inky come. It was the only way to feel connected to her lover, this six-degrees-of-Kevin-Bacon not even close, but all she had.

Remnants of him left behind.

"Where the fuck are you," she demanded.

OMEGA.

Clear as day, she could see the letters crudely depicted on the wall of her lair, the Book communicating to her what she had been too dense to understand until it was so obvious that it was, quite literally, right in front of her face.

The truth of her lover's origins had tantalized her.

They were also going to define his future.

His goal, now that he'd broken free of her, was inevitable, and she told herself that it came with good news. He was going to stay in Caldwell.

Because that was where the vampires were.

That fucking Lassiter might have broken the spell the Book made for her, but those fanged assholes Lash was going to be so determined to kill were the diversion that was in her way. If her lover didn't have them to worry about, he would see her, he would be with her, with or without the Book's bullshit. They had the sexual compatibility. They could have built on that.

But noooooooooooooo. He had to go Van Helsing on everything.

Her hatred swirled away from the neighborhood's architects and former residents and toward that race of night dwellers. Then she thought about that fucking angel and his shouldn't-have-ever-happened reunion with his beloved.

Fuck.

But surely, if there were no vampires, then her lover would fall in line . . .

"Oh, who am I kidding," she muttered.

Lash would likely move on to something else to conquer. Just as, for her, there had always been something else she wanted to buy: It wasn't about the acquisition. It was about the struggle, the hunt. The capture and own.

Tilting her head back, she measured the amount of light in the sky. It was such a gray, overcast day, you wouldn't need sunglasses, but the illumination was still going to be too much for her lover—at least from what he told her. There had been a time when he'd been able to withstand it. No longer, however.

Where was he hiding?

She needed to get to him, but again, that lock of hair hadn't worked. She was the one who had the tie to him, not the other way around—so she couldn't draw any energy from him and pinpoint his location. He was giving nothing to her now that he was gone.

"Fuck."

If she could only find him, though, she could talk some fucking sense into the motherfuck—

It was as she went to duck back under the tape, without having any concrete next-destination in mind, that she caught sight of a gleam over on a stairway. So subtle, the reflection of light, the kind of thing that should have escaped her notice.

Frowning, Devina walked to the set of steps. There were hunks out of the poured concrete contours and also a variety of stains and weathering on them, but she ignored all that.

It was the drops that dotted the scuffed surface, so shiny in the dull daylight, so stinky. Leaning back, she looked up the facade of the Victorian four-level. Where was the yellow tape around the entrance? The cops had either missed the drips or they'd cleared the building because they'd found nothing.

Or maybe the inky stuff in the middle of the road was as far as they were willing to take things in this war-zone part of town.

Either way, she was going inside.

There had to be a basement.

Had to.

CHAPTER SIXTEEN

When Lassiter pulled back from their kiss, Rahvyn could not breathe. Staring up into his beautiful, oddly colored eyes, her heart was hammering and she had no voice. Not that he was speaking, either. The angel seemed as transformed as she was.

His hand shook as he brushed a lock of her hair over her shoulder.

"My first kiss," she whispered.

He closed his eyes, and as his features tightened, she wished she had not spoken. The truth had to come out, however—and she imagined it was going to be hard for him to reconcile her fumbling with the fact that she was no virgin. Meanwhile, on her side, she was going to struggle with the aftereffects of the violence that had been wrought upon her two hundred years ago by the calendar, but mere nights past for her experience.

Fortunately, here in this netherworld, with him . . . all of what had been done unto her seemed far away.

The challenge was going to be to keep it at such distance. With the way he'd just melded his own mouth with hers, and how she was feeling the now, so hot and hungry, things were going to progress to places where making sure that she stayed where she was in this vital present, and not regress to where she had been in that castle, might become more difficult.

"Rahvyn . . ."

As he opened his lids and focused on her, the yearning in his voice was so intense, it was a physical caress, and she reclosed the distance that had bloomed between their bodies, fitting herself to him. When her hips came up against his, she felt the hard length there—and she cursed that sadistic aristocrat who had taken from her that which she would have chosen to gift Lassiter.

But the cruelty shown to her had been the final key to her coming into her own. And that which had been forged in pain was stronger than what was nurtured, as it turned out. At least in her case.

"Yes," she replied to the question he had not asked. Not with words, at any rate. "I need to be with you, and I have this troubling sense . . . that time is running out."

Just as he frowned and seemed prepared to argue the point—

The double doors at the far end of the library opened, and what appeared, silhouetted against the pastoral landscape, seemed a threat, even though he was not one. Not in the conventional sense, at least.

The Brother Vishous stepped inside and walked toward them, his heavy boots making a thunderous sound he did not bother to dim.

With a shiver of anxiety, she heard the echoing beat as a countdown of whatever hours remained for her and Lassiter.

"I'm here for Rahvyn," the Brother announced.

Lassiter stepped around, placing himself in front of her, blocking her with his body. "Why."

Except Rahvyn was not inclined to have anyone speak on her behalf, not even him. Moving out from under the lee of the angel, she focused on the Brother's chest. No daggers. No weapons on the male at all, as it turned out.

"Whate'er may I do for you?" she said quietly.

The icy eyes that bored into her made her feel so uncomfortable, she looked to the bookshelf she and Lassiter had come to stand before, to the tome he had taken out and flipped through. It was not precisely back in line with its ilk, and she had an odd thought that it would probably resettle itself, the perfection of arrangement in the library, in the Sanctuary as a whole, as self-perpetuating as the flora.

"Nate."

As the name reverberated up into the high ceiling, her eyes flipped back to the Brother's. "Is he all right? Has something happened—"

"What you did to him, to bring him back."

Rahvyn immediately began shaking her head. "No, if you're asking me to do that to someone else—"

"We need you."

She put both her palms out. "Forgive me, but I will ne'er do that for anyone nor anything e'er again. It is a violation of the natural order and a curse more than a blessing."

"It's the miracle that we need right now."

Before she got into a proper argument with the fighter, she glanced up at Lassiter for some assistance. He was staring at Vishous as if he were attempting to read tea leaves, and after a moment, he put his hand to his face and passed it over his features with exhaustion.

"I don't think you understand," Vishous said, "how important this is or who it involves."

"It does not matter." She thought of Nate. Her cousin, Sahvage. Herself. "Death can be cruel, but it is, along with birth, the basis of the Creator's construction, and ultimately, a blessing. Tampering with that is wrong and certainly not for me to undertake. I should not have done what I did—"

"It's Wrath."

Abruptly, the portrait the Book had shown her was all she could see, the image of the great Blind King's face consumed by darkness, by evil, the tide rushing in, claiming.

Lassiter looked down at her from his greater height. Then he said grimly in the Old Language, *"Whither the King goes so goeth the species."*

A strange feeling of arrival cut through her anxiety. What if this was the reason for her powers, the mission she had always wondered about: All those times, when she had lain awake, consumed by confusion as to why she had been gifted with so much she did not understand, when she had grappled with implications she could not comprehend . . . what if it all came down to this moment here.

The Book had certainly sent her back down here for a purpose.

What if the Creator had been working through the ancient tome, just as He was working through her now by presenting her with this messenger of need?

So many disparate instances suddenly stitched together, including the torture of her body by that aristocrat, when he had unleashed the evil within her, providing the balance required for her powers to be fully present . . .

Yet the more she sought to construct her destiny, the more she returned to a core question that could not be skirted: Who was she to determine a King's fate?

"It is not right," she said as she stared back at Lassiter. "You yourself just told me thus."

+ + +

Back down in Caldwell, in a cluttered, filthy storage room in the basement of the Victorian walk-up, Lash sat with his back against a rough stone wall, his legs stretched out before him and crossed at the ankles, the cold-and-clammy wrapping around him like a blanket just pulled out of a foul pond. With a hunting knife he'd stolen from that Dick's Sporting Goods store, he whittled a broom handle that he'd broken free of its shaggy head. The *shht, shht, shht* was loud in the silence, a beat that played contrapunto to a leak in the far corner.

From time to time, a rat scampered across the dirt floor—or maybe it wasn't dirt as in earthen, but layers of dust packed into a solid over concrete slabs you'd have to dig down to find. Either way, to his sensitive ears, the rodent's padding of paws reminded him of dice rolling on a backgammon board.

There was one other sound.

When another groan hit the airwaves, he said without looking up, "Forget about him."

"How the fuck is he still alive," a male voice asked.

"That's the point. He's not."

Lash glanced across the drafty darkness. His second and third inductees were sitting together on top of an old freezer that was a horizontal opener, their lower legs dangling at right angles, both sets of hands gripping the lip on either side of their knees as if they were about to get pushed off and prepared to fight the shove.

You already fell, Lash thought to himself as he resumed his even passes of the blade off the tip of the broom handle, little shavings flying free to join the loose pile by his thigh.

"So this is it? This is all we gonna do?"

Mr. Mouthy, who'd been the driver of the blacked-out Suburban, had had a rough time with the induction. Then again, his buddy had been the first to get his veins opened, so he'd gotten a gander at what was coming. To keep things tidy—a first in this basement, evidently—Lash had emptied the contents of their vascular systems in a claw-foot tub out in the hall. After that, he'd slit his own wrists and had them feed from him. This had been a new method of transmitting the essence of his father, but he'd felt as though he'd needed to make his mark on the process.

This was his time now, his turn to dictate how things were going to go.

After their hearts had circulated their new blood— after he had stood over them as they had writhed and retched—he had taken the cardiac muscles, burrowing his bare hands under each one's sternum and pulling out the still-beating muscle.

The hearts were in the tub with the red blood. Enough with the stupid fucking jars.

"Yo, man, hello?" Mouthy demanded.

The Suburban's driver, whose name didn't matter, was getting grating. Lash had much preferred when the guy had been in too much pain to talk, but he had to remind himself: After facing an eternity in *Dhunhd*, he'd never expected to be back in his sire's game. So this annoyance shit was a more-than-fair trade-off for—

Up above, the apartment building's entry door opened and someone set foot in the shallow foyer.

As his acolytes looked up, he ignored their twitching nervousness. He'd learned something from that brunette with the pneumatic sex drive and all the clothes. Hiding in a parallel plane of existence was a good trick, and it was a damned shame he couldn't pull it off to the extents she could. What he was able to do—and he'd learned this when the cops had searched everything earlier—was project an image of a-okay that disarmed the curious. It wasn't as complete a cover as the demon whipped up, but it was enough to have things appear as if there was nothing going on.

Come to think of it, his Band-Aid over reality was similar to what he'd done to secure the SUV. That vehicle he'd coveted, which was now his, had been moved two blocks away and stored under a tarp.

The reality patch he'd pulled over the tub out in the hall and this room here with the three of them was just the same.

He glanced over at the oozing mess of the *lesser* on the floor in the corner.

Okay, fine. Three and a half.

The incompetent security guard, who'd been pumped full of lead out on the street, was still restless and ever-leaking, the movements of his arms and legs slow and unceasing, his suffering manifest. Lash could have just left him where he'd collapsed, but like with the inductions, he'd been compelled to be tidy about things, throwing the sack of undead down here with the rest of them. The stink was horrible, the moaning pitiful—

Lash lowered his knife and looked to the off-kilter door. As the pair on the freezer likewise came to attention, he flared his nostrils.

And smelled Poison.

Tossing his broom handle aside, he got to his feet and jacked up the camo pants he'd stolen. "You stay here."

"We ain't stayin' shit, man—"

As Mr. Mouthy went to get off the fridge lid, Lash threw a blast of energy at him, pinning the subordinate sonofabitch right where he was.

Leaning forward on his hips, Lash met him directly in the eye. "If you want to try that out for fun"—he pointed to the slayer in the corner—"go right ahead."

Mouthy's buddy spoke up. "Nah, we good. He good. Chill."

"I thought so."

As Lash walked out of the storage area, he shut the door with his mind and waited by the tub full of blood. The fact that his cock thickened between his legs was exactly the kind of reaction he wasn't looking for, and he put faith in his temper as it also rose to attention.

He was not about to let a good fuck screw him.

The brunette started down the basement steps, and as the *clip, clip, clip* of her heels preceded her, he pictured her legs descending, shapely and lean, and her manicured finger-tips tickling the top of the old balustrade, and her tits casting shadows even in the darkness. The fact that he fully hard-ened made him think of the *lessers* he had just spawned.

They were now impotent, a little fact that— oopsie—he might have forgotten to mention in the pre-amble. But their sexless lives were a saving grace for them right now.

Lash might not want to be with the demon all twenty-five, eight. But he sure as shit wasn't going to put up with anything looking at her with ideas—

Devina emerged at the base of the stairs, and as she stopped, he looked her up and down. Well . . . fuck.

Literally.

Her dark eyes sought out where he was standing, as if she could see him even though he remained hidden behind his optical illusion of vacancy. It was galling, to not face her legitimately, but he didn't understand how he'd ended up so locked in on her, with her.

Until suddenly, for whatever reason, he'd been set free.

So no, he wasn't rolling any dice with getting re-caught. He had a war to restart and a King to murder. He was too fucking busy to get entangled, no matter how hot the rope—

The demon started coming toward him, her strides slow, her eyes drifting to the tub, which would appear dingy and dust-covered to her, not filled with the blood and pair of hearts that were actually in there: She was just like the cops, blind to whatever he didn't want her to see.

He liked that he had some power over her.

When she paused by the porcelain bath and leaned in to inspect its belly, her winged brows dug in over the bridge of her perfect nose. Then she faced him and the door he'd closed behind himself. Two steps forward and she was directly in front of him, chest to chest.

Then she walked through him, the passage of her body into and out of his own making his balls clench like he was about to come.

The door creaked as she opened things, and he twisted around as she went inside the storage—

"Whoa . . . what a piece of *ass*."

And that was why he'd shut the door, he realized. He knew what the demon looked like, and didn't want the new inductees to see her.

"You want some, bitch." There was the sound of a pair of boots hitting the floor. "Mmm, girl. Get it—"

Lash's body moved before he was aware of deciding to change where he was standing—and then he was past the demon and right in front of Mr. Mouthy.

He slapped the slayer so hard a spool of black blood went flying from the busted nose. "You don't fucking look at her. You don't fucking talk to her."

"What the fuck—"

Lash picked the *lesser* up by the throat and spun around, walking him through the demon's body. Then he threw the slayer down with the leaking undead lame-ass, grabbed Mouthy by the back of the hair, and shoved that face riiiiiight up close to the security guard's.

"You want to be him? I can make you be him for eternity—he's not getting any better and he's not dying. *Ever.* You want to ride that wave?"

As the bullet-ridden sad sack's eyes bugged at the news flash about his own destiny, Lash dragged him forward, too, so that the two *lessers* were almost kissing.

But he was only concerned with the asshole who'd thought he had any chance with the brunette. "Look at him. You want this? No? Then you *never* fucking talk at her again."

Mr. Mouthy raised his hands like he was in a stickup. "No problem, man. She yours. Whatever. Fuck—"

Lash released the pair so abruptly, their noses punched together, and Mouthy cursed and covered the bottom half of his face. The security guard merely moaned and fell back into his slump against the cold stone wall, like another slice had been added to his shit sandwich and what did it matter.

Lash turned around to the other slayer, the one who'd stayed out of it. That *lesser* had his eyes locked on the floor, and he just shook his head back and forth, staying exactly where the fuck he was.

"That's right," Lash snapped as he marched back into the hall.

Putting his hands on his hips, he glared into the tub and wished he could drain them all over again—

Creeeeeeak. Click.

He looked over his shoulder. The demon, who'd remained oblivious to the drama, had stepped back out of the storage room and was standing with her fine ass to the closed door, her hand still on the tarnished brass knob.

Her eyes lifted and seemed to meet his own. "I know you're here," she said softly. "I don't know exactly where you are . . . but you're close. I bet you can even hear me."

Those black eyes, dense and bottomless as a well, roamed around.

"You're a fucking pussy, not being able to handle me. A spineless coward." She smiled in a nasty way. "But you already know that, which is why you're hiding now."

Fury tightened his chest and shot down into his throbbing cock.

Just as he was about to reveal himself so he could tell her he wasn't afraid of a fucking thing, much less a female—she up and disappeared, only the scent of her purple perfume lingering in the dank, nasty air.

"Goddamn it," he muttered. "Goddamn . . . you."

CHAPTER SEVENTEEN

As Lassiter re-formed in the training center's corridor, he told himself that technically, he hadn't asked Rahvyn to do anything. Sure, he'd pointed out that one thing, about Wrath's destiny being the species', but that was hella different than a flat-out entreaty.

Like . . . *Will you please use your whatever-the-hell-it-is and pull Wrath out of whatever mortal injury is going on?*

Now, *that* was tampering as well as putting her in a totally bad situation. And he himself certainly wasn't getting overtly involved. No matter how dire, how tragic, how sad and unfair, he was resolved to stay out of—

Rahvyn arrived beside him, and he willed her to look at him. She did not. She stared at Vishous, who'd come back down here first. Then she walked forward, to the exam room door the brother was standing beside. As he opened the way inside, she stopped dead.

"Shit," Lassiter said under his breath as he peered over Rahvyn's platinum head—

"George? Wait . . . what?" he blurted.

He glanced at V, but just got a shake of the head in return. So when Rahvyn entered the exam room, Lassiter took the brother's arm and pulled the guy away from the door as it shut on its own.

"What the hell is going on?" he demanded.

V took out a hand-rolled. "The dog's got cancer."

"This is about *George?*" As he got a level stare in return, he put his palms up. "I thought Wrath was the one who needed help—"

"You mean Wrath isn't in trouble if that dog dies?"

Lassiter went silent and then turned to the closed door. "What about your sister, Payne. She healed her *hellren*'s horse, right? And—"

"The last time she used her gift, she was down for two months. I wasn't sure she was going to recover at all—and that was even after we took her up to our *mahmen*'s Sanctuary—sorry, *your* Sanctuary. The next time, it will probably kill her. So not an option."

He thought of Nate. "You want Rahvyn to—"

"The King can't lose that dog. Remember how we found that pesky evidence of a *lesser* induction downtown last night? Lash is going to walk right in his father's footsteps, mark my words. Now is *not* the time for the species to lose our leader."

Lassiter had a sudden image of Wrath sitting at the

head of the mansion's mile-long dinner table, Beth to his left with L.W., Tohr to his right, the golden in his lap—so the King could hand-feed choice pieces of roast beef to the dog.

"I thought it was Wrath who was hurt," Lassiter repeated numbly.

"It will be. And you're right, where he goes, we all go. This war with the Lessening Society? It's entering its second phase, and my gut says it's going to be worse. We're going to need everybody on deck, especially Wrath."

"Have you had a vision?"

"No, but you want to do the math when civilians start dying? How about if another round of aristocrats get murdered? The King's democratically elected now, which means all that power that is supposedly absolute, ain't so absolute anymore."

As the brother exhaled off to the side, Lassiter closed his eyes. "She says she's not doing it again for anybody or anything—"

Up along the ceiling, the inset fluorescent fixtures started to blink—and then everything went pitch black.

V's voice was close to reverent in the dense darkness: "Thank fuck—"

There was a sudden *boom!* and an explosion of light inside the exam room that was so bright, it bled through the tight seal of the door, creating the outline of a rectangle. And then the glow slowly faded, the electricity coming back on with a whirring sound as the HVAC restarted.

Lassiter looked up as the ceiling lights flickered before going steady.

He didn't wait for permission to enter. He shoved the door open, and jumped inside. Rahvyn was at the exam table in the center, her hands hovering over George, her eyes rolling back in her head as her body went loose.

He lunged for her at the same time Wrath did, but the King retracted and not because there was no way he could be sure where she was in space. He knew Lassiter was the one who should care for her. They all . . . knew.

Rahvyn's body was so light as he caught her, and then he pulled her in close to his chest, stroking her silver hair out of her face. Her lids fluttered and her lips parted as she breathed wanly, and he wondered if he needed to scream for medical help.

"Is she okay?"

Lassiter looked over. As Wrath spoke, he was draped across his dog, that massive warrior body a blanket covering the golden. Meanwhile, George's head was up and moving around and he was blinking as if in confusion— but also wagging his tail. On the far side of them, Beth was brushing tears from her eyes and hugging her young on her hip.

And it was the oddest thing.

L.W. was staring at Rahvyn. As if he understood, somehow, what she had done and why. Not that that was possible, of course. The kid was still, in the slow-grow manner of vampires, all but an infant.

Lassiter refocused on the female in his arms and answered the King. "I don't know. I'm going to go lay her down somewhere—"

Wrath's long arm reached out and he locked a grip on Lassiter's shoulder, the wraparounds he always wore angled as if he were staring forward. "I'm going to come check on her. I owe your female."

For some reason, Lassiter looked at the tattoos that covered the insides of those heavy forearms. The lineage of the last purebred vampire left on the earth was a measure of time, so many souls coming before him and establishing his legacy—and he was keeping it going through the blood that coursed through his young son's veins.

All those books in that library, metronomes of lives lived . . . and lost.

As an eerie pall came over him, Lassiter glanced at Beth and L.W. They were just passing through, too, he thought. Someday . . . these people were going to be gone, nothing but memories and echoes of times long past in the minds of those who survived them.

Meanwhile, Lassiter would still be here. So would Rahvyn.

Assuming . . . would she live forever, too? It seemed inconceivable that she could save others with eternal life and not possess it herself. Yet any relief that might have come with the idea she wouldn't die got wiped out quick as he thought about what he'd done with the demon, and how that might make Rahvyn run from him—in which case he'd be forever without her even though she remained in existence.

An eternity of mourning.

Was that why the Scribe Virgin ultimately had decided to leave? Had she lost too many of her young? The heart could only bear so much, and though immortals didn't have to worry about dying, they had something even worse looming over them.

No way out.

He thought of Nate, the young male who had been saved, and wondered how the kid was getting along in his new reality. Someone needed to check on him because the repercussions of his situation were going to come home to roost, maybe sooner rather than later.

Rahvyn was right not to share forever anymore.

With anybody.

+ + +

In one of Caldwell's nook-and-cranny suburbs, in a neighborhood full of nicely maintained, modest houses that were vacant not because they weren't lived in, but because they were inhabited by humans who went to school and work, Nate, adopted son of the Black Dagger Brother Murhder, sat in his bedroom underground.

It was a nice crib, as his best friend, Shuli, would have called it, with a connected private bathroom, and a king-sized bed, and a set of matching, rustic furniture that included a bureau, two side tables, and a desk. The walls were painted navy blue, the wall-to-wall carpeting was a speckled brown that went with all the oak or whatever hardwood, and the loo, as the Old Country people would have called it, was done in navy blue, cream, and brass.

It was the nicest place he'd ever stayed. Then again, that lab he'd grown up in, with all its clinical equipment and horrifying experimentation, had been a low threshold to beat.

This cellar he and his family stayed in during daylight hours was basically separated into two parts. The other half, on the opposite side of the open living quarters in the middle, was where his parents slept in their big master suite. Down on this end, there was his room and a guest bedroom that his mom had converted into her off-site office. There was also the reinforced entrance to the escape tunnel.

Of course there was another way out, in the event of an infiltration or a fire—because safety first. All of the off-site homes associated with the Black Dagger Brotherhood were modified not only to house vampires during the day, but to make sure there were really good alarm and monitoring systems in place as well as defensive protections and B plans built into the layouts.

He looked over to the desk across the way. His computer was shut down, the monitor's screen black, the keyboard sitting on the little platform that slid out from underneath the top. He'd chosen everything in the room, and assembly had been required. He and his father had worked together on the furniture and the setup, not only of his quarters, but his parents'. It had been the first thing they'd done together, while Sarah had been kitting out her lab at the training center.

Getting up, he went to the closet and slid back the mirrored door. Hanging from the rod, his anemic collection of sweatshirts and t-shirts was elevated in terms of formality by one button-down and one pair of slacks. With a steady hand, he made sure all the plastic hangers were equidistant from each other, then he closed things up and double-checked the rest of his stuff.

His bed was made with all the precision of a watchmaker, and he went over and straightened the pillows even though they were precisely aligned with the headboard, the two meeting in the middle, like the part for hair in a bowl cut.

He'd vacuumed earlier, right after he'd said good day to his parents, the three of them breaking off and going their separate ways.

Heading for the bureau, he opened the drawers one by one, from top to bottom. His underwear were folded, his socks color coordinated and in paired-up bundles, his shorts and bathing trunks sequestered down at the lowest level.

In the bathroom, he made sure his toothbrush was still in its holder, and the toothpaste in the little set of shelves behind the mirror. Then he closed the medicine cabinet and looked at his reflection.

Well, he looked into the reflective glass. He didn't focus on his face.

No, it was the background that captured his attention. The desk, specifically.

He thought about the only other time he'd put furniture together. It hadn't been with his father. Nate had been at Luchas House, setting up a bedroom for a female who had mysteriously appeared from out of nowhere . . . and made him feel like she was the only person in the universe.

There had been an instant connection, for him.

And Rahvyn had connected to him, too.

That one time in her bedroom, when she'd somehow seemed to step inside of him and see all his secrets for herself.

As inexplicable and incredible as that moment of communion had been, especially as she had hugged him and seemed like she didn't want to let go, little had he known that there would be another, even more incomprehensible, event waiting for the pair of them.

In his mind, he returned to that night they'd gone out to that club. The drive-by shooting hadn't had anything to do with them—until he'd become collateral damage in someone else's fight. He could remember just standing there on the sidewalk as the black car screeched by and the popping sounds had echoed and he'd felt this blaze of heat go through his stomach.

He'd called Rahvyn's name at least once. And then his knees had gone out from under him as he'd grabbed his sweatshirt where a red stain was spreading. He didn't remember much after that, other than snippets of her scrambling over to him and holding him. His last thought had been that she was very beautiful, even in her distress, her silver hair a cloud around him as she leaned across his chest, her eyes so luminous with terror.

And then later . . .

He'd replayed what had happened many times, him

becoming aware that he was in a foggy landscape, a
door materializing before him, his hand extending out
and opening that portal. There had been such a draw
for him to go to the other side, a pull sure as if there
were a rope around his waist.

It had been the Fade, of course. Except just as his
body had started to move through—

Snap!

The sound had been like a clap of lightning and clash
of cymbals at the same time—and suddenly, he was
being sucked backwards, his body pulled out of the aperture, out of the foggy landscape . . . back to his corporeal
body. As his eyes had fluttered open, his adopted mom,
Sarah, had thrown herself at him, smothering him in an
embrace that carried the scent of her tears, just as Murhder had reached out with tears in his eyes, too.

Nate had not immediately understood exactly how
he had been saved . . . or what it all meant. In the aftermath, when he'd finally been able to talk to Rahvyn, he
had been confused and grateful. And a little afraid of
the female.

But she had been the same, beautiful and shy.

How could he not fall in love with her?

After being released from the training center's clinic,
he had gone to the local supermarket and bought her a
bouquet of flowers. He hadn't known what they were
called and they weren't particularly expensive, but he'd
liked them because he'd thought she would appreciate
the yellows and pinks of the petals. He'd then gone out
into the country, to Luchas House, where she was stay-

ing, his heart in his throat. He had always worried she'd be gone as abruptly as she'd arrived, his gut telling him that she was not long for Caldwell, New York.

Even though he'd known she was a kind of forever for him, no matter where she was.

He'd been relieved to be told by the staff that she was out in the meadow, and even though he'd tucked the bouquet behind his back, he hadn't done that much to hide the flowers—and as the female on shift had seen them, her gentle smile and nod of approval had given him some tailwind courage as he'd gone out the rear of the farmhouse.

Where he had seen thousands of flowers. An entire field of them.

He'd had a momentary confusion and wondered if he were hallucinating—but then he'd seen the two figures standing in the middle of a swirl of colors so bright, they had even glowed in the night.

Lassiter and Rahvyn had been looking into each other's eyes, and there was no forgetting the rapt way she had stared up at the angel.

Nate had let his measly bouquet fall to the ground.

He'd had to walk around the front of the farmhouse and out the lane quite some distance before he'd been able to dematerialize.

Rahvyn had left him a voicemail the night after—or a couple nights afterward, he couldn't remember: Finally, she was leaving. And hey, that was her right, just like it was her right to be in love with Lassiter. No doubt the happy couple were going to go live on a cloud up in the heavens, passing eternity eating bonbons and staring into each other's eyes.

Good for her. He was happy for her—

As his cell phone started to vibrate on the bedside stand, he remembered how he'd always jumped before, hoping it was her calling. Now he let things go to voicemail without checking the screen.

He already knew who it was. And a split second later, sure enough, Shuli called back again.

Or at least he assumed it was Shuli. Who the hell else called him.

Stretching his arm out, he didn't pick up the phone. He opened the narrow drawer of the stand and took out the nine millimeter Glock he'd tucked in there. As he sat down on the bed and put the weapon in his lap, he stared at its molded metal contours, felt the weight on his thigh, touched the textured grip.

It was time to find out just how far this immortality thing went, and he hated the fact that he had to wait until the sun set and his parents left for work.

But maybe Rahvyn was wrong. Maybe she'd only brought him back, like as in resuscitation rather than resurrection.

Which was why he'd made sure his room was clean and tidy.

And why he was going to wait until he was alone.

The fact that he didn't care one way or another what the outcome was probably meant he was in a bad way.

He couldn't give a shit about that either, however.

CHAPTER EIGHTEEN

At the Brotherhood's training center, in the break room, Eddie was sitting across from his partner in time, watching Adrian work his way through a Hershey bar, when he sensed bad news had landed once again: As the ripple of warning went through him, he knew his buddy felt it, too, Ad's eyes leaving the TV and its episode of *The Simpsons* and focusing on the door across the way.

"Shit," Eddie muttered. "Lassiter's female is back. I can feel her presence."

When Ad just shrugged and broke off two more squares, he felt compelled to underscore the obvious. "This is a fucking mess. With him, with her."

Ad resumed watching Homer, in all his yellow, rotund glory, shove donuts in his face.

"We've got to split them up." Eddie waited for a response. "We have a job to do for the Creator. Hello? All that chocolate gone to your brain?"

"I've only had four."

Glancing to the guy's elbow, Eddie measured the collection of mangled plastic wrappers that looked more like six or eight to him. "I think we just contain him and drag him back to the big boss."

"Like throw a burlap sack over Lass's head?" Ad cocked an eyebrow and didn't break focus as a commercial for Tums started rolling. "We better use something a little stronger—and we're going to need to duct tape. The screaming and cursing will hurt my ears. You know how sensitive I am."

"Will you get real."

"Hey, do you remember"—the angel finally glanced over—"when Hershey's wrappers were made of tinfoil and proper paper labels? Now everything is so disposable."

"Whatever, the old kind weren't keepsakes, either." The "oh, pulease" went unspoken, but was in the tone. "And I'm done. We've been chasing after that angel for how long now? I'm ready for a vacation, and that only happens if we—"

"Yup, it's been three years. Three hundred and sixty-five times three—"

"What a relief that you can still do math—"

"—is one thousand eighty-five days."

Eddie rolled his eyes. "Guess not. It's ninety-five. One thousand *ninety*-five."

"You ever wonder, why now?" Ad murmured. "The

Creator knows all, sees all, and we've been banging around Caldwell for however much time? Suddenly, we're led right to this group of vampires, where Lassiter's been putting his feet up—and at least initially, they were as confused about where he was as we were."

"To be fair, that's probably because that angel has never had a sense of direction," Eddie muttered.

"I think we're supposed to be here."

"Yeah, to take Lassiter back. That's our fuc—" He stopped himself. "Frickin' job."

Ad gestured with his chocolate. "If I've told you once, I've told you one thousand and whatever times. Fuck. It's FUCK. I don't get this no-swearing thing."

"Well, I did call Devina a cunt."

Ad perked up, like someone had told him Santa was real. "You did? When?"

"Back at that travel agency. To her face."

"Look at you." Ad fanned next to his eyes. "I'm getting misty with pride over here."

"You're weird."

"I'm not a grown-ass angel going church lady with the syllables." Ad shook his head, the piercings that ran up his ears glinting in the overhead light. "And I'm telling you, we're here for a different reason—"

"The Creator was very clear—"

"—and we need to chill until we find out what it is—"

"—about what He wanted us to—"

The electricity began to flicker, the fixtures on the ceiling blinking on and off, the TV going dark and then rebooting. And then it all went pitch black.

"Like I said," Ad muttered dryly, all disembodied, "I think we need to stick around."

Eddie opened his mouth to point out that none of this was their problem—

The sonic *boom!* reverberated through the break room, loud enough to stop the argument in its tracks, the energy shock waves so great that they rattled the door into the corridor.

Eddie got to his feet so fast his chair went flying, and as he put his hands forward, he was ready to fend off an attack—he didn't know from what, but given the cast of characters? Could be anyone from the Creator Himself to Elon-frickin'-Musk.

Silence.

And then the lights came back on in a flicker.

Ad was right where he'd been, sitting there with his half-eaten chocolate bar and all those wrappers. "Wow. Freaky."

As he threw another square into his pie hole and went back to staring at the TV, there was a temptation to smack him upside the head just on principle.

"I do *not* trust that female," Eddie snapped.

"That's okay." Ad shrugged as he chewed. "It's not like you're going to date her."

◆ ◆ ◆

"Wait, before you go. Are you sure Rahvyn is all right? Does she need Jane?"

Down the corridor in George's exam room, Lassiter repositioned his female in his arms and looked over his shoulder at Beth. The Queen had risen out of her chair with her son, and was looking like she wished she could do anything to help.

"I think we're okay," he said, even though he had no idea whether that was true or not.

Rahvyn still hadn't come around properly, her head lolling in the crook of his arm, her eyes roaming and seemingly unable to focus.

The dog, on the other hand, was a rock-solid rebound. George was nuzzling his master's hand and wagging his tail and trying to get up and at'em. Wrath, meanwhile, was running his hands all over the animal, like he was trying to reassure himself that the turnaround was real—and the scent of tears surrounded the King, though nothing escaped the rims of his black wraparounds.

"What a miracle," Lassiter said as George shoved off his master and got up on all fours.

The shake was so vigorous, blond hairs went everywhere, and then he sneezed emphatically, as if he were putting a pin in the experience and moving on.

"Yes," Wrath said with a laugh. "It is amazing."

The King then focused on Rahvyn. "She has saved all of us."

As if in response, Rahvyn moaned and stretched—and Lassiter got his shit together. "I've got to let her rest."

"I'll send Doc Jane," Wrath announced.

Lassiter made some kind of response; he didn't know what came out of his mouth. And then he was through the door and out in the corridor. There were all kinds of members of the Brotherhood loitering around, but he didn't look at any of them, and fortunately, none of them asked him anything. Instead, a way was parted for him, the fighters making space so he could carry Rahvyn onward. Someone even jumped ahead to open the door to the next recovery room, and he nodded his thanks—

It was Vishous. And then the brother shocked him again: "She's one of us now."

"*Whither the King goes so goeth the species*," Rahvyn mumbled.

V's harsh face softened. "That's right. You recover. We're here on guard."

As Lassiter stepped in and waited for the door to close behind them, he wondered what the hell he'd gotten her involved in. Then he remembered what she'd unleashed—for the second time—and wondered about a whole lot of other things.

"Come on, let's get you settled," he whispered.

Over at the hospital bed, he laid her out with care, which seemed stupid given what she was capable of— but she was so small and appeared so fragile. When he pulled back to unfold the blanket that was at the foot of the bed, her hand gripped his arm.

"Please . . ."

He hesitated. And then she urged him forward.

Powerless to resist her, he lowered himself onto the mattress—and the way she curled in against him made him stiffen . . . but not because he didn't like it.

Moving slowly, he slid an arm under her head so that his biceps was her pillow, and then he brought his body against hers so that he was her covering. The ragged sigh she let out made him feel important.

In a way that being responsible for the destinies of all the vampires on the planet didn't come near.

He smoothed her hair, marveling at the way the silver gleamed in the low lighting of the recovery room. Funny, how even though they were in a clinical setting, this felt like a private suite just because they were lying together.

"I could not . . . not help him," she said with a kind of defeat.

"You did the right thing."

She propped her head up and stared at a framed oil painting of a weeping willow beside a still pond. Her eyes were dead tired.

"I did not know that it was a dog." She took a deep breath and exhaled slowly. "I had a rabbit once. I loved her. I called her Mallie. I fed her fresh grass . . . and made sure she had a soft nest to sleep in. She lived with me in my room. One night when I awoke, she was curled in the corner away from her bedding. She wouldnae drink . . . wouldnae eat. My parents were still alive then. There was nothing they could do."

"I'm so sorry." He reached out and squeezed her hand. "That must have been rough."

"I put her in a box. My father dug a deep hole. We buried her . . . under the moonlight, behind the stable. Even my father cried. Animals have a way of being closer to our hearts than people, sometimes." Her pale eyes watered, becoming even more luminous. "Did you ever have a small animal who relied upon you for care and succor?"

As she brushed at her tears, he wondered if she hadn't saved her own pet in that room next door.

"No," he said. "I didn't."

"Where did you grow up?"

He hesitated. "I was begotten, not born. There was no . . . growing up for me. No childhood or transition like you vampires go through."

"You are wondrous," she breathed.

"I am nothing . . . compared to you."

"Do not say such things."

As she flushed and hid a yawn with the back of her hand, he stroked her hair again. He told himself he wanted the contact because it comforted her. In truth, it eased him.

"You want to ask me," she said. "What that was . . . that I did."

"We don't need to go through all that now."

Rahvyn nodded. There was a pause. "I am sorry you did not know the joys of a young who is loved."

"Not all that long ago, I was taken in for a time, by humans." As she seemed instantly aware, he shook his head. "It's not a happy ending, though."

"Tell me." She touched his arm. "Thus I would ease you if I could?"

He scrubbed his face with his hand. "I have told no one this, actually."

"Then I shall keep your secrets."

"It's not a secret. Just nothing I like to talk about." He shrugged. "There have been a lot of falling-outs between me and the Creator, and during one of my expulsions, I was wandering the earth, not really all that bothered . . . when I decided I had to do something with myself. I ended up volunteering at a church—if those humans had only known, right? It was back in the fifties, down north from here in Manhattan. One of the families who ended up staying at the shelter there was from across the ocean. They were refugees and had just recently lost their son on the journey over from India. They took me into their hearts . . ." He cleared his throat. "They insisted on giving me the only thing they had of value—it was a collection of gold jesses they had smuggled onto the boat. They had saved and saved to buy them for their son, for when he got married, as they called it. But he . . . passed."

Lassiter pictured the man and the woman, their sorrow a tangible weight they dragged with them wherever they went. "They had nothing of material wealth. I tried to get them to keep it all. I mean, they needed the money to set themselves up."

When his voice got rough, he arched back and tried to hide his emotions by stretching his spine. "One night, they took off. I came in for the start of my shift at the shelter, and they were gone . . . they'd left the jesses behind, though. In a shoebox with my name on it."

As Rahvyn murmured something, he looked at her. "Their most prized possessions became mine, and I vowed, if I ever got married, I would wear them."

It was so easy to picture Rahvyn in a traditional human wedding gown, standing up with him in front of Wrath as they took their vows.

"The jesses were stolen," he heard himself say. "I shouldn't have kept them at the shelter, and I blame myself. I tried to find them for years, even though that was stupid. There were so many people in and out of the church, most of whom were good, honest folk, but clearly not every one of them. It hurts, even after all this time."

"Oh, Lassiter, how terrible."

"Human goodness coexists with cruelty, both of the casual and the conniving kind." He shook his head. "I went out and bought gold chains afterward. Wore them for years as a punishment and a reminder that things need to be kept safe."

He thought of the satchel he'd thrown into the view of the valley. He would have loved to wear the original set with her, he really would have. Or his own, he supposed, although it wasn't the same if you'd bought something like that yourself.

It was the gift from the man and woman, more than the intrinsic value of the gold, that had made the necklaces, bracelets, earrings, and chains so priceless.

"Anyway, enough of that." He forced a smile. "Let's talk about something else or let you rest."

But his mood had landed like a boulder between them, and it wasn't just about him playing peek-a-boo with a sad part of his past. He had a lot of regrets tonight—

"You did not ask me to help the King," Rahvyn said abruptly. "You should not feel as badly as you do."

"So you can read my mind, huh." He smiled a little, but not because he was about to yuck it up. It was more like how much worse could he feel? "I have to point out that I didn't tell V to back off, either."

"You merely framed the situation. You let me make my own decision."

Had he, though? He'd hoped she would help. He had wanted her to.

"I need you to know something," she said as she turned his hand over and ran her fingertips across the lines of his palm.

"What's that?"

Her eyes flipped to his and her stare was disarmingly direct. "I am not the Gift of Light. I need you to understand that."

He smiled a little. "As you say—"

"I am not. And you must know that truth, not merely in your mind, but in your heart."

"Shh. Just rest." He stroked her cheek, then brushed her chin with his thumb. "You don't need to worry about all that—"

"You have to believe me."

"As you wish."

"I am serious, Lassiter. I do not want to be made more than what I am. Because that will break your heart, and I shall not be a party to such meanness."

Lassiter didn't bother to hide the fact that the corners of his mouth were lifting once again. "So you are not indifferent to me, then."

She pursed her lips. "Do not be daft."

He thought of V. "Some would say I have no choice but to be daft—"

"Of course I am not indifferent to you."

Lassiter's heart stopped. And then began to pound.

"Good," he said gravely. "I can build on that."

As a flush bloomed in her face, her voice became husky. "What do you wish to construct, angel mine."

His eyes traveled to her mouth, and he felt a rush of heat at his hips. But then she tried to hide another yawn and he knew now was not the time.

Under the guise of a repositioning, he moved his lower body back from her own.

"Rest now. I won't leave."

Rahvyn licked her lips, as if she were tasting his kiss—and he braced himself for what he was going to do if she asked him . . . for what he wanted. She was totally spent, though.

"Yes, I beg of you, please do not leave," she said as she laid her head down on his arm and closed her eyes.

It was not long before she was breathing deeply, and it was only then that he mirrored her total recline. He didn't relax, though, and there was going to be no sleep for him.

He had no idea why she was denying what she was. Maybe it was a self-protection she felt she couldn't afford to ditch? But she didn't need to worry about defending herself. She had worked a second miracle today, and V was right. The Brotherhood were going to adopt her like one of their own blood from now on.

You did something for Wrath? You did it for all of the brothers.

And Lassiter was relieved. If anything were to happen to him? They might have been grateful for her saving Nate.

But for the gift she gave Wrath . . . they were going to protect her to their deaths.

CHAPTER NINETEEN

"Does my dog glow in the dark now?"

As night arrived, Wrath put the question out there as he stroked the pad of one of George's paws. The golden was lying on his chest, the pair of them stretched out on the bed beside Beth and L.W.

"No," Beth said with a laugh. "He doesn't."

"I wouldn't care if he did." Wrath fanned his fingers through the long locks below George's throat. Then he passed his palm over what had been shaved for the ultrasound. "Maybe L.W. would appreciate the night-light."

He was pretty sure his son was asleep because otherwise, there would have been the soft clacking of blocks being stacked over and over again. The kid had a weird thing for making towers with those old school wooden cubes, the letters and numbers whittled out so that Wrath could feel the patterns whenever he picked them up.

There had been some of them on the bed earlier. Maybe they'd ended up on the floor.

"L.W.'s finally sleeping," Beth murmured.

"I was just thinking that."

"You're always right about him. The two of you have a connection."

Wrath turned his head to his *shellan*. He could hear the smile in her voice. It was in the easy way the syllables came out, the softness in the vowels, the slow cadence. It was also in her scent, unmarred by anything fearful, sad, or anxious. It was in her words, affirming and kind.

"You know what, *leelan*," he said.

"What."

"This is what I hope the Fade is like." He moved his hand up to George's head and rubbed a silken ear back and forth between his forefinger and thumb. "An eternity of the four of us, right where we are now."

"Wrath . . ."

"Hmm?"

"What was that. Down in the clinic. What happened?"

He paused with the ear. "I don't know. But what I'm clear on is that now, George has nothing in his spleen. Doc Jane couldn't find anything."

"Who is that female? I mean—" There was a rustle,

as if Beth were rolling over onto her side; sure enough, her voice's signal sounded closer. "And is it true Lash is back?"

Wrath tried to hide his frown. "Ah, yeah, I think he is."

"So is the war starting up again?"

Please don't do this, he thought. *Not here, not now.*

Except how else was she going to get any information, given that she didn't attend Brotherhood meetings? And besides, they'd had all afternoon to lie next to each other, holding hands, stewing in gratitude, the release of stress so great he felt like he was buoyant inside his own skin. But like he'd just told her, he could have used an eternity of these hours, and maybe that was something he needed to think about. When was the last time they had done this? Dawdled. Loafed. Had a lie-in. The grind for him down at the Audience House, as important as meeting with the civilians was, had become a suck zone of pressure and distraction—to the point where even if he had been lying next to his mate, his mind was always partially somewhere else.

"Yes," he heard himself say. "I think the war is restarting."

"Then we're lucky to have Rahvyn."

He thought of those angels showing up on the front lawn, looking for Lassiter. It did seem as though fate was beginning to swirl around, the cycling pulling things in, gathering them together: The demon, Lash, the Book, Lassiter . . . Rahvyn. Another era getting off the ground like a 747 barreling down a runway, gathering speed and rattling its bolts until, at long last, loft occurred and the journey began.

But who the fuck knew how it was all going to go.

"I want to head down to Manhattan with you, *leelan*. Soon."

The purr that came out of his mate was exactly what he was after. That bolt hole in the Big Apple was their private sanctuary—although he couldn't remember the last time they'd been there: Real life had intruded on *their* life and taken a helluva lot of liberties.

It shouldn't take a tragedy to remind him of how much he needed his family. Both those up on two legs, and those who were on four.

"I would love that, *hellren* mine."

Wrath smiled to himself. "Let's make it happen. And I don't want you to worry about the war or me. I've made it how long? I'm good for another nine hundred years—if you can put up with my—"

"Charming personality?"

"That's it. That's me," he muttered. "Every night, I wake up and choose joy."

"Ah, you're not so bad. You just don't have much patience. And you don't suffer fools very well. And then there's the hangry thing—"

"Okaaaaaay." He put his dagger hand out, and a split second later felt Beth's palm slide onto his. "I'm a peach."

"Well, one thing's for sure." Her voice deepened. "If we're talking fruit, you do like peaches."

"Mmmm." Doing a little purring of his own, he deliberately licked his lips. "I do."

There was a tug on his arm, and then he felt his mate's kiss on the inside of his wrist.

"Any more of that," he murmured, "and I'll be telling George to lie in the bathroom and you to put L.W. in his crib."

"I think that's a fine idea—"

The sound of a cell phone vibrating on the bedside table snapped Wrath's head around. Baring his fangs, he hissed at the thing, curled up a fist, and—

"Nope," his *shellan* said. "I'll get it. At least that way, we won't need to replace it because you broke the screen."

As Beth stretched over him, he said, "Don't feel like you have to."

"What if it's something important—"

He palmed the side of her throat and pulled her face into his. Finding her lips was not hard. He'd been doing it without vision for how many years now? And oh, fuck, her mouth was soft and warm and—

She broke off the kiss, and then a second later the ringing stopped. "Hello?"

George let out a chuffing sound, as if he too were interested in who was calling. Which made just the pair of them.

Wrath was not on that list.

"Hey, yes," Beth said in a serious way, "he's right here, hold on."

"Who is it."

"It's—"

"Actually, I don't care." He put his hand out, and when the phone landed against his palm, he whipped it up to his ear. "*What.*"

Tohr was as unflappable as ever: "Are you coming to the Audience House tonight, or . . . ? I mean, it's fine either way, we're just waiting for you. The civilians are arriving in about fifteen minutes."

Wrath swallowed curses. "What time is it—"

"Oh, my God," Beth exclaimed. "It's nine! How is it nine? It can't be n—"

"I'll be there, ASAP," Wrath said. Then he snapped, "No, don't cancel anything. I'm fucking coming."

As the call ended, like Tohr was in a hurry to stop being the messenger, Wrath was in the mood to chuck the Samsung across the room. But then he petted his dog, and replugged into the gratitude. Without Rahvyn, he wouldn't be bitched about a forgotten schedule of civilian meetings.

He'd be heartbroken and staring off into space with his blind-ass eyes.

"Soon," he vowed as he went in to kiss his mate again. "You and I are going to Manhattan together *soon.*"

◆ ◆ ◆

Down in the training center's clinic, Rahvyn awoke alone in a hospital bed—and for a split second, she was confused. Was this after she had saved Nate . . . or was this—had it been a dream that she had been called to see about the King's dog?

Sitting up from the pillow, she turned to the door. Had Lassiter even been here—

The panel opened wide, and there the angel was, appearing in the jambs as if she'd summoned him. In his hands, he was holding a tray that was piled so high with snacks and drinks that the mountain nearly reached his chin.

She moved to get to her feet. "Let me help you—"

"Nope," he said briskly. "You stay there. I'm coming to you."

As he marched across and put the load down on a rolling tray, the carefully balanced order devolved into chaos, things falling everywhere—and she rushed her hands forward to try to keep the pile intact. There were so many little bags slipping off, however, and the more she attempted to corral them, the more determined they seemed to be to explore the virtues of the tiled floor.

And suddenly she was laughing because Lassiter was batting at them, too, the pair of them playing a silly slap game that turned into some kind of volleying as the chips and pretzels became like balls.

When a fragile equilibrium was finally reestablished, she collapsed back against the pillow, her hands flopping onto her chest as she giggled. "At least I know that I did not dream this."

Lassiter's eyes grew serious. "No, it all actually happened."

As a curl of anxiety tightened her stomach, she resolved to focus on what she might like to eat, and as if the weight of her decision destabilized the forces of snack adherence, one of the bags fell to the floor.

The angel caught it before the Lay's chips hit. "I may have gone overboard, but I was worried you haven't eaten for a while."

While he straightened, she found herself measuring him—and resisted the urge to reach out and touch his arm. Or his shoulder. This *is* real, she told herself. Her subconscious would not be so inventive as to edit this— what did they call them, again?—*vending machine* feast into a dreamscape.

"Oh, what to have," she murmured as the labels registered properly. "And you should have some, too."

"It's all for you." He sat at the foot of the bed. "After you're done, I'll eat."

"No, we share." She took the bag of chips from him and motioned to the others. "You must eat with me—or I shan't eat at all."

"Well, this is actually just hors d'oeuvres. I'm going to call Fritz and ask him to bring you a proper—"

"Oh, please do not trouble anyone." She held up the bag, then opened it. "This is all I need."

As she put the first chip into her mouth and bit down, she made an *mmmmm* sound. "Indeed, they did not have food like this where I am from."

Lassiter went still, and she would have taken the words back if she could have. She wanted no talk of the past. Or the future. Or . . . the present, actually. Outside of snacks.

"What shall you have," she said quickly. "Lay's like me?

Or no, how about these. Pretzels with cheese in the middle."

When she went to pass the "Combos" to him, he tilted his head and studied her. But then he took what she offered. "Thanks. And I really do want to feed you something more than empty calories."

"How can you not call this profusion a sufficiency— and oh, you brought a Sprite. I do enjoy its fizz."

As he cracked the top of the green can for her, he said, "Females cannot live by junk food alone. Especially ones as beautiful as you."

She flushed and covered her pleasure by accepting the soda from him. And then she said, "I liked sleeping beside you."

The stillness came over Lassiter once more. "Did you."

"I felt safe." She took a sip, the bite of the cold and the sweetness of the bubbles a combination she had not liked at first, but had come to enjoy. "It has been a very long time . . . since I have slept and felt safe. Even in Luchas House, I did not truly rest. So I thank you for that. And for this."

Lifting the soda in salute, she bowed her head in gratitude.

"I didn't sleep," he said.

"Did I keep you up?" She winced and covered her mouth with her hand. "I did not—what is the word— snore? Did I?"

"No." He extended his long arm and brushed her hair back over her shoulder. "Never."

"It could happen." She took another sip because his eyes were burning as he stared at her, and an answering heat inside of her body came up too quickly for comfort. "Tell me, though. Why did you not sleep?"

"I was too busy making sure you were safe."

More heat kindled within her. So much more heat. "Surely the Brothers ensure proper defenses here."

"They do." Lassiter shrugged. "But sometimes a person wants to make sure that another person . . . is safe."

She brought the soda halfway to her mouth. Then she lowered it.

He was not so much sitting as poised, his upper body tilted forward, his elbows on his knees, his weight steady but on the verge of a shift in position.

Over the hours of the day, she had felt the warmth of him, a banked fire that had been up against her back on some occasions, and then something that she curled into on others. There had been a temptation, even in her repose, to touch him. To bridge the sanctity of his physical boundaries. To have him reciprocate.

Yet he had held off as they had first lain together and he could be hard to read.

"Rahvyn . . ."

As the hunger in his voice registered, she thought . . . well, not *that* hard to read.

And yet, in the crackling air between them, anxiety threatened, a wolf at her hedges. Would he even want her if he knew that she was unclean? There was much different in the modern world, but from where she hailed, a female who had been used by any male prior to a proper mating, consensual or not, was not considered of worth.

"I need to tell you something," she said roughly. "Which well may cause you to rethink who I am—"

"Not possible."

"Do hold your judgment," she countered, "until the details are known unto you. I—I feel that you must know . . . I am not a virgin."

There was a pause, as if her words were sinking in for him. Then he cleared his throat. "Well, I mean, you lived a life before now. I, ah—are you still in love with him? Or, like, with him? Do you have a mate?"

She took another chip out of the bag, but there was no way she could chew it in her dry mouth. Much less swallow it. "No. I was not mated. I . . . it was not . . . it was not by choice on my part."

The change in him was immediate, his brows lowering over his iridescent eyes, his shoulders seeming to thicken, his hands tightening into—

Pop!

The sound was so unexpected, she jumped. But it was just the bag of Combos in his hand, the pressure of the grip he had made causing a breach of its structure, brown nuggets falling to the floor between his bare feet as a waft of cheese bloomed in the suddenly tense air.

And then he just sat there on the end of the bed, breathing.

"Perhaps I should have told you previously." She looked down—and wished she could return to mere minutes before. But this collision had been inevitable, ever since the first flare of their attraction. "I just did not know how . . . to tell you. Or explain the—"

"I only need to know one thing," he said in a low voice.

Rahvyn took a deep breath and swallowed past the lump in her throat. "Yes, I am afraid the . . . breaching . . . was complete."

When he made no response, she put the soda and the chips back on the tray. "Shall I go?" She glanced toward the door, which seemed a great distance away. "Yes, I believe I should go—"

"Is the motherfucker still alive. Because I will *destroy* him with my bare hands."

CHAPTER TWENTY

Now, *this* was more what he had in mind.

Not in terms of interior decor, Lash thought as he glanced around the shitty apartment. When it came to *Architectural Digest* standards, the current environs were on par with that shitty walk-up.

But as he considered the lineup of fresh meat before him, there was an improvement with regard to manpower.

"Man, what the hell, you not washin'? You stank."

As the olfactory conclusion was announced to the collective, Lash stayed behind Mr. Mouthy and Silent Bob, as he had come to think of them, the latter a reference to the movie, not because the fucker's name was Bob. His two slayers were standing in front of him, and the group of young human men they'd called together were typical punks, unremarkable except for the strength that came not with training or discipline, but rather the sloppy confidence of youth.

He would take it, however. Any night of the week.

"Fuck you," Mouthy said to the one who had the fussy nose. "So you want to work or not. You want to chill in this shithole or—"

"Hey, fuck you. I pay twelve hundred a month for this."

Did *everything* have to start with "fuck," Lash wondered. Then again, he wasn't inducting them for their vocabulary, and frankly, it was—to take an f-page from their book—fucking ridiculous to talk about smelling anything bad. The couch over there was so stained, it was impossible to tell what color it had started out as. Red? Blue? And who would have thought that that would be the subject of any debate. The rest of the rank rathole was no better, the wall-to-wall carpeting raw from tread traffic, stained like the sofa, peeling up in the corners. Likewise, the windows were so dirty, it was like there were privacy curtains over the panes, and through an archway, the kitchen had more flies than a cow pasture.

And the sonofabitch—sorry, "fucker"—had the nerve to criticize anything?

"So who the fuck is he," one of the lineup asked.

Lash stared at the man. He was short and stocky, with narrow hips badly balanced by heavy shoulders and a thick neck, like the guy only worked out the top half of himself at the gym. Up on his head, his hair was dark and floppy, his eyes dark, the shadows under them dark, his brows and lashes dark.

Depending on his answer, that was all going to change. Over time, *lessers* lost their pigmentation, everything turning pale.

"You talkin' or what?" the stumpy one asked with the kind of cockiness that came with being a prick by nature.

And being armed under that leather jacket.

They were all armed, bulges under coats, in ass pockets—but then they had things to protect. There were drugs under wraps on the chipped table in the corner, a couple different piles of white powders, along with dusty scales and crumpled bills, solving a mystery that required little, if any, sleuthing. Lash had gotten a gander at the display before they'd pulled a tarp over the setup after Mouthy had knocked on the door with the butt of a shotgun and not waited for an answer. As he'd busted in, the punks had scrambled to attention all around the room, their drug-addled minds trying to catch up with the surprise visitors. Meanwhile, Mouthy had taken control, something that was easy when you had a double-barrel on your side of persuasion, and some kind of relationship with the infiltrated.

"I asked you a question," Stump said as he jabbed a forefinger at Lash. "You're gonna fucking answer me—"

"He don't have to talk," Mouthy cut in. "You want to dick around here or be a part of something bigger. You want more? Or you want this shit."

Mouthy kicked a jug full of what could have been apple juice, but was more likely piss. "What do you want, Muggs. What do you want, Bullz. What do you want, Dollah . . ."

He went down the line and asked the question, made the demand, whatever. Just like Lash had told him to: When it came to the Lessening Society, there were two rules. Only two. One, the inductees had to choose of their own volition; Lash wasn't allowed to influence them.

The second rule only came into play when they were in the field. Number two bridged the divide between enemies, uniting the hunter and the prey—no human involvement, and if there was any, you cleaned that up, whether you were a slayer or a vampire.

Nobody wanted humans getting involved in the private business of the war.

"We doin' okay," Stump tossed back. "We eat good—"

"Power. Real power." Mouthy pointed the shotgun at the drug table. "Not this middleman bullshit. I'm talking clout. Like you own Caldwell. Or you wanna be under Big Tony 'til you get your fucking top blown off. This man right here's your answer."

All eyes on him. Like Tupac said. And Lash stared back.

"And it's forever," Mouthy pressed it. "For fucking ever."

The tipping of the scales occurred at a different rate for each one of the men, and Lash could tell by their expressions when the click was made, the consent given, the choosing over, the decision set. They didn't have to respond verbally because their bodies suddenly projected a different energy, yet their lips did clap together in confirmation, their heads nodding as they spoke to Mouthy.

But that slayer's role in this was over now. Lash had what he needed from them.

"Step aside," he said softly.

Mouthy shut up, cutting off his own words, whatever they were. And Silent Bob didn't fuck with it, either. They got out of the way, moving over to the door to bar any escape, good ol' Bob getting a chair and bracing it under the doorknob.

It was a subtle thing. Cute, really.

"What you doing?" Stump demanded.

"Don't worry about that," Lash said as he stepped forward.

There was an unobstructed wall behind where the group had loosely shoulder-to-shouldered themselves, the expanse as stained and marred as everything else was. How convenient.

"What the fuck you looking at us like that—"

Lash swept his hand, and the movement translated to the bodies, slamming them back against the grimy vertical, pinning them in place.

The lineup of punks struggled, trying to pull and kick free of the invisible bands that held them aloft and mounted them as moving sculptures. And as they were of different heights, he made his job easy and evened them up. At throat level.

Then he shifted his eyes to the side and measured the dirty windows. The apartment was stacked on top of more of the same, the ten-story building teetering on a condemned notice—just like the pair of look-alikes on either side of it. The development was on the fringes of downtown, an attempt from the eighties at reinvigorating a declining part of the city. Maybe there had been an initial success with some urban professionals, but that time had passed, and now things were back where they had started.

Economic challenges aside, there were neighbors. Lots of them.

He was not going to deprive himself of this experience, however—so he was just going to take for granted that mind-your-own-business was a universal tenet for the other tenants.

Taking out the hunting knife he'd whittled with back in that basement, he held the stainless steel blade up. The response in the inductees was satisfying, and he inhaled, drawing in the tangy scent of fear sweat as they began to beg.

At which point, he decided he had to silence their commotion. That second rule was pesky, but practical, and this was going to go well beyond usual levels of disturbance in the building.

Pity, really. His favorite sopranos were the ones singing for their very lives.

Walking up to Stump, he enjoyed the flapping mouth, the peeled-wide eyes, the flushing panic and fruitless struggle. And he didn't read lips, but he could dub in the gist of the speech. Wonder how many f-bombs there were now—although he was rather thinking the one on the far end, with the tattoo of a cross on the front of his neck, was praying.

Twirling the knife in his fingers, Lash gripped the handle so that the blade could stab most effectively, but that wasn't the motion he was going to use. He crossed the weapon over his pecs, placed it at the correct level, and held on tight for the ride: With a long stride, he walked down the row, the sharp edge doing its work sure as if it were going for a gold star.

A set of second mouths opened freely across each of the necks, a chorus of them, and the blood that ran out of those jugulars was a glossy show, red and vital. When he got to the religious one on the end, he loosened the lockdown a little so that, as he licked the blade clean with his tongue, he could enjoy the show.

Talk about puppets. All the arms and legs clapped against the filthy wall with a fine show of herky-jerky, the heads bucking, the gurgling quiet.

With a curling anticipation, he knew he was going to do this a hundred more times. A thousand.

The good thing about humans, for his purposes, was that they were easy to come by, and equally easily exploited, their modern-life ennui a perfect entry point for promises of power that would come at a very high price.

Breathing in deeply through his nose again, the copper perfume was nuanced as each of the drug dealers brought their own particular tilt to the common scent—and he knew, as he measured the puddles forming under the boots and sneakers, that this was going to take a long time. They were just beginning the inductions. Add the recovery time afterward? He wouldn't be able to use these new *lessers* tonight at all unless he hurried shit up.

Stepping into Stump, he reholstered his knife and went for the button and zipper on the front of those jeans. As he took care of business and then yanked the waistband down to the knees, blood dropped on the backs of his hands and he paused to lick it off. It tasted like crap, watered down and contaminated with chemicals. Whatever.

Ah, yes, commando. Of course. And it appeared, given the open sores on the flaccid penis, that someone had been getting busy without using proper protection.

What was going to happen next would take care of that. Not the herpes, but the dipshit's ability to spread the virus—

Lash re-palmed the hunting knife and plunged the point into the sinew just below where the thigh plugged into the pelvis. In response, the body did a siezure-jump, everything animating for a brief second, and the same thing happened when he sliced into the femoral artery on the other side.

"That's better," he said, as the blood flowed even faster.

With Stump's puddle immediately doubling in size, the punk next door knew what was coming, and as Lash stepped up to him, the guy fought hard, so very hard, until he choked himself out, his eyes rolling back as he lost consciousness.

"This won't take long," Lash drawled. "Don't worry."

As he went on a pants-down repeat, he thought of his father. The Omega had had a special way of welcoming his inductees into the Lessening Society, but Lash had no interest in that sexual shit. This was absolutely not a turn-on for him, and there was a shot of superiority that he remained detached.

Sloppy, really, to fuck your acolytes.

"Say cheese," he said just before he made the cut in the left artery first.

As the dealer woke back up, his face stretched like Silly Putty, the features elongating as he hollered for help and made no sound at all. And things got even more strain-tastic as Lash sliced into things on the right side.

Continuing on to the third punk, Lash checked on Stump—and decided not to forge ahead. Things were getting bone-dry in the circulatory system over there, and he didn't want the cardiac muscle starved for oxygen for too long. He needed it in good pumping order.

"You'll have to wait," he told the third in line. "But be ready. I won't be long."

Back at the head of the class, Stump was on the verge of losing consciousness, but the surge of adrenaline that came with Lash returning was enough to perk him up into a panic.

"Open wide," Lash said.

Bringing his own wrist to his mouth, he scored his

vein and thought that his sire had had his own way of doing this part, too. But as he'd resolved the night before, it was a new era, and he felt like honoring his vampire roots. Feedings, after all, were a necessity for the species that had taken him in and raised him.

So this unnatural event felt more natural this way

Willing the human's head back, Lash went to put the puncture wounds over that goldfish mouth. "Drink and join me in forever."

The black ooze that came out of him gave him a pause, and he had the sense that he was never going to get used to it. His blood had been red, once. Like the humans' in that regard. And it had smelled of copper, too.

Not anymore.

Curling his lip in disgust, he told himself to refocus. Some gifts came with complications, and did he really want to be powerless and mortal? Did the appearance and odor of what was in his veins matter so much?

"The fuck it does," he said softly as he pressed his bite to the human's mouth and made the man start swallowing, even as he choked.

Because hello, there was a slice across his windpipe. Enough got down, though, and the thrashing was nearly instantaneous. These movements now were different from the struggle to get free, the epileptic activity repetitive and spastic in its uncoordination, no larger purpose to it—

Vomiting presently. Red blood and bile first.

And now . . . black.

Yes, good. His essence was taking over, propagating,

magnifying—and he felt a stirring, a thrill that he imagined was like watching conception happen.

"Fuck," Mr. Mouthy whispered behind him.

"Surely you haven't forgotten how this works," Lash countered dryly.

Thrusting his hand forward, he clapped his open palm on Stump's chest, directly above the sternum.

"Come to me," he commanded.

The heat was instantaneous, leaping up to greet his hand, not a kindling but a flame without fire. The vibration came next, the calling answered by a need to respond—

The scream was so loud and long, it broke free of the imposed silence, the ringing, high-pitched auditory explosion something Lash drank with his ears—as the rib cage broke apart and the muscle popped out, steel to a magnet.

Except unlike metal, it was warm, soft . . .

And wet.

CHAPTER TWENTY-ONE

R age was a dark magic, really. Or maybe "evil" was the word.

As the vengeful emotion swept through Lassiter, it was transformative, taking him away from what he knew of himself and making a monster of him: Sitting at the foot of Rahvyn's hospital bed, with her admission ringing in his skull, he was ready to commit murder.

And draw the shit out.

"Does he live," he repeated, in a voice that did not sound like his own. "The male who hurt you, does he live."

"No," Rahvyn replied roughly. "He . . . does not."

The answer should have satisfied him. Instead, he felt his fury thicken. Who had done the duty? Sahvage? Or another male relation of hers—

"Do you still . . ." She touched her mouth. "Do you still want . . . to kiss me?"

It took him a moment to translate what she was saying through all the fury. And when her words finally processed, they were probably the only thing that could have cooled him off.

Refocusing, he cradled her face in his hands, searching her beauty, wondering how he could express himself. "Of course I do. What happened to you—it's not you. It was something that was done to you, by someone who was wrong."

Someone who needed to be skinned alive, inch by inch. And yes, the irony of giving her earnest, heartfelt advice that also applied to himself was resolutely and firmly lost on him. She was different.

"What is it," he said as she grew tense.

"I am changed now. Foree'ermore."

"Yes," he said. "But at your core, you are still you."

"No, I'm not. And I am afraid to tell you this . . ."

As she hesitated, he took her hand and put it over his heart. "You can tell me anything. *Anything.*"

Her ragged inhale, her pale face, the way she held herself so tightly, made him want to start looking for a weapon. But he already knew without checking under the hospital bed or looking in the cabinet above the little basin, that the recovery room had no guns or knives, no flamethrowers or grenades. No axes, no hammers, no saws or crowbars.

Also, no target.

Just the damned bed. The rolling table with his absurd attempt to feed her piled high. The TV in the corner, suspended from the ceiling. The medical equipment that was not in use.

Goddamn, why did the asshole have to be dead? He wanted to kill him.

"Tell me," he prompted. "I promise you, there is nothing that you can say or do that will make me see you in any other light than I do now."

As she lowered her head, her platinum hair fell forward like a veil. "The truth of it is . . . though it was terrible, I am strengthened from what was done to me."

When her eyes darted to his, as if to check his reaction, he nodded. "That's because you survived." He tucked her hair back so he could keep seeing her properly. "You know, I've crossed paths with a lot of survivors in my line of work. Only a few have scars on the outside, and even if they do, it's what is on the inside that's always been harder to heal. But you're right. They are stronger for what they've endured."

"You do not judge me, then."

"I don't." He touched her chin and lifted her face. "I think you're even more beautiful. Because you're a survivor."

There was a long silence, and he imagined she was testing his words, his tone, his vibe, for the truth in what he was saying. And just as he was wondering what else he could say to reassure her, she cleared her throat.

"Will you do something for me?" she said. "If it is . . . agreeable to you."

"Anything."

As he had done to her, now she did to him, her free hand rising up, her fingertips moving over his face, brushing his jaw, his cheek, his hair. The wonder in her eyes, the reverence, humbled him—and he almost told her it was misplaced.

"I want you to clean him out of me." She looked down at her sweater and jeans. "I want the memory of . . . what he did taken from me. I want to think of you, never . . . him. Please . . . make that go away."

Her hesitant request, and all it implied, took his fucking breath away.

Holy hell, he'd sat at the foot of the Creator, had seen the earth from another dimension, had felt the shifts of births and deaths alike—and never, *never*, had he been so moved, never had he been so resolved. And as he imagined doing exactly what Rahvyn had asked, Devina's specter was instantly raised, and he slapped that shit down. He was going to lock that nasty in his vault and never think of it again.

Wiped clean. Erased. Gone, as if it had never happened.

After all, why burden Rahvyn with what he'd gone through.

As a sense of peace came over him, it was unexpected—and he brushed her lips with his thumb. "I'm going to kiss you. Now. And you can tell me . . . whatever else you want me to do. Or if you change your mind, we can stop—"

"I am not going to stop." Her eyes went to his mouth. "I think I decided the first moment I saw you, at

Luchas House, in the garage. I chose you then, I choose you now."

Fucking hell, he couldn't breathe. "I remember that moment. You captivated me. You were standing there with Sahvage, and I couldn't take my eyes off you."

"Kiss me . . ."

Lassiter leaned in and got lost in her eyes, the world around them disappearing—and this kind of magic, so different from what came with rage, was something he was into. He'd been so destroyed by the demon, left demoralized and unsure on how he could recover, but Rahvyn was showing him the way: In service to her, he was given a further purpose that made him whole in a way he couldn't have foreseen.

Saving them both.

I love you, he thought just as he put his mouth on hers.

Lassiter kept the kiss soft and slow, giving her all kinds of opportunity to pull back, rethink, pump the brakes. When she just made a pleading sound—that went right down between his legs—he tilted his head and deepened the contact, stroking his lips over hers as he cupped her nape. She was the one who lay back, and when he went with her, their bodies stretching out together, he threw the lock on the door with his mind.

Lifting his head a little, he took a moment to soak in the sight of her, her silken hair flowing over the pillow, her hungry eyes roaming around his face and shoulders—as if she didn't know what to expect.

And that was when it dawned on him. This was a first time for them both, in a way.

God, he hoped he could make it good for her, and as he worried about whether he was going to know how to pleasure his female, shadows of that nightmare with the demon prowled around the periphery, sure as there were versions of Devina stalking the bed.

Kissing Rahvyn again banished the threat, and he learned what she liked, what made her surge up to him, what caused her to press her breasts into his pecs. But he still kept his hips back because he was hard as a two-by-four, his body instantly ready to mate.

"Can I touch you?" she asked against his mouth.

The groan that came out of him was all anticipation. "Anywhere."

More with the kissing, as her hands rode up his biceps and drifted across his shoulders. Then they were in his hair, sinking in, bringing him even more firmly to her mouth. Following her need, he was careful as he entered her with his tongue, licking inside of her, going gently—

He was so in tune with making sure he was treating her lips with the attention they deserved that he didn't immediately notice she was pulling his scrubs top up his chest. Eventually, however, the cool air hitting his hot skin got through to him, and he eased back again.

"May I see you," she whispered, her silver eyes shimmering.

"Whatever you want." He sat up. "Do you want to do the undressing or should I—"

She answered the question before he finished it, her hands going back to the hem of the blocky blue shirt, and as she lifted the bottom, he put his arms up.

Higher, higher, higher—

Just as his head was swamped in the folds, she made a purring noise—and then he could see again. As she saw the top half of him.

She dropped the shirt to the floor like she forgot she was even holding it—and put her hands on him, starting at his collarbones. The wonder in her face made him feel more masculine than anything else ever had, and he wished he were wearing all his gold chains now so that he could feel them move over his skin and hear the sweet chiming as she explored his pecs . . . and followed the links down to the piercing in the head of his cock.

But that was no more.

"Where are your necklaces now, angel?" she breathed. "You used to wear many."

Gone. "Maybe I'll put some back on sometime."

"I would like that. If only because I could take them off you, one by one." She flushed and dropped her eyes. "That is silly—"

"It's a date." As her stare flipped back up to his, he nodded. "If I didn't have to leave you, I'd go get some chains right now."

And then he realized—

"What is it?" she asked as her hand went down to his sternum. "What troubles you?"

"I, ah . . ." He captured her hand and kissed her palm. "I don't want to freak you out."

But he wanted to take off her clothes, and kiss her in places he wasn't sure she was ready for. Holy fuck, he wanted to go down on her, right now.

"Without meaning any offense," she said dryly, "I saved a dog earlier in the day. My threshold for surprise is quite high at the moment, thank you very much."

He laughed. Then pressed his mouth to her hand.

When the silence became awkward, her brow lifted. "I would rather hope you will see your way out of this current dearth of words."

"I love the way you talk and your accent. You roll your r's and it goes right through me."

"Oh?"

He looked at her mouth. "It makes me wonder what else you can do with your tongue."

With surprising boldness, she met him directly in the eye. "Let us find out, shall we?"

CHAPTER TWENTY-TWO

As Rahvyn waited for Lassiter to respond to her rather blatant invitation, she enjoyed exploring his upper body, the feeling of his skin, so warm and smooth, the expanse of his shoulders and chest, so vast and hard, all of it a landscape she was compelled to touch. And as she imagined him with his gold on properly, she was tantalized with what it would have been like to have the links under her hands as well.

"So will you kiss me some more," she said in a husky voice that did not sound like her own. "I like your tongue inside of me."

"Fuck, yes," he groaned as he closed his eyes for a second.

Gripping his shoulders, she used his body to pull herself to him, and as she closed in on his mouth, she heard herself purring in satisfaction. The contact started gentle, as it had before, but it did not stay that way. His arms came around her, and there was a crushing sensation she only wanted more of as he held her against him, fiercely. Running her fingers into his blond-and-black hair again, she wanted to get out of her own clothes. She wanted to be naked underneath him. She wanted . . .

Pulling back, she was breathing hard, and her eyes latched on to his neck, where the thick vein ran up the side. As the tips of her fangs tingled, she felt a compelling need to know what he tasted like—

"Do it." When she recoiled in shock, he cupped the back of her head and held her in place. "Take me, in your way. I want you to mark me. I want to know what it's like to have your fangs in me."

Rahvyn's heart thundered—and yet she hesitated. "I do not want to hurt you."

"You can't, don't worry—even if you did, I don't care." His hand ducked underneath her hair and stroked her nape. "My blood may not offer you the sustenance you need, but I want to give you a part of me. Even if it's not enough."

Her mind told her no. Her body told her yes.

Her hunger told her *now*.

The decision was made before she was conscious of coming to any conclusion, and her fangs descended all the way down in a rush. Rearing back, a hiss came out of her mouth—

She struck with a violence that should have bothered

her, but did not because she was just that starved to drink of him. On Lassiter's side, his bark of an exhale as the punctures were made sounded like triumph to her ears, and then she wasn't hearing anything. She was drinking, swallowing, taking of him.

He tasted of a piercing white wine, his blood cutting into her with a sizzle, the path of it burning down her throat and hitting her stomach with a blaze—that went right into the juncture of her thighs: Her core seemed to open upon the command of his flavor, and the response got even more intense as she nuzzled into his vein and sucked upon the source, pulling more and more of him into her—until her body was so hot, she fumbled with her clothes in an attempt to get them off.

"Shh," he said from what seemed like a vast distance. "I'll take care of it—"

The next thing she was aware of was a cooling on her skin, all over her, as if what she was wearing had melted off. She paid no attention to the hows or whys of that. Instead, she pulled him onto her, shifting his weight as she made space for him between her legs—

"Rahvyn."

He said her name as the hard length at the front of his hips fitted itself into the juncture of her core, the pressure bringing a piercing echo of pleasure throughout her entire being. But she had only a moment of the exquisite weight of his strong body on top of her own. As soon as the sensation registered, he rolled his torso to the side, her mouth's seal moving with his neck—and she had a feeling he was repositioning himself so she wasn't pinned or trapped.

But she knew who she was with.

What she was worried about was harming him. She was not sure whether he understood the danger he had put himself in. He was relying on her to stop drinking, when with every swallow, she became more charged for taking from him—and then there was the urge to mate, which was redoubling as well.

A firestorm was owning her, one that was incompatible with making rational decisions.

As an alarm began to sound at the base of her brain, she knew she had to act fast. With a self-control she did not know she possessed, she forced herself to relinquish the lock on his vein—and as she pulled back, she was astonished to see a silver flash around the wound.

"Your blood . . ." she said with wonder as she touched her mouth.

"Don't stop. Take more of me. Take all of me—"

The frenzy she felt was likewise in his eyes, and that was even more dangerous. He was not going to halt this.

"No, I will not." She touched his face. "It is not safe."

From the puncture wounds, tendrils of silver rivered down his throat, and in a quick surge, she licked the wound closed—and became conscious of a tingling throughout her body. Indeed, this was like no feeding ever before, the sensation of strength coming upon her, and yet there was something else. A shimmer. As if his blood brought her nutrients she had never had before, never even knew she needed.

"Lassiter . . . I want you," she breathed. "Please, I ache."

"I'll take care of that, don't you worry—" His eyes drifted down. "Oh, God, you're beautiful."

In the back of her mind, she was surprised she was so comfortable being naked with him. Then again, that was how you knew you were with the right male. That you were safe. That you were cherished.

As he dropped his head toward her, she went for his mouth—and something was unleashed. In her. In him. The kissing became intense, his lips grinding on hers, and then his tongue was inside of her as she dug into his back with her short nails. This time, as she tugged at him, he went where she wanted him: Fully on top of her, his hair falling around her face, all blond-and-black waves, the thickness between his thighs pressing into her again.

Only this time, with no barrier on her side, and just the scrubs bottoms on his.

So no barrier at all, really.

Pushing her knees up, she tilted her hips and—

The moan that came out of her was so loud, she probably should have been more quiet about it, as walls and doors were thin. But then Lassiter swallowed most of the sound.

Things got hotter from there.

The movement. Dearest Virgin Scribe, he began flexing his lower back, and then releasing it, flexing and releasing, and with every surge forward, that arousal of his stroked her sex. Soon he would be inside of her doing that, and then he would fill her up. She had hated that from before, the essence of that aristocrat pooling inside her.

With Lassiter, she wanted to be his receptacle.

Needed his release in her core just like his magical blood had gone down her throat.

◆ ◆ ◆

Just how far did she want to take this? Lassiter wondered.

He hadn't been sure how Rahvyn would feel with him on top of her, but with the way she was moaning? Especially as he started to ride her a little? She seemed to want this as badly as he did—and after she'd taken his vein, he was next-level hot for her.

Nearly coming right now.

Breaking the kiss, he lifted himself off her. Beneath him, she was flushed and panting, her head going back and forth on the pillow in frustration. When she'd wanted her clothes gone, he'd obliged, whisking them off with his mind . . . so that he was now what clothed her, only the bottoms of his scrubs separating them.

"Rahvyn," he said as he stared at her spectacular breasts.

Her eyes fluttered open. "Yes . . ."

"Watch me."

When he was certain that she saw him properly, he dipped his head and kissed her shoulder. Then her collarbone. Then the top of her sternum. Sweeping his hand down the side of her ribs, he moved himself lower on her body.

"You're so damned beautiful."

Her bare breasts were rosy-tipped and perfectly proportioned for her body, and he had to touch them, his hand shaking as he cupped one and brushed his thumb over her nipple—

Rahvyn cried out again and arched up into his hand.

He couldn't resist. Leading with his tongue, he licked at her—and was rewarded with her holding on to him as he sucked on her, treating her as she should be treated, making sure she knew who was doing her so right. Yet she seemed to know. There didn't appear to be any confusion with what had happened to her before, and he was struck by her courage. He didn't need the details to know the violation had hurt and traumatized her, but here she was, enjoying him while he enjoyed her.

She inspired him. And by her example, he felt himself separate even more from what had been done to him.

Rahvyn was his healing.

And at the same time she was his undoing in the best possible way—

Knock. Knock. Knock.

Lassiter lifted his head from her breast and glared at the door. "No," he snapped. "We're *not* here."

The voice that came through the panel was the last

one he wanted to hear: "Too bad. We need to talk to you."

Ah, Eddie, he thought as he squeezed his eyes shut with frustration. *What perfect, piss-poor timing, you schmuck.*

Knock. Knock.

"Lassiter, we're in the break room. Let's get this over with."

He popped his lids and looked down at Rahvyn. She was fucking resplendent, a high flush to her cheeks, her lips swollen from his mouth, her nipples tight and hungry for more of the attention he wanted to give them.

"I'm sorry," he whispered.

"You should go speak unto them," she replied at an equally low volume.

"See you in a minute down the hall," Eddie announced on the far side of the door. "Or I'm going to pull up a chair and put my knuckles to use until they bleed."

In the aftermath of what Lassiter assumed was the angel's departure, he interviewed a variety of curses—and not as in swear words, as in actual hexes you could put on someone . . . many of which, if set into action, would have required Eddie to go to an ER. Stat.

Michael Scott's voice went through his head: *I got you both beat. I'm a proctologist, so I drive a brown Probe.*

"I won't be long," he muttered.

Taking a last look at her breasts, he hovered his hand over her and summoned her clothing back—which felt like he was rewrapping a gift.

Rahvyn glanced down at herself and smiled. "Oh, you are a trickster indeed. And I shall wait for as long as you need."

"Female," he said as he got off the bed. "The last thing I want to do is make you wait—"

"Lassiter . . . you are *phearsom*."

For a second, he had no idea what she was talking about. Then he caught the drift of where her eyes were and looked at himself.

Actually, the word was maybe "obscene." Because his erection had punched one helluva tent in the front of the scrubs.

He covered himself. "Sorry—"

"Do not apologize for *that*." Extending her arm, she said, "Before you go, may I touch you—"

Jerking his hips out of range, he double-palmed himself. "I'll come." Matter of fact, he was about to orgasm right now. Between her eyes and the pressure of holding himself, he was going to fucking lose it. "Like, I'm going to orgasm. Immediately."

"Please. I just want to see, I want to watch—and you are short on time, are you not? So there is a convenience to alacrity, is there not?"

Well, put like that, it would almost be stupid not to.

"Rahvyn." His capitulation was all over the syllables of her name. "If you're sure."

"I shall beg. If that shall further persuade you?" As his eyes bugged, she lowered her voice. "Please . . . Lassiter. Allow me to see you achieve your pleasure . . . *please . . .*"

She topped it all off with licking her lips, nice and slow.

As his eyes rolled back in his head, he stepped toward her. And when he didn't feel her touch, he wondered if she had changed her mind.

As he opened his eyes, she smiled. "I thought you might want to watch. I know I liked witnessing you upon my breast."

Oh . . . fucking *hell*.

Her hand was tentative as she reached forward—and then she made contact with his hypersensitive head. The sound he made was explosive, and his hips thrust, bumping him into her palm.

"I want to see," she said roughly.

Lassiter covered his face with his arms. "You're killing me, female."

"I thought you were immortal, angel mine."

"Not when I think—oh, *fuck*."

Her fingers brushed against his lower abdomen as she freed the bow he'd tied in the front of the scrubs—and the friction of the loose cotton fabric was enough to drive him right to the edge. Then new torture showed up. The bump, bump, and shift of the waistband stretching over the length of him ground his molars.

After which his erection broke out.

"Ohhhh," she sighed. As if she approved of what she'd found.

Dropping his eyes, he looked down his pecs and his abs, to his enormous arousal just as Rahvyn's hand circled his shaft. He barely had time to bark out her name before he was tackled by the most powerful orgasm he had ever had. Throwing a hand out blindly, he grabbed on to something, a blanket, a sheet, whatever, and pulled it over his cock.

He caught the jets just in time.

He couldn't say the same for his balance. As he listed to the side, the bed came up and kept him from hitting the floor—of course it was the other way around, but he was absolutely off the damned planet so it sure as hell seemed like he was still on his feet. And the flop was not the most manly thing, but Rahvyn didn't seem to mind.

As the initial spasms passed, she moaned in the back of her throat and then did some exploring of her own. Which made him start to release all over again.

Stretching out across the foot of the bed, he watched her face as she peeled the blanket off him and stared at his ejaculations with rapt attention as they marked up his six-pack.

Fuck it.

Those angels could wait a little longer.

CHAPTER TWENTY-THREE

Arcshuli, son of Arcshuliae the Younger, was done with the waiting. Pulling his Tesla into the shallow parking area of a modest ranch house, he canned the car and glanced around the quiet neighborhood. Vampires hiding in plain sight. It was genius—and banal as fuck. Middle America, with its average joes who liked football and porno and books about war, sitting in their average houses with the nice hardwood floors, didn't really interest him. But then, he was an asshole.

Probably why he knew all the words to Denis Leary's magnum opus.

Getting out, Shuli jacked up his fawn-colored suede pants, then brushed at the thighs just because he liked the feel of the supple leather. And maybe because he was nervous. After that, he fucked with the collar of his animal-print silk shirt. He was pulling a neo-sixties, mod vibe tonight, but he wasn't sure he was feeling all the Harry Styles style.

The lights were out in the house, which wasn't right, and he checked his phone just to double-triple-hundredth-time check the no-texts, no-calls state of things.

None. Still.

"What are you doing, Nate," he muttered as he shoved the cell into his ass pocket and got walking.

Heading around the side of the garage, he noted the coiled garden hose, green as a lawn should be, and the orderly arrangement of recycling and garbage bins. Out the far side, the backyard was narrow and shallow, the porch that anchored the rear of the ranch free of all furniture as part of the winter lockdown that persisted.

No lights on in the kitchen, either. Not even for security.

Then again, the inhabitants lived mostly in the basement, except when it was, hello, dark out, so shouldn't there have been some lamps on? Unless of course, everyone was at work—

Brrrrrrrrrrriiiiiiiiiiiiiiiiiiiinngggggg.

"Fucking finally," Shuli said as he jammed his hand around his phone and whipped it out of his ass.

Not Nate. Their boss.

He answered. "Hey, yeah, I just pulled up to Nate's house. I still don't know where he is—what? . . . no, it's cool. I have the codes. I'm just going to—no, his parents gave them to me. They're chill . . . yeah, I'll call you back after I'm inside."

As he ended the connection, he shook his head. Great, so their boss was looking for Nate, too. Then again, the guy always showed up for work. Always answered calls, even when he didn't want to. Always was willing to hang out. Even when he didn't want to.

Stepping up onto the pressure-treated porch, Shuli went over to the sliding glass door. He'd heard that the Black Dagger Brother Vishous had kitted out these satellite homes with all kinds of security—so he was well aware, as he entered a numeric sequence on a keypad, that his breaching the seal would be recorded, and maybe even followed up on.

But Murhder had given him access because they all knew that Nate had some special circumstances he was dealing with.

All of which had gotten even more special a couple of nights ago.

And yeah, sure, he thought as he stepped through and slid the door closed behind him, he could have just hit up the 'rents and flagged the fact that it was weird he hadn't heard from his best friend in twenty-four hours—but what if he was merely being paranoid? What if he was wrong to be worried?

What if Nate was perfectly fine, going about his business, just not feeling like talking to his ol' pal Shuli and late for the extra shift he'd picked up to make more moolah. Or what if the guy was turning over a new leaf and getting better friends, and there had just been a miscommunication with the construction company's work schedule?

Inside the house, everything was neat as a pin. Which was one of those sayings, like "happy as a clam," that he wasn't sure he understood. Were pins neat? Could they be messy?

Had clams really been properly assessed for depressive episodes?

Whatever, the counters were free of clutter, no dirty plates in the sink, no pans in the drying rack. The subtle whirring noise suggested the dishwasher was running, or maybe there was a washer going somewhere.

"Hello?" he called out.

No answer. So he went over to the cellar door. Like all vampire homes of this ilk, the sleeping quarters were down below and there was another code he had to put in. When he got two of the numbers mixed up, he had to reenter the sequence before he heard the dead bolt retract.

Finally. Light.

As he opened up the steel door, he was relieved by the illumination and thought it was funny how a ceiling fixture could elevate your mood. Of course, it was artificial optimism: In the same way a dark room could be perfectly safe, he knew that just because you could see didn't mean the boogeyman wasn't waiting for you around the corner.

You did have a better chance of defending yourself, though.

"Nate?"

He was halfway down the carpeted stairs when he got a sickening feeling in his gut—and as he reached the bottom and stepped off into the lower living area, he figured out what it was.

Gunmetal.

He smelled gunmetal.

Cranking his head to the left, he looked down the hall. Nate's bedroom was the first one and the door was closed.

"My man," he said loudly. "Whatcha doing?"

As he headed across the living room carpet, he sniffed the air some more. Definitely . . . a gun. Maybe it was Murhder getting ready for the night? That had to be it, right? The Brother was always armed when he left the house, and that meant making sure his weapons were in working order and in their holsters.

"Nate?"

At the closed panel, he knuckled up and rapped. "*Nate.*"

Putting his hand out, he watched from a distance as he gripped the knob. "I'm coming in. Right . . . *now.*"

Shuli threw the door wide and braced himself for—

"Nate?"

Stupid question. The navy blue room was relatively small, and the guy wasn't in it. Not unless he was hiding in the closet: The big bed, which was required for Nate's size, was pushed flush into the corner, so there was no "other side" for him to be on the floor behind. The

244 ' J. R. WARD

dresser was shallow—not the kind of thing someone
like Nate could play hide-and-seek with. Same with the
desk. And as for the closet?

Shuli went over and pushed the slider aside to reveal
the t-shirts and sweatshirts and the lonely button-down
hanging on plastic hangers.

Nate hated bureaus for some reason. Said he liked to
see his clothes all at once or he didn't know what he had
to pick from.

"As if there's a huge difference," Shuli muttered.

Just as he turned away, he saw the cell phone. It was
sitting on the bedside table, next to the pillows that
were set up neatly against the headboard.

With a fresh shot of dread, Shuli stepped back out
of the room and looked farther down the narrow
corridor.

As he breathed in through his nose, he caught the
scent of his friend, although it was impossible to know
whether it was from the bedroom or if the guy had
really just gone through the hall.

"Nate?"

Continuing on, he passed by a couple of other closed
doors that he'd always assumed were guest rooms because Nate's parents' master suite was down at the other
end. And then he came to a flimsy pair of folding panels. Separating them, he exposed a vault-like portal
made of reinforced steel.

His hand shook as he entered the code, and when
the lock released, there was a hiss and a shift. Pulling
the heavy weight wide, he got a clear view into the es-

cape tunnel thanks to the banks of fluorescent lights in the low ceiling. Breathing in deep, he smelled fresh drywall—and the fabric softener Nate used on his clothes.

Later, he would wonder why he stopped calling his friend's name.

Moving silently, he tracked the laundry scent and noted that fresh air had mixed with it. He couldn't really find any more of that gunmetal smell, and he told himself that it was all fine. Nate had just forgotten his phone, not left it behind intentionally. Nate was just leaving out the back way of the house, after having made sure his parents were gone for the night, for no particular reason. Nate was totally not depressed because of the female he'd lost, even though he'd never actually had her.

It was all . . . fine.

Shuli repeated the pep talk to himself as he went down the two-hundred-yard-long chute—and somewhere along the way, he realized he'd only come here once, back when he and Nate had first started hanging out. They'd met on a construction job, Nate working because he needed money, Shuli because his sire had determined that character building was the new black.

Those lectures from Arcshuliae about how getting some calluses on his hands was going to turn his life around had been so tedious, it had been easier to just pick up a hammer and learn the difference between a nail and a screw than sit through another litany of his lack of value. And the thing was, his pops was not wrong. Shuli was a lazy piece of shit who just wanted to look good and hook up with females. Women.

Even humans were fine for him.

Nate wasn't like that.

He'd liked only one female.

At the end of the tunnel, there was another vault-worthy steel barrier, and when he entered the code and heard the clunk, there was the hiss of a vapor lock being released.

With his heart starting to pound, he was cautious as he opened things.

On the far side, there was a shallow concrete room lit by pods of illumination and a set of stairs. It was colder here. The night air was stronger here, too.

At the top of the steps, he entered another code at another door. And then he was in a structure that was built to appear to be a shed.

As he emerged from it, he was in a stand of trees at the far end of the neighborhood's development. The lot was vacant, the branches and trunks thick, the ground cover just as packed in. In fact, the flora had been delib-erately cultivated to deter attention and create inconve-nience of passage.

The path Nate had taken was obvious, the distur-bance of a set of footfalls and a big-ass body clear in the moonlight.

Shuli followed along, tracking snapped branches and crushed new growth. The smell of dirt was thick in his nose, and there was nothing else. No fabric softener now, or gunmetal. Then again, the wind was blowing at the side of him.

After what felt like a forever-distance, he finally found his friend up ahead. Through the network of budded branches and fluffy pine boughs, in the icy blue illumination that streamed from the heavens, he caught sight of the male's head and shoulders, the back of the hoodie a clear telltale that it was Nate.

Facing away from Shuli, the male's attention was trained on something in front of him—

The gun came up to his forehead, the suppressor lengthening the barrel, the grip steady.

Just as Shuli started to yell—

The trigger was pulled.

CHAPTER TWENTY-FOUR

I'm not going back, just so you know."

When Lassiter finally arrived in the break room, Eddie was not surprised by the angel's announcement. And also not really shocked that the guy had felt the need to delay things by having a scrub and changing his scrubs. After all, that female had been in the room with him.

What was the saying? *Save water, shower with a friend.*

"As if you have a choice?" Eddie indicated the vacant chair at the little table he and Ad were at. "And do you want to have a seat while we talk or just stomp around like a toddler."

Guess we have our answer to that, he thought as the angel marched over to a vending machine.

Given the glare on the guy's face as he considered his options, it was like the Frito-Lay Company had insulted his mother. Not that he had one.

"Look, don't get pissed at us." Eddie shrugged. "We're just the messengers here. This is between you and the Creator. You got issues with this situation, talk to the one in charge."

Although they all knew how that was going to go. Lassiter and the font of all life made oil and water look symbiotic, and not for the first time, Eddie wondered why, if an entity was in charge of creating things, He would volunteer for the likes of what He had with that fallen angel.

You'd think the Creator would have made things easier on Himself.

Lassiter jabbed at the keypad, something went whirring, and there was a drop. When the angel turned around, he had a Snickers in his hand.

Well, at least the hangry train was pulling into Satisfied Station.

As the wrapper was ripped apart, Eddie remembered when he'd first met the angel. He and Ad had just gotten out of Purgatory, and the three of them had bumped into each other in a way that could have been predestined, but might have been chance.

It had been a fender bender of sorts. Go figure.

"Do you think we're lying about you being called home?" Eddie said. When there was no reply, he could feel himself ramping up. "Really. After everything we've been through. Or have you forgotten the past."

Lassiter took a shark's bite out of the Snickers. "None of that matters now."

"Of course it does." Eddie leaned forward over the table. "And there are no coincidences. We've been looking for you for three years, and suddenly we're led to you? He wants you to come home now. You don't belong in"—he glanced around at the tables and chairs, the TV, all the food—"whatever is happening here."

"I am the spiritual successor to the Scribe Virgin—"

"And maybe you shouldn't be. Maybe that's why we've connected here and now."

As Lassiter looked over his shoulder to the exit, like he was getting ready to use it, the side of his throat was exposed.

The bite mark was obvious.

"Jesus Christ," Eddie muttered with exhaustion.

"Still not my name," the angel ground out. "Never was."

Eddie rose to his feet, and motioned for Ad to stay put. When he got a nod in response, he walked over to the other angel and reached up.

Lassiter slapped his hand away. "Don't touch me—"

Ignoring that, Eddie swept the blond-and-black hair back again. "You know why He wants you to return. And worse than hooking up with some female, you've been playing God, haven't you. You're supposed to be the eyes of the Creator, only a witness, never a participant, and that means you shouldn't—"

The shirt-grab was right at the pecs level, and he let

himself get spun around and slammed into the vending machine.

"Stay out of my fucking business—"

"So stay out of theirs!"

Slam. Slam. *Slam*—

The sizzling sound of an electrical malfunction was coupled with a furious blinking of the machine's inner lights, the strobing hitting Lassiter's furious face and making things go Claymation freeze-frame.

"You don't know what it's like," the angel said hoarsely as a whirring noise played soundtrack. "Watching them suffer."

"The hell I don't."

There was a momentary confusion. "So how can you sit back and do nothing."

"Because that is *not* my role." Eddie fisted the front of the angel's scrubs because two could play that game. "And it's not yours, either. Savior is a term of art, not a definition for what we are."

"Or maybe you just don't give a shit anymore."

Things started dropping inside the vending machine, landing in a clapping rush that was easy to ignore in all the tension.

"Don't try to get in my head," Eddie snarled, "or pretend to know where I've been. Don't *fucking* do that."

"Why? Hiding something—"

Just as Eddie was about to toss something nasty back, maybe even a punch, Ad pried them apart and pushed Lassiter off to the side.

And what do you know, getting pissed at the interruption was the only thing Eddie and Lassiter had in common. They both turned on the guy.

"I told you to stay out of this—"

"You want some of this, too—"

"Fuck you both," the other angel said. "I could give a shit about whatever you two are dick-tossing about." He indicated the waterfall of snacks that was still happening. "This thing is throwing up its guts and I think I want a Snickers because you have one."

For a split second, Eddie couldn't follow. Then he realized that the machine's motherboard was flashing an SOS as all of its corkscrews rotated at once, its wares dropping into the bin at the foot, a pile of calories dressed in colorful bags and wrappers.

Kind of a parallel for the situation.

A fucking mess.

Ad bent over, shoved his arm into the slot, and came back out. "Crap. Milky Way. Guess it'll do."

Leaning up against the Plexiglas window, the last of the pretzels and the M&M's fell down as he peeled the bar with considerably more restraint than Lassiter had.

His utter lack of concern was enviable. And annoying.

"The Creator already knows we've found you," Eddie said with defeat. "He knows everything."

"Then why hasn't He pulled me off the planet." Lassiter cut off any argument by throwing up a stop-sign palm. "He's all-powerful and all-knowing. So if He wants me, why is He sending the two of you. He should just manifest me home."

"It's our fucking job, okay? That's all I know."

"Hear me out," Lassiter said. "What if you're right, and there are no coincidences. You were supposed to find me *now*—after how long? Maybe He doesn't want you to bring me home, He wants you to *help* me here."

Eddie massaged the ache at the base of his neck. "I'm not interested in arguing with you about this."

"I'm not arguing with you, I'm asking you to look at this situation in a different way. He's all-powerful? He'd call me home. Instead, you two find me here and now. He chose to give all of us free will, and you have it. So does he." Lassiter nodded at Ad. "So do I."

"I'm not lying for you."

"I'm not asking you to do that." Lassiter glanced toward the door. "Come with me. I want to show you something."

"I'm not negotiating on this."

"So what are you going to do." Lassiter put up his hands, all now-what. "I'm not going anywhere with you—are you going to drag me into the next dimension? Huh? How's that going to work."

"Why does everything with you have to be difficult."

Ad bent down to the floor. "Either of you want his Snickers? This floor's so clean, you could eat off it."

When Eddie and Lassiter looked over at the other angel, Ad offered left, then right, with the one-bite-off candy bar that had been dropped when things had gotten physical.

"No? Cool, more for me."

While Ad went ham on the Snickers, Eddie closed

his eyes and prayed for . . . shit, he didn't even know anymore.

◆ ◆ ◆

Out in the woods behind the human neighborhood, Shuli fought his way through the undergrowth and the branches in a panic, his shirt getting snagged, his slick-soled loafers skating over the damp ground and roots. Grabbing on to thin trunks, he pulled himself forward—

The wind changed direction and he got a nose-full of the gunpowder and the blood.

"Nate!"

Off in the distance, he heard a dog bark, and something with prickers on it slapped his face. And then he saw the body, facedown in a patch of spring grass in the middle of a clearing that permitted the moonlight way too much access.

So the exit wound that had blown out the back of the skull was glistening, black and gray, in the heaven's wash of blue illumination.

"Oh, *fuck*," Shuli choked out as he fell to his knees. "What the fuck . . . Nate. Oh, God, *Nate*—"

Patting around for his phone, he couldn't remember which pocket he'd put it in. Then he dropped the thing. Lost it in the scruff. Couldn't make his hands work because they were shaking so badly.

"Why did you do it . . . Nate . . . why, oh God . . . why—"

Except he knew the why. Rahvyn. Although maybe

it was more than just that: All those years in that human lab, being experimented on. His *mahmen* dying in captivity. Real life being no great prize on the far side.

He tried to dial. Failed. Forgot he had voice commands.

"I can't do this," he blurted as tears fell. "Hold on, Nate, stay with me—"

He glanced at the back of that skull again and couldn't catch the vomit that rose up in his throat. As he started to heave, he pitched himself onto all fours and tried not to hit the phone. The hurling seemed to go on for hours, and he told himself to cut it out.

Help. He needed to get help. *Now.*

Determined to get control of himself, Shuli shoved himself back so he was sitting on his ass. As he hyperventilated, he passed a dirty palm down his face and felt the calluses his father had been so determined for him to get as a sign of character. Yeah, well, all that manual labor wasn't doing shit for him at the moment. He and Nate had never made sense on paper, an entitled elitist and a quiet survivor of the kind of thing people never got over. But they'd been best friends—

The body jerked. Flopped.

"Nate?" Shuli lunged for the guy. "Are you—"

Shuli couldn't understand what happened next. According to what his eyes saw, it looked like the body rolled over onto its back. Which would be hard to believe, given the injuries. And then Nate sat up, his torso rising off the ground to the vertical, a little trail of blood leaving the circular entry wound at the center of his forehead.

"Nate . . ." Shuli said softly. "What you doing, man?"

Like something that had reanimated from the dead, Nate's head swiveled on the top of his spine toward him. Then the guy reached up and touched the bullet wound, catching the trickle of plasma on his fingertips.

Shuli wiped his mouth with the back of his hand. Where was the phone, where was his fucking phone—

"I'm going to call the Brotherhood," he mumbled as he patted around at the grass and weeds without looking away from Nate. "Just like your father told me to. He said if there was ever a problem"—and this was a *big fucking problem*—"I was to call this number, and, and—"

"Don't call anyone."

"W-w-what the fuck are you talking about. Nate, you don't look so good—"

"Don't. Call anyone. Just gimme a minute."

Nate's eyes closed, and holy shit, fuck the give-him-a-minute. Shuli threw himself into the phone search, slapping around the ground, wondering why in the hell, with how much moonlight there was, he couldn't find his fucking—

"Got it!" Okay, his hands were still shaking like he was in withdrawal, so this was going to . . . be . . . fun . . .

"Nate," Shuli breathed. "What are you doing."

"Standing up."

Sure enough, the guy bent his knees under him, steadied himself with a hand on a stump, and slowly, as if he didn't trust his balance, rose to his full height. Then he tilted his head back and looked to the heavens.

Blood streamed from the exit wound, not black now, but deep red as the moonlight penetrated the translucent flow.

With an awkward hesitation, Nate reached behind his skull and touched the gaping hole in what should have been solid bone.

"I'm calling—"

That head snapped in Shuli's direction. "No calls."

For a split second, a thread of fear wound its way around Shuli's throat, tightening things up but good, making it impossible to speak or breathe.

The eyes that met his were not his friend's.

He didn't know whose they were.

CHAPTER TWENTY-FIVE

And now he hunted.

As Lash stepped out of the drug dealers' shitty apartment, he closed the door and locked it with his mind. No one was in the hallway, but he could hear the other humans inside their little rat cages, *scurry, scurry, scurry*. He started walking without paying any attention to which direction he was going. It didn't matter.

Striding along, he heard TVs, video games, cursing. Smelled food that actually made his mouth water, some kind of meat that was seasoned well—also scented weed. A lot of weed.

By the time he got to the battered stairwell, he was aware someone was following him. They were good at the stealth, their footfalls muffled to the extent that, had he been a human, he wouldn't have heard them.

But he wasn't human.

He knew they'd strike at the landing, and wheeled around just as the switchblade was raised. He had a brief impression of dark hair, light eyes, and black clothes—and then he was taking control of the arm, bending it back, breaking the wrist. As the weapon dropped with a clatter and the scream started to rip, he slammed his palm on the front of the throat and pinned the slick bastard to the concrete wall.

Right by a stretch of red and orange graffiti that read: PUZZY.

Which suggested, as talented as the artist had been, they couldn't spell for shit. Zhit. Whatever.

Unholstering his hunting knife, Lash leaned in and got eye to eye with the guy, which was only possible because he was holding his attacker about a foot off the ground.

"This was stupid on your part," he said softly as he watched the slack mouth click.

With a vicious thrust, he drove his blade into the guts, twisted it sharply, and jerked up until he hit the base of the sternum.

A warm blanket of blood tickled his hand on the grip of his weapon, and he had a thought the thing had proven quite handy in the last twenty-four hours. Too bad they couldn't use any of the ways he'd put it to work in a commercial. Retail price was about a hundred dollars. Considering the number of slices he'd made? Stabs? He'd be down to four or five bucks a job.

Of course, he'd stolen it. So the economics worked even if he'd just been using it as a paperweight.

"Very stupid."

He let the man drop and stepped back as the crumple happened, the limbs drawing in on themselves as his victim curled up around vital organs that had been breached, ancient lizard-brain instincts overriding the logic that would have informed the dumbshit it was too late: The mortal wound had been made, so there was nothing to defend against anymore.

Shifting his weight, Lash lifted one of the hunting boots he'd boosted, and as it came up, he noted that the things were waterproof. How handy.

He placed the tread on the side of the face and skull, right at the ear, and as he transferred a little of his heft, there was an immediate intensification of writhing, a muffled holler bubbling as bloody hands clawed at the chipped tile and one of the legs bobbed up and down, like a dog getting its belly scratched.

Lash relented the pressure, watching the movements ease. Then he brought it back—

"What . . . the . . . fuck . . ."

Twisting his head, he looked behind himself. A young kid, about the age of the punks who'd been inducted, skidded to a halt in the doorway of the first apartment on the left. In his baggy clothes, fresh kicks, and waft of cologne, he was clearly ready for a good night.

"Do you want some of this," Lash drawled.

"No, sir. Sure don't."

As the interloper backed the fuck up and shut his

door, there was the clunk of a dead bolt getting thrown and then the skitter of a chain. Cute, really. Like any of that would keep Lash out if he wanted to infiltrate. Yet respect had been paid, and therefore respect would be shown. For the moment.

"See?" he murmured to the dying guy who'd had all the bright ideas. "That's what you should have done. But no, you wanted to dance with me."

With a quick hop, he transferred all his weight onto his raised boot, going ballerina, balancing himself with the help of a palm on the PUZZY. Beneath the treads, the body spasmed wildly, everything clapping on the stained linoleum tile, one hand getting thrown out and smudging through the bright red blood. But two hundred and fifty pounds wasn't enough. At his will, his specific gravity increased to industrial standards—

The crack was so satisfying that Lash closed his eyes and parted his mouth.

He was a little less satisfied with the results when he stepped off and had to kick free all kinds of glistening debris.

Leaving the body, he went back to the head of the stairs, and as he assumed his descent, his left boot made a squeak or two, which was rather annoying. By the time he bottomed out in the front hall, however, things had worn off or dried off, and he walked silently out the building's entrance. He was aware that along the way, he passed a couple of humans. They didn't bother with him, keeping their heads lowered and moving on their way quickly.

So he did not bother them.

On the street, he assessed his surroundings as he took out the burner phone he'd taken off one of the new inductees. The text he needed was right on top, and a quick check of the time informed him he had to hustle.

Dematerializing across the Hudson River to Caldwell's other side, he re-formed in a parking lot that had only a couple of cars slotted close to a white marble-faced block of a building. The glowing cursive sign over the door gave him a moment's pause of nostalgia.

Saks Fifth Avenue.

Back when he had been with that family he'd thought was his own by birth, he had gotten some of his clothes here. Most of what he'd worn had been made for him specifically, imported from England, Italy, and France. But he had also come to this store, and had always liked the orderliness and subservience of the staff.

He couldn't go to the appointment he had tonight as he was dressed now.

A quick glance down at himself was intended to confirm that this was not a self-indulgent waste of time—and all he saw were the stains. Cursing, he whisked the dried red and black blood off the hunting clothes and boots—just as a well-tended man in a suit stepped out of the glass doors.

As the guy approached, he gave Lash an up-and-down that suggested disapproval on a moral scale—and wasn't that something that was going to get dealt with right here and now.

Except as his upper lip peeled off his fangs, Lash caught sight of the name tag.

Edward.

Oh, so that was staff, leaving after they'd finished cleaning up the dressing rooms, and counting pennies, and checking that the bathrooms were clear. This was not a customer, not someone for whom the store had been kept open after hours for an exclusive shopping experience.

No, this was a worker getting into a BMW 2 Series that was no doubt leased, going home to his mommy's basement, where he hung up his wishful-thinking clothes on a rack by his twin-sized bed.

The judgmental fuck's life was already ruined. Short of a Powerball win, he was going to spend all his four seasons aspiring to be where the customers he served were, forever jonesing as he acquired almost-theres along the way to a condo and a used Mercedes G-Wagen.

At the end, his grave would be marked with a pretentious quote from some dead English poet that he'd heard about online—as opposed to studied at an Ivy League.

So really, killing him was redundant.

Besides, if Lash was honest, he didn't have time to truly enjoy the fun. In a half hour, that real estate agent would be waiting for him at a mansion that was in a right and proper neighborhood, ready to show him a property of worth. He was so done with the shitcodes he'd been in, and thus he was going to have to play the *Homo sapiens'* game to get what he needed.

Fresh start. New home.

And anyway, if he got sidetracked every time some human was a fucking asshole, it was going to be decades before he could look at real estate.

Continuing onward, he approached the locked doors. The store had closed at eight, and he would have come earlier, but it was the strangest thing. In this current incarnation of himself, he could not tolerate sunlight. He'd tried it again first thing this morning. The stinging wasn't exactly a mortal threat, but he hadn't liked the way he'd become instantly weaker.

That was dangerous.

At the entrance, he caught sight of his reflection in the glass and took a moment to pull his jacket down and run his hands over his hair. Although why he bothered, he didn't know. The interior was dimmed, and it appeared that judgy fucker Edward was the last to leave. Who cared what he looked like anyway?

Dematerializing into the store, he looked around and felt right at ease. There had been a redesign since he'd been here last, everything now white and airy, with linear black accents, like it was a museum or a gallery. Handbags and accessories took up most of the space around an atrium, the bigger name brands anchoring their own freestanding boutiques located farther in.

Walking forth, he approved of the spit-and-polish clean of the glass cases and the marble floor, and every time he breathed in, he got more of the multi-layered perfume bouquet that was drifting over from the acre-sized cosmetics department. The fact that only security lights were on gave the place a campfire-like glow, and he reveled in the privacy of the moment, especially given the company he had currently been keeping.

The solitude was a double-edged sword, however. He'd always had a personal shopper before, and as he proceeded around to the base of the escalator, he hated the inefficiency of having to find the men's department and weed through the merchandise himself—

Lash stopped. Rubbed his eyes. Wondered if he were seeing things.

About twenty feet away, standing underneath the silver Gucci header, a very familiar brunette in a black bodysuit and high heels was staring through a chained barrier at a display of floral purses with the iconic red and green striping.

"What the *hell* are you doing here," he demanded.

✦ ✦ ✦

"I'm sorry you had to see that," Nate said as he shoved a branch to the side and then let it go.

Walking behind the guy, Shuli defended his face against a slap he probably could have used; then he put his hands in the pockets of his ruined suede pants and wished he weren't wearing them. They were the cut-glass of bottoms, the kind of thing that had to be treated with care. Moisture, dirt, rough handling?

A hike out of the woods with your good buddy who'd managed to throw off a gunshot wound to the brain like a head cold?

More than they could handle.

He knew how they felt. He was ruined, too, and no amount of dry-cleaning was going to save him, either.

On that note, he glanced at the back of Nate's head again. Everything was fine and dandy, the catastrophic injury all bye-bye, never-been, a-okay.

"I don't understand what's happening here," he muttered.

As they continued through the trees, Shuli marveled how they could be so close to a suburban neighborhood and yet feel like they were in the middle of the Adirondack Park, miles away from anything civilized. Although he supposed he could have currently been in a mall at Christmastime and felt totally isolated.

"It's hard to explain," Nate said eventually.

No shit, Shuli thought.

"That night after what went down at Dandelion . . ." Nate held another branch off, this time waiting until Shuli took hold of it before continuing. "I was revived."

"Back at the clinic, yeah. It was a miracle."

"Literally." In the moonlight, the guy's shoulders lifted in a shrug underneath his SUNY Caldwell hoodie. "I'm not supposed to be here at all. She brought me back. And now things are . . . different."

There was no reason to ask for a clarification on who the "she" was. The tone alone said it was Rahvyn—and on the subject of "brought back," Shuli had assumed things had been more along the lines of CPR, just-in-time, *conventional* revival stuff.

Not . . . whatever the hell made you immortal, or some shit.

As they came up to the shed that camo'd the escape route out of Nate's house, Shuli hung back. "I left my car at your place."

"So come on." Nate indicated the door. "I have to go to work anyway. I'm late."

The guy still had the same wholesome looks, all that boy-next-door handsome definitely the type for a certain kind of female or woman, the eyes clear and blue, the face nice and regular, the hair cut for practicality rather than style. The sweatshirt and jeans were Nate's regular Joe Schmo uniform, too, comfortable and casual, yet emphasizing his big build.

But the vibe was dark as a black cape and a vendetta against a hero.

"What?" Nate said.

"Did you know that was going to . . ." Shuli motioned lamely up around his own head. "Did you know that was going to fix itself."

Not a question. Nope, that was a demand, because he had to understand—because the implications were mind-blowing. In a way that wasn't bullet-driven, but might as well have been.

"I told you," Nate countered calmly. "I needed to know how far it went."

"What if it hadn't—what if you had . . ."

"Then I would have known the answer."

The logical way the response was framed was so chilling, Shuli felt compelled to spell everything out in words of one syllable.

So he did: "But you'da been dead."

"Yeah, pretty much." The guy nodded to the entrance of the shed. "You coming with?"

Shuli reached out and put his hand on a heavy shoulder. "Do you understand what you're saying?"

"Of course I do. Why do you think I cleaned my room before I came out here?"

"You honestly believe that is what we would have all cared about? That your clothes were fucking folded and your bed made?"

"Hung."

"What?"

"I like to hang my clothes. Not fold them."

Shuli rubbed his face, and entertained the idea that this might be some kind of fucked-up dream. But then he dropped his arms . . . and nothing was any different. They were still out in the woods, and the little word volley was still in the air between them.

"Nate. What the fuck has gotten into you—and please. Don't bullshit me. You need to be alarmed by all of this, and instead, you're . . ."

"What am I alarmed by." An eyebrow raised. "Tell me."

"You just shot yourself in the head—and you don't seem to be bothered by the fact that you don't care whether you lived or died."

"Yup, that's where I'm at. You want to sum it all up for a third time? Would it make you feel better?"

Shuli wanted to grab the guy by the sweatshirt and shake the shit out of him. "If you'd died, and I'd found you, what the fuck do you think it would do to me?"

"You weren't supposed to be out here."

"So fine!" He threw up his hands. "I'd have gotten a phone call—whenever they found your body. What about your parents—"

"They're not really my parents. They're just giving me a place to put my head—"

"That night in the clinic when you came in on a stretcher, they were *weeping*."

"Were you there? Did you see it yourself? 'Cuz if I remember, you were still back in the club, fucking humans in the bathroom, while I was getting shot and bleeding out on the sidewalk. So how the hell would you know what those two people did next to my hospital bed better than me."

"They love you," Shuli said roughly.

"Or maybe they just have savior complexes that have nothing to do with me. In which case, it's not my problem if they get all twisted."

"Are you listening to yourself? What the *fuck*."

As Shuli's voice went up an octave and projected like a loudspeaker, a night bird flushed off into the darkness, but that was the only reaction he got. Nate just stood there as if he were a bad actor in a *Dawson's Creek* remake.

Shuli shook his head. "I need a drink."

"Good, I'll go get my phone and call in sick to work." Nate shrugged in that offhand way again. "I didn't feel like going in anyway. And I think I'd like to get drunk."

"This isn't right. You need to talk to someone."

"I just found out I'm a fucking superhero, and you're upset? Really? This is not bad news." Nate turned back to the shed and opened things. "I'm going out for a drink. You can come or not. I don't really care."

As the shed door clapped shut behind the guy, Shuli looked up at the sky and decided that whoever the male was who had just up and left without a care in the world, he was not his friend.

He only happened to be inhabiting Nate's body.

CHAPTER TWENTY-SIX

Sometimes, you had to show and not tell.

Aware that those pains in the angels were waiting for him out in the corridor, Lassiter ducked back into Rahvyn's recovery room, and kept as quiet as he could. She had curled onto her side facing the door, her hands under her chin, her feet tucked in. A blanket had been pulled up from the base of the bed, but he imagined she'd been half asleep when she'd gone looking for extra warmth, because the thing covered only part of her legs and none of her back.

He would have given anything to be able to join her.

Whispering across the cool, tiled floor, he carefully lifted the blanket and rearranged it so that—

"You return," she said in a husky voice.

As her eyes fluttered open, he laid the thin covering

properly over her body. "Just to check on you. I have to go out."

"For a while . . . or foreermore?"

"Just for a while." He brushed her cheek. "Don't worry."

At least that was the plan.

Rahvyn rolled over and stretched, and his eyes went to the soft swells of her breasts. She had changed into a fresh set of scrubs, the loose fabric hiding her curves from him, but also from others if anyone else came into the recovery room—and yes, maybe it made him a prehistoric, bonded knucklehead, but he was not in any kind of hurry for another male to see what she looked like naked.

Mostly because they were likely to lose their minds at how beautiful she was, and then he was going to have to murder the poor bastard.

Ah, yes, bonded males were *such* fun.

"Where are you going?" she asked. "If I may inquire."

"Of course you can. I'm going to the Audience House."

"Oh." She pushed herself off the pillows. "Will you be safe?"

"I promise. And as soon as I'm done, I'll come back here."

So they could finish what they'd started, he thought to himself.

"Please be careful."

Her smile was the worried kind, the one you put on when you were trying not to show how anxious you were.

Bending down, he pressed his lips to hers and lingered with the contact, his body instantly flaring back to life—which, considering how fucking distracted he was with all the shit going on? Was an indication of exactly how desperate he was to have her.

"I'm always careful." He kissed her again. "Just rest. I'll be back before you know it."

Rahvyn nodded and resumed her tuck-in, but she didn't look like she was going to sleep any more, her stare too fixed on the door—as if she knew who was waiting for him on the other side of it.

"Don't worry about Eddie and Adrian," he told her. "I'm taking care of it."

Now she sighed. "All right."

He waited until her lids got low again, and honestly, all he wanted to do, maybe for the rest of his immortal life, was just stand over her like this, guarding her as she caught up on the rest she clearly needed. But nooooooo.

He was going to play tour guide. But shit, maybe if those two angels could see what the Brotherhood and the King did every night, maybe they'd understand why he had to stay here.

"Sleep well," he whispered.

Lassiter kept the "my love" to himself as he headed back for the exit.

He was careful to shut things up behind himself. Then he looked at Eddie and Adrian.

"Give me your hands," he said.

Eddie shook his head. "I am not do-si-do'ing with you."

"I'm in." Ad popped the last of the Snickers he'd picked up off the floor into his mouth. "Let's do this— and Eddie, will you just relax. Fuck—sorry, *fudge*."

The angel grabbed Lassiter's palm and then stared at Eddie like there was something wrong with the guy. And wasn't that the most endearing thing Adrian Vogel had ever done.

"You know exactly what's at stake here," Eddie muttered.

But out came his broad palm, and as Lassiter took it, he nodded at Ad to close the circle.

The moment contact was made, up, up, and away they went, the three of them swept into a swirling draft, their corporeal forms reduced to a whiff of smoke that dissipated. Traveling as ether, he led them out of the training center through the ductwork, and when they were off into the night, he piloted them away from the mountain's base, across the Adirondack Park, and past the farms that ringed the suburban skirt of Caldwell.

When they were finally in the right neighborhood, he reconstituted himself, and in doing so, them as well, all their bodies reappearing in the shadows on the front lawn of a gracious Federal house.

Ad whistled softly. "Nice digs. You thinking of buying it or is this an aspirational thing?"

Leading the way to the door, Lassiter paused and glanced over his shoulder. "And you're both going to have to remain hidden, too, 'kay?"

Though Ad was sticking right with the program, Eddie was still out on the grass, his boots planted like he was some kind of heavy-duty, hard-ass garden gnome. With his thick braid, and those ready-to-fight clothes, he fit in—but only with the people on the in-side.

Some of the people, that was.

"Eddie." Lassiter motioned for the guy to come on up. "Let's go."

After a moment, the angel approached the shallow steps. "You're bargaining with the wrong people. You don't need to convince us."

"I know, I know. You're just the messengers, doing your job. Well, I'm trying to do mine and I want to show you a part of it. And can you lose that disapproval stew you're marinating in? You'll scare the fucking children." He glanced at Ad. "Or . . . is it frickin'?"

"He doesn't swear anymore." Ad shrugged. "Don't ask me."

"Wow. New leaves getting turned all over the place. So how about you work on your attitude, Blackhawk."

Eddie hit the steps. "I am not responsible for what my face does when you're talking."

"You know," Lassiter muttered, "you and Vishous are soul mates."

Passing through the door, he waited on the far side, wondering whether either of them—

Thank God, he thought as Eddie and Ad ghosted through.

The Audience House's foyer wasn't anything like the Brotherhood mansion's enormous cavern of marble and mirror and crystal, but it wasn't dogshit, either.

The generous space separated what had once been a dining room capable of sitting twenty-four, easy, and a parlor that was now a waiting room. A formal staircase in the middle accessed the second floor, and hallways on either side led to the library and study to the left, and Fritz's second home, the kitchen and pantry, to the right.

Leaning into the waiting area, he wanted the angels to look at the civilians cooling their jets before they saw their King: There were three groups sitting on the silk chairs and antique sofas, all of them fidgeting and re-crossing legs, the females checking their makeup in compacts, the males on their phones or staring off into space. Two guys were up on their feet and pacing—and assiduously not making eye contact or getting in each other's way.

The receptionist, a lovely female with an easy smile and a knack for staying calm and organizing things, was not at her post. But there was an empty spot on the coffee table where the Danish were always served at the beginning of the night. Maybe she'd taken the platter back for a refill, although Fritz was not going to approve of that.

"Come on," Lassiter murmured.

The closed dining room doors were no barrier at all to him—yet as invisible as he was, the instant he was on the far side, Vishous straightened out of his lean against one of the sideboards, the brother's hand going to one of the black daggers that were holstered, handles down, on his chest. Likewise, Rhage, who was over between the windows that faced out the front of the mansion, stiffened and swept the room back and forth with his Bahamas blue gaze.

There was an audience in process, and Lassiter stayed just inside the entry, crossing his arms and tuning in to the other end of the room. The young couple who were huddled together on the Persian rug didn't notice anything. Then again, they were facing the hearth—not that they were interested in the modest fire that crackled and sparked in a friendly way. Their attention was consumed by the pair of armchairs angled in toward each other.

Only one of the seats had been called into service, and Wrath's imposing royal form overfilled its high back and generous contours. Dressed in black leathers and a muscle shirt, with those black wraparounds hiding his blind eyes and his long black hair falling from that widow's peak, it was easy to understand why a pair of civilians would be shitting their knickers.

And the King was aware something had altered in the environment.

Like the two brothers who were guarding him, Wrath knew other interested parties had entered the proverbial chat. His head tilted up ever so slightly, as if his eyes were in working order and he was searching exactly where Lassiter and the other angels were. And then his nostrils flared as though scenting the air. As well, George, who was very hale and hearty at his feet, lifted his boxy head and pricked his ears.

After a moment, the King refocused on the couple.

Extending his dagger hand, the black diamond he wore flashed as he motioned.

"Bring the young to me," he commanded.

The female glanced at her male, and then she repositioned the bundle in her arms. When her *hellren* nodded, they both approached cautiously. Made sense. Sitting the way he was, with his hard jaw up, and all those muscles showing, Wrath looked like he could go either way, aristocrat or aggressor.

And that was a really tiny little baby in the burrito of pale blue blanketing.

"G-g-go on, then," the male stuttered as he gingerly moved his *shellan* in front of him. "Bring him up."

The guy didn't abandon her. He stayed connected to his mate, keeping his hands on her shoulders, pressing his chest into her back.

Such a fragile young family, Lassiter thought. Just starting out and scared to death—because everything they were in life was wrapped in that cotton bundle.

"Go ahead, *leelan*," the male whispered.

The female was trembling so badly, it seemed like she could barely stand, and Lassiter glanced at V and Rhage, hoping one of them would step in, do a solid, and make it so the young didn't hit the floor and crack open like an egg.

But neither of them moved, and Saxton, the King's solicitor, was nowhere in sight, his desk, with its neatly arranged paperwork and volumes of the Old Laws, vacant for the moment.

Fine, Lassiter thought as he went to step forward.

He might as well demonstrate exactly how he helped—

Wrath's face softened and he leaned to the side, placing his broad palm on George's head to stroke the dog.

"That's what I call my mate," he said as he fiddled with one of the blond ears. "*Leelan.* She is my beloved."

"The Queen," said the male with awe.

Nodding, Wrath kept his face angled in their direction. "We have a son, too. I remember how scary it was in the beginning. Do you watch over him when he sleeps? We did that constantly for the first month."

The female glanced back at her *hellren.* Then cleared her throat. In a wavering voice, she said, "I'm afraid he won't wake up. I almost prefer him fussy and crying."

Wrath nodded again. "Oh, I remember those days. They're really long. L.W. is past that now, but you never forget it. They're so small. How many nights old?"

The female said with a little more gumption, "Three nights."

"Are you okay?" Wrath lifted his hand toward the male. "If you'll permit me the inquiry of your *shellan?*"

The civilian seemed dumbfounded that the ruler would ask his permission. Then he nodded furiously—before seeming to recall the King could not see.

"Yes, I mean," he said. "Please."

"I am well," the female answered. "As long as he is well."

Now, when the King held out his hands, the female went forward, and as she transferred the young, there was a rousing and a squawk. A proper crying commenced, and as the couple rushed forward, the King secured the infant in the crook of his arm and started gently batting that diaper.

Pat. Pat. Pat. Pat.

The young settled in almost immediately, and the male and female fell back a little, holding on to each other.

Wrath murmured to the infant, his low, deep voice weaving throughout the room. After a little bit, he moved his free hand up and parted the folds around the face. Blunt fingers traveled over the tiny features.

In the Old Language, he said more loudly, "*What name hath been given unto this young?*"

"*Rohn the Younger,*" the *hellren* replied with a choked sound.

"*I hereby proclaim this fine-born male as Rohn, son of Rohn, pride of his* mahmen *and father, anchor of his bloodline. May he find all blessings in this life, and carry forth unto further years the love and honor of his family. In accordance with the right and proper way, and as my royal sire before me and his before him, I welcome Rohn unto the world corporeal.*"

And then the King smiled.

Not in a perfunctory way. Not in a just-doing-my-job fashion. He well and truly beamed, the warmth transforming that harsh, autocratic face into something altogether approachable.

Well . . . almost approachable.

When he held the infant out, the *mahmen* took

Rohn back—and then the couple fell onto their knees with bowed heads, the scent of their tears of joy wafting up. That dagger hand was extended, and both of the civilians kissed the black diamond, words of devotion and submission whispered over the ancient King's ring.

Lassiter glanced at Eddie and Ad. They were staring across the long room, their faces serious.

Good. He was glad he didn't need to state the obvious. Generations of vampires, in the midst of their fragile mortal lives, had fallen in line with this private ceremony, a linkage that went from the current moment to all the ones that had gone before . . . back to the very first King and the very first young who had been recognized, welcomed, and approved of.

Turning back to the hearth, Lassiter's eyes shifted over and down to George.

The golden retriever had angled his head toward the exchange, and with his jaws open in an easy pant, it seemed as though he was also smiling at the baby. For certain, he was alert and tracking everything, his blond fur and kind eyes like a second banked fire warming the room.

Lassiter tried to imagine the scene without George's gentle presence.

And couldn't.

God . . . he loved Rahvyn so damned much.

CHAPTER TWENTY-SEVEN

Down in the Brotherhood's training center, the knock upon the recovery room door was soft and respectful—yet Rahvyn sat up in a rush and put her hand to her skipping heart.

"Yes?" she said over the thumping in her chest.

Although what exactly did she think was coming through that door?

Ehlena, the clinic's nurse, put her head in. The female had strawberry blond hair and toffee-colored eyes, and always seemed, with her warm smile, a calming and competent presence.

"Hi! You still okay?" When Rahvyn nodded, the female pointed to the bedside table. "You've got a call on the phone there? It was transferred in from the main switchboard. Just push the blinking light and pick up."

"Oh." She glanced over at the unit. "Oh, thank you."

"No worries. And remember, I'm just two doors down if you need anything."

After the female gave a little wave and ducked out, Rahvyn looked at the telephone that sat on the bedside table. She had seen such landlines in use at Luchas House, and yet she had to remind herself how to pick up the heavy handheld unit that linked one's ear and mouth. When there was no sound, she remembered— the light. She pushed the little square and there was a clicking and a quiet hiss.

"Hello?" she said.

"Rahvyn?"

She frowned. "Shuli?" As the male started speaking, a distortion cut into the connection. "Shuli, I'm having difficulty hearing you—"

"—where are you?"

"In the Brotherhood's clinic. Is there something wrong?" Stupid question. She might not be able to hear all his words, but the tension in his voice was obvious. "Are you okay—"

There was a crackling that made her flinch and take the phone away from her ear. When she put the unit back, he was much more clear.

"I need your help with Nate," the male said. "He's gone off the rails. Maybe you can talk to him."

"Where is he?" Another stupid question. "Where are you, rather?"

"Outside his house. He just took off." Now with a fuzzy sound, as if perhaps he were in a breeze that had just intensified. "He says he's going to go get drunk. I think you're the only one who can reach him. He's fucking lost it."

This was *all* her fault. "But wherever did he go?"

"Out to the clubs somewhere. Do you know his address? Come here and meet me, we'll look for him together."

"I'm afraid that at one point, he told me where he lived, but I disregarded the coordinates?"

There was a pause. "Okay, meet me at Dandelion. You remember where that is, right? We'll start there."

As her gut tightened, she thought about suggesting they convene somewhere, anywhere else. "All right. I shall leave the now."

"You're sure you know where the club is?"

Between one blink and the next, she saw Nate falling to his knees onto the sidewalk, a small hole in the front of his sweatshirt, a haunted look in his eyes, her name leaving his lips on a gasp.

"As if I can forget," she said roughly.

"Okay, I'm going to move my car and then dematerialize over. Gimme ten minutes."

She was about to tell him to be careful when the call was cut.

After replacing the heavy plastic communicator in its cradle, she shifted off the bed and looked down at herself. She had put on some of those baggy blue clothes for comfort, but her jeans and sweater were folded on the chair, and she quickly changed back into them.

When she stepped out into the hallway, she heard people talking a couple of doors down, but she was disinclined to ask for directions to depart from the facility. Closing her eyes, she carried herself away, not in the method of dematerialization, but in her fashion, whereupon she stepped through time and molecular space, entering that nether region of a boundary that buffered and protected the here and now from existential manipulation, similar to how the atmosphere insulated the earth from the cold void of space.

Having transferred her energy thus, it was the work of a moment to step back out of the boundary.

Across the street from what would always be a place of horror to her.

The club Dandelion was as it had been that night Nate had been shot—but as if she should have expected it to be different? It was the same spring green entrance, the same human man in the green and brown uniform, the same wording over the door and line of people awaiting admittance.

"Hey."

Rahvyn jumped and spun around. "Oh. Hello."

Nate's best friend was as different from him as could be, and as with Dandelion, that had not changed, even though, given the course of events, it felt as though everything should be altered, the bellwethers of the young male's appearance and countenance transformed in material ways.

Alas, the tiger-print silken shirt and the fine suede pants, like the gold watch that gleamed upon the wrist, were exactly the sartorial theme of wealth and eccentricity she associated with Shuli. His face did seem to have aged, however, the jocular insouciance nowhere to be seen in the well-bred planes and angles that stared back at her. And the pants had dirt stains on the knees and tendrils of foliage clinging unto their soft nap. He rather looked as though he had been through a physical trial as well as a mental one.

"I need to know something first," he said.

"Whatever is that?"

"What did you do to him back at the clinic," the male demanded. "And before you tell me it was CPR, I just watched him shoot himself in the head tonight and then walk away like it never happened. That ain't normal."

Rahvyn put her hands over her eyes, sure as if such violence was before her and she was seeking to avoid its gruesome visuals. "Oh, Nate . . ."

"That night the meteor supposedly hit the ground out in the forest behind Luchas House—that wasn't a fucking rock from space, was it. That was you, coming from fuck all knows where. He and I saw you in the crowd that night and you were the only one who wasn't ooh'ing and ahh'ing. What the fuck are you and what did you do to my friend."

Dropping her arms, she looked across the street at the club just as a line of automobiles came at once, released at the head of the block by a light that had gone green.

"He's lost himself," Shuli said gruffly. "You brought back somebody different than who he was."

"No, his soul is as always the one you knew." Although she feared the experience had irreparably reshaped him. "But now is not the time for inquiry. We must find him."

As she started to cross the street, Shuli grabbed her arm and loomed over her. "You owe me an explanation."

She nodded. "After we make sure he's safe."

Having arrived at an accord, together they jogged across the four lanes, and as they approached the human who guarded the entry of the club, the man winced and put his hand up to his head as if in pain: Ah, yes, erased memories, trying to surface. They were always uncomfortable.

Shuli stepped forward, and took something out of his pocket. "My guy."

When he held his hand out, the guard put his own palm forward, even as he blinked like he was having difficulty focusing his eyes.

"G'head," the man in the green shirt said.

Rahvyn looked the human in the face, remembering how, just prior to the shooting, she had rushed over to him when he had been lying on the concrete no more than a couple of feet away. And then the gun went off and Nate fell unto his knees and said her name—

"Let's do this," Shuli muttered as he pulled her through the door after him.

Inside, she had the clear sense of a beat of music and the vague impression of all the flowers. The latter were on the walls in vases of countless varieties, and along the base of the counter that ran the entire length of the club. Behind that divider, more were slotted between the bottles of libations that lined a long set of shelves, and the ceiling was likewise bouquet'd with them.

They were all fake, however, just silk petals and plastic stems. She had investigated them during that fateful night, and had been disappointed that they were but an illusion.

Meanwhile, encouraged by the electronic rhythm, humans were pec-to-breast on the dance floor, moving to the waving music that was unlike anything that had been produced during her time. Among the density of bodies, she searched for Nate, his height and broad shoulders a combination that should have been easy to spot, and she was aware that there were vampires interspersed with the other species, her kind unnoticed by the men and women, but instantly recognized among those who were like her.

No Nate, however.

"Come on, we need to go down the bar," Shuli announced as he drew her forth.

All kinds of patrons were crowded up to the counter, bunching in mini-groups of two and three, the ones in pairs looking into each other's eyes as they waited for drinks that were pink, green, and yellow. There was such a chaos to the environment, with all the people milling about, a charged air of anticipation buzzing along with the strange treble notes and thunderous bass percussions piped in from overhead. When she had first come that night, she had wondered how such noise would facilitate greeting and socialization. But then she had realized that the deafening volume required the men and women to lean into each other to hear and be heard.

And that was the point.

At the far end, where money was exchanged for the drinks, Shuli shook his head. "He's got to be here. He hasn't been to any other clubs really, and none of the hardcore ones are his vibe. Wait while I check the bathroom. And don't leave if you find him."

Shuli urged her over to the start of a hallway, and as she resumed her scanning, he strode into the dim chute and disappeared through a door.

Crossing her arms, she felt within her a restlessness rooted in her regrets. Unable to stay where she was, she processed down the hall a little—and was promptly interrupted by a pair of women emerging from the females' bathroom in a collective giggle and whiff of mingled perfume.

"Oh, sorry—"

" 'Scuse us—"

Tripping and recovering their balance by turns, they collaborated their way back to the dance floor.

Rahvyn looked to the door Shuli had pushed through, but knew she could not breach its barrier.

"—my ex. That's who—"

"Ah, fuck, you're a pussy-whipped fool—"

"You don't know what she's like."

"No, I remember *all* the reasons you broke up with her."

As the pair of male voices registered, she glanced back toward the club proper. Two vampires were coming toward her, and they were dressed . . . well, like Shuli, in pastel silk shirts and thin-legged slacks. They did a double take when they noticed her, but nodded as they passed. Acknowledging them with a dip of the head, she watched them continue all the way down to a solid steel door with a glowing red EXIT sign above it. There was a brief flash of light as the portal was opened, and in the glow, one of the males took out what appeared to be a small pipe. Then things closed, the illumination cutting off—

A woman came out of the males' room, and stopped in the process of pushing her breasts back into place under a tight pink bodice. Her blond-streaked hair was tangled, and after adjusting her upper body, she attended to her tresses, her hands shoving the waves around in a similar fashion.

Her perfume registered first, fruity and overpowering. But under it . . . there was a scent that was instantly recognizable—

Nate didn't so much exit the males' room as he was pushed through the door by Shuli, and his stumble in the hall was something he didn't right with any alacrity. He just let the momentum take him where it did, the opposite wall of the corridor halting him.

There was lipstick around his mouth and his hair was tousled. Unlike the woman, he didn't bother fixing either. His cologne was . . . gin, she believed it was.

"—don't know what you're bitched about," he was saying as he shoved himself around. "This is what you always want me to do. Come out and drink. Get fucked. Bust my cherry—"

Nate broke off the tirade as he saw her. Then he glared at Shuli. "Fuck you."

With an abrupt coordination, Nate marched off in the direction of the red EXIT sign—and Rahvyn didn't need any urging to follow him.

"Nate," she called out. "Wait!"

As he punched his way free of the club, there was that flash of light again, and Rahvyn caught the door as it started to close. Absently, she noted there was a red and white sign on the panel: "Emergency Use Only—Alarm Will Sound."

There was no ringing to be heard against the back-drop of the dimmed music. Then again, there was enough of a warning screaming in her head so she could cover it on her own.

Outside, there was an open area of asphalt on which a collection of rather battered vehicles were parked, the rears of the other buildings facing on other streets forming a gritty, dirty courtyard. The two vampires who had gone by her were in a tight clutch over on the left, huddling in the shadows around the smoking instru-ment which they passed back and forth.

Nate was heading in their direction, and when she called out his name again, he spun around and jabbed a finger at her.

"No. I'm not doing this."

She rushed over, and tried to catch his hand. "Nate, listen to me—"

"Oh, I listened plenty." He held his arms out of her reach. "I got your voicemail. Real poignant shit, thanks for the sign-off. So what the *hell* are you doing back here."

"May we go somewhere to talk—"

"You've said plenty. We're done—"

Shuli came up to them. "Look, I'm just worried about you—"

"I am not your problem!"

As a fetid scent came over on the breeze, Rahvyn glanced back toward the other vampires, and thought perhaps it was whatever they were imbibing in.

No, that wasn't it.

"Shh," she hissed as Nate and Shuli got louder in their argumentation. "What is that smell."

It was like a dead animal . . . and a certain . . . *sweetness*.

"That's a *lesser*!" she exclaimed.

"Nah, the war is dead," Nate said in a bored tone. "I got to hear alllll about the triumph."

At that moment, something came around the corner of the club. Bent over, shuffling, oozing a black, glistening substance, the undead stopped beside the pair of vampires who were passing that pipe back and forth. Its hair was dark, its clothing stained, its condition such that one wondered how it remained upon its feet—

As Shuli cried out a name, the deadly attack was so fast, neither of the males had time to react.

CHAPTER TWENTY-EIGHT

tanding outside the Gucci boutique in Saks, Devina wondered whether she'd conjured an image of Lash out of thin air, her unassuaged angst creating its own kind of Band-Aid on things she couldn't control or change by making him the fuck up. Except then she scented him and watched as his eyes narrowed like he was as surprised as she that they'd run into each other.

And come on, if she were pulling this shit out of her ass, her created-Lash would have prostrated himself on the polished marble floor, gone into a seizure of forgive-me-for-being-a-douchebag, and kissed her feet.

As opposed to stand there all annoyed like she was some stranger killing his vibe.

"What the hell are *you* doing here." In response to his rude demand, she tossed his question back at him. As if this Saks Fifth Avenue was her own private backyard and he was the one crashing the party.

Her lover's autocratic brows arched. "I'm getting a suit."

With a spear of pain, she thought of him showing up to her lair with those red roses. It had been mere nights past, but felt like a lifetime ago. "You already have one."

"You ripped it off me, remember."

"That was you—"

"Maybe I did the shirt. But tearing the pants was all you."

Memories of them naked and straining, sweaty and desperate, made her blink quick as she wondered who he was dressing up for. And fucking hell, but he looked good. His blond hair had been tousled by the wind, the waves thick and pale over his high forehead. Likewise, his cheeks were flushed as if he'd been outdoors, and she wanted to know what he had been doing for the last twenty-four hours with an aggression as if the information, like him, was her property.

"Why are you here," he said.

"Excuse me? This is *my* store."

"I was unaware your last name was Avenue."

She pointed over his shoulder, toward the exit. "You can go get what you need at Macy's. Matter of fact, you can get the fuck out of Caldwell."

"So can you."

Devina leaned forward. "The reason you're back on this planet is because I summoned you with that spell."

His eyes dipped down to her cleavage for a split second. Then he looked at her breasts again—and everything about the involuntary movement was a weakness on his part.

Well, what do you know. The antidote to her anger was him wanting her, even if he didn't like it. *Especially* if he didn't like it.

"Why do you need a suit," she said in a calmer tone.

"I have a meeting."

"Job interview? As a fuck boy?"

As he cocked that arrogant eyebrow of his, she wasn't about to tell him that if he said "date," there would be a whole lot of ruined retail space around them both. And what a loss of some good Italian leatherwork, the chain barrier notwithstanding.

"What kind of meeting," she pressed.

"Have a good night," he drawled as he started walking for the escalator.

"You still want to fuck me," she ground out.

She assumed he would just ignore her, but he stopped. Put his hands on his hips. Stared off toward the Prada kiosk like if he could have changed one thing about himself, it would have been the fact that, yes, he wanted to bang her until they were both dripping.

Smiling to herself, Devina approached him from behind and looked his body up and down. The back view was, as always, absolutely exquisite.

"What kind of suit do you need," she murmured as she came around so that she faced him.

Oh, look. He was hard in those hunting pants.

"Business, is it?" She stared at the bulge in front of his hips. "Something dark blue or gray, then. With a bright white button-down."

Reaching out, she touched the front flaps of the hunting jacket and thought of that Dick's. She'd been right. He was the one who'd broken in—and he'd been in that Victorian walk-up, too, even though she hadn't been able to see him.

"A red tie—or no tie at all," she continued. "Maybe leave the collar unbuttoned, so that they see . . . your . . . throat."

His eyes locked on her lips, and she gave them a little lick. Just so she could watch his eyes follow the tip of her tongue.

"Come with me," she told him. "I'll take you to the Tom Ford section—or maybe Ermenegildo Zegna. And we'll find something that fits your size."

At that, she put her hand between his legs and felt the arousal straining at his hips. As he sucked in a breath through his front teeth, she watched his fangs descend. She'd learned of late that she had a thing for vampires, and he did not disappoint.

He was long in a lot of places.

"Or would you rather do it yourself," she taunted as she stroked him and then released her grip—

The snarl Lash let out was the sound an animal made when you took away its food, and the hold he snapped onto her arm hurt in a delicious way. Jerking her to him, he put her hand back where it had been.

His eyes narrowed like he hated her, but oh, man, that stare burned with something other than the enmity.

Leaning into him, she tilted her mouth as if she were about to kiss him.

A millimeter away from his lips, she whispered, "Sorry, it's just about the suit, lover boy."

Then she ripped herself free of him and walked over to the escalator.

He was going to follow her.

No doubt. Whatsoever.

✦ ✦ ✦

Lash focused on the demon's ass as she hipped away, her swizzle clearly intended to give him a taste of what, yes, he had been missing, fuck him very much. But damn it, after all those inductions, and the killing by that PUZZY stairwell—he wanted an outlet for the bloodletting buzz that was still rushing through his veins.

And she wasn't looking back at him. Like she was so fucking sure he was going to trail after her like a dog.

He told himself he wasn't going to follow.

Except then he was reminded that he was better

with a personal shopper. He'd never bought anything here without one. Plus she gave good head.

Reaaaaally good head.

Falling into her wake, he closed the distance, the blur of merchandise and well-familiar luxury brands lost to him given the view he was being treated to. When they reached the escalator's base and all of its static, interlocking, metal levels, he expected her to ghost up to the second floor. Nope. She took those steps like a champion, swinging her cheeks, the skintight black leather pants doing absolutely nothing to diminish those assets of hers.

The fucking heels were a nice touch. Louboutins, of course, the soles red as the blood he'd spilled tonight. And the night before.

It was his favorite color, he decided.

At the second floor, she took them straight ahead, and as he glanced around at all the displays of clothes, he was reminded of her place with the racks and the couture—and he knew why she'd come here. Selfmedicating was real. She was missing him.

And couldn't handle it.

He probably should have felt a shot of superiority at that, but he didn't. All he could think about was getting into those leathers of hers—and the suit he needed.

He was here for a fucking suit, he reminded himself as they came up to the men's section, which took up most, if not all, of the back of this part of the store. The suits were in the far corner, lineups of designer names mounted above differently branded kiosks and nooks.

The demon pivoted around and swept her hands from side to side, like she was Vanna-fucking-White.

"Is there a designer you prefer?"

Her spoken words to the contrary, she wasn't actually asking about the clothes. Everything about her hooded eyes and her stance with her arms out was about her body, especially her breasts in their bustier. Man, she could fill the fuck out of those cups, the swells of creamy flesh so tempting, her already gravity-defying tits pushed together so that her cleavage was spectacular.

"Tom Ford," he said in a low voice.

Now she walked backwards, her stare locked on his. "Double- or single-breasted."

"Double."

"Double vents?"

"Of course."

"Silk or light wool."

"Wool. Silk suits are nouveau rich. And you must have eyes in the back of your head."

"I know where everything is." She halted and lifted her chin. "You were in that basement today. I could sense you."

He debated lying, but that was weak, even if he was the only one who knew he was fibbing. What, like, he couldn't handle her?

"Let's just say I took a page out of your book."

Her black eyes narrowed. "You could have at least greeted me properly."

Lash stepped in close to her and looked down into

that face. As he opened his mouth, he was going to tell her the fuck off. Demand to know who the fuck she thought she was to reprimand him for a lack of manners. Dismiss her because he could find not only a good suit, but another lay—

"How the fuck are you so beautiful."

When he heard his own voice, he would have taken the words back if he could have—except they were true. The demon was exquisite, her eyes topped with brows that arched as if by aesthetic engineering, her nose an unobtrusive straight shot to her mouth, her cheekbones high and prominent and balanced by her jaw, and her red lips . . . well, they were a goddamn work of art. She was Angelina Jolie and Gal Gadot and Elizabeth Hurley ca. the Versace safety pin dress, all rolled into one.

Her true secret sauce, though, was what was under that skin she clothed herself in.

She was a nasty piece of work, and to him, that was her biggest appeal.

Snapping a hold around her waist, he yanked her against him—and she pushed at his chest.

"What are you doing."

"Greeting you properly."

He took those lips with the aggression he'd been banking, and the moan that came out of the demon was exactly what he was after. The second he heard it, he released her mouth and spun her around, grabbing a hunk of her hair and pushing her forward until she ran into a display and knocked a mannequin in a maroon suit off the block on which it had been mounted. As the crash reverberated through the empty store, he bent her over and popped her hips.

Then he got out his hunting knife.

As Devina turned her head and looked back at him, he lifted the blade up so she could see it. And even though there wasn't a lot of light, the flash of the steel gleamed like her eyes.

She threw out her hands and locked on to the edges of the cube he'd sprawled her all over. Then she bit her lower lip, her sharp white front teeth bearing down on the plump softness.

Planting his palm in between her shoulder blades, he held her in place as he took the knife and put the point right at where his cock was going to go. The sharp tip pricked into the leather seam, locking into the hide, and he added pressure into the grip, pushing the—

The demon gasped and arched up, her brunette hair swinging free.

"It is not just about the suit tonight," he growled.

Twisting the hilt back and forth, he needled through the overlap and the stitches, working his way in, boring through the barrier.

The scent of her arousal exploded in his nose, and as he kept going—

The orgasm took her hard, her pelvis working, her sex seeking the hunting knife, and as she writhed, he slapped her ass, the tight black leather translating the impact of his palm right into her. As she cried out his name, the breach happened, pink, gleaming flesh peeking through as a seam opened. Reholstering the knife, he took his two forefingers and inserted them in the hole, widening it—then he kept going so that they teased her core.

Crooking a hold on either side of the aperture, he started to rip, and the leather cut into him as it fought the separation.

Millimeter by millimeter, he exposed her flesh, and the more he saw of it, the harder the heartbeat in his cock.

He didn't make it all the way. He'd intended to part the leathers completely.

He couldn't wait.

Rearing up over her, he tore his zipper down, palmed his rock-hard shaft, and lasered into her sex—

The demon let out a holler as he took another grab of that hair and started slamming his hips into her, using the hold to help with his rhythm by pulling her tresses like a rope. The clapping was loud, and he liked the way her torso jerked back and forth, how she had to hold on to the display block even tighter. How she strained to take him, her arms bowing out. How she orgasmed and milked at him.

Lash started coming immediately, and he rode the sensations, his upper lip peeled off his fangs, his body taking over.

When he could, he looked down and watched his cock go in and out. His black come was dripping free from her, glossing him up, puddling on the white floor.

But not everything was leaking free. Some of him was staying, deep inside of her.

Not that he cared about that.

No, really. Not at all.

CHAPTER TWENTY-NINE

Right before the attack, Shuli couldn't understand what his eyes were seeing. Even though he'd known about *lessers*, as a precious son of an aristocratic family, he had been sheltered from so much. But the smell, that baby powder smell, he'd heard about that—and then there was the oozing black blood that covered a camo jacket and trailed behind the undead on the sidewalk.

How was the thing that injured and still moving?

And then he did the math.

"Theox!" he called out. "Alfie!"

The two vampires who were smoking hash were too into their drugging to notice the slayer, and even him yelling their names didn't—

The *lesser* grabbed on to Alfie's shoulders and yanked him back, a Bic going airborne, the little flame extinguishing on the fly as Theox shouted and jumped away. Even though the undead was in a decayed state, it was still strong enough to overpower its prey, and Shuli was halfway across the parking lot to them when he realized he had his gun on him.

The nine millimeter that he barely knew how to use.

Unholstering the weapon from the small of his back, he palmed it and tried to get a clear shot while Alfie fought to shove off the slayer. Meanwhile, Theox stumbled toward the door back into the club and started yanking against the locked handle.

"Stop!" Shuli yelled at the *lesser*. "I'll fucking shoot!"

The slayer had Alfie by the throat, the vampire clawing at the hands locked around his neck—and then they were down on the pavement, rolling around until the enemy was on top—

"I'm gonna shoot!"

Shuli circled the struggle, until he dropped to one knee and aimed. He knew he needed to hit the *lesser*'s head straight on, without any angle to the bullet, or he risked wounding Alfie. But there was too much—

A flash of movement went by in front him, and then Nate threw himself at the *lesser*, knocking it away—but the undead took its prey along for the ride, a tangle forming among the three of them. There was a scream, the scent of fresh blood, and suddenly Nate was cast off as if he'd been shot out of a cannon, his body flying toward the back of the club with such force that he traveled far enough to bowling-pin Theox—

Shuli pulled his trigger once. Twice. Sparks lit off on the asphalt across the parking area, and the stench of baby powder exploded into the night air. But if he'd hit the thing, it wasn't slowing down. It was still choking out Alfie, the undead once again on top of the vampire.

He had to get closer, and so he moved in a little bit more, but there was such a flurry of arms and legs, the positions constantly shifting as Alfie kept fighting the assault to get a breath.

"Let go of him!" Shuli barked.

Abruptly, he made a decision that went against every selfish thing he had ever done, all the narcissism of his nightly life, every cloistering he'd had as the privilege-born son of his *Princeps* sire, flushing out of him, his body moving on its own volition.

He closed in on the violent struggle, getting close, too close, so close that he could see the hellish expression of the *lesser* and the sweat on Alfie's pale, shocked face. Keeping his gun up, he knew he had to train the muzzle on the slayer's head at point-blank range. It was his only hope. Bouncing back and forth on his feet, weaving the nine-millimeter around, he tried to find the opportunity. Almost. Nearly. Almost—

And then it came.

Alfie went limp without warning, his eyes rolling back as he passed out, and the abrupt lack of defense collapsed the hand-to-hand combat, the slayer pitching forward—and that off-balance required a recovery: The undead's head popped up, and provided a split second of perfect target.

Shuli put the muzzle directly on the temple.

Just as he pulled the trigger, the slayer swung his arm up and deflected the shot. With the weapon going wide, their eyes met, and it was like staring into an abyss—and Shuli froze. Which provided an opportunity for the *lesser*. With a surge, it tackled Shuli backwards, and grabbed the autoloader.

The strength in the slayer was a total shock. As black blood speckled his face, Shuli battled against an unfathomable brawn to get his arm free—

The gun discharge was a pop right by Shuli's ear and he instinctively recoiled, bracing for a blaze of pain. When none came, he pulled at his arm, and as the hold on it released, he felt a wave of triumph.

That didn't last.

The slayer had the gun and it squared the muzzle off in Shuli's face.

The world slowed down, as it did in the movies—a realization that he felt a weird, detached surprise at—and as he stared up into the face of evil, he couldn't believe this was how he died. Behind a club. By a slayer turning his own weapon on him—

Fresh air.

All of a sudden, Shuli was staring up at the darkness that blanketed Caldwell. No gun. No *lesser*. Just the night sky.

In confusion, he turned . . . his . . . head.

For the second time, he couldn't understand what

was happening. The slayer was up off the pavement, suspended on high as if it had spontaneously levitated. Had one of the Black Dagger Brotherhood come from out of the blue—

The *lesser* was slammed into the ground, the impact sending black blood in a splatter all around.

When he saw a figure standing over the undead, he couldn't process what he was looking at.

But it *was* Rahvyn. And she wasn't finished.

Somehow, she picked up the slayer again and drove the undead into the asphalt once more. And as the *lesser* flailed uselessly, the female went down to his waist with her hands. There was a heartbeat of stillness—and then she lifted her arm over her head.

She had a knife in her grip, and its stainless steel blade gleamed for a split second.

The female cast the razor-sharp point downward, right into the center of the *lesser*'s chest.

A brilliant flash cast daylight all over the parking lot, the rear of the club, the huddle of two bodies by the back door—and with it came a popping sound that was so loud, Shuli's ears hummed from the sting.

After that? Nothing but a scorched patch where the slayer had been, and the female standing there, panting.

"Jesus," Shuli said. "How did you do that?"

"He's hit! Shit, he's bleeding out!"

As Nate spoke up by the club's exit, Shuli scrambled toward the rear door while he went for his phone. "What happened—"

Just as he took out his cell, he got in range and his

heart stopped. Nate was bleeding from a head wound—
again—but that wasn't the real problem. Theox was lying
flat on his back, his lax hands flopping around his chest,
his mouth open while he gurgled for air.

The front of his throat was glossy with blood.

"Oh, my God," Shuli stammered. "I shot him. I
fucking shot him."

CHAPTER THIRTY

S o you bought the car for how much?"

Back at the Audience House, while Wrath tossed the question out there, Lassiter really wanted some popcorn: As he and the other angels watched from the corner of the dining room, he had a thought that something of the salty, finger-food-persuasion would be perfect—and the idea he was worried about snacking while he was watching a good show was a welcome return to normal.

Up by the fire, Wrath was still in his armchair, but instead of a happy couple in front of him, the two males who had been prowling around the waiting area were front and center. Both were twitchy, cracking their knuckles, shifting their weight in their Nikes. Considering that they were each wearing themed outfits from the Buffalo Bills winter collection, and were also sporting the same mullet haircut, you had to wonder why they didn't get along better.

"I paid seventy-five hundred for it," the guy on the right said as he glared at his twinsie.

"And what kind of car is it?" the King asked.

The one on the left crossed his arms over his chest. "Toyota Corolla."

"How many miles?"

"Fifty-eight thousand—"

"Fifty-*nine*," the buyer shot back.

"Year?" Wrath reached down to the floor and picked up his dog, settling George in his lap. "And manual or automatic, if it's an older model."

The seller went full-in on the proverbial floor space. "It's a twenty-twelve automatic. Look, it's in good working order, the paint's tight. Engine's solid—"

"The problem isn't the car," the buyer snapped. "It's the fact that I can't get it registered because I don't have the goddamn title."

"I told you, I lost it."

"Bullshit—" The male slapped his palm over his mouth. "No offense, Your Majesty."

Wrath inclined his head. "I've done worse. Continue."

The buyer threw up his hands. "He stole the car. And I know this because not only do I *not* have the goddamn title, I got pulled over by a cop tonight on the way to work. The plates pop up as stolen—"

"So you wipe some memories," the other guy said with a shrug. "Big frickin' deal—"

"Third time. *Third*, this month. I'm tired of erasing those rats without tails—and you should have disclosed this first—"

"You got a good deal—"

"Enough," Wrath snapped—and the subjects went dead quiet, like they weren't sure whether beheadings were still a thing or not. "Saxton."

"Sire," came the response from the desk.

Lassiter glanced over. The King's solicitor, who'd just come in, was looking like the proper gentlemale he was, all waistcoated and blazer'd and cravat'd on the far side of his leather-bound books on the Old Laws.

"Make an appointment with that garage we use," Wrath said as he played with one of George's paws, rubbing his thumb into the pads and then stroking the nails. "Switch out the VIN, get a title, and register it for him." As Saxton took notes, Wrath looked at the seller. "And you're giving him a thousand dollars back for the trouble."

"Now, wait a minute, I sold him a good car—"

"You stole the fucking thing and got free cash. And you're now giving him two thousand dollars because you're a pain in his ass and mine." Wrath lifted an eyebrow over his wraparounds. "You want to make it three? We can do that—"

Phones started to go off around the room, the

vibrations quiet, but pervasive, and V and Rhage both straightened and went for their cells.

Vishous immediately started texting, then looked up from his screen. "We are stopping now."

The King put George back down to the floor and turned his head in the direction of the buyer. "We'll take care of the car." Then he appeared to look the seller right in the eye. "You get him the money and you won't have any problems. You have seven nights. I will be personally checking on the disposition of the funds, and if they're not where they should be, I'm going to show up at your back door and—"

Saxton cut the King off with a loud clearing of the throat, and in the tense silence that followed, Wrath glared over at his solicitor. Then he pressed his lips together like he was holding his tongue on a number of subjects.

"Just fucking do it, okay. Your life will go better."

As the civilian nodded like he was having a seizure, Saxton hustled out from behind his desk and led the Buffalo Bills fans from the room. As the doors shut, Wrath sat forward on the armchair.

"What."

"There's been a *lesser* attack downtown at Dandelion—"

"Ah, *shit*—"

"—and Nate's there along with an aristocrat and Rahvyn—"

Lassiter heard the name, and instantly became corporeal. Confronting the brother, he demanded, "Is she hurt."

V's left eye twitched like a seizure was coming. Then his diamond stare narrowed. "You know, you could have told us you were here—and I don't know if she's hurt."

The up-and-leaving was an instantaneous thing, an act of desperate will that shouldn't have been possible given his panic. And as he ghosted, he didn't think of Eddie or Adrian, or even the brothers.

Speeding toward downtown, he couldn't understand how the female had gone from curled up on that hospital bed, safely in the training center, to out in the field, caught in the crossfire of the war. Who the *hell* had let her go there?

He re-formed in front of the club, and there was no chaos, no disruption, in the wait line. But no bouncer, either, that Pete guy with the shit-brown pants and the GF problems nowhere in sight.

Lassiter sank into his thighs and leapt into the air, landing on the roof and ignoring the gasps and shouts of the humans at his superhero routine. As he strode across the tar paper, he heard the thumping bass of the music and felt the vibrations come up through the soles of his bare feet—and he just wanted to scream for them to shut that shit off and stop the dancing. Didn't those men and women know that something had happened? Something fucking dangerous, and Rahvyn was somehow in it? Didn't the whole world know—

At the far edge of the roof, he looked down. "Oh, God."

Jumping to the ground, he landed with a booming impact that startled Shuli and Nate, as well as a male who'd been roughed up. The three were kneeling over Rahvyn, who was clearly bleeding out, and Lassiter fell to his knees—

"Is help coming?" one of them begged. "Is—"

Wait.

Hold on, it wasn't Rahvyn who was hurt.

This wasn't Rahvyn on the ground; it was not her blood, not her clothes . . . it was a male who'd apparently been shot in the throat.

"Where is she?" Lassiter demanded as he looked around. The fact that there was a scorched spot on the pavement made his heart skip beats. "Rahvyn, where is she—"

Shuli pointed at the door into the club. "I made her go inside. She's okay, she's in the hallway—but is help coming? He's dying."

No, Lassiter thought. *He's dead.*

"Yes," he said gently. "The brothers are on the way."

"It's my fault." Shuli brushed his eyes. "Oh, fuck, I shot him, I—"

"That's not how it happened," Nate cut in. "You were defending us."

"It was still my bullet."

Jumping up to his feet, Lassiter yanked at the back door, and when he found it locked, he had to force himself to concentrate so he could flip the dead bolt with his mind. The instant he got the thing open, he saw Rahvyn. She was standing just inside in the hall, next to the bouncer who should have been out front with the wait line—and though they were of totally different species, the two of them looked the same, both staring ahead of themselves, him because he'd clearly had memories wiped, her because she was in shock.

She didn't even look over as Lassiter entered.

"Rahvyn." At the sound of her name, she snapped to attention and swung her head his way. "Are you hurt?"

"Ah, n-no." She covered her mouth as if she might be sick or was trying to hold in a sob. "No, I'm not."

There was black blood on the front of her sweater, and the stink of the *lesser* wafted off of her—and holy *shit*, the idea she'd gotten that close to one of those undead slayers made him dizzy.

"Stay here." When she nodded in a herky-jerky way, he wanted to curse at all the could-have-happeneds. "I'm going to make sure they're protected out there, okay? I'm right on the other side of this door. Do *not* move from here."

More nodding. "Is Theox okay?"

"Just stay here. So I know where you are—"

"I am not bringing him back," she said in a low warning. "Do not even ask me."

Tears gathered in her silver eyes, turning them luminous, and as she wrapped her arms around herself, everything about her tangled hair and her stained clothes came into sharp focus.

"You shouldn't be out here like this. What the *hell* are you thinking."

She wiped under her eyes, clearing tears from her cheeks. "I am not a prisoner."

"No, instead you'll get people killed while innocent

males are trying to make sure you're not hurt. Come on, Rahvyn. This is wartime, not playtime—"

"That is so unfair!"

He jabbed his thumb over his shoulder. "That male out there is dead. You want to tell me what was so fucking important that you had to come out here, to this club? With those two kids? Just stay where you are, for fuck's sake, while I make sure this situation doesn't get even worse."

Back outside, he forced the door to re-close and searched the parking lot, in case there were more slayers on the periphery—or some of those shadows that had been showing up in various places, at very inopportune times. Then he looked at Shuli, who had sat back on his ass.

The poor bastard. He was barely out of his transition, a newly minted adult, and not from any kind of family or situation that would have prepared him for this. And yet he had manned up when it had counted and made sure Rahvyn wasn't hurt when the consequences of her bad decisions had put the three of them, as well as others, in danger.

Lassiter went across and put a hand on Shuli's shoulder. "Give me the gun, son."

Eyes that were confused raised up. Then the kid looked back down to his lap with surprise—like he had no clue what was in his grip.

"Here," the kid said as he offered the weapon forward. "I got it back."

Taking the nine millimeter, Lassiter flipped the

safety on. "Just hang tight. The brothers are coming with medical help any second."

"I didn't mean to shoot him," came the tortured reply. "Oh, God, I know his family and—"

A massive vehicle with a set of headlights bright enough to light up a football stadium trundled into the parking area, and Lassiter had never been so glad to see Vishous as the brother materialized on the other side of the victim.

"Let me get a look," V said as he crouched down.

Manny Manello, the Brotherhood's personal surgeon and medical officer, jumped out of the mobile surgical unit with a black bag, just as Tohr, Z, and Phury arrived to set up a guard formation.

"I killed him," Shuli said to no one in particular. "It was my bullet. I killed him . . ."

Nate said something that was too low to hear, and then the kid crab-walked over to his friend, pulling the guy into an embrace, his bloodstained hands wrapping around the other male's shoulders.

As Lassiter stepped away to give the medical types room to work, he looked over to the burn spot on the pavement again. Then he went back to the door into the club. Pulling it open, he was in mid-sentence as he—

Only the bouncer was standing in the hall.

Rahvyn was gone.

CHAPTER THIRTY-ONE

Okay, fine, it *should* have only been about the suit, Devina thought.

But really, since when had she been into "shoulds."

As the demon re-formed on a gracious, tree-lined street, she kept herself invisible, but that didn't mean she wasn't corporeal. The instant her body habitus came back into being, all kinds of aches registered and there was a glorious wetness between her legs. Smiling to herself, she enjoyed a brief flashback-buffet of images of her getting pummeled from behind in the men's department of her now absolute-favorite store of all time.

Maybe there was hope for them yet, she thought as she glanced left and right. Assured that there were no cars coming—not that it would really have mattered—

she crossed the lane and paused in front of a tall pair of iron gates that were just re-closing. On the far side of them, extending into some very nice formal landscaping, a driveway wound about and disappeared over a rise.

A pair of taillights was following its way along, glowing red until the car was consumed by darkness as it surmounted the little ridge.

Devina walked forward and passed through the iron barricade, the coldness of the metal causing her body to shiver as the shafts penetrated her and came out her back side.

Striding forward, she wanted her stilettos to make a sound as an auditory way of pissing on fences, but Lash wasn't going to appreciate her following him so she kept herself completely camo'd. As far as he knew, they'd gone their separate ways: After she'd gotten him into a very nice suit, and executed the tailoring with an I-Dream-of-Jeannie snap of the fingers, he'd taken off from the Saks.

But she'd slipped a lock of her own hair into his breast pocket.

So if he had the jacket on, he was as good as microchipped.

Cresting the rise herself, she stopped and felt her inner Zillow swoon. The grand house was a lovely sprawl, with two wings extending out from a central core, the whole of it painted a pale yellow, its shutters and doors black, its roof deep-gray slate. Discreet upward-focused lighting enhanced the visual impact, as did the approach of the driveway through mature plantings and full-time-gardener-maintained flower beds.

"What a money shot," she murmured as she checked out the drapery-framed windows.

There appeared to be about seven thousand lamps in the place, and all of them were on, beacons of sunlight fighting back the darkness inside and out. And yup, wow, the interiors were professionally decorated, none of the hodgepodge, happy-hands-at-home stuff she supposed she'd have been surprised to see in such spread: This estate was not just venerable, it was lived in by humans who had money and knew how to spend it.

Or had inherited all those antiques.

The silver Mercedes sedan that had gone through the gates ahead of her pulled up right in front. After a pause, both the driver's and passenger's side doors opened.

And what a suit it was.

As Lash extended his powerful frame out of the car, his blond hair caught the glow that surrounded the mansion, and she refreshed her very keen memory of what she had picked out for him. The Tom Ford was the color of all that slate, a resonant gray that perfectly complemented the aura of power he gave off, and the double-breasted, double-vented cut was traditional— the subtle black stripe was not. And neither was the open collar of the fine white cotton shirt.

He looked wealthy. As if he could afford a place like this.

"Well, here we are, Mr. LeRoi," the woman said. "Quite an impressive exterior, don't you think? The sellers are motivated, but cognizant that whoever purchases the property should be . . . how do we say, appropriate for the neighborhood. They've entrusted me with the listing, but of course I can represent your interests with proper disclosures. Shall we go in?"

As the smooth voice carried over on the breeze, the only thing that saved the real estate agent's life was the fact that she was over sixty and had had a bad facelift. Jesus, she looked like she'd been in a car accident and gotten put back together by a pathology resident.

Well, and then there was the fact that Lash completely ignored her. Hell, he didn't even acknowledge her dumbass rhetorical.

"I'll just—ah." The agent looked back and forth between him and the front door. "I'll just open us up, shall I? You know, I must point out that we're very happy to provide this kind of after-hours service for clients such as yourself. Please keep us in mind for your colleagues?"

The woman double-checked with him one last time, and got nothing, not even a nod. So she walked up a handful of marble steps and worked some kind of locking system, the entry's matched set of brass lanterns bathing her in a pool of light that was not kind to that puss with all its pulls at the ears and along the hairline at the forehead.

Meanwhile, Lash just stared at the central portion of the house, his hands in the pockets of the slacks, his weight back on his heels. As he was mostly facing away, Devina changed her position, materializing off to the side.

She was surprised when she got a look at him. His

perfect profile seemed tense. But he had set this appointment up, and it wasn't like he couldn't conjure the money.

Was it possible he missed her?

The thought was a tantalizing relief—and as she replayed how they'd fucked in the men's department . . . well, clearly she was under his skin in a way that had shit-all to do with a spell.

Lash wanted her. And he hated it.

If that wasn't the basis for every one of her best relationships, she didn't know what was. So yes, maybe it was time to let the spell go . . . and take another approach.

Although murdering Lassiter's chippy, as always, was in her back pocket.

"Do you want to come inside?" the realtor prompted as she stood to the side and motioned with her French-manicured, old lady hand.

Lash waltzed by the woman like he already owned the place.

And two could play that game.

+ + +

As Lash crossed the threshold of the mansion, he thought of all those human horror movies about vampires. *The Lost Boys. Blade. Dracula,* the one from the seventies, and then the Francis Ford Coppola update with Gary Oldman.

What was that one with Colin Firth—no, Farrell. *Fright Night.*

Where the hell had the rats without tails gotten the invitation-into-a-house-first thing?

Same place garlic came from, he supposed.

As he looked around the foyer, the woman he'd called from the listing he'd found online prattled on about various architectural features, historic whatevers, and hand-crafted thises and thats. It was as easy to tune her out now as it had been in her car, and for a moment, he was tempted to break some glass with her head just to get some peace and quiet. He refrained—because he liked the antique window panes with their bubbles, and the chandeliers and mirrors that had been placed with care.

If the woman only knew how narrowly her life had been saved. And by what.

Walking where he chose, he approved of the simple and elegant layout, multiple parlors offering different areas for entertaining, the dining room generous, the study a masculine haven, the kitchen kitted out for a professional staff.

Everything was in fine condition, the old molding freshly painted, the Zuber wallpaper applied with ex-pertise, the floors varnished and covered with fine car-pets from the Middle East. He even liked the drapes, the pops of coral, red, and blue silk damask elevating the restrained colors of the furniture.

It was all just what he was looking for—at least until the future he envisioned for himself on the property fell apart as he got to the base of the stairs. Staring up at the second floor, he was reminded that this was not a vam-pire house, one fortified with shutters that would come down for the day or living quarters underground that were something so much more than a bomb shelter built in the forties. Likewise, he was forced to confront the fact that he was no longer an aristocrat, with a cohort of social equals swanning around in finery while dissecting all manner of discourse in search of slights and misappropriations of status.

He was the son of evil.

Here to conquer Caldwell.

With an army of streetwise killers who wouldn't know a salad fork from a pair of sterling tongs.

Exactly what did he think he would use a place like this for? It wasn't as if he could desert his subordinates. They were too shocked to act independently right now, but they were aggressive enough to start to get creative when they felt more at ease. Besides, there were plans to be made, weapons to buy and store, perishable skills to develop.

"Don't you want to go upstairs?" the realtor asked.

Looking over at the woman, he—

The sensation tackled him from behind, and his body arched like someone had shot him in the back, right between the shoulder blades. As he barked a curse and contorted, the realtor put her hands forward.

"Mr. LeRoi? Are you—"

He cried out and went down to his knees, the black-and-white marble floor cracking his caps as a rocketing pain sliced through the center of his chest. With fumbling hands, he undid his suit jacket, and when he couldn't see the exit wound of a bullet on his fine white

shirt, he yanked the goddamn thing apart, little pearl-
ized disks flying free.

His sternum was intact, the hairless skin unmarred
over his pecs.

"Should I call nine-one-one?" The realtor leaned
down. "Mr. LeRoi? Are you all right?"

Absently, he noted that her fake posh accent had
been ditched in favor of a much more appropriate,
lower-class twang.

Opening his mouth, he intended to answer her, but a
sudden weakness overcame him, his eyes rolling back in
his head. As he went limp, he thought about his sire.
The fucking Omega and his self-interest was legion.
Was this an attempt for the father to come forward
from the abyss?

Was Lash's presence up here on the earth all just
some kind of stepping-stone out of oblivion, a loophole
in the *Dhestroyer* Prophecy—

"I'll take it from here," a familiar female voice said.

Oh . . . *great*. Just what he needed.

The demon in charge of him when he was like this.
And how the hell had she found him?

Unless she'd followed his ass.

Shit.

"You can go now, sweetheart," Devina said to the
realtor. "Unless you want to make friends with me?"

Lash's last thought, before he lost consciousness,
was a piece of advice for a human woman he couldn't
have given less of a shit about: *Do yourself a favor, lady.
Don't make friends with the bitch, she'll eat you alive.*

CHAPTER THIRTY-TWO

I have to go to his parents. No, I have to—I have to tell them—"

As Shuli rambled and gestured with his hands, the Black Dagger Brother Tohrment leaned down so that the only thing Shuli could see was the warrior's face and his deep blue eyes.

"We will take care of notifying his bloodline, son. You're injured and need treatment."

"You don't understand. I know the family. It's my responsibility—"

"No, it's not. You're staying right where you are."

When a heavy hand landed on his shoulder, Shuli realized he was lying on a gurney—and with that, the rest of the interior of the mobile surgical unit came into focus. Bench seats ran down either side of the open bay, and all around, medical supplies in see-through-fronted cabinets were within ready reach. Above him, a set of bright lights made him blink.

Or maybe that was the tears.

He grabbed on to the Brother's leather sleeve. "Please. It's my fault so I have to go to the family."

The Brother Tohrment sat down on the bench and took his hand. "Listen to me. You saved Nate and Rahvyn, as well as the other male. If you hadn't stabbed that *lesser*, God only knows what would have happened—"

"No, no, no." Shaking his head, Shuli didn't want to be a party to any kind of stolen valor. "That was Rahvyn. She was the one who saved us. The slayer overpowered me and got my gun. He put it to my head and if she hadn't thrown him off me, I'd be dead." He'd be like Theox. *Oh, fuck.* "She somehow got his knife—and when she stabbed him, there was an explosion of light and this popping sound—"

"Wait, wait, slow down. You're saying *she* was the one who—"

"It wasn't me. It was Rahvyn." He put his hands over his eyes, as if he could block out what had happened. "Right before she tore the *lesser* off me, that was when . . . I was trying to shoot the slayer and that was when I hit Theox—"

In the background, something started beeping furiously, and someone said something in a sharp warning.

"Shh," the Brother Tohrment said. "Lay back and relax, son. You're bleeding."

"I don't care about that—where's Nate?" At least he hadn't had to worry about that guy dying. "I need to talk to Nate—"

"He's with his dad. Murhder came right away." The Brother Tohrment squeezed his hand. "Listen to me, son. You'll get a chance to talk to your friend, I promise. But right now, I need you to breathe nice and slow with me. You have to calm down, okay?"

"I don't feel so good."

There was some whispering, and then a human took the Brother's spot. It was the one who had done the assessment on Theox, the one who had subtly shaken his head at Vishous and then moved on to take Shuli's vitals.

Oh, right. That was how he'd ended up in this high-tech OR. The human had ordered the Brothers to get the gurney.

"I'm just going to take a look," the man said in a calm, confident tone.

"At what," Shuli mumbled.

And that was when he saw the blood. Jesus . . . his whole arm was stained red.

"My shirt is ruined," he noted absently.

Like that mattered. Like his clothes ever should have mattered as much as they had.

"I'm going to have to cut the sleeve off, okay?" the human asked.

Shuli nodded, because what the hell did he care— "Oh. Shit."

As a pair of snub-nosed scissors made quick work of

the stained silk, a deep, jagged gash on the inside of his arm was revealed: The thing ran up from his elbow nearly into his armpit.

"How did that happen?" he wondered out loud. "I didn't feel anything."

"Sometimes," the doctor murmured as he looked over the wound from various angles, "you don't know what you run into when you're fighting. The parking lot has a lot of broken bottles. I think you caught the sharp edge of one and stayed with it."

"It will heal."

"Only with stitches—"

One side of the back double doors opened, and a Brother with a skull trim and a scar on his face leaned in. "He's here. Can I let him in?"

When the human nodded, the other Brother stepped back—

"Father," Shuli said numbly.

His sire was dressed in a tuxedo, Arcshuliae's fine black jacket set off by a pop-collared white shirt and a bow tie, his dark hair slicked back, a pocket square of white and black sitting with a jaunty pouf at his breast. He was still handsome, even at his age, still very fit and alert, as the patriarch of a noble bloodline should be.

Shuli turned his face away. He had been a disgrace before with all his loafing and his partying and his not taking anything seriously. Now . . . he was a curse. And in a way, perhaps his father would be happy that he now had an excuse to kick out—

"My son."

The anguished cry was a shock, and as Shuli looked back to the sound, the male he recognized, and yet did not know in this moment, jumped up and pushed his way forward, elbowing the healer aside.

"Oh, my son," Arcshuliae said as he bent down and gathered Shuli up in his arms. "You live."

After a moment of utter confusion, Shuli hugged back—"Oh, no, I've got blood on your shirt—"

The male touched Shuli's face. Then his shoulders and his chest. Finally, he inspected the arm. "You will tend to this?"

Shuli was about to answer the question, when the human who was actually being addressed nodded. "Yup. He'll be fine—provided I can close it right now. Otherwise, it's going to heal wrong and he might end up with irreversible nerve damage."

"See that you do your best." Eyes that were the precise color of Shuli's refocused on his own. "I am just glad you live, my son. Praise unto the great Virgin Scribe."

"I'm sorry, Father," Shuli choked out. "I am so sorry—"

His sire put a trembling hand on the side of Shuli's face. "I still have you. That is all I care about the now."

◆ ◆ ◆

Standing just outside the mobile OR, Nate couldn't get the smell of blood out of his nose, and every time he blinked, he saw fragments of the fight in slow motion: The *lesser* making an appearance around the corner, shambling along like something from *TWD*, that horrible fucking smell floating over and cutting out the metallic undertone of city stink in the air. And then Shuli yelling those names, and the slayer attacking that civilian, and . . .

But all of that was just a preamble to what stuck with him the most.

He was never going to forget the image of that gun pointed in Shuli's face, the *lesser* in complete control of the ground game. The jolt of fear that had gone through Nate had been violent enough to break through both his anger at the world and the ringing concussion he'd suffered when he'd been thrown across the parking lot. Yet even as he'd been determined to jump back into the fight, his body had refused to listen to any commands, his legs useless as ribbons, his arms slapping at the pavement under him.

If Rahvyn hadn't exploded onto the scene when she did?

Cursing, he shook his head and stared at the ground. How was she that strong? And how had she known about what to do with that knife? It wasn't something she'd just magically thought up in that split second of chaos. No, she had known exactly what to do, not just to incapacitate, but to end, the undead. Meanwhile, he and Shuli had gotten snowed, and an innocent person had been killed, and . . .

"Son, do you want to go back with Shuli in the RV?"

As he heard Murhder's voice, he couldn't look at the Brother. Shame, thick and sour in his throat, cut off his air passage, and he couldn't believe—couldn't comprehend—what the fuck had been going through his head earlier in the night.

Like leaving his room clean could have made up for him killing himself? With a gun he'd stolen out of this male of worth's arsenal in the basement of that home?

And what the hell had come out of his mouth when he'd been talking at Shuli, about his . . . parents.

"Nate."

At the insistent tone, he reluctantly shifted his eyes over. When the familiar, harsh face in front of him got wavy, he thought, *Ah, shit, I'm crying. What a pussy.*

"Come here."

Heavy arms pulled him in, and he resisted only because he knew what he had done earlier in the night, and guilt was a physical barrier to the kindness shown by the ones you'd betrayed, wasn't it.

"I'm just glad you're okay," Murhder said. "And don't worry, I called Mom. She's at the clinic working, and I told her to stay put. That we'd be there soon."

Pushing himself free, Nate scrubbed at his face and paced around. When he finally stopped, he realized he was standing over the burned spot on the pavement where the *lesser* had exploded. Between one blink and the next, he saw Rahvyn's arm rise above her head. The arc with which she'd brought that steel blade down had been perfect.

Couldn't have been any better if she'd practiced it.

Maybe she had.

Fuck. He had to pull it together somehow. If she

could keep her mind in the game under those circumstances, he was a total loser if he fell apart now, surrounded by Brothers who were packing more weapons than an army battalion.

Then again, what was scrambling his eggs wasn't about any mortal threat—

The box van that presently arrived on the scene was shiny and black, and had no windows in its rear compartment. After bumping up the lip of the parking lot, it did a couple of turns to reorient itself for an exit, and then it backed in close to the rear of the club. As the driver's side door opened, a little old male in a butler's outfit emerged.

Fritz, the Brotherhood's most trusted servant, had come on a grim job that he clearly took solemn responsibility for.

Around at the back, he opened the double doors, and subdued lighting came on in the interior. The gurney he pulled out had stainless steel fittings and a black padded plane, and its wheels dropped down and grabbed the ground to form a rolling support.

"Over here," the Brother Vishous said.

Nate backed away, even though he wasn't obstructing the path, and he watched as the body, which had been draped in a couple of white sheets, was head-and-footed and lifted off the asphalt. After the male was settled on the gurney, Vishous went around and tucked the sheeting in.

Red stains seeped through at the neck immediately.

And the body wiggled as they rolled things over to the back of the van.

Nate wanted to turn away. He made himself stay right the fuck where he was.

He hadn't exactly known the victim. Shuli had been casual drinking buddies with the guy, both of them cut from that aristocratic cloth of privilege and wealth, and so Nate had run into Theox in a peripheral capacity.

Had the family been told yet?

A bottomless pit opened in his gut as he imagined what that was going to be like, and he looked at Murhder. The Brother was staring back at him—and it was clear. In spite of everything that was going on, with all the dynamics of dealing with the fallout of the attack, Murhder had one, and only one, true priority: The stupid fucked-up fool he considered his son.

More tears now. Loads.

All Nate wanted was a do-over of the night. But that wasn't how time worked, was it.

What the *hell* had he been thinking? About everything?

Vishous closed up the back of the van, then went around to the driver's side, getting in behind the wheel. After the butler hopped into the passenger seat, the vehicle, with its heartbreaking cargo, started forward on its departure.

Nate braced himself and looked over to the left. Lassiter, the fallen angel, was standing with two other males Nate didn't recognize, the trio watching the body get driven off.

Funny, he expected to feel hatred that was rooted in jealousy as he stared at the sacred entity with the blond-

and-black hair. He didn't. Maybe he was just too numb at the moment.

Nate jacked up the waistband of his jeans, ducked his head . . . and went over to the angel.

He couldn't meet the male's eye, but his voice was strong and sure. "I overheard through the door what you said to Rahvyn when she was in the hall. You got it all wrong. The slayer was going to shoot Shuli in the face when she pulled the undead off him. She was the one who saved us by stabbing it, not the other way around."

In the stunned silence that followed, Nate's stare lifted, and in some distortion of reality, he didn't see Lassiter up close. He saw the angel across a field of wild flowers that had somehow sprouted in full bloom despite the fact it was April in upstate New York.

And the male was standing with Rahvyn, the pair oblivious to the world around them.

Oblivious to the heart that had been broken on the sidelines.

Earlier in the evening, there would have been a subtle satisfaction in letting the angel get it all wrong, the wedge of misunderstanding driving the happy couple apart. But Nate only had to glance at the blood red taillights of that now-hearse, and he was reminded that there were enough bad things out there waiting for everybody. Creating a false one was just nasty.

"You owe Rahvyn an apology."

At that, Nate turned away. He didn't have enough energy in him to care whether he was believed or not. If

Lassiter couldn't recast his cooked-up version of events? That was his problem.

It was as Nate walked back to Murhder that the mobile surgical unit's engine flared to life, and then the RV also trundled off.

For a split second, all of the Brothers who were left on scene looked at him. Murhder. Zsadist and Phury. Rhage. Sahvage.

He knew them from having been invited into the First Family's mansion. He had sat with them at Last Meal, shared food with them, listened to them tell stories and laugh, witnessed them looking deeply into the eyes of their mates. He had also seen them with their young, if they had them, and watched them play with the young of their brethren.

"Son," Murhder said. "What do you want to do?"

From a vast distance, he heard himself say, "I want to learn from you all. I want you to teach me how to fight. I want to be trained properly in the ways of the war so that I can protect people who need protection and so that something like this doesn't happen again." He looked at Murhder. "I want . . . to be like my father."

CHAPTER THIRTY-THREE

The wild flowers had all died.

As Rahvyn walked over the meadow's soft bed, she remembered the blooms as they had been when Lassiter had conjured them, full of color and fragrance, a feast for the eyes and the senses. She had spun around in joy at the visual display, the thoughtfulness . . . the male who had presented her with such an unexpected gesture.

But then she had looked up properly into his face.

It was in that moment that she realized he was marking a goodbye, not the start of something, and her heart had been crushed.

Later, whilst she had been with the Book far from earth, she had wondered what would happen to the fragile flowers. Would they disappear after he left?

Or, once brought into being, would they suffer a life cycle?

Now she had her answer. Like all things manifested into the physical world, the figment that had been made corporeal was subject to the reality it had entered. Out of season was out of season, and the fresh beauty had been unable to sustain itself in the harsh, cold nights.

Glancing over her shoulder, the farmhouse she had once resided in for a short time was like something from a fable, a curl of smoke lazing out of its chimney, vampires moving around inside the cozy rooms. It would be about time for the nightly Toll House cookies, handmade and fresh from the oven.

She had met Nate under its gabled roof. He had been working on the garage, putting up panels that smelled like flour and painting around windows. He had been as shy as she, and thus he had been easy to approach. He had also seemed to know that she was not long for Caldwell.

He had been correct. She had come forward through time just to reassure her cousin, Sahvage, of her persisted existence—and also, if she were honest with herself, to ask for his forgiveness. Following that, the Book had given her a purpose that had defined her choice of next destination.

Rahvyn refocused on the forest at the far edge of the meadow . . . and presently she had returned to the juncture of decision. What now? Did she go back to the Book? Or did she stay here and—

She wheeled around. When she saw who it was, her breath slowly departed her lungs.

Yet she wasn't surprised.

With purpose that appeared grim, Lassiter walked forward through the dead flowers, his eyes on hers rather than the ruination upon the ground, his bare feet surely chilling to the bone.

"How did you know I was here?" she said roughly.

He stopped in front of her, his blond-and-black hair teased by the cold spring breeze. "It was a gamble."

Turning away from him, she went back to staring at the trees. She thought about her landing in the forest, the fireball of energy created by her breaching the boundary of the calendar gouging into the earth, her corporeal form emerging from the great divot like a young newly born.

Lassiter cleared his throat. "I came to apologize. I know now what really happened behind the club and I—"

She put her hand up over her shoulder. "Stop." As the angel fell silent, she cleared her throat. "I want you to listen to what I am about to say, so that I do not have to repeat it."

"All right."

It was a moment before she could continue.

"I want you to know who killed the male who took my virtue, who raped me until I bled. Who intended to hurt and humiliate me, who wanted me to feel sullied and used." Rahvyn looked back at the angel. "It was me. I killed him."

As those iridescent eyes flared, she faced him once again. "He had left me for dead on his bedding platform, quite satisfied with himself and the condition in which he left me. Whilst he celebrated his victory over his prey with a meal delivered unto him, I gathered my strength even with his chains still upon me." There was a long silence. "And then I went after him. When I was done with the flaying, there was barely any life within him, and I impaled his remains on the standard pole above the entryway of his castle."

The gruesome memories were so vivid, she could smell the copper of the blood in her nose anew, feel the cooling of the sweat from her exertions on her flesh. "In rendering him thus, I was not sending a message to those within the castle walls who had heard me scream and done nothing. It was not for the villagers, either. It was because he was so proud of all his power, so sure about how he wielded it and what was his due. His standard colors had always flown over his grand castle. I thought his skinned corpse was a better representation of him."

Lassiter closed his eyes briefly.

"Look at me," she demanded.

His lids slowly lifted.

"I need you to know something about me, something you should never forget." She leaned in, so there was absolutely no mistaking her words. "I liked killing him. I breathed in the scent of his fear and suffering, the rank stench of his body odor as he vomited and lost control of his bladder and bowels. I relished both the sound of him begging me for mercy and the denial to him of that which he refused me. Further, his testicles were in his mouth when I put him on his flagpole. I was cruel and I do not regret it. I sleep well during the day, and there is naught on my conscience."

"Rahvyn—"

"What is more, I believe that I owe him a debt of gratitude. Before him, there was no balance to me. I was of virtue, but I had no power because I was without aggression. And then . . . he captured me because of my gifts and sought to subdue me. He had heard about me rescuing crops and livestock, aiding with births, healing with my hands and presence, locating the missing. He feared losing his authority, that others would bow unto me. So he endeavored to destroy me by forcing my physical body to submit unto him in the basest manner. In the aftermath, as I was bound by chains and in pain, I realized I had a choice. Either I retained the virtue of my character, and submitted to my body's ruin—or I sacrificed all of what I was, and *ahvenged* myself and my cousin. I. Have. No. Regrets. I am balanced now, the healer and the killer, the virtue'd and the cursed, and I will not hesitate to draw upon either side of me, as it suits or is required."

In the silence that followed, she was aware of a deep-seated release, an uncoiling of the tension in her body. It was hard to imagine how she would have told Lassiter the details under any other circumstances, and she was glad it was done.

"When I tell you," she intoned sternly, "that you do

not need to worry about my safety, I mean it. I will not hesitate to defend myself and I have the power and strength not just to do that, but to make those who would seek to aggress upon me or those I protect rue the night they were born. I am not the Gift of Light, I am a scourge held in check by a conscience that is very easily dissuaded from its supremacy."

+ + +

There was a plane traveling overhead.

In the resonant quiet that followed Rahvyn's stark revelations, Lassiter looked up to the night sky with an essential detachment and tracked the slow, lazy passage of a commercial aircraft from west to east. But the lack of evident speed was just about perspective, wasn't it. From where he was standing on the ground, the 747, or whatever it was, seemed to be strolling. If the thing were going by him? At eye level? It would have been a blur that knocked him off his feet.

"And your apology about this evening is not re-quired," she concluded, "because I know what I did and what happened behind the club, and that is wholly suf-ficient for me. I do not need your version of events to align with reality. That is your issue, not mine."

He re-leveled his head, and as he met her silver stare, he remembered when they had stood out here together that night of the flowers—all of which had died in the cold. She had been so diminutive, so fragile . . . or so it seemed. And it was that impression of her, as delicate and precious, that had fueled his anger at her autonomy tonight. He had imagined her in the dangerous alleys of Caldwell, surrounded by *lessers* and shadows and humans who were out to hurt her.

Fear over what could happen was what had made him snap.

Especially in light of what he knew had already been done to her.

"I am balance," she reiterated, as if his silence made her feel that he was marshaling arguments. "Not innocence. And balance does not need protection to survive. It regulates itself, no matter what, and no matter who, seeks to upset the equilibrium."

Lassiter closed his eyes—and yet he saw her on the backs of his lids, standing there in front of him, her platinum hair teased by the wind, her face composed, her voice unwavering. In her jeans and sweater, she seemed nothing like what she truly was.

No civilian, this female. But something else entirely.

Come on, though. Like he didn't already know she was powerful after what she'd done to Nate. To George?

"I realize this changes your opinion of me," she said. "It changed my opinion of myself."

A stiff breeze came in from the opposite direction and swirled around her, and he thought of his showy display with the wild flowers. He had wanted to impress her, but also to pay tribute to her. And he realized that part of her mystique, part of what he had been attracted to, had been an illusion, his mind filling in her characteristics—and downright creating others—until she was a construction he'd projected, a melding of her physical beauty, the allure of her grace, and also what he imagined she would seek to feel secure in this world.

He'd enjoyed what he'd created: If she was weaker than he was, then he was required. Want was a choice. Need was more forgiving out of necessity.

"You ended us out here first," she said roughly. "Thus I end us now."

At that, she pivoted back to the woods, crossed her arms over her chest and nodded, as if all his quiet was speaking for itself—and she was getting ready to walk off.

"Rahvyn."

When she made a noise acknowledging him, he said, "Do you want to know what's going through my mind at this moment?"

As she glanced over her shoulder again, that wind caught some of her hair again and carried it out from the crown of her head, the platinum waves glimmering in the moonlight.

"I love you," he gritted. "The real you is even more beautiful than the illusion I manufactured. I'm not scared of you, and I don't judge you. If I'm not talking, it's because I'm worried I'm less necessary, and I don't fucking know what to do about that."

Her mouth opened. Then closed.

He continued. "I'm sorry that I created some kind of image of you. I wasn't even aware of doing it, and you're right. You are free to come and go. I was just . . . worried about your safety and it came out all wrong." He glanced around. "Look, I'm just going to leave now because I've said waaaaaay too much tonight already. I'm going back to the clinic to check on Shuli and Nate, and I'd like to see you there. I'm sure they would as well. I'm assuming you know how to get to the training center from here. If you don't, all you have to do is go into Luchas House and call me, and I'll come back and guide you, if you want. I hope . . . well, I'd like you to see me when and if you're ready. And if you decide you don't want to . . . I get it, I really do."

He wanted to touch her face. He kept his hands to himself.

"I bonded with who I thought you were," he whispered. "But yeah, I'm in love with who you actually are."

With that, he up and dematerialized, leaving her in the field of dead flowers.

Where the beauty of the moonlight was no match for the female who was bathed in heaven's illumination.

CHAPTER THIRTY-FOUR

When Lash came back to consciousness, his eyes flipped open, and for a split second, he had no idea where he was. The room was wholly unfamiliar, but not unpleasant, from the luxurious silk drapes and ceiling fresco of a woodland scene to the Ming vase on a display pedestal and the Flemish still life of flowers over the French marble mantelpiece.

No fire crackling in the hearth, but the ambient temperature was nice and toasty enough.

Potpourri was simmering in a dish somewhere.

"You're back."

He looked to the voice. The demon was seated in a silk chair and wearing a glittering black evening gown that had a slit all the way up one side. With her long legs crossed at the knee, there was plenty showing, but in a tasteful way—and to top it all off, she was holding a Herend teacup with her pinkie extended so far out, it was like it had been broken and healed wrong.

Her chignon was a little dated, maybe, but her face was so beautiful, the sweeping style really worked for her.

Lash sat up and discovered he'd been lying on a tufted sofa that was covered in a coordinating blue and green. As a patterned throw pillow fell off, he bent down and picked it up.

God, he loved Scalamandré.

"So are you going to buy this house?" Devina motioned around with the teacup, her red nails fresh from a manicure, an Art Deco diamond bracelet he didn't recognize twinkling at her wrist. "You don't strike me as a male who wastes time window-shopping."

"No." His voice was rough so he cleared his throat. "I'm not buying it."

"Too expensive for your bank account? That surprises me."

"I have plenty of money."

Placing his feet on an Aubusson rug, he stood up slowly and conducted an internal function review as he went vertical. Everything seemed to be working okay.

What the fuck had happened.

Devina smiled, her red lips lifting. "It's easy when you can just conjure the cash, isn't it. And humans think crypto is the way."

"My bank accounts survived me. From before. I don't have to conjure anything."

He was aware that he was answering more candidly than he normally would, but the subject of finances didn't particularly interest him, and he wanted to understand his collapse without drawing more attention to it. If she was inclined to compete over who could pull more dollars out of thin air? Fine. What the fuck did he care.

"That's a different outfit," he commented as his eyes traveled down her thighs, her calves.

The Louboutins she'd changed into had thin straps that highlighted her delicate ankles. And good ol' Christian was right. Toe cleavage was sexy.

Garbed as she was, she fit right into the house, all lady of the manor. But like the past he'd been thinking he could return to, there was no depth to her in that role.

"You know," the demon said, "I keep thinking about that mess outside my lair, that inky, stinky mess. You're creating an army, aren't you. You're recruiting humans to fill out the Lessening Society."

Jesus, if she expected an A+ for that math, she was really reaching. Any idiot could deduce that goal.

Putting the teacup off to the side in its saucer, she got to her feet as well. With those heels, she was almost as tall as he was.

As she approached him, he caught the scent of her under the Poison she wore. She was aroused, but he wasn't going to fuck her. Even as he hardened in the slacks of the suit she'd found for him, he wasn't about to get into any habits that were going to be a distraction.

And if she'd somehow been able to find him here, he didn't need to encourage her stalking.

Bringing her breasts against his pecs, she eased her body into his. Then she locked mouths with him, the kiss ending in a bite of his lower lip that, if it had been any sharper, would have drawn blood.

"I have an idea for you," she drawled. Before he could don't-bother that, she continued, "I'll meet you in the basement of that nasty-ass walk-up with the bathtub at nine o'clock tomorrow night. If you want more humans to turn, I'll get you some. Feminine intuition tells me you're missing an opportunity. Have a good night, honey. Loooooove you."

She backed off and then drawled out of the room.

"I don't need your help, *honey*," he muttered.

Tilting to the side, he watched her leave through the front door, and when he sensed her presence was gone, he sat back down, crossed his legs knee to knee, and looked around. The silence bore upon him like a physical weight and his mind churned over things he could not change.

He didn't know how long he stayed there, in the elegant drawing room, breathing deeply of the scents and feasting upon the beauty around him with his eyes.

In his soul, he wanted to return to where he had started. Nostalgia did not come with a rewind button, however, no matter how powerful the yearning. And even if it did, jumping backwards in time would not undo his own evolution—

Why was he wasting time with this introspection.

With an emphatic push into his Ferragamos, he rose and walked out to the front door. Opening things up, he stepped outside and noted that that Mercedes was gone. Which suggested the realtor had been safely released back into the human wild, but who knew. Who cared.

It would be more efficient to ghost away, but he put his hands in the pockets of his slacks and strode down the walkway. Hooking up with the drive, he continued along, and it was as he ascended the rise that he realized he was providing the demon with a chance to give away her presence. Either because she couldn't help herself or because she didn't mean to.

He wasn't looking for a partner in the war.

He didn't need help.

Period.

As he came up to the gates, he willed them open, enjoying the parting of the way before him, imagining that on the far side, victory awaited.

After he passed through, he paused and listened to the clanking as things closed in his wake. Maybe later he'd buy a proper place like this. Right now, there were too many things to get organized—

A vehicle approached on the street, moving slowly, and at first he didn't pay any attention to it. Except then, as it passed, he noticed that it wasn't a Rolls-Royce or a Bentley. Not even a Benz or a Beamer. It was a blacked-out box van, the kind of thing that a security force or servants might be driving.

When it paused at the barricaded entry that was across the street and down a little to the right, he imagined whoever was at its wheel was lost, but then they pulled in next to a video checkpoint. Which made no sense. Why would servants or employees use the front entrance? That would never be allowed—

The driver's side window lowered.

And revealed in the security lights a hard face Lash recognized.

As if he could ever forget that goatee ... or the tattoos in the Old Language that marked the temple.

Vishous, son of the Bloodletter.

♦ ♦ ♦

Lassiter didn't immediately return to the clinic. First, he went back to the parking lot behind the club. He wasn't sure whether Eddie and Adrian would have waited for him as he'd asked, but there they were, sitting on top of the building to the rear, their feet dangling off the drop of the roof. Side by side like that, they reminded him of a couple of schoolchildren in some old-fashioned TV ad for lunch boxes.

A matched pair, not misbehaving.

For the moment.

As he came into his corporeal form, they glanced at each other and then jumped down to walk over to him. He met them halfway—or intended to. Two steps in and he stepped on something sharp. Cursing, he lifted his bare foot and looked at the bottom of it.

A piece of glass had carved a jagged hole in his sole, and he picked it out with a grimace. As silver blood welled, he tossed the shard over his shoulder.

"You okay?" Ad asked. "You need a Band-Aid?"

"I'm good." Staring at the wound, he watched as it sealed itself up. Then he looked at the pair. "So that happened."

And he wasn't talking about his boo-boo.

Eddie's expression was reserved, his burgundy eyes hooded, his mouth tight. "Helluva night."

"Nothing out of the norm." Lassiter put his foot back down on the cold pavement. "Sometimes I feel like Caldwell, New York, is the starship *Enterprise*, everyone grabbing on to consoles to stay upright, shields failing, Scotty screaming that he's giving the engines all he's got as Kirk barks orders and redshirts die."

He glanced to the exit of the club. The bloodstains were still on the pavement where the male had died.

"So, no," he said gruffly, "I'm not going to leave this. And it's not just about Rahvyn."

The words that came back at him from Eddie were soft and defeated: "I feel for you. I really do."

But clearly, the angel was going to hold his course with his mission, even if Ad was next door, shaking his head like he disagreed with that decision.

"Okay, fine." Lassiter shrugged. "But I'm not going with you. Tell the Creator you found me. Tell Him where I am, even though He obviously already knows it. He's going to have to come get me Himself, and I'm going to fight Him tooth and nail."

In the pause that followed, he was ready for an argument. Instead, Eddie just nodded once. "Will do."

Then the angel put his hand out.

After a moment, Lassiter clasped the palm that was offered, "Thank you."

Eddie shrugged as they released their grips. "It's not exactly a gift."

"But at least you see where I'm coming from. You know my history. I've been a fuck about for eons. Finally, though, I'm where I can do some good, even if it breaks the rules on occasion."

Off in the distance, a siren bubbled through the night. A human shouted a greeting. A car was started. And meanwhile, in the club, the thumping music continued, and he thought of the men and women inside—and vampires—all of whom were still drinking and yukking it up and dancing.

Like nothing had happened.

Then again, in their lives, nothing had.

Talk about different planes of existence.

"I didn't think it was going to end this way," Eddie said, "I gotta confess."

Lassiter smiled at the other angel. "Oh, come on. When have I ever done anything I was supposed to."

"No, I didn't think you'd find . . . a family. With anybody. And that's what this is, for you. For them. The vampires have embraced you and you the same. It makes this hard because what are they going to do after you're gone."

Goddamn, he didn't want to think about that.

"Could you do me a favor?" he said.

"Yeah," Eddie replied. "I'll wait to tell Him for a little bit. But I can't keep it to myself forever."

"Twenty-four hours. If you could just give me a full day and night."

After a moment, Eddie nodded. "You got it. Twenty-four hours."

Ad stepped up. "It was good to see you again."

As the guy pulled things in for a hug, Lassiter said over that heavy shoulder, "You're lying now."

"Not this time."

As they stepped back, they both looked up. Overhead, and in spite of the ambient illumination of the city, a shooting star flared in an arc, bright enough to beat the glow of electricity.

He knew damn well that Rahvyn had arrived on the night that a meteor had supposedly landed in the forest behind Luchas House.

With a sickening dread, he thought . . . it looked like she had left in similar fashion.

Maybe his going back to the Creator wasn't such a bad thing after all.

It wasn't like he had death, in the traditional sense, to look forward to.

CHAPTER THIRTY-FIVE

Tracking the box van into the property, Lash was very careful to stay downwind and out of sight as he re-formed behind a hedge that had been pruned into the shape of a rabbit up on its hind legs. With his aggression firing on all cylinders, disappearing himself wasn't possible, so he was glad that his new suit was dark gray—and to make sure that he wasn't seen, he unbuttoned his white shirt and pushed it into the jacket's confines so it didn't create a visual clue. Then he disappeared himself up to the next topiary—a lion. And after that, the third in line, which was a—well, he wasn't sure what it was.

Maybe the gardener had had a stroke halfway

through the trimming. There was a gopher feel to things, but also a raccoon vibe, although neither was the kind of fauna typical of pretentious property owners.

As he continued on, he was careful to stay waaaaay back. He was alone and there was no backup coming, and as much as he would have loved a fight with one of the Brothers who had taught him everything he knew, he needed the intel more. Members of the Brotherhood were precious commodities, so if Vishous was out and about in the world?

This had to be important, and he had to know what was going on.

The estate's layout was not dissimilar to that of the one Lash had just tried on for size, the drive long and winding, the gardens professionally cultivated and maintained. The mansion was a Tudor replica, but it had been built in the early twenties—of the previous century—so there weren't the cheap materials, distorted angles, and rinky-dink details of new McMansions. And this was a vampire house. Had to be, if Vishous himself was tooling up and making some kind of a delivery.

A *glymera* family that had somehow escaped Lash's raids.

He must know the owners from his previous life, but he hadn't ever been here before—so this had to be something that had been purchased as a relocation after all the aristocratic landholdings had been compromised when he'd attacked them.

The van drove directly up to the front entrance and the mansion's door was opened, not by a servant, but by a female in a gown. She was all done up, her hair in orderly waves, diamonds at her throat and wrists, even white gloves to her elbows. Her makeup was a mess, however, black streaks melting down her face, her lipstick partially wiped across her jaw. She stumbled as she ran out to the back of the van, one of her heels flipping off her foot, her stride going entirely lopsided. A male in a tuxedo quickly caught up with her, and all but carried the female the rest of the way.

Vishous disembarked from behind the wheel, and as he went to meet the pair at the rear of the vehicle, he scanned the environs. He was heavily weaponized, those black daggers on his chest, multiple guns holstered on his waist, extra ammo locked in at the small of his back. He wasn't wearing a Kevlar vest, and there was no leather jacket to cover the show.

He had come directly from the field.

One by one, other Brothers arrived, re-forming out of the darkness, and he recognized them from his time at their training center: Zsadist and Phury, the twins who looked alike except for the hair and that scar; Tohrment, the second-in-command who had disappeared for a while, but was clearly back; Rhage with his movie star looks and blond hair. They formed a protective semicircle around the tableau of suffering.

To get a better look, Lash dematerialized to another position, ever mindful of which way the wind was blowing. And as a gurney with a body in a bag was rolled out the back, he caught the scent—

Baby powder and rancid meat.

"What the fuck," he breathed.

As a shot of pure fury went through him, his hand instinctively went to the hunting knife at his belt. But he didn't follow through on any attack—because what the hell had his subordinates gotten into while he'd been at Saks?

See what happens when you bang demons in department stores? a disapproving voice pointed out in the back of his head.

And then he realized . . . the sinking spell he'd just had. Had one of his *lessers* been stabbed back to him? If that was the reason for his collapse, he was going to need to get over that shit quick.

As a trickle-down of implications made him growl softly, he cut the sound. What he did *not* need right now was a one-on-five fight with the Brothers. Yes, he was the very definition of special weapons and tactics, but he'd just weebled his wobble and he was monstrously outnumbered.

Plus it wasn't like there was any cavalry he could call. Not yet.

God only knew what the Lessening Society had gotten into behind his back.

The body was rolled over to the entry of the mansion by Vishous, the other Brothers processing behind what had to be the parents at a discreet distance as *doggen* spilled out of the glow of the house, the weeping audible, many of the maids, cooks, and chauffeurs grasping on to each other.

In this moment of sad arrival, there was unity between upstairs and downstairs, and as the remains were taken inside, the wave of grief receded along with the deceased into the interior, the door shutting behind them all, including the flanks of Brothers.

With the cargo transfer complete, an elderly figure got out of the passenger front of the van, walked around the rear, got behind the wheel, and started off on a departure.

Well, wasn't this an unexpected gift.

Lash recognized the old *doggen* from the training center program. His name was Fritz, and he had not only supervised the cleaning of the facility, but performed the pickups and drop-offs of trainees, and provided food for breaks. He was the Black Dagger Brotherhood's butler.

And servants went home.

Didn't they.

◆ ◆ ◆

As Rahvyn stood before the last of the training center's barricades, she still wasn't sure whether she was going to go inside. Though she had come through all of the previous gates, from the ones that were made to look like nothing more than rotting wood rails to the later, far sturdier constructions, at each pause point, her internal debate had escalated.

And now she was here, in the oddly buffered forest landscape, before the most vigorous of the collection, the concrete and steel-meshed fortification so intimidating, so vast, so solid, surely an army could not breach its dimensions.

She supposed she could have tried to enter through the venting system by dematerializing. That seemed risky, however, given that there had to be steel mesh set within it. And yes, she could have returned as she had departed, working through the planes of existence. The truth was, she felt like she needed the time to think.

'Twas fortunate that she had surmised the physical location from her previous excursion.

As an owl hooted overhead, and a cold breeze curled around her legs, she hunkered into her sweater and glanced up the towering expanse of the gate. As she felt minutes go by, she thought, alas, it appeared she was going to have a sufficiency of rumination opportunity unless someone permitted her entrance. There were plenty of cameras mounted where she could see them— and undoubtedly where she could not—

The *clunk* and quiet whirring suggested that she had been approved for entry, and as the reinforced panels slowly slid back, she did not need to wait for them to complete their retraction. She was not a double-wide vehicle and could fit well enough with only a narrow space.

She waited anyway.

No more dithering, she thought. *In or out.*

Yes . . . or no.

In the end, her body made the decision, her feet starting to walk again, her mind and her emotions following suit because, no matter how many powers she possessed, she had yet to be able to separate the two.

As soon as she cleared the threshold, the great gates began to close once more and she glanced behind herself to watch them. When they resealed, she faced what was before her, a gradual descent, the stretch of road continuing forth. Flat banks of lights set into the ceiling, and also the concrete walls, illuminated the way, and as she proceeded forth, her footfalls echoed all around, a lonely sound. The air smelled like chalk, and the farther she went, the warmer things became, and the louder the conversation in her head grew.

Pros and cons, though the decision had already been arrived at—

Rahvyn stopped.

The figure ahead was unmistakable, that blond-and-black hair a dead giveaway—and then Lassiter's scent reached her nose. She breathed it in deep.

And liked it.

They were both silent as they came forward, and when they finally were face to face, she had a thought about the two halves of the gate behind her finding home, locking together, solid.

Looking into the angel's oddly colored eyes, she had one and only one thought.

She was glad she'd come.

"Hi," he said.

"Hi."

"I'm glad you came."

"You know . . . I was just thinking that, too."

It was hard to know who reached out first, but suddenly, there was no more division between them. Closing her eyes, she turned her head to the side and rested it upon his pecs. The sound of his heart was strong and even, and there was comfort in the beat.

"You truly do not judge me," she choked. "Neither for what was done unto me nor for what I wrought."

"No, I don't."

The relief that flooded through her made her head feel as though it was full of fizz, like the soda she had learned to enjoy.

"And I really am sorry," he murmured as he stroked her back. "That I underestimated you and got all up in your face about leaving the clinic. I was a bonded male off his rocker. It won't happen again."

Bonded? she marveled. *For true?*

Pulling back, she reached up and touched his face in awe. "You know just what I want to hear, don't you."

His smile was wry. "It's not that hard to apologize for being a douche canoe."

"Douche . . . canoe?" She frowned. "Does that involve oars?"

"Paddles." He slipped an arm around her shoulders and guided her farther underground. "On my own ass."

"Oh. Well . . . one hopes your posterior survived." She hesitated. "May I ask you something?"

"Anything."

"I saw you . . . in a cave somewhere. There was firelight, I think, and rock walls behind you. Where is that?"

He glanced over at her. "How did you know about that?"

Up ahead, the drive widened into an open area where vehicles were parked among concrete columns that anchored a low ceiling.

"It was just a vision I had," she answered lamely.

There were reasons why even he could not know about the Book. She trusted Lassiter's intentions always, but minds could be read and sometimes secrets were shared in the hopes of improving situations. It was safer for everyone.

Besides, the Book was done being used, and it had earned its privacy. And safety.

As they reached a reinforced door that surely led into the training center proper, Rahvyn stopped and took the angel's hands. "I want you to know why I left here tonight. Shuli tracked me down on the phone and begged me to come out and help with Nate. The male is struggling, and part of that is my fault. I have offered him no help with the transition after . . . everything that happened to him. I have a responsibility unto him, for I am the reason he is the way he is."

Lassiter nodded. "I get it, and I didn't think about that until later. What's going on with him?"

She started talking, and the words just kept coming—yet it was weird, she wasn't sure exactly what she was saying. She could tell by the way Lassiter's expression kept getting grimmer and grimmer, however, that she was accurately conveying the situation.

"Do we need to talk to Murhder?" he asked. "If Nate's playing around with guns, his parents need to know."

"I never got a chance to speak with Nate. Things happened really fast with the *lesser*." And the male hadn't exactly been glad to see her. "Where is he now?"

"With Murhder. He's gone home."

"First thing tomorrow, I shall reach out to him. If he won't talk to me, let's go to his sire."

"Deal."

Dropping one of her hands, he turned away and reached for the handle—

"Lassiter . . . do you think you might take me to your cave? And show me . . . the firelight?"

CHAPTER THIRTY-SIX

Just down the road.

The blacked-out box van went less than a quarter mile away from the Tudor mansion before it pulled into a far shorter drive. The Federal house on this property was of the same caliber, however, old, grand, and kept in meticulous order and condition. In the rear, a detached garage was set way back, and the butler proceeded right to it.

As the panels of the left bay retracted up their tracks and the van disappeared into the darkness, Lash perched on the top of the next-door neighbor's cupola. There was no way he was touching down on what potentially could be Brotherhood property, and the viewpoint was perfect, allowing him to see over the hedges that separated the two parcels while staying totally out of the way.

After the garage was shut back up, he waited. And waited. And . . . waited.

No butler. Was there an underground tunnel access to the house?

Studying the manse's structure, he noted the three floors, the kitchen in the back, the gracious, fenced-in yard that was planted with some really good, well-tended-to fruit trees. Unsurprisingly, there were monitoring cameras set under the eaves of the roof, the units discreetly hidden in the architectural details, and he was willing to bet there were more inside. On that note, all of the windows were unshuttered, only drapes pulled in some of the rooms, but that didn't mean there weren't interior fittings for the daylight barriers that were absolutely necessary for vampire homes—and especially common in a place like this, where there had been so much money invested into things.

From what he could see, no one was moving around inside, and he eyed the roof of the garage for a different vantage point—

The butler came out of a side door located under the stairs to the outbuilding's second story. Giving his black uniform a tug at both sleeves, he walked briskly to the rear door of the main house, in a manner that belied his aged appearance. Using a key—that had to be copper—he let himself in and shut things up.

Nobody else appeared to be on the property.

Surging with a hunter's instinct, but not as juiced as he'd been when he'd seen his enemy's protectors in the flesh, Lash was able to obscure himself and drop down to the neighbor's grass so he could walk over the property line. Passing through one of the gaps in the black wrought iron fence, he got an unobstructed view of some of the windows of the first floor: The butler was washing something in a sink, his body tilted forward as he appeared to be scrubbing at a pan or perhaps a large platter.

No, it was a pan. And he set it in the rack when he was finished—but did not leave it there. The ancient male went for a dish towel, dried the thing, and put it away under a gas cooktop.

He spoke to no one. No one came in to interact with him. Nobody appeared to be in any of the other rooms.

So did the butler live here? Like . . . it was his private residence? Impossible. A traditional *doggen* wouldn't stand for that. They would have to be with their master, and besides, this was far too grand a place.

This *had* to be one of the Brotherhood houses, the fighters hiding in plain sight, just like Lash's "parents" had done . . . just like the owners of that Tudor who had lost a young to a rogue *lesser*.

So whose estate was this? Not the King's. No way. The First Family would be in something far more removed, far better defended than this. Lash, after all, had been in the Brotherhood's training center. That place had been a state-of-the-art fortress, and Wrath's crib would be nothing less.

But that didn't mean this wasn't a property owned by one of them, and maintained by a trusted *doggen* . . . who had the keys to all the other houses.

And who knew where his true master stayed.

Studying the butler through the windows, Lash knew that he had a good hundred pounds on the *doggen*, and then there were the tricks of his trade as the Omega's son.

He stepped forward and remained invisible, making a slow circuit of the house's perimeter. As he stared through into a parlor with a massive oil painting of a French aristocrat, the layout of the rooms was as he expected it—and though he hadn't noticed it at first, he now saw a subtle distortion in the panes of the old blown glass: Every one of them was covered with a fine steel mesh, and he was willing to bet there were sheets of it inside all the walls, across every ceiling, embedded in the foundation itself.

A surge of triumph and purpose was a heady buzz as he rounded the corner to the front. But then . . . he peered into what should have been the females' drawing room. All mansions from this era had one, so that the males could retire after Last Meal to cigars and talk of serious matters, while the fairer sex nattered on elsewhere about gossip and jewelry.

The room on the left as one entered the house was in the correct location for après-meal chatter of the feminine variety, the walls painted a lovely lemon, the pastoral oil paintings intended to soothe and provide a suitably subtle background to the true beauty of the chatelaine and her guests. But instead of dainty silk love seats and maybe a marble-topped console table or two, there were matching chairs all around the periphery against the walls. And that wasn't the only oddity. A desk—not an antique one, but a modern sort, with a computer and a phone on its blotter—was set just inside the archway.

Like it was a waiting room.

Continuing across the front lawn, he stopped again and peered into a long, narrow room kitted out with sideboards, a chandelier the size of a car, and enough carved wooden molding to qualify the square footage as a sculpture. But where was the dining room table? Things were obviously set up for the serving and consumption of food, especially given the flap door in the back right-hand corner. The weird thing was, the whole space was vacant except for two armchairs in front of the hearth and a desk set with leather-bound books.

He thought of the waiting area.

Was it possible . . . that this house was used by the great Blind King to meet with his subjects? Why else would it be set up like this?

It wasn't like there was a dentist chair up by that fireplace.

Could this mansion be the key to what he really wanted: Death of Wrath, son of Wrath. Destruction of the Brotherhood.

And dominion over all vampires.

The last part of his credo shocked him, because that hadn't been part of his original playbook. Yet now, as he stared into this fine home, he realized that, unlike his true father, he didn't want to destroy the species for destruction's sake, in the fulfillment of some private battle over creation.

He pictured himself in that mansion he had seen with the realtor who had talked too much and had a bad facelift.

No . . . he rather thought, considering everything . . . he should like to rule the vampire world.

The bolt of purpose that went through him was so vibrant, so powerful, he got hard, the impulse downright sexual in its intensity. And he rode the wave of power and focus back to where he had started his promenade, by the rear entry.

The butler was leaning into the refrigerator, putting something in. Maybe taking it out.

The solution to the unknowns about the precise utility of this incredible discovery was simple: He could just borrow the butler for a little while. And after he got his information? Well, things could just as easily be erased, couldn't they.

A little Trojan horse in the mix. Just in a penguin suit.

How positively Homer-ific.

The Greco-Roman, not the Groening.

Cupping his hand to his mouth, he called out, "Fritz."

The *doggen* instantly straightened and looked to the back door.

When Lash repeated the name, the servant, ever loyal, ever prepared to be helpful, went to the rear entry . . .

And opened it.

❖ ❖ ❖

"Right through here."

Standing back from a collection of boulders the size of small houses and sheds, Lassiter indicated the passageway that was in their midst. He also lit the fire down in the cave with his will so that Rahvyn had a light source to follow.

"Thank you," she murmured.

She ducked down even though she had plenty of headroom, and he double checked the vicinity before following along. There was nothing moving in and among the pines, no scents on the air, no sounds except for the wind as it whistled through countless boughs. Indeed, the mountain was quiet in the moonlight, and he decided he was going to take her out to the summit clearing at some point, so she could see the valley.

But not right now. Falling in behind her wake, he had to turn sideways to fit his shoulders, and there wasn't all that far to go before the cave presented itself as an open area created by a stroke of nature-luck, the confines established by a random fall of enormous rocks that just happened to leave a nice, cozy living space beneath them.

Well, there had been some *Town & Country* comfort added, of course.

"Oh, this is so . . . warm," Rahvyn exclaimed as she went to the smokeless fire and put her palms out. "And luxurious."

"The latter is a Fritz thing."

Rubbing her hands together, she investigated the bedding platform that had been made up with Egyptian cotton sheets, a cloud-worthy comforter, and pillows that were soft as a summer breeze. There was also a table and two chairs, and fine china and glassware. A candelabra. A battery-run mini-fridge. A storage box packed with nonperishables and bread.

How Fritz had the time and energy to do everything he did was a mystery.

"There's an escape hatch behind there." He pointed to a tapestry that had been hung up with hooks pounded into the rock. "It's another passageway that penetrates deep into the mountain. So there are options during the day if something uninvited was to show up."

Pivoting, she met his eyes over the fire. "Can you go out into the daylight?"

"I have to regularly, as a matter of fact."

He went over to the bed, intending to plump the pillow he'd used so that the imprint of his fat head didn't ruin the look of it. Except then he decided to leave things as is because he didn't want to seem like he was taking for granted that she was staying over day—or that horizontal was where they were going to end up.

"Does it recharge you in some manner?" she asked as she bent to check out some books on a mahogany shelf. "Oh, my, I do not recognize these authors, I'm afraid. Sue Grafton? There is an alphabet of them. Lisa Gardner. Steve Berry."

"Yes, on the sun. And I'm not a big reader, I'm afraid. Now, if there were a TV . . ."

Well, he'd still be watching her, wouldn't he.

As she took one of the novels out from the lineup, she had to tuck her hair behind her ear, and he loved the way a little frown of concentration appeared between her brows as she fanned through the pages.

"I was never much of a reader myself." She glanced over. "Father insisted I learn, however. Many females in my era were not so lucky. The disadvantage to them was substantial."

"What happened to your parents?"

"They are in the Fade." Her gaze dropped back down to the words, but he'd have bet she didn't see anything on the page. "They were left for dead by *lessers*. My cousin, Sahvage, was tasked with overseeing me, and it was a role he fulfilled very well." She paused. And then shook her head with a sadness that pierced his heart. "It was not his fault I was captured. He told me to run, you see. When the aristocrat's guards came for me . . . Sahvage screamed at me to run, but I knew they were after me, not him. I thought if I stayed where we were, if he was the one to flee instead of defending me, then at least one of us would survive. In the end, however, we both came through."

"And you did to him what you did to Nate."

She nodded and replaced the book. "That was how he knew to ask me the night Nate was killed."

There was a subtle hesitation about her, a fiddling with her hands. Then she turned to him.

Her face in the firelight was a different kind of eternity altogether, something that was, to him, so beautiful that it was as if he had memories of looking at her that spanned his whole life.

"I'm glad you suggested coming here," he said hoarsely.

"The clinic is wonderful. But not . . ."

"Private."

Rahvyn nodded. And then her voice deepened. "I truly have this strange sense that time is running out. I cannot shake it." As he cocked a brow, she shrugged. "I find myself wondering what would have happened if you had not come out and found me in that field earlier."

"I would have kept looking for you." He shook his head. "I wasn't leaving things like that between us. No way. Even if you didn't want to be around me, I had to apologize."

"I am glad you sought me out." She smiled a little. "You took a gamble and won."

"I just wanted to go back to a moment I didn't fuck up. Get some inspiration, you know."

There was another pause from her. "I can think of another time you didn't . . ."

"Mess up?"

"Yes." She laughed. "That verbiage is a bit more my style."

When her face grew serious once again, the air between them changed, thickening with an anticipation that he prayed he wasn't misinterpreting. But he'd already put his foot in his mouth once tonight. He had no intention of making things epically worse by reading her wrong and throwing a pass at—

Rahvyn went over and touched the soft bedcoverings, her fingertips running over the duvet that had been folded up at the foot of the platform's mattress. "I feel better that I told you . . . everything."

"Me, too."

"It is more honest that way." She glanced back at him. "To keep my deeds from you is a kind of manipulation."

"I'm still here—"

"Did you mean what you said. Did you *truly* mean what you said unto me."

Lassiter nodded. "Yes, I did. I love you."

"Even with all that I—"

"I'm not afraid of you, Rahvyn." He shook his head again. "If that's what you're worried about."

"Sometimes . . . I feel as though all I do is worry. And I am afraid of you, you know."

Jerking back in surprise, he looked around. Which was dumb. Like there was someone else she was talking to? "Why? I'm not going to hurt you. I might be an idiot from time to time, but—"

"I love you, too," she whispered. "That is why you scare me."

CHAPTER THIRTY-SEVEN

As Vishous, son of the Bloodletter, stepped out of the mourning family's mansion, he had a thought that he was going to need to go back and retrieve the gurney at some point. Not that it really mattered. Who the fuck cared about a piece of equipment, given the circumstances.

Still, he was thinking that that *mahmen* and sire weren't going to want the thing kicking around their basement somewhere, considering the memories attached to it.

As he took out a hand-rolled to light up, he glanced back at Rhage, who was just emerging.

"We left the gurney," the brother said.

"Was just thinking that." V put the cigarette in his teeth, but he left his lighter where it was, in his ass pocket. "I sure as shit wasn't going to ask them for it."

"No, me neither."

Tohr joined them. "You guys talking about the gurney?"

"Yup."

"Uh-huh."

Behind them, the door was shut softly by a *doggen* whose eyes were so swollen, you had to wonder how he saw anything at all, much less a brass doorknob. The other fighters who had come to pay their respects had already left to go back to the Brotherhood mansion, and not just because the long night was grinding to an end and Last Meal was getting organized: Wrath was looking for a report, and once condolences had been shared, they'd gone along to update the King.

"That poor kid," Rhage said as he ran a hand through his blond hair. "Wrong place, wrong time."

Tohr stayed silent on that one. Then again, he'd lost his Wellsie and unborn son in a similar situation, regular life turning into a goddamn nightmare at the drop of a hat. The turn of a car wheel. The choice of one club over another.

V checked the time on his phone. "We gotta go."

As the other two nodded, they all dematerialized. When they re-formed, it was just up the street about a quarter of a mile, at the Audience House—

The second Vishous resumed his corporeal form, his instincts started firing and he palmed one of his guns.

Fritz, who, like him, always checked this place at the

end of the night, was standing frozen in the open doorway into the kitchen, his foot poised on the top step like
he was about to leave . . . his attention fixated on the
hedgerow on the far side of the driveway.

"Get back in the house," V barked. "Right now."

The servant snapped to attention, like he was coming out of a trance, and as he'd been trained, immediately shot inside. Two seconds later, the shutter protocol
was engaged, everything locking down.

That fucking *doggen* was a star.

V slowly scanned the driveway, and then looked out
to the street beyond. As Rhage and Tohr both outed
weapons, Tohr spoke softly into his earpiece.

A moment later, three other brothers came on scene.
No one moved.

Spitting out the hand-rolled, V flared his nostrils.
No scent anywhere. Nothing moving on the property.

Somewhere to the east, a dog barked, and then the
wind swirled by, carrying the smell of fertilizer like
some gardener had started prepping for annuals planting. A car passed by out on the street, heading deeper
into the neighborhood. Then another car approached—

And stopped at the end of the driveway.

Its turn signal started flashing, after which the tiny,
road-legal-for-no-good-reason Matchbox entered onto
the narrow stretch of pavement that led right up to
Vishous.

The gray-and-black Mini Cooper came to a halt, and
the sound of its passenger's side window getting put
down seemed loud as a scream.

Eddie, the fallen angel, stuck out his head. "You still okay with us parking here while we're gone?"

V glanced around. "Yeah."

"You sure about that?" The angel's brows went up. "Because if it's really a 'yes,' I think you need to lower your weapon and take a step back out of the way?"

With a nod, V got his reverse on, but he kept his gun right where it was.

When the proverbial coast was clear in front of the Mini, Eddie put his window up, and the pocket-sized vehicle was piloted so it went grille in to the left bay of the garage. Then the engine was killed.

The two angels both got out—and V knew exactly when they keyed into the disturbance. They went statue, and swiveled their heads around to stare across at him.

It felt like an eternity, all of them static in their boots, so many weapons up, nobody moving their bodies, everyone's eyes roaming over the house and yard. At least Fritz was well off the property by now. Per protocol, the butler would have gone down to the subterranean bedchambers, hit the escape tunnel, and proceeded underground.

He should be three estates over to the east at the moment, getting into a bulletproof Range Rover and driving away—

All at once, the warning sensation was gone. Sure as a light was extinguished when power was lost, so was the cutoff that distinct: Here. Gone.

Binary.

And they all felt it at once, tension easing in shoulders, Adrian the angel muttering a curse of relief.

Except no one seemed to be able to recognize what the presence had been.

V went over to the back door. Putting his forefinger on a discreet keypad, he disengaged the lock, opened the way in, and peered into the kitchen. It was weird to check out the all-normal, the counters free of clutter and wiped off, the cabinets shut tight, none of the burners on the stove sporting flames.

He felt like the Audience House was now a mess, everything ransacked like a robbery had taken place.

Entering, he swept his gun left to right, even as he realized that was stupid. For bullets to work, even the ones he had in his magazine, ones that carried not just lead but water from the fountain in what had been his *mahmen*'s private quarters, you had to have a physical target to shoot at.

There was none that he could see.

At the pantry, he back-flatted himself and reached out to push open the door. Willing the lights on inside, he popped his head around the jamb.

Nothing but commercially canned goods, homemade jars of preserved peaches, boxes of pasta, and bags of flour, sugar, and coffee.

As he continued on through the meal staging area and into the dining room, all of the other brothers went out the far side of the kitchen, proceeding down the hall that led to the front entrance, foyer, and staircase. He tracked their progress through the creaking of old floors, just as he knew they were doing the same for his footfalls.

The dining room was empty.

Everything where it should be.

He strode across the great Persian rug to the partially open double doors. Peering through them, he saw Rhage working the waiting area like it was a crime scene, those baby blues assessing everything.

When he and Hollywood reconvened at the front door, John Matthew and Qhuinn came out of the back parlor and held up a closed fist for "clear." V did the same.

Tohr was the one who went upstairs, but he wasn't alone. Sahvage dematerialized up ahead of him, reforming on the top landing.

As Rhage looked over, the question in that brilliant aqua stare wasn't something V could answer.

He had no fucking clue what that had been out there.

Or whether, when it had seemed to disappear, it had gone into this house or not.

CHAPTER THIRTY-EIGHT

Rahvyn surprised herself as she spoke the three most powerful words in any language.

And yet saying "I love you" to Lassiter had seemed inevitable, in a way.

In fact, all of this suddenly felt inevitable, from her having been honest with him to them being alone together in this cave, the world so far away. His acceptance of her had offered her an unexpected healing, and she was going to embrace the relief from pain she had not been aware of harboring.

There were other things she wanted to embrace, too.

As if he read her mind, he came around to her, his big body shifting with power, his eyes hooded and hungry. She knew what was going to happen next—and not because she was looking into the future in some prescient way. Lifting her chin, meeting his beautiful, unusual eyes, she knew what else was inevitable.

Their kiss was chaste yet firm, a sealing of the commitment they'd entered into when she had given back to him the words he had first expressed to her, her syllables the turn of the lock that she knew, deep down inside of her, would bind them for their immortal lives.

Lassiter eased away a little. Then he stroked her hair, his eyes roaming around her face.

"Please," she said, before he asked the question.

"We don't have to do this."

"Yes," she whispered, "we do."

There was no going back now, and even if she had a chance to reverse this fall, she did not want to—and certainly her consent was the center of gravity for them, the thing that presently pulled them down onto the soft bed, his body moving on top of hers, his hair falling around her in a shimmering wave with shadowed undertones.

Now, as he kissed her, there was true passion. His lips caressed hers with heat and intent, his tongue licking into her mouth, as she arched into his chest and spread her legs—

She cried out as he came to rest right where she needed him to be, his hard length once again pressing into her warm, wet core. Rolling her hips, she stroked herself against the arousal that told her exactly how much he, too, wanted this—and then her hands were finding a way under the loose blue top he'd put on what felt like a lifetime ago. And although he could easily have disappeared what covered him, like her, he seemed to want to enjoy the gradual unveiling at her own doing, his torso pulling back as he lifted his arms to help her get it off the old-fashioned way.

His upper body was extraordinary in the firelight, his muscles flexing and releasing as he tossed the cotton away, a cloud the color of a bright daytime sky from her pretrans youth. Turning back to her, his face became fierce as he balanced himself on his forearms.

"What is it?" she said as she stroked her way up his ribs.

When he shook his head, she was having none of that. "You will tell me. Now."

Closing his eyes, he seemed to grit his teeth. "I want to kill that male who hurt you. Even though you already did. And that is the last thing either of us needs to be talking or even thinking about at this moment."

"Lassiter. *Lassiter*, look at me." As those lids opened, she touched his face. "Just because I can take care of myself doesn't mean that I do not appreciate you wanting to be there for me. It is a lovely gesture."

"I don't want to think about the past."

"So kiss me some more and let's put it far away from our present, where it belongs."

There was a moment of hesitation on his part, and then he seemed to gather himself. His lips were very light on hers when they returned—but they didn't stay that way. Soon enough, he was kissing her with heady desperation, and as she dug her grip into his hard shoulders, she did not think they could get closer.

Yet she needed that—

The world spun without warning, and suddenly

their places were reversed, she above him, his body the thing on which she lay.

"Take your clothes off," he said in a guttural way. "I want to watch."

Sitting upright on his hips gave her a shot of pure pleasure, his hardness digging into her sex to the point where both of them moaned. And then she was grabbing the hem of her sweater—oh, how efficient: The shirt she was wearing underneath rode up with the knitted cables, going along for the ride. There was a slow-up when she got to her head, her hair getting tangled, her arms twisted, the cowl neck becoming caught on her chin.

As she wriggled to get free, his hands gripped her hip bones and he started to move rhythmically against her, that rigid shaft of his pushing into her so that she lost track of what she was doing and why.

"Rahvyn . . ."

Whilst she tugged at the hold of her clothing, broad hands circled her waist and went farther, until the twin weights of her bare breasts were cupped. That was the clarifier she needed. Finishing what she had started, she yanked the layers off and let them drop to the carpet that covered the cave's dirt floor.

Lassiter's eyes were on her, and then his hands were all over her, caressing, exploring.

And finally, he pulled her nipples down to his mouth.

Now his lips . . . were on her.

As the pleasure ran through her, Rahvyn gave herself up to the waves of heat. In the back of her mind, she realized that this space they were creating, not merely by their isolation in the cave, but by what they were doing with their bodies, was like the netherworld where she had sequestered the Book. This was an alternate reality, one that was impenetrable for its duration, the sensations a boundary that none and no one could break through, the powerful heat burning through her, through him . . . and yet causing no pain.

Magic, she thought.

This was magic and why it was true:

I love you were indeed the most powerful three words in any language.

♦ ♦ ♦

Lassiter wanted to slow it all down. But with half of Rahvyn's clothes off, and the tip of her breast in his mouth, and his hands on her body, and her thighs once again parting for him . . .

He was a fucking freight train.

She was right with him, though, clutching his shoulders, arching into his lips, her scent blooming in the cave until all he could smell was her. And God, even though this had been the position Devina had favored most, there was no confusion.

He knew exactly who was riding him—and that was why he'd put Rahvyn on top. Though the demon would never know it, he felt a surge of triumph that the abuser was not the master of him or his body any longer.

"Please," Rahvyn groaned. "I want you . . ."

As he let himself fall back, her nipple popped out of

his mouth, and holy fuck, she was on the verge of unhinged, her hair a tangle from her writhing on the pillow, her breath coming in a pant, her fangs descended from a hunger that had nothing to do with blood.

And everything about him coming inside of her.

As he was well aware of exactly what she wanted, he might have been tempted to tease them both some more. But not this time. No, the teasing and the begging would come later.

Rolling them once again, he kept his weight only partially on her, and had to grit his teeth in frustration as his erection went in the wrong direction, away from her core—and his hand trembled as he went for the button on her jeans. When her head jerked up, he froze in case he'd alarmed her.

"Yes . . ." she said. "Please . . . take them off."

Yes, ma'am, he thought to himself as he went back to work.

To get at the zipper properly, he had to sit up, which was good because he could take her jeans down her—

Fuck.

She wasn't wearing underwear.

As he froze, she flushed. "I am sorry, but I do not have proper undergarments upon myself. I had no clean—"

"Are you kidding me? This is the sexiest goddamn thing I've ever seen."

Her abrupt laugh made her breasts bounce, and talk about spoiled for choice. There was so much he wanted to explore on her body, so many things he wanted to do, but at least they had time—

Or do we, he thought with a shot of dread.

Eddie and Adrian had better keep that promise.

As he started to tug at her jeans, the going was tough, those creamy thighs of hers getting better and better looking the farther down he drew the denim— and in the end, he decided that, however efficient disappearing clothes was? This was better.

The torture just made the sex more intense.

And then she was naked, the soft comforter puffing up around her body, the firelight over her skin and her platinum hair, her innocent sensuality making him feel more male than anything else ever had.

"What about you," she whispered as she looked at the bulge in the front of his scrubs.

"Are you sure?" he said harshly. "I can stop now . . . but there's a point of no return."

Of course he would never do anything to her that she didn't want, but an orgasm was already right at the tip of his cock—and that was something he would not be able to control for much longer.

"Very, very sure," she said as she nodded. Then she licked her lips, like she wanted to—

Nope, he couldn't think like that. Not while he got up onto his knees in front of her. He was liable to come all over himself—and he wanted to save it for filling her up. On that note, he looked down his bare chest to the tie that was earning every bit of its keep trying to prevent a structural breach that would get him arrested for public obscenity if he were anywhere else.

More with the hand shaking now as he futzed around with the bow and the knot under it—and then the tie was loose and the waistband was going lower—

Well. There you have it.

His erection broke out of confinement with a bobbing thrust that absolutely, positively, did not look like it was raising its hand to get called on in a master's class on erotica.

"I want to touch you again," she murmured. "Let me . . . touch you."

Before he could respond properly—on account of all the *OMG, she's going to touch me!!* going around in his brain—Rahvyn's hand circled his shaft—

Lassiter jerked his hips back and nearly cracked all of his molars. "I'm going to come."

"I know. I want you to."

He had to stay perfectly still on his knees after that, for a good minute—and yes, he looked like he was directing traffic, his arms out in front of himself like there was about to be a car crash. Meanwhile, his chest was pumping up and down, and didn't that not help anything at all: It created a sway at his hips.

"Come into me," Rahvyn said. "My love . . . come inside me."

Lassiter looked up at the arching ceiling of the cave, as if he could see the heavens. He'd never been one to worship the Creator—or even give Him much credence. But it was with utter reverence that he thanked the entity.

For this female.

When Lassiter once again mounted his female, he kept his hips off to the side and found her mouth. Even though he was, quite literally, panting for it, he forced himself to—

Without warning, she repositioned her pelvis, shifting over so that his sex was on hers, and the slick feel of her made something in his brain snap.

It was all instinct after that . . . reaching between their bodies, grabbing himself, putting his head on her. As she cried out his name, he nudged forward ever so slightly.

Rahvyn took it the rest of the way, a roll of her hips and a push of her lower spine making the penetration real. Looking into her face, he wanted to make sure there was no pain for her—and her tight expression was hard to read.

"Rahvyn?"

Her hands traveled down his body to his ass, and when she gripped him there and pulled forward, he followed her cue, sliding himself all the way home.

Her tight, slick, hot hold was a constriction he felt all the way through him, and he couldn't help it. He retreated in an achingly slow glide . . . and slid back in, all the way . . . inside of her . . .

The scent of tears panicked him, horror turning the tables on his passion, taking his hot need for her to an icy cold regret—

"I am sorry," she mumbled as she started to shake.

"Oh, God, Rahvyn, I'm withdrawing—"

"*No.*"

At her sharp command, he stilled. Not knowing what to do for the best, he watched helplessly as she brushed under her eyes.

"I'm not crying because it hurts," she said hoarsely. "I'm crying . . . because this is how it should have been for my first time. With you."

CHAPTER THIRTY-NINE

I deally, they would be doing this one-on-one.

Back in the Brotherhood's mansion, up in the pale blue study that had been decorated for dandies, as opposed to a bunch of males of war, Wrath was sitting on his sire's throne and praying like hell that the collection of hotheaded fighters, who were testing the structural integrity of all that antique French furniture, would for once—just once, in their ever-loving lives of aggression and territoriality—shut the *fuck* up.

"No, Fritz," he said in a voice that was, for him, pretty fucking calm, "you're not in trouble. I just want to know what happened, that's all."

The silence that followed was not good news—and neither was the scent floating over. The *doggen* was careening into an ocean of self-admonishment and guilt, and if he drowned in it, there was no amount of self-esteem-boosting CPR that was going to bring him back.

"Fritz." He sat forward on the throne. "Listen to me. Like I said, you didn't do anything wrong, but it's a real problem if you don't talk to me. Don't think about all of them. Just talk to *me*."

To emphasize the point—like he really needed a "Hello, my name is . . ." badge?—he put his dagger hand over his heart.

In the quiet that persisted, he pictured Fritz in the study. Though he couldn't see anything anymore, he re-membered the layout of the room from when Darius had once guilted him into coming for a tour shortly after the building had finally come to a conclusion and all the fur-niture and stuff had been moved in. The mansion had been constructed to house the Brotherhood and their mates, a goal that no one, except for Darius, had ever thought would be realized—so Wrath, for a whole host of reasons, hadn't paid a lot of attention to the decor, all of which was top-notch old crap, and lots of damask this and satin that, and oh, hey, yeah, let's hang some more crystals from everything because, by all means, the three hundred thousand pounds ya currently got ain't enough.

Of all the spaces, he did remember this particular one clearly, however—not just from that specific night, but from when he'd moved in and had a little sight left—the Versailles furniture and pale blue walls something Darius had taken pride in for some unknown reason. He'd chided the brother that it was better suited for a knitting circle than anything involving real business.

Because he'd been a prick.

God, if he'd only known then that not only was that fighter right—life was better and safer with them all under one roof—but that he himself, as a properly serving King, would be regularly convening meetings of the Brotherhood in the aforementioned powder blue, knit-one-purl-two four walls and a ceiling ... maybe he wouldn't have been such a jackass.

In any event, he could picture exactly where all the furniture was orientated, where the brothers and fighters were sitting or standing or pacing—even knew the position of the two angels who, given what they'd likewise sensed at the Audience House, had seemed like a value add and worthy of trust.

Fuck, even Boo approved of the pair, and that cat—who wasn't really a cat—was pickier than Butch choosing a new suit of clothes.

And with all of that in his mind, Wrath also knew where his *doggen* head of household was standing on the other side of the great carved desk. He could scent the elderly male's nearly paralytic worry, the disappointment, the crushing concern that he had not protected the sanctity of his master's property.

This was the thing about *doggen*. They had to be handled carefully.

And when kid gloves didn't work, you had to fall back on the one constant that always would: "Fritz, it is your duty to speak to me. I therefore command you to do so right now."

Annnnnnnd cue one hell of a monologue deluge.

"Sire, forgive me, I should not have departed the back of the Audience House as I—"

"Don't be ridiculous," V cut in. "You have every right to walk out of that house anytime you want—"

Wrath shot a death glare across the space, and for once, Vishous took the fucking hint.

"Go on," Wrath prompted. "Don't worry about them. Just tell me what happened."

There was a clearing of the throat and some shuffling of clothing, and Wrath imagined the butler tugging the cuffs of his starched sleeves down. "Verily, I had entered the property to return the van from its very sad duty. After parking in the garage, I tidied some things on the workbench and then I proceeded to go unto the house. After letting myself in with the key, I was upon the kitchen, ensuring that all was in preparation for the shift of pastry chefs to come the following afternoon." The old male took a deep breath. "Having ensured there were sufficient provisions, I intended to walk through the house to make certain it was properly closed up for the daylight . . . but then I heard my name being called out on the drive. I assumed that . . . well, I thought perhaps I was needed by one of you all. I proceeded unto the door, opened it—and I just felt rather frozen. Directly at that moment, all and sundry arrived and—"

"Wait, did you see anything?"

"No, my Lord, I did not." There was a shifting of clothes, as if he were bowing. "And there was a sufficiency of light. Naught was there in the drive or anywhere about in the backyard. As soon as Vishous gave me the order, I jumped back into the house, initiated the shutter protocol, and removed myself from the vicinity, utilizing the underground passageway."

"Good, you did the right thing," Wrath praised.

"Verily, I did endeavor to execute the evacuation procedure as it had been explained unto me." When there was a pause, Wrath imagined that Fritz was bowing in V's direction. "After I rushed forth through the escape tunnel, I arrived at the remote garage three estates over, and I did drive away in the Range Rover. I would have returned here right away, but we had a shortage of heavy cream and that was important to rectify for Last Meal."

Behind his wraparounds, Wrath closed his eyes. The butler's life was worth so much more than whatever the hell he'd picked up at Hannaford, but he wasn't going to point that out. For one, if you ever showed any affection toward the guy, he was liable to need a crash cart to recover. For another, the current shame spiral was plenty for one night. If he criticized the side trip, suggested it would have been better for Fritz to just come right back here?

Total molecular breakdown.

"You did well." Wrath held up his palm. "And I don't want you to think of it again."

"But of course, my Lord," the butler said weakly.

"That's another order, Fritz. You put it all out of your mind. You did nothing wrong, and this is over. Am I clear enough?"

"Yes, my Lord."

There was another pause, and as Wrath pictured the elderly butler bending at the waist, he flared his nostrils and breathed in deep—and then he just . . . felt the energy rolling off the *doggen*.

Fritz hadn't lied. Thank fuck. Not that the butler would have done so intentionally, but V had been adamant something had been on that property, and therefore things had to be objectively assessed.

"You may be excused," Wrath murmured.

"Thank you, my Lord. May I bring anyone a libation? Or perhaps an hors d'oeuvre? I will be holding Last Meal until I am informed your meeting is over."

"Thank you, Fritz. That is just perfect."

◆ ◆ ◆

Standing with Ad just inside the fancy study, Eddie watched the old guy in the tuxedo bend so far down, it was like he was inspecting the carpet for missing threads. Then the butler went to leave, his shuffling stride taking him to the door, his head angled to the floor as if he felt like he'd ruined everything, and not even a direct order from his master could make him stop rehashing it all.

The whole situation kind of made you feel sorry for him—hell, even the King over there, sitting on his throne like something out of a Mad Max movie, had clearly been choosing his words carefully around the guy.

And not because his royal grand pooh-bah'dness was worried about some kind of argument. More like he hated to see the butler cry, and if he pushed too hard, he was worried about a Kleenex event the likes of which even *Bambi* and *Old Yeller* put together couldn't level up.

As the poor old guy reached the door, Eddie tilted to the side to open it for him—

An enormous blond mountain stepped in and blocked the exit, Eddie's hand getting slapped back by a carton of mint chocolate chip ice cream.

The Brother's headshake and bugged eyes were as clear a set of nonverbal cues as Eddie had ever seen, and as he flashed his palms in an I-don't-get-it, the butler opened the door for himself and slipped out of the room.

The blond vampire then motioned around the assembled with an ornate silver spoon. "Jesus, you guys. You should have asked for a drink or two. Or at least let him bring a Brie or something."

"And you could have asked for hot fudge," the one who always smoked muttered from a love seat.

"Fair enough," Rhage said as he leaned back against the door. Poking his ice cream with his spoon, he frowned. "Well, crap. Actually, now I want fudge."

The big boy on the throne popped up those black wraparounds and rubbed his eyes like he had the business end of a clawhammer in his frontal lobe. "Enough with the food. So where are we?"

"We searched the grounds and the house," the calm vampire directly to the right of the King said—Tohrment was his name. "There was nothing we could see."

Vishous, the smoker, added, "And I checked the security feeds. Nothing in the drive or on the lawn. Fritz did what he said he did. He was in the kitchen, he looked out the window, like someone had called his name. He exited the back door, glanced across—and we arrived."

"You're sure nothing was caught on video?"

"I looked at everything twice."

"But we all felt it," someone said.

When there was a grumble of agreement, somebody else chimed in, "There was a presence, like a person, standing there."

"Yet all we got was thin air," a third concluded.

"What about you two."

For an instant, Eddie didn't realize that the angels in the room were being addressed. But when no one else spoke, he swung his gaze back to the throne—come on, that *had* to be a throne, otherwise George R. R. Martin was missing one of his living room chairs.

"What did you males sense?"

Eddie glanced at Ad. When the guy nodded a g'head, Eddie put his hands in his pockets, all non-threatening, and took a step or two toward the center of the room. He wasn't going to get much farther—the furniture was delicate, but there was a lot of it, and the bodies were huge, with more than a dozen squeezed in together.

It was like wading through a defensive line trying to have a tea party. But at least no one was trying to tackle him.

Taking his hands out of his pockets, he looked around at the vampires. They were from different bloodlines, he thought they called them. Colorings were various, but body types were pro-wrestler without any of the fat, and all the intelligence was clear.

And then there was the King. Wrath seemed bigger

than the lot of them, and not just because of his size advantage.

Eddie thought of Lassiter. No wonder the rogue had come home to roost with these hard-ass guys.

And he wanted to get involved, too. He really did. It was just . . .

"I didn't sense anything. I'm sorry."

Turning away, he caught the one with the goatee narrowing his diamond eyes—and nearly said, *Well, what the hell do you want me to do. We don't belong here and we have to go*—

"You're lying."

Eddie froze. Looked over his shoulder.

The King had lowered his chin, and holy fuck, for a moment it was like Dracula was alive and well—and about to work some fang action.

Then the male touched the side of his nose. "I can smell it. You didn't lie when you first came to my home." That forefinger shifted away from the harsh face to point to the door the blond mountain was still leaning against. "Out there, in my courtyard. You were surrounded by my private guard, but you did not lie. What's changed."

Fucking hell, Eddie thought.

He pivoted back around. "I told you why we came. It's not to get involved with your business, it's to finish our own."

"As of tonight, the two can't be disentangled."

"Sure they can. All we did was leave our car by your garage down in town. With your permission."

"You have intel that is pertinent to that property. Tell me what it is, and you're free to go."

Eddie glanced back at the blond. "No offense to what he can bench-press, but your boy—or boys—aren't going to stop us."

"Oh, I'm aware you can leave right now." On that note, the blond made a gallant bow and stepped aside with his ice cream. "You'll just have to deal with your conscience. And given that you're immortal, you've got a long runway ahead of you to carry guilt-related baggage. Probably already have some weighing you down. More the merrier, though, right?"

"You don't know me," Eddie snapped.

As there was a collective growl around the room, like a pride of lions had woken up hungry all at once, the King made a dismissive swipe with his hand.

"Relax, ladies. The angel is just getting defensive because he doesn't like a stranger walking around the inside of his skull. And now he's going to take his little buddy and go out our front door. Maybe even return to that house of mine in town and squeeze into his car. Drive off—and pretend that not sharing material information with people who treated him with respect doesn't bother him because he's a fucking tough cookie."

Eddie muttered to himself. And then glanced at Ad.

When the angel just shrugged, all what-can-you-do, Eddie wondered why—*why*—everything on earth had to be such a G-D struggle. Three years of searching, they finally find Lassiter . . . and now this sh—

Stuff, he corrected.

"You know what it was," he said roughly to the males who had searched the house. "Why are you going to make me put a label on it."

None of them moved—which told him that they still had slim hope, very slim hope, that the conclusion they hadn't yet put into words would somehow remain invalidated. Provided no one talked about it.

Funny, he felt the same way.

"You fucking vampires," he muttered as he let his head fall back in defeat. "Why you gotta be like this."

"Can I shoot him?" someone asked. "Just on principle—"

"No," the King snapped. "You can't fucking shoot him. Fritz has enough going on tonight without having to shop-vac silver blood off the fucking carpet."

Well, excuse me if my arterial breach ruins your butler's night, Eddie thought.

"I bleed red, for one thing." He re-leveled his head, having found no cogent advice in the ornate ceiling. "And fine. I believe you call him the Omega. Ad and I know him by another name, but that doesn't matter for your purposes."

There was no argument from anyone. And the King didn't move a muscle, that face composed as a mask.

"That's not what you're really worried about, though, is it." Eddie nodded at the door. "The butler's fine. There's nothing in him that shouldn't be in there, in a spiritual sense. But I'll tell you this: If you hadn't showed up when you did?" He glanced at the goateed vampire, and then the other two who had been there first. "I can't imagine what would have happened."

"I let the cat check him out," Vishous added. "As

soon as Fritz pulled up in the Ranger Rover. Boo went right over to him. I figured he had to be okay."

"He is." Eddie inclined his head. "And if the evil had tampered with him in any way, I would know. I've seen it before, and no matter how cleverly disguised, I always know. So does that feline, apparently."

The King's obvious relief broke through all that composure, and the guy leaned to the side and stroked his golden retriever's flank.

"See," Wrath said as he straightened. "That wasn't so bad."

Actually, it was. Because the goddamn long-haired, widow's-peaked bastard was right. Eddie's conscience *was* getting to him. For a bunch of tough guys, there was something about them that just made you want to roll up your sleeves and help row the frickin' boat.

Man, humans had it all wrong. The most dangerous thing about vampires wasn't the fangs. It was the codependency.

"That thing at your other house is true evil," he heard himself say.

"No shit," someone tossed back. "And here we thought it was Avon calling."

As the King shot a glare in the direction of the ass-slapper comedian, Eddie pulled himself together. "Ad and I really can't get more involved in this. We already have bad news to share with the Creator, and I am not looking for complications or another demotion."

"So leave." The King motioned to the door again. "And thank you for the intel."

Eddie stared them in the face, one by one—and the males stared back at him.

"Goddamn it, I have a job to do," he bit out.

The blond one stepped up, and for a split second, Eddie wondered whether there was going to be some kind of throwdown.

Instead of a punch, the vampire offered the ice cream, which was melting by the moment. "You can use my spoon if you want. I'll wipe it on my shirt."

"What are you talking about?" Eddie said.

"Here." The blond mountain forced the Breyers over, even as Eddie no-thank-you'd with his hands. "I just find when I have my ass in a crack, a nosh helps."

"You eat all the time," one of his cohorts pointed out.

The blond assiduously scrubbed the spoon with the tail of his black shirt. "True, but especially when I'm about to make a decision that I know is the right thing to do, but that I'm also aware will complicate the ever-living hell out of my situation. Ice cream is a total stress-reliever."

The vampire put out the spoon.

"I am not stressed"—Eddie snapped the thing from the guy's hand—"and I am *not* making any decision that will 'complicate my fucking situation,' thank you very much."

On that note, he fired up a heaping load of the ice-cold, creamy bullcrap—and shoved it into his mouth.

"Frickin'," he groused as he jabbed the spoon in for another round.

CHAPTER FORTY

Looking up into Lassiter's face, feeling a part of him deep inside her body, the sense of completeness was something Rahvyn had never experienced before. The idea that they had been two, but now were briefly this combined one, was so powerful, she knew she would never be the same again.

Like her first experience, this too was going to transform her.

And better her, in a different way.

"I can stop," he whispered.

What needed to stop was this stupid crying, she thought. She just had to pull herself together. Tears? In this situation? They were about as romantic as a broken leg, as sensual as a trip-and-fall.

"Never," she shot back.

Even though he was on top of her, she began to move, her hips pushing her buttocks into the soft mattress, then bringing them back up. Down. And up. Again . . . and again.

It wasn't much, but the friction was incredible—and suddenly, he was taking over and filling her so deep, and moving away, and filling her again. Before she knew it, there were no more tears, only pleasure, and whereas she thought she'd been at some kind of pinnacle, that there was no more sensation to be had, no more possible, nothing further she could contain within her body or her mind . . . he took her higher.

There was vigor now, and she only wanted more of him—and as if he sensed that, he grasped the back of one of her knees and moved it into an even tighter bend. Something about the angle changed—

"Lassiter?" she cried out, partially in fear—for she did not know what was going to transpire.

"Let yourself go," he groaned. "I've got you. You can trust me."

He continued to penetrate her, ever faster, ever deeper, and the cresting wave that was coming for her, inside her skin, seemed liable to swamp her rather than carry her forward. It was only Lassiter's voice in her ear, telling her she was safe, that—

And then it happened. Something broke, but the splintering was a glorious relief from the nearly intolerable pressure that she only wanted more of. As her core contracted in sequence, and the agonizing on-the-verge culminated, she felt a flying, soaring, sweet freedom.

That, rather than taking her away from the male who was loving her so fiercely, brought her closer than their physical bodies—

Abruptly, the rhythm changed again, the pumps becoming shorter and faster, Lassiter breathing hard now, as if he were running. After that . . . a growling in his chest.

Which was not threatening, more like he was exerting a self-control that was causing him pain.

"You can trust me, too," she whispered. "You can fly, too."

As if he'd been waiting for her to give him permission, his hips locked into her and she felt a kicking in her core. He was filling her up.

Just as she wanted him to.

"Don't stop," she begged as the twitching inside of her created a new and different friction. "Keep going."

Lassiter immediately resumed the ancient movements, and now, because she knew what to expect, as the curling need coalesced and began to build again, she let herself go with it—knowing that with him, she was safe.

+ + +

Lassiter lost count of the orgasms. All he knew was that as long as Rahvyn wanted more, he was going to give it to her—and that was not hard to do. Her sweet cries, the way she held on to him, her pleas and her releases, all of the sex was a grounding motivator for him.

When they were finally still, he rolled onto his side and took her with him. As she curled into his chest, she was warm and drowsy. So was he. His eyes closed and he let himself drift, listening to the crackling of the fire, feeling the softness of her body conform to the hardness of his own, scenting her arousal, which still lingered, thick and heady, in the cave's air.

He stroked her back. Murmured things, as if he were a poet, as if his words were worth anything more than the breath that carried them to her ear. In return, she replied in a similar way, her syllables too quiet to be heard, her meaning fully obvious to him.

"Will you stay the day with me?" he asked.

As he waited for her reply, he was aware of tension creeping up his spine and clawing him in the back of the head—

"There's nowhere else I want to be."

Lassiter smiled and opened his eyes. "Good."

He wanted to remember everything about this moment, the cave he had been indifferent to but now revered as a landmark, the gentle glow of the flames, the quiet chatter of the logs being consumed, the quiet sound of her breathing, a symphony.

The female in his arms, his forever.

Twenty-four hours, he thought.

"Rahvyn?" When a *hmm?* came back at him, he drew his fingers through a length of her hair. "Will you go on a date with me tomorrow? After nightfall?"

Her head lifted and her eyes opened. "A date?"

Nodding, he touched her chin, urging her in for a kiss. As their lips met, he said against her mouth, "It's where two people go somewhere, usually to eat and enjoy each other's company."

Her smile was innocent and sensual at the same time. "I rather am enjoying yours right now."

Laughing, he caressed her lower lip with the pad of his thumb. "Are you now?"

"I like it when you come inside of me—"

As he choked, she sat up in alarm. "Lassiter, are you well?"

"No, no—it's fine," he sputtered.

"Did I speak out of turn in some way?"

He slowly shook his head. "Nope, not at all. You just didn't warn me ahead of time you were paying me that kind of compliment."

"I am not being charming. It is the truth, I can feel you in me when you—" As he made the same noise again, she frowned and patted his arm. "You are sure I may speak as such?"

"Female, you talk like this all you want. I just have to be honest, it's having an effect—"

"Oh, I want to feel it."

Her hand burrowed between them, and he arched back as she wrapped a hold around his shaft.

"Is this too much?"

"No," he moaned as his hips instinctively punched forward.

"May I be on top this time?"

Lassiter opened his mouth. Closed it. Laughed. "You are . . . amazing."

By way of answer, he eased over on his back—and he was not prepared for the sight of her parting her glistening thighs across his hips and standing his erection up to her bare cleft. As she looked down at what she was doing, her hair fell forward in a gleaming platinum wave, and her breasts swayed, the nipples swollen from when he'd sucked on them, the creamy curves so full compared to her waist.

"Yes," she said huskily as she paused. "I should very much like to go on a date with you tomorrow. I accept your very kind invitation."

He stretched up and kissed her. "I am honored."

Her smile was pure happiness, so radiant it overshadowed the fire. Hell, it overshadowed the sun, as far as he knew.

And then she got a serious look on her face, like she was going to get to work. Hissing in a deep breath, he locked his molars in preparation for the—

She sat right on him. No gradual descent.

Impaled would have been another word.

With a moan, she arched back, and as all the oxygen in his lungs exploded out of him, he marveled at the sight of him buried in her core. And the view got even better as she figured out how to move, her lower body starting to swivel as she set the rhythm, those breasts swinging back and forth, his gleaming shaft appearing and disappearing inside of her.

Her eyes stared ahead briefly.

But then they locked on his . . . as they began to orgasm again.

Together.

With no one and nothing else welcome in the sacred space.

CHAPTER FORTY-ONE

I t was an earthquake.

That was what went through Beth's mind as everything in the whole world seemed to go haywire. In a panic, she threw out a hand for the lamp beside her mated bed—

"Wrath! What's going on?"

In the dim glow from the bathroom, she caught a pretty unforgettable image of her *hellren* springing out from under the covers, his enormous body contorted as if every muscle he had was charley-horse'ing at once. As he landed with absolutely no grace at all, the booming sound reverberated through the First Family's quarters, the jewels on the walls going into a sparkle as if he had rocked the very foundations of the mansion.

For a second, he stayed in a crouch, like a monster

under the bed was coming out to get them and he had to protect her. Then he wheeled around for the exit and took off.

Beth scrambled after him—and so did George, who bolted up out of his Orvis bed and four-paw'd at a dead run after his master.

"Where are you going? What's happening!" she exclaimed.

"I'm fine, it's fine, I'm fine—"

Wrath kept repeating the mantra as he broke out of their suite, hit the vault door like a wrecking ball, kept going down the staircase.

"You don't have any clothes on!"

He didn't seem to hear her or maybe he didn't care. At the base of the steps, he exploded onto the second floor loggia across from the study. Skidding on the carpet, he tore off along the Hall of Statues, passing the ancient Greco-Roman sculptures of athletes and warriors like one of them come to life, his black hair streaming behind him, his naked ass a money shot that nobody was really looking for at this hour of the day—

Crap, she probably shouldn't take note of how good his butt was, not in this situation.

As Wrath led the panic parade, with her and George bringing up the rear—natch—people's heads poked out of bedroom doors. Rhage. Qhuinn and Blay. Zsadist.

"It's fine," she said over her shoulder. In a strangled voice. "Everything is fine."

Wrath hit the double doors at the end of the corridor, and kept on going—to the unadorned hall of rooms on the left. Unlike the rest of the mansion, there were no paintings, no bouquets of fresh flowers on period console tables, not even any rugs, along its straight shot.

He stopped at the first set of quarters, and before he could knock, things opened up.

In his Charles Dickens nightshirt and cap, Fritz was alarmed to begin with, no doubt on account of all the noise, but when he saw his master, unclothed and disheveled as a wild man, his shock transformed into full-blown terror.

"Master! Whate'er—"

Wrath paid no attention to that. His hands started patting all around the *doggen*, going over Fritz's thin arms, his wrinkly neck, his sunken chest. Then Wrath popped that cap right off and tossed it, touching the butler's head as if he were searching for structural deficiencies, before moving on to the wrinkly face.

As he searched for God only knew what, the great black diamond he wore flickered in the low lighting—

Fritz gasped and covered his mouth with both hands.

At first, Beth had no idea what he'd seen in her *hellren*'s face, but then she realized . . . no wraparounds. Wrath never showed his eyes, ever, but in his rush, he had not stopped to put on the blacked-out sunglasses.

"Sire . . . ?" Fritz breathed, transfixed.

"Fuck." Wrath's body wobbled. "Fuck . . . you're okay. Shit."

That was when the collapse happened, the great

Blind King falling to his knees at the feet of his most loyal servant, his massive muscles bunching up as he bent over and struggled to keep his emotions—and maybe his stomach—in check.

"Sire . . ."

Fritz bowed down so he could see that harsh face, and when Wrath put his palms up and covered his features, the old *doggen* looked around as if searching for a rescue. He had plenty of spectators, all of the staff now out of their rooms and approaching cautiously, their distress obvious—and meanwhile, behind Beth, the Brothers were gathering, most of them in boxers, a couple in flannel PJ bottoms.

But there were no saviors.

Everybody was frozen, with no clue what was going on.

So Fritz did what a butler should. He dealt with the mess that was before him.

Though *doggen* eschewed physical contact with their superiors, for they deemed themselves—irrationally—as unworthy of such affection, Fritz brought forth shaking hands and gently placed them on the enormous bare shoulders of his King. Wrath clearly sensed the contact because heavy arms, tattooed on the inside with his ancient royal lineage, shot out and locked around Fritz's waist.

As the other servants came a little farther forward, Fritz nodded curtly.

On cue, the *doggen* of the household closed in, linking arms, forming a circle around their King, and there were so many of them, Beth had to inch back to give them space.

"George," she said, patting her thigh. "C'mere, baby boy. Come on."

The golden looked back and forth, clearly concerned he was needed in the mix, but when she shook her head, he obeyed the command, walking over and planting his butt on her bare foot as he faced out and kept an eye on his master.

All of the *doggen* wore the same white shifts, but the males had those caps and the females wore bonnets on their heads. Standing shoulder to shoulder, they formed an aura of adoration, insulation . . . and protection around Wrath.

Beth glanced back at the Brothers. A couple of them were wiping their eyes with quick swipes of their thumbs, all nah-I-ain't-cryin', it's-just-dust.

Even though Fritz, with all his high standards, would never allow such a thing, even in the servant wing of his house.

CHAPTER FORTY-TWO

As night fell on Caldwell, Shuli sat on the foot of his bed in his room at his parents' mansion and watched the shutters retract. With no lights on around him, the details of his chamber were muted to the point of disappearing, and his eyes sought the shapes and shadows of the gardens outside. Funny, how the familiar could look so different, so foreign.

There had been no sleep for him during the day. An endless reel of everything that had happened behind Dandelion—*lesser* attack trying to intervene fighting for control of the gun *pop!* The ox injured dying . . . death— had been a relentless battering, mental in origin, physical in effect. He felt sore all over.

Then again, maybe some of that was from wrestling with that slayer.

As yet another image of Theox going down at the back of the club speared through his brain, he covered his eyes. Which was stupid. What he was seeing was not in front of him—

The sound of a text hitting his phone was the last thing he was interested in. He'd been getting all kinds of DMs and shit throughout the day as word of what had happened spread. Everyone was touting him as some sort of hero, which was fucked up. Theox was gone, and the idea that Shuli now had some kind of war cred was obscene.

Flipping his phone over, he just wanted to clear the screen so he didn't have to look—

It was Nate.

Frowning, he went into his phone . . . and he had to read the message twice. And a third time.

The knock on his door was soft, and he twisted around. "Come in."

Probably a *doggen* with a tray from First Meal, not that he had any appetite—

It wasn't a *doggen*. Shuli's sire stood in the jambs, the illumination from the crystal-strung ceiling fixture behind Arcshuliae turning him into nothing more than a dense black hole that conformed to his body's distinguished outline.

Years of careful training came back as Shuli jumped up and made sure his hands were down at his sides.

"Sit, my son."

Collapsing his spine, Shuli fell back down onto the bed. As his father entered, he had a thought that he couldn't remember the last time the male had been in his room.

There was an awkward pause. "I am . . . checking upon you."

"Thank you, Father. I am well enough."

It was a *glymera* answer to a *glymera* question. And his sire acknowledged the response in the aristocratic fashion, inclining his head.

Then there was a clearing of the throat, but it was not a reprimand for once. "If you think you perhaps shall eschew First Meal, that would not be inappropriate."

Shuli inclined his head. "Thank you, Father."

His father inclined himself again. And wasn't this proof that *Princeps* families could have full-on conversations about tragic things using nothing but eyebrows and the occasional hand gesture.

"Very well, then." On that note, his sire turned away—

"Father," Shuli said as he burst up again.

As the male pivoted back around, Shuli slapped his hand on his phone and surged forward before he was aware of moving.

"*Father*," he repeated.

"Yes?"

Now it was his turn to go silent. Off in the distance, he heard strings playing and pictured the quartet that came in regularly for the hour before First Meal all set up in the corner of the red parlor downstairs. His *mahmen* and brother, his sister-in-law, and his three cousins would be there, all dressed formally, but not in tuxedos or gowns. That only came at the end of the night, at Last Meal.

Shuli lifted up his cell, even though the lock screen was showing. "I want to go into the Black Dagger Brotherhood training program. I just got a text from Nate. They want to talk to us about . . . coming in and learning. Things."

His sire tilted his head. "What manner of 'things.'"

Glancing down, Shuli blinked and was instantly there again, behind the club. "I want to learn how to fight, Father. In the war."

His sire's torso shifted back ever so slightly, which was the equivalent of anybody else screaming, *WHAT THE FUCK!*

"I know that you and I have always had our differences." Shuli noted his father's handmade alligator shoes for no good reason. "And until last night, I don't think I appreciated the message you've been trying to give me all along. I don't want to waste my life. I have everything I could ever need, and more than that, I have everything I could ever want. But I've been pissing it all away, haven't I. And too busy arguing with you to see the merit in what you were saying. I didn't sleep all day. I can't . . ." He grabbed the front of his monogrammed silk bathrobe. "I can't hold this feeling inside me. I need to let it out by doing something . . . worthwhile. Finally. And I want to fight in the war."

He exhaled long and slow and got ready for all kinds of frustration and resistance, the cash-and-carry of the way he and his father had been interacting for how long now? Years. He hadn't been quite as recalcitrant as the male believed, but he hadn't been anywhere near as justified as he himself had believed—and in any event, neither extreme mattered because they just couldn't relate. Even when they met in the middle. And so the cycle had ground on, separating them even further, relegating them into roles, him the ne'er-do-well, spoiled disappointment of a son, his sire the out-of-touch, demanding father, and never the twain should meet.

As his father opened his mouth, Shuli interrupted him. "Actually, wait." He drew in a deep breath. "I'm not asking you for permission to do this. I'm telling you, this is what I'm going to do. I'm going to learn how to defend people who can't defend themselves . . . against the enemy. And I'm going to be good at it, even if it kills me."

Long silence now. Or at least it felt that way.

Then his sire put out his palm.

For a moment, Shuli just stared at the thing, having no clue what it meant or why that arm was just hanging out there.

"Oh," he said with surprise.

Extending his own palm, he clasped what was offered.

"I am proud of you, son." His sire bent at the waist in a bow and spoke in the Old Language: "*You bring honor upon this bloodline, and pride within my breast. May you go forth and know that your family awaits your safe return. Always.*"

Shuli's throat got tight, and he bowed in return. "I

*shall endeavor to deserve your faith, Sire mine. I shall do
my level best."*

"Just be of care, my son," his father said urgently. "Be
safe."

The embrace happened spontaneously, and as Shuli
closed his eyes, he did not see the blood and death
anymore. He saw the image of his father's palm
extended across the divide between them, an accord
offered . . . and an accord struck when he put forth his
own.

"I'll do my best, Sire," he murmured over his father's
shoulder. "My very best."

CHAPTER FORTY-THREE

A *shower*, Rahvyn thought as she returned to the training center upon nightfall.

How lovely.

As she walked across a tiled floor, she was rather interested to find three separate berths, the trio kitted out with identical overhead faucets and crank handles—and in front of each was a small ante-area that, given the benches and the curtains that had been shuffled to the side, was obviously for changing one's clothes.

Glancing to the opposite wall, she noted the three sinks with shelves over them, perhaps for one's toothbrush. Overhead, the ceiling fixture had a cage around it, as if the builder had been concerned someone would be throwing a ball about and did not wish to risk the bulb getting broken; the walls were likewise in a hearty tile that would withstand much wear.

Everything was a dark gray and white.

"Here, I have some fresh clothes for you."

At the sound of Lassiter's voice, she pivoted and departed from the showering alcove. Out in the larger room of the facility, he had propped open the entry with his foot and thrust something through the crack, only his muscled arm showing.

Ah, yes, she thought as she recalled the symbol upon the door. They only allowed females herein.

"Oh, thank you," she said as she went to take the bundle from him.

He poked his head in and smiled. "I figured you'd want something a little more substantial than scrubs."

"Whomever do I owe for this," she murmured as she riffled through the fresh jeans, shirt, and fleece.

"Beth is awesome."

"Oh, how kind of her. Is there any chance that perhaps I could express my gratitude in person?"

"Absolutely. She headed back up to the big house, but when I'm there, I'll have her come down again." As his eyes sought hers, they dipped to her mouth—and with a flush, she knew exactly what he was thinking of. "I'm sorry I've got to go. I just feel like I need to check in with the Brotherhood."

"Oh, but of course." She put her hand in his. "You must. And take your time. I should enjoy a shower in this—what is it called again?"

"Locker room. And you should feel free to explore

the training center. They've got a pool down here, classrooms—have a snack, even though I intend to take you to dinner, remember?"

Yes, our date, she thought happily. "I shall explore."

There was a pause. Then he lowered his head such that he stared at her from under his lids. "I wish I were showering with you."

As a flush warmed her through and through, she purred. "There is always later in the night."

"Indeed."

The kiss started with a peck, but didn't end that way. The next thing she knew, she was in his arms, and he was pushing her back with his body, and the clothes were slipping out of her grasp. When she and her lover finally came up for air, both of them were breathing hard.

Lassiter brushed a length of her hair behind her ear. "Make yourself at home. I'll be back in a little bit."

"Do take your time."

He kissed her quick again. Kissed her a third time.

Then bent down and gathered up the things that had fallen out of her hands.

"Be back soon," he murmured.

As he walked off, she leaned out and watched him go. His stride was long and purposeful, and his hair flowed behind him. When he disappeared through a glass door, she wondered how far they were away from the First Family's house. Not far, she was guessing, if the loaner of the clothing could just "go back up" or however he had phrased it. Indeed, there was probably an underground tunnel somewhere that provided linkage, and for that, she was grateful.

She had hated what had happened last night at the club, and if one of the Brothers' females was kind enough to lend clothes to a stranger, Rahvyn had to imagine there were many good people in this community. Kind, good people. She would hate such violence e'er to come upon them, especially in their home.

Ducking back inside the locker room, she glanced around at all the metal vertical cabinets. Then she returned to the showers' enclave, chose the first stall, and closed the curtain. Changing out of what she had on was a bit of a relief, and, oh, the hot water.

Soap, shampoo, and various other supplies were in a metal basin upon the wall, but she just stood under the rush for a while, enjoying the sensations of the gentle fall of rain and the warmth and the humidity. Her body was sore in places that made her smile, and when she finally took to the cleansing, she felt a kind of wonder as her hands passed the bar over her breasts, her stomach . . . between her legs.

With everything washed, including her hair, she gave herself a little longer, but then began to feel guilty at how much hot water she was using. Back in the Old Country, such a luxury was rare and precious.

When she got out, she took a white towel off a little ledge in the dressing part of the stall and she dried herself off. As she reached for the shirt to put on, a packet slipped out of its folds. It was a plastic bag that read "Hanes," and inside were three pairs of fresh underwear.

"How thoughtful."

She chose the red ones, and imagined, as she put them on, Lassiter removing them. And didn't that make her flush.

The shirt was soft and white, the fleece was a light-weight cotton layer with a zipper in front, and the jeans were a little long, but otherwise perfect. She collected her own clothes—or rather those that had been given to her at Luchas House—and left them on the bench in the cabinet area.

As she went to the exit, she had a thought she would pick them up on her way home—and stopped.

Glancing back, she regarded the little pile and realized that she had no home. Luchas House had been a stopgap. The alternate plane where the Book was sequestered was not a residence. And the rustic cottage in that field, back in the Old Country, was no doubt long gone by now.

And yes, Sahvage had told her that she could live with him and his new *shellan*, but she did not feel right about that. He had done his duty caretaking her, and now he should be able to live without the burden of—

She considered the cave. And Lassiter.

Yes, she thought. When she considered the subject of going home, that place she had only been to once before was what was in her heart. Although that had more to do with where the angel was . . . than the location itself.

◆ ◆ ◆

Striding down the subterranean tunnel that connected the training center to the main house, Lassiter was nervous as hell. Given his personality and the whole immortal thing, him being this kind of stressed was a new experience. He'd known despair, sure. Generic sadness. Boredom—often. Panic—when he hadn't been able to find Rahvyn the night before.

But this twitchy, vibrating anxiety was a new one.

Yay. Personal growth.

Stopping in front of a steel door, he punched in a code, went up a short-stack stairwell, and entered another code. Emerging from under the mansion's grand staircase, he took a deep breath. He'd always liked the way the big house smelled, all lemon wax, old-fashioned floor polish, and homemade bread in an oven.

Man, if there was a way to bottle this, it could be called *Mom's*.

Not that he'd had one.

Although he wasn't exactly sure what time it was, it was clear First Meal had come and gone: Not only was there no one eating in the dining room, he could also tell by the scent of dishwashing liquid wafting through from the kitchen, and the sweet chiming of silverware being scooped up off the big table as place settings were swapped out.

He went to the right, to the foyer. At the base of the grand staircase, he looked up. The red carpet and all the gold leaf of the balustrades made him think of the tsars, and so did the crystal sconces and the marble columns. The art installations weren't bad, either: Under his feet, the mosaic depiction of an apple tree in full bloom was a masterpiece, and overhead, three stories up, the fresco of great warriors on stallions was also one for the history books.

But all was not museum-serene.

Up on the second-floor landing, the double doors of Wrath's study burst open, and the sound of male voices in a full-on argument exploded out and echoed around. The chaos was cut off as the panels were re-shut.

Sahvage appeared at the top landing all dressed for war, the black daggers on his chest not just a symbol of his status but the tools of his trade. With his hair freshly shorn and his eyes hyperalert, the brother was exactly who anyone would want on their front line.

"You rang," the male said as he came down, light on his feet, in spite of his heavy weight. "And I'm surprised you're not up there with us."

"I'll join in after you and I . . . you know, talk. How's it going?"

Sahvage jumped off the last two steps, landing with a muffled boom. "They're arguing about whether or not to close down the Audience House. Permanently or otherwise."

Lassiter frowned. "Why would they do that?"

The story was told efficiently, and when the brother was finished, Lassiter had a pit in his stomach. "And they think it was the Omega's son? How the hell'd he find the place?"

"Don't know. But between that drive-by of Fritz, or whatever the hell it was, and the *lesser* in the back of that club last night, we're clearly back in business in the worst possible way." Sahvage narrowed his eyes. "Hey, are you all right?"

Nope. He didn't want to think about evil, or any of its forms, not tonight. Not any night, actually.

"Ah . . . yeah." As a vacuum started *whirrrrrring* in the background, Lassiter glanced toward the billiards room. "Can we, ah, go in there for a minute? This won't take long and then we can head upstairs."

Sahvage nodded, and the two of them side-by-side'd their way into the other space. Walking around the green felt tables, Lassiter eyed the leather couch he'd spent so much time on. The remote was on the arm, just where he liked it, and there was a sealed bottle of his favorite Tropicana orange juice on the coffee table.

"I love Fritz," he murmured as he touched the whacker and pivoted to the massive flat-screen.

So many days he'd sat here and fired up that TV, tuning out the world to Betty White.

"That *doggen* is something else for sure." Sahvage deliberately stepped in front of him. "Let's not fuck around, shall we—and frankly, I don't know why, if you want a QT conversation, it's not with Tohr. He's not only the King's right-hand male, he's a helluva lot more stable than I am—"

"This isn't about the war. Or the Brotherhood."

Across the foyer in the dining room, his peripheral vision picked up a maid in the house's black-and-white uniform as she started pulling out chairs and running an old-school box broom under the table to make sure there were no crumbs anywhere.

In his mind, during the day in the cave, he'd pictured a much more private scene for this.

Sahvage's brow went up. "Well, if you're looking for advice about what to watch on your boob tube over here, I'm not your guy. You'd better ask Rhage. Or if you want to turn over a new leaf and try some stuff that doesn't melt your brain, Mary is the way to go—"

"It's about Rahvyn."

All at once, everything about the male changed. No more jokey-jokey, and those eyes got real focused. "What."

Lassiter took a couple of steps toward the TV. Came back. Then he rerouted and headed for the bar—remembered he didn't drink, reconsidered the abstinence thing. Came back.

Meanwhile, Sahvage stayed right where he was, his expression getting grimmer.

Finally, Lassiter just threw his hands up in defeat. Then again, why had he thought this was going to be easy? "Look, I know I don't have the best reputation for being a serious guy. I fuck around a lot and you don't really know me outside of my poking the shit out of V or chilling on that sofa. But the reality is . . ."

When he couldn't go on, Sahvage took a step in. "Have you seen something about her? In the future? Is it bad? What's going on—"

"I'm in love with her. And I want your permission to ask her to mate me. I want to be her *hellren*."

In the aftermath of the announcement, Sahvage was so dumbfounded, there was a temptation to call Doc Jane for a stroke eval.

Then the brother opened his mouth. Shut it. Leaned in even closer. "I'm sorry . . . what?"

CHAPTER FORTY-FOUR

I n the training center, Rahvyn stepped out of the locker room. The corridor that ran through the facility was empty, but she could hear people talking down where the clinic was. She imagined the healers and the nurse with their heads together, discussing something that would make someone feel and function better, because the infirmed had an injury or a wound or an illness.

They had been so kind to her.

A rhythmic noise that she couldn't place drew her attention, and she decided to follow the sound. As she passed by the glass door Lassiter had used, she glanced into an office space, and reflected that in her short so-journ here in this current time, she had learned so much. New words, new things, new places.

Continuing on, she came to a set of doors with little windows in them, the glass of which was striped with some kind of wire. On the far side, a broad, high-ceilinged space was revealed, one with a glossy honey-colored floor, sets of shallow stairs flanking both sides, and a pair of net-ted baskets suspended by arms at each end.

There was a male at the far station, bouncing an or-ange ball. Which explained the sounds.

And she knew who it was, even though his back was to her.

When she opened one half of the doors, the scent confirmed what she already knew to be true, and though there was no squeak of hinges, the male cap-tured the orange ball and swung around. Dressed in a sweatshirt and loose bottoms, Nate nevertheless looked older somehow, though in fact, none of his features had changed. Mayhap it was in the eyes, she decided.

"Hi," she said as she lifted a hand in greeting.

He bounced the ball once. Twice. "Hi."

"I, ah . . ." She indicated the door she'd just come through. "I was just down here and I heard this noise."

"I'm warming up." He bounced the ball again. "I'm not any kind of basketball player, though."

Rahvyn nodded at the netted circle suspended behind him. "That is the target?"

"The rim, yes."

"Rim."

Crossing her arms over her chest, she glanced across to the steps that seemed, in her view, to offer spectators places to sit and regard the game. Then she lifted her eyes upward and noted that as with the locker room, the ceiling lights were caged.

"I'm sorry about last night—"

"I don't blame you for being mad at me—"

There was an awkward shared laugh as they both spoke. And then Nate took the lead, his voice deeper than she remembered.

"I was rude. I'm sorry for that. I've been having . . ." He rubbed his forehead with his thumb. "I haven't been sleeping and my head's all fucked up—screwed up, I mean."

"I understand why. And I wish I hadn't left after that night. I had to . . . it was required of me to help with something."

"And now you're back?" He wasn't quite meeting her eyes, his stare hovering off to one side or the other. "In Caldwell."

"Yes, for a little while—"

"Do you love him." Now he looked at her straight-on. "Lassiter. Just tell me, please, even though it's none of my business—and I already know the answer."

Rahvyn opened her mouth. Closed it. Finally found her voice. "I do, yes."

Nate nodded and started walking toward her, that ball trading places between the flooring and his palm, the sound like a healthy heartbeat, slow and regular.

"I saw you two in the meadow with all the flowers."

As her brows popped up, he shrugged. "It was after—well, I went to Luchas House to see you, you know . . ."

He stopped in front of her, his eyes roaming around before they re-locked on hers. "Actually, I think I'm just going to be honest here, so we clear the air. I brought you flowers that night. Nothing like the ones all over that field—just supermarket flowers because they're what I can afford."

"Oh, Nate . . ." As she released an exhale, she blamed herself for not noticing and being more sensitive to any feelings he might have garnered for her. She had been so heedless in that regard. "I am so sorry."

Putting up his palm, he said, "No, don't apologize. In a way, if you love him—I mean, honestly love him? It kind of makes it easier. At least you're not with me for a big reason, an important one. Not because you think I'm a five out of ten, wouldn't recommend."

"Five out of ten?"

"Never mind, just a saying."

As he palmed the ball and glanced down, she rushed into the silence. "I think you are a wonderful male, Nate. And you are going to—"

"Please don't patronize me. I know you don't mean to be demeaning, but that's what it feels like on my end. Besides, you don't owe me anything. It's not like a person can change their emotions. They are what they are."

He was right about that. But she hated that he was hurting—and to tell him that she hadn't been aware of his side of things seemed insulting, as if she hadn't seen him properly.

Which she had not.

"But I am sorry," she told him. "That you have any kind of pain, and that is a truth which shall endure."

Nate bounced the ball using both his hands: left, floor, right, floor, left. Then he caught it again.

"Does he love you? I mean . . . really love you?" When she inclined her head, he took a deep breath. "That's good. That's the way it should be."

"You shall find someone, Nate, I promise you—" As he tried to interrupt, she shook her head. "Let me finish. I did not believe that I would ever discover someone to love me for what I am. So convinced was I that I did not even look. And yet destiny provided me with my soul mate. The same shall be true of you."

"So you guys are going to get mated and live happily ever after?" He looked at her. "And I'm not saying this to be a douche."

There it was, that word again. "Indeed, there is no reason to paddle yourself."

Nate frowned. "Excuse me?"

"Douchedinghy? Is that the word?"

He laughed a little. "Canoe. I think you mean douche canoe."

"Ah, yes, that is the saying." She smiled at him, forcing the expression because she desperately wanted things to be okay between the two of them. "And, no, there are no plans for us to be mated. Our situation is not like that."

"Because he's the new Scribe Virgin, huh."

She nodded. "And I am—well, I do not know how long I shall be around."

Nate's brows united over the bridge of his fine, straight nose. "Where will you go. If he's here, if Sahvage and Mae are here?"

"I take things evening by evening. That is just the way things are." She hesitated. "Listen, Shuli and I spoke and . . ."

"He told you. About last night in the woods." When she nodded, Nate blew out a long breath and looked at the other netted circle, the one that was quite far away. "Nobody needs to worry about that. My head was really fucked up. I have clarity now, though."

"What has changed?"

"I'm going to fight the Lessening Society, that's what changed." He laughed harshly. "Okay, so your expression says it all. It's the same one both my parents had at different times when I told them. Do I look like such an incompetent ass? A weakling?"

She shook her head. "No, we just care about you that much."

For a split second, as he stared across at her, the hurt he felt showed. And she would have done everything to make it go away or relieve it in some way.

"Thanks, Rahvyn," he said hoarsely.

"Do everyone a favor and believe the sentiment, please. When you are out there in the field, and I believe you will go on to fight for our species, just remember, there are so many who truly care for you. You hold the hearts of an entire community in your hands."

He nodded and blinked quickly as his eyes glowed with emotion—

"Oh, hey."

At the sound of the voice, they both jumped. A female in leggings and a t-shirt, with long brunette hair and a young on her hip, was standing just inside the double doors. Rahvyn remembered her from the time with George—

As realization struck, Rahvyn looked down at the clothes she had on. Looked back up at the female . . . Beth.

"Hey, Nate!" the female said as she came forward. "And I heard you wanted to see me, Rahvyn. Can I just say, those jeans look great on you—"

The squeak Rahvyn let out made her stop. "Are you okay?"

Rahvyn threw a hand out as her balance shifted alarmingly, and thank heavens Nate's upper arm happened to be in range.

"Rahvyn," he said urgently, "what's wrong? Come here, let's sit down—"

"No, no, I'm fine." She rubbed her eyes, and glanced at the massive ruby that was on the female's finger. With an utter lack of sophistication and grace, she said, "Is that . . ."

Oh, why was she asking. She knew what it was, who the female was—who the young in those arms was.

The female winced a little. "Ah, yeah. That would be the Saturnine Ruby."

"Which means you are . . ."

"Wrath's wife. *Shellan*. Mate."

"The Queen. And your young is . . ."

"Little Wrath. Thus the L.W."

"The next in line for the throne. Dearest Virgin Scribe." Rahvyn lurched into a bow. Then curtseyed with all the coordination of a drunk. "Forgive me. When I was with you and the King previously, I was so consumed by taking care of the beautiful dog, I did not consider the repercussions of who . . . —oh, God, I am wearing your pants!"

Promptly, because she had not embarrassed herself enough, she went for the waistband and started unbuttoning the jeans.

The Queen reached forward, waving her hand. "Oh, sweetheart, you don't want to do that—"

Nate joined in on the *no-no-no*, dropping his ball and putting one arm over his eyes and the other straight out in front of him as he turned away.

Rahvyn stopped what she was doing. Stopped . . . everything, actually. Almost including her own heart rate.

"I am . . . so sorry. I am just making this all worse, am I not."

Beth laughed, and put her free arm around Rahvyn for a squeeze. "It's okay. I can't believe I've got any title other than mom, either. Do *not* worry about it—besides, you saved the thing my husband loves most outside of this little guy and me. And some nights, I'm not sure I've got that order right!"

As the female stepped back, Rahvyn smiled a little, and looked at the young—only to become even more self-conscious. Instead of being one of those happy, burbly little males, the son of the King and Queen stared her right in the eye, as if he were judging the merits of her character. Then he reached out, took her finger, and gripped it briefly like he was shaking her palm properly.

Something of her surprise must have shown, because his *mahmen* let out a sigh.

"I know, he's a little intense. He takes after his father." Beth smoothed his black hair. "Isn't that right, L.W."

Rahvyn nodded. "He is quite fierce, but I do believe that is a good thing for the future of the race."

"Some nights, I'm not sure what his destiny is . . . or even what I dare hope it to be."

As the words drifted, Rahvyn got the impression that the female knew exactly what was coming her son's way, and she was seeking to avoid the thoughts of warfare and governing during these years of his innocence.

To change the subject, Rahvyn wrapped her arms around herself—and by extension, the fleece and shirt. "I shall take very good care of your clothing."

"I know you will, but don't worry about that, either." Beth glanced over her shoulder. "And now, I have to take this man down to Doc Jane for his checkup. It's good to see you both, and Rahvyn, if you ever need more clothes for any reason, you know where to find me. Say bye, L.W."

After she waved her son's hand, the pair were off, the door closing behind them.

Rahvyn glanced over at Nate. "I cannot believe I just did that."

His brows went up, and then he laughed in an easy,

genuine way. "You know, if I was feeling sorry for my-self? You've just done me a tremendous service."

"Indeed. Whatever challenges you may face, at least you did not try to get naked in front of the Queen."

"Amen to that."

As she regarded the male balefully, he was smiling. And she smiled back, thinking that the humiliation was worth it if it cheered Nate up.

Totally worth it.

◆ ◆ ◆

"I can see you're surprised by this."

As Lassiter threw that no-shit-Sherlock out there, he waited for something, anything to come back at him. Instead, Rahvyn's cousin, Sahvage, just stood there with his eyebrows up at his hairline and his head tilted to the side like he was a German shepherd who'd heard a dog whistle.

Meanwhile, across the foyer in the dining room, a *doggen* rolled in a cart full of porcelain to complete the table-setting process for Last Meal. Thank God the staff were busy with their own jobs. Otherwise the im-minent humiliation that was about to come in for a landing on his head was going to have one helluva pea-nut gallery.

"I . . ." Sahvage started. And didn't finish.

"I'm going to be honest with you," Lassiter said as he raised both his palms. "Straight up, I'm probably not a good bet, time-wise. There's another plan for me, and I don't know how long I'll be here, in Caldwell. But here's the thing. Even immortals can die in a way, and if the last twenty-four hours have taught me anything, it's that time isn't relative, it's rare and precious. I want to be that female's *hellren*, and maybe she'll have me like that, maybe she won't. I want to ask her, though, and I want to do it in the right and proper way. You're the eldest male in her family—and back in the Old Country, in her time, it's customary for the permission to be requested. If you don't want to give it to me, that's fine. It's her decision anyway. I just thought it would be important to her that I pay her bloodline the respect you and she deserve."

Sahvage's brows lowered. And so did his voice. "She told you . . . about the Old Country."

When Lassiter nodded gravely, the brother said in a voice that cracked, "Just so we're clear, I tried to protect her."

Lassiter reached out and squeezed the fighter's thick shoulder. "I know you did."

"I'm surprised she talked to you about all that."

"I want to kill that male, even though he's already dead."

"That line forms at the rear." Sahvage scrubbed his face with his dagger hand. Then he dropped his arm and looked off to the side. " 'Scuse me."

The brother headed over to behind the bar, grabbed a tall glass, and threw his palm out in a distracted way. Bringing over a bottle, any bottle, it seemed like, he poured himself not so much two fingers as an entire fist. Then he tossed it back. The whole thing.

As he righted his head, he grimaced. "I hate gin," he muttered as he poured himself another serving.

After that also went down the hopper, he nodded and came back around. "Okay, sorry. I didn't expect this."

"I get it."

"Do you love my cousin?" Sahvage asked. "I mean, bonded love. Like the real, core feeling, not any of that surface attraction bullshit."

"Yes, I do. I knew from the moment I saw her standing next to you in the garage of Luchas House. That first night I saw her . . . I knew she was the one for me."

"All right. And what does she feel for you?"

"She told me she loved me last night."

Sahvage nodded. Then he took a deep breath. "Okay. You have my permission to ask her. Whatever she wants to do is okay with me—but it's her call."

"I agree. It's up to her."

"Okay."

"All right."

"Deal."

"Roger that."

Having run through the list of yuppers, they both nodded back and forth like their foreheads were tennis rackets. And then they stood there.

"Sooooo . . ." Lassiter glanced around.

"What do we do now?"

"I've never done this before. I don't know."

"Me either."

There was another long pause. And then they both shrugged and started walking out.

Halfway down the lineup of billiards tables, Sahvage

glanced over. "You mess with her, I'm gonna kill you. Doesn't matter that you're immortal, I'll find a way, even if it's just making you wish you were dead."

Lassiter started to smile and put out a fist for bumping. "I knew I liked you. And I'd expect nothing less."

CHAPTER FORTY-FIVE

As Lash considered whether or not he was going to meet the demon at nine o'clock, he was clear on one thing: He did not want any help from her. Firstly, he wasn't interested in anything's opinion as to what he needed for the Lessening Society, especially something that shopped, fucked, and went psycho for a living. Secondly, if what actions he did take just happened to overlap whatever it was she babbled on about, she'd feel like he owed her, and who the hell needed that complication.

In the end, however, he did decide to go back to that Victorian walk-up. He had another reason he had to head over there, and if she showed up, fine. He didn't have to hear her out. Besides, what was he saying, that he couldn't handle her?

That was fucking weak.

Re-forming on the front steps of the decrepit apartment building, he glanced around at the abandoned street, then proceeded through the door. The cellar stairs were right there, and as he descended, he could smell the days-old blood before he even bottomed out in the lower corridor.

Coming up to the bathtub, he wasn't surprised to find that everything had congealed into a semi-solid. Soon, it would start turning brown.

The door to the storage room was open a crack, and as he flared his nostrils and caught the scents of dirt, mineral deposits, dank mold, and something vaguely meth-lab-ish, he was not happy.

No sickly sweet stink.

Inside, he immediately looked to the black ink puddle in the far corner. *Fuck.* That permanently dead, miserably stupid security guard had up and left. And as he considered the remains that had been rolled out of that van at the Tudor mansion, he came to the only possible explanation there was. Somehow that slayer had dragged himself off, traveled somewhere—likely still in downtown given all his bullet holes—and found a vampire to kill.

So where was he now?

"Fucking hell—"

Overhead, the entrance he'd just used opened and footsteps proceeded into the walk-up. Lots of footsteps.

Stepping out of the storage room, he waited by the tub—with one of the three guns he had on him in his palm. His second batch of inductees, the drug-dealing punks, had had a nice stash of weapons at their disposal, and now that he was their new boss, they'd shared.

"Share" was probably the wrong word.

He'd left them behind at that apartment building to get him a list of names for the next wave. Then it was going to be training time. He just needed enough warm bodies—

Sorry, *cold* bodies.

And then he could . . .

His thoughts drifted as what came down the stairs started to fill the hallway.

What the . . . *fuck?*

Instead of all kinds of human men, gathered by the demon after she'd fucked them, he was confronted by a bevy of . . . street beauties. And not as in prostitutes.

Female gang members were more like it: The human women wore leather jackets of a similar style, and every one of them had a tattoo on the front of her neck, the design of a skull bifurcated by her windpipe. Their hair was all types, blond, black, curly, straight. Many had earring holes that took up their entire lobes, but there were no hoops or studs in them. No rings, bracelets, or necklaces, either.

The scent was a combination of hash, crack, and drugstore perfume.

Which was not to say they weren't hot. As his shock abated, he recognized that though they looked like the last thing in the world they needed was a man, that didn't mean they weren't fuckable.

And there was his demon, bringing up the rear.

Not that he was claiming her in any way.

Devina had her hair all coiled up again and she was

wearing a business suit, her vibe like a beauty queen CEO about to get rolled for her heels and her gold watch.

Yet the women readily parted for her as she came down to him. "I'd like you to meet my friends. I believe you'll find them well qualified for your work."

Lash took the demon's arm in a hard grip and pulled her into the storage room. Kicking shut the door, he hissed, "What the fuck is this."

"Are you saying you won't deal with women?" An arched brow lifted even farther. "How chauvinistic."

"I'm not asking them to a fucking tea party."

"Do they *look* like they'd know what to do with a cup and saucer? Unless it was breaking the latter and using it to slice someone's throat open."

"I don't need this—"

"You are so *stupid*."

Lash recoiled as if she had struck him. And he was so affronted by the statement that he couldn't throw back a retort immediately—which gave the demon time to continue: "I handpicked these women from over a hundred. Most of the vampires who go out in Caldwell at night are males, and most of them are heterosexual. If you want to get at civilians, they can be seduced. And I know your Lessening Society's history—all *lessers* have started as men before they were turned, so none of the Brotherhood are going to expect slayers who are women—which is a tactical advantage. Plus you can still keep recruiting men. Why limit yourself and your strategy?"

Lash rolled his eyes. "Do you think I want *them*

fighting against the Brotherhood? You think that matchup is going to go well—"

The impact of a knee to his groin was so swift, so targeted, he saw stars as he jacked forward, covered his nuts, and debated whether he was going to throw up.

Devina grabbed the back of his hair and ripped his head up. "Oh, whoops. Did I do that? I guess I don't know my own strength. Tee. Hee."

Lash shoved her off and paced around with a stiff leg as the pain faded. When he was sure his voice wasn't going to squeak, he faced the demon and said, in a voice that was absolutely not any higher than his normal one, "Be careful, you like what I can do with that shit."

The demon smiled and licked her lips. "I do."

"Then keep both your fucking feet on the ground."

If it had been anyone else, he would have blown them apart. But knowing her, she'd enjoy that, and he was not in a mood to make her fucking happy.

And what was worse than getting nailed in the privates? The bitch had a good fucking point. Maybe not about fighting the Brothers with women who had been turned, but certainly about civilian vampires and sex. There were still a lot of traditional families who sequestered their females, that double standard making it many times more likely that males would be out alone—and in the mood.

The more civilians he could kill off, the greater the civil unrest and the less stable Wrath's throne was.

He went back over to the door, opened things up, and eyed the women.

They weren't chatting, taking selfies, or scrolling through Instagram on their phones. They were staring down at him, their bodies still . . . like they were ready to do whatever was required—even if that included some hand-to-hand. On him.

Clearly, they weren't the kind to be played.

The demon's hand curled onto his shoulder. "You know I'm right. And you should also know the Brothers are going to have a real hard time fighting women. They're not going to want to kill them because they're a bunch of Boy Scouts. That's another advantage."

Lash took note of each face, meeting each one's eyes. "Do they know what they're in for."

"Not any more or less than any of the men have." The demon squeezed. Hard. "I wouldn't fuck them, if I were you."

Lash glared into her black eyes. "I'll be the judge of that."

"You'll just waste good soldiers. 'Cuz I'll fucking kill them."

"Jealousy is boring."

"So is infidelity."

"We are *not* in a relationship."

The demon's exquisite face froze into a mask, and he enjoyed the hurt she couldn't hide, no matter how much she tried.

Lash refocused on the women for a long moment. Then he raised his voice. "Ladies, this way," he said as he indicated the storage room. "Four at a time."

It was, after all, a new era.

Wasn't it.

+ + +

Up on the second floor of the Brotherhood's mansion, Lassiter got to the study first and did the duty with the door for his future cousin-in-law. Assuming Rahvyn would have him. And as soon as he opened things, all the heads in the room turned to him, except for Wrath's because the King was already staring straight ahead.

After Sahvage went ahead, Lassiter followed and had a thought that he couldn't imagine not walking into yet another of these meetings and seeing all these faces. Add Rahvyn to the mix? There had to be a way out of the Creator's—

In the far corner by the hearth, two males who shouldn't have been at any kind of get-together in the mansion lifted their hands in a wave—and Mike Myers went through his mind: *Exsqueeze me. A baking powder?*

No, wait, that was the other guy with the rubber face. From *In Living Color. The Mask.* That pet detective movie . . .

"So we move the venue," Vishous said into the silence, like he was continuing a discussion. "That's the answer. We don't stop the meetings, we just go somewhere else."

No, it was *Wayne's World,* Lassiter thought as he started to make his way over to the other angels. But goddamn, why couldn't he remember the other guy.

Then again, like he didn't have a couple of things on his mind?

Phury stepped back to give him a little room, clapping him on the shoulder. Then Butch gave a smile from where he was sitting on the pale blue love seat next to his roommate. After that, Xcor nodded and leaned to the side so he could squeeze by. There were other acknowledgments, too, as he made progress through the crowded-subway-SRO, and he couldn't help thinking that, in spite of his best efforts to be a jackass, they valued him and they wanted him here—

"*Ace Ventura*," he hissed as he arrived at his destination. "And Jim Carrey."

"No, I'm Eddie," the angel said as he put his thumb to his sternum. Then he pointed next door. "And he's Adrian."

"Nice ta meet ya." Ad stuck out his hand. "It's been *ages*—"

As they got *shhh*'d, Lassiter put both palms up, mouthed WTF?, and then motioned back and forth between them.

"Long story," Eddie muttered. "And I'm not talking about it."

A sudden lift in Lassiter's mood made him feel like he'd gone to see Dr. Now and "made good progress." And then Eddie was repositioning him so that the three of them were standing shoulder to shoulder and he could see out into the room.

As new sites for the King to meet with civilians were discussed, Lassiter kept glancing over at his immortal buddies. But every time he did, they were still there, Eddie looking like someone had just made him eat a rotten egg, and Ad, as always, pierced and happy, rolling along with whatever.

You're supposed to be going to the Creator, Lassiter thought at Eddie. *My twenty-four hours is almost up.*

Eddie's lower jaw started grinding. *Not talking about it.*

So you're staying? To help? When nothing came back at him, he looked at Ad. *Hello?*

For once, Ad looked him in the eye and got really fucking serious. *The Omega was on their property last night. So there are two malevolent entities in this town now, and our prime directive has always been to engage evil.*

Lassiter again went palms-up. *But that was true last night and you were determined to finish your mission then.*

How do we know there aren't more coming, Ad thought. *What if one of the barriers between planes has opened and there's going to be a run of demons? Besides, do you want to argue with this? Really.*

Nope, sure don't, Lassiter thought back.

Plus hey, at least they would all be in trouble together— and under the theory that there was only so much of the Creator's wrath to go around? Divide and conquer had always been an effective strategy, and at least now the pissed-off from on high was going to be split three ways.

"So that's what we do," the King announced from behind the great carved desk. "We move locations—and I want all rotations out in the field. Let's go looking for *lessers* again."

There was a growl throughout the room, low and threatening. Also annoyed, as if none of them could believe they were up to their daggers in the war again.

"I'll get the word out about a change in venue," V said. "And no one goes back to that house. If it was Lash—and

454 J. R. WARD

it has to be because he's the only part of the Omega left—he'll stake out the site, and while we watch him, I don't want any collateral damage or distractions."

"That's right." Wrath held up his forefinger to emphasize the point. "I do not want *any* of the *doggen* going there."

"Not a problem, I'll take care of it."

The King nodded. Then swept the room as if he were sighted, his face turning from side to side. "Any other updates."

When there were just mumbles that were I-got-nothin' in nature, the King banged the desk with his dagger hand. "Roger that. I'm calling this meeting adjourned. Get back out in the streets then, and find—"

"He's going to ask my cousin to mate him."

As Sahvage's word-grenade landed in the center of the study, everyone looked at him. Then followed where he was pointing and stared at Lassiter. Every eyeball. In the room.

Well.

"Ahh . . ." Lassiter glanced around and then mouthed his second *WTF?* of the night in Sahvage's direction. "She hasn't said yes yet—"

A surprisingly hearty cheer rose up and resounded, and then the brothers and fighters swarmed in for high fives and *attaboys*.

Hello, it was *an update*, Sahvage mouthed back across the chaos.

"Let us know what she says," Wrath called out over the din with a smile. "Fritz is always ready to plan a party."

CHAPTER FORTY-SIX

As dates go, this was not quite what I had in mind."

As Lassiter spoke, Rahvyn squeezed his hand. "Well, I can't think of anything I'd like more."

The pair of them were up in the sanctuary of temples and tulips again, strolling side by side over the bright green, cropped grass. She didn't know where in the extensive landscape they were headed, but she didn't care. They were together and things were peaceful—and after the previous couple of nights, that was perfection in her view.

"Can I tell you what I was thinking? You know, date-wise," Lassiter prompted.

She glanced up at him. "Please."

"I wanted to razzle-dazzle you."

With a laugh, she indicated around the bucolic envi-rons. "We are in paradise. I can assure you my razzle is very dazzled indeed, whatever that means."

He tilted down and kissed her. "Well, first I rented out the Palisades movie theater for us."

"Oh! As in the moving picture show palace?" An image of gold-leafed grandeur and red velvet curtains came to mind. "I read an article about it whilst at Lu-chas House. It was very lovely, the interior. Quite fancy."

"Yup, that's the one. A little grandeur never hurts, even if we're in jeans, you know? Also, if it's good enough for Elvis, it's good enough for me."

"Elvis?"

"Long story. And I'd arranged a screening of one of my favorite movies of all time. *Sixteen Candles.*"

"Whatever is it about?"

"The guy gets the girl in the end—and there's a red Porsche involved. It's a defining movie of the eighties. Molly Ringwald. Jake Ryan. Anthony Michael Hall. Rice Chex. Farmer Ted. Totally outer limits. Amazing."

Even though he spoke in a different language, she smiled broadly. "I should very much like to watch it with you."

"I will make that happen." He squeezed her hand back. "And afterward, I was going to take you to this 24-hour diner all kinds of people rave about. Apparently the place serves an apple pie that if consumed after mid-night guarantees a religious experience."

"Oh, I've never had one of those. But I look forward to it."

Lassiter laughed in that way she liked to hear, deep and in his belly. Then he leaned in. "Are you talking about the pie or the religious experience? Because I've got another way I can give you the latter."

As a flush went through her body, she remembered what they had done in that cave during all of the daylight hours—and decided, whilst looking around at all the privacy they had, that this was indeed the very best place for their date.

"I anticipate that even more," she murmured.

"Preeeeach." He kissed her again. "So anyway, that was my plan."

"What made you change it?" When he didn't reply, she felt anxiety take a bite of her stomach. "Lassiter . . . what aren't you telling me."

She stopped and pulled him to a halt. "Is it because of what happened behind that club? Or something else?"

As his eyes did not meet hers, she thought . . . *dearest Virgin Scribe, something else.*

"I should like to know," she said as she released his hand and crossed her arms over her chest. "Right the now."

Lassiter broke off from her and paced around, as if his body could not contain his worry, and as a sickening pit formed in her gut, she told herself that whatever it was, they could deal with it: The Brotherhood. Lassiter. Herself and those two angels who did not care for her very much, but who certainly would be useful in a fight. They had resources, and they could deal with anything.

"I am not afraid." She lifted her chin. "And I am not helpless. Remember?"

"That doesn't mean I like talking about this with you." He shrugged. "Or anyone, at any rate."

"So . . . ?"

The angel she loved more than anything or anyone else in the world looked around one last time, as if he were searching for words. Or a different reality.

Then he spoke with firm authority. "The Lessening Society has found the place where the King meets with his civilians. How? They don't know for sure—but it's down the street from the parents whose son died during that *lesser* attack. Maybe there's a connection, who knows. It's just a really shitty coincidence otherwise." He shook his head. "Add to that *lessers* back on the streets? And how many inductions we don't know about? There's this bad momentum coming to Caldwell, you know? And I'm worried—everyone's worried—that we're heading for a culmination nobody's going to like . . . that maybe, nobody's going to survive."

Rahvyn thought of the portraits the Book had shown her, especially the image of the King, those symbols swamping in and consuming the features of his face.

"Yes," she whispered. "It is a very dangerous time."

"And then there's the fact that the Creator called me home three years ago, and Eddie and Adrian have been in Caldwell, looking for me, all that time—but surprise! They just found me. It's a helluva convergence."

The thought of him leaving filled her with fresh

dread. "The Scribe Virgin made you her successor, however. Surely that responsibility cannot be usurped."

"No one is above the Creator. And somebody else can do the job." He paced around again, making a circle in the grass. Then he stared off to the forest boundary. "Right now Eddie and Adrian are joining the fight— and I am so psyched about that. It's the best fucking news. But like everything in existence, there is a higher power who is going to do what He will."

"So they are not turning you over to the Creator."

"Not tonight. Not tomorrow. Who knows in the future—and in any event, it doesn't really matter. I'm on borrowed time for other reasons." Lassiter looked up at the milky sky. "The thing is, the vampires need me. The demon and the Omega's son together? Fucking hell, what if they have kids. And because of . . . certain circumstances, I'm in a unique position to help keep them apart. I can make sure that the pair of them don't collude and turn what is a dangerous situation into an untenable one."

"So they are . . ."

"I'm not sure demons and the seat of all evil can be called a 'happy' couple, but yes."

"Oh." Abruptly, she clasped both his hands. "Then you must stay. You must do whatever it takes."

After a moment, he leveled his head and looked at her with a strange detachment. "I agree. Whatever it takes."

◆ ◆ ◆

As Lassiter spoke the words, he knew his female understood the gravity of the situation, even if she didn't have all the details or the backstory. And he thought of the Book and its spells. Who'd have thought his life would change for the better because of something that demon did.

But here he was.

Slowly, he sank down on one knee.

"Are you unwell?" Rahvyn asked with alarm.

Staring up at his female, he saw her silhouetted against the sacred, milky sky of the Sanctuary, the diffused illumination like a halo all around her. And God, with her platinum hair falling forward and her body strung like a bow, she was impossibly beautiful. Except for the anxiety on her face.

He would have changed that if he could. Then again, he would have created for them all a different reality. If he could.

"Rahvyn . . . this was also not how I'd planned."

"I beg your pardon?" With impatience, she pushed a wave of her hair out of her face. "Planned what."

"You know I love you."

"Yes, and I love—"

"Will you take me as your *hellren*?" he blurted.

When she just stood there, stunned, he wondered what exactly it was about him that made everybody freeze like that when the whole mating thing came out of his mouth.

"I talked to Sahvage earlier," he rambled. "It's your decision, but I wanted to do things right. Well, some of them, at any rate. I wanted to ask you on top of one of the bridges that span the Hudson. The city at night looks like diamonds that fell from the sky, and with the stars overhead—I wanted you to feel like you were my universe, you know? Cheesy, I get it. But I stayed up all day thinking of a place that was special. I even thought up a poem—but I can't remember the words. I was going have a little music playing—except I forgot my phone in the cave. I just . . . I wanted this to be perfect for you because I was hoping if I had the right combination of elements, you were more likely to say—"

"*Yes.*" She closed the distance between their mouths. "Yes!"

Now he was still as a statue as she kissed him—and he wondered if he'd heard her right.

"You said yes?" he asked against her lips. "Wait, really?"

"Mm-hmm. That was a yes. *Is* a yes."

Closing his eyes, he started to kiss her, and then he was pulling her down into the soft grass. As they stretched out together, their bodies getting flush, his arousal was instantaneous and urgent.

Yet he pulled back and looked at her. Stroking her face, he whispered, "I am so relieved."

"You are?" She smiled. "As if I would say no."

He thought about all they were facing. "I can't do this without you."

What's more, he didn't want to.

And as he thought about the alternative, she shook her head, like she was reading his mind. "Whatever happens, we face it together."

"I just wish I had more to offer you."

"You have given me yourself. That is all I should ever need."

They started kissing again, and their clothes were not long for remaining on. Rolling her onto her back, he stared into her eyes as they were joined.

The pleasure had never been so intense.

Then again, he couldn't shake the sense that though this was supposed to be a beginning for them . . . somehow it was also the end.

He thought back to the meadow and all those flowers.

Maybe this time, it would be different.

CHAPTER FORTY-SEVEN

After the meeting in the King's baby blue study broke up, Eddie followed some of the members of the Brotherhood down the grand stairs, across the mosaic depiction of the apple tree in full bloom, and out through a vestibule into the night. Standing on the stone steps with Ad at his back, he looked across a courtyard to the smaller structure, then glanced out to the view from atop the mountain. The wind was persistent and strong, the cold creeping in through his leather jacket and his heavy flannel shirt, and as he took a deep breath . . .

He felt alive.

Which was about so much more than being immortal and not subject to death's dispositive void.

He had missed this, he realized. Sure, he and Ad had

had a purpose in finding Lassiter, but that was different from engaging an enemy. With a cadre of other fighters who were up to the task.

Fighting was in his blood. Avenging angel, indeed.

"Thanks for being here with us."

Eddie looked over his shoulder. The goateed Brother—Vishous was his name—was lighting up, a gloved hand circling the fragile flame that he'd popped up at the tip of a Bic. As he exhaled, smoke drifted back toward the gray stone mansion.

"No problem," Eddie murmured.

Ad leaned in to the vampire. "We like being useful as well as decorative."

The Brother Vishous nodded. "And we'll take the help, for sure."

When the group on the steps had filled out to all of the assigned members, one by one the vampires dematerialized to the location they'd agreed on.

Eddie looked over at his best friend. "You ready for this."

Ad was steady and sure as he nodded. "I feel like I'm back on track, actually. I'd rather be a soldier than a scout."

"Me, too."

"AWOL it is, then."

They clapped palms and shook on it, the deal that they had been tap-dancing around sealed on both sides.

Then they followed the vampires, ghosting off into the night, traveling back to the neighborhood of fancy houses, and humans who were clueless . . . and demons who were trespassing. As they returned to their corporeal forms, it was not beside the white Federal mansion with the detached garage. It was in front of a Tudor-style house that was set very far back on grounds that were worthy of a garden party. Or twelve.

Eddie scanned the landscape—and Ad did the same. It was only after both of them nodded that the Brothers went up to the front door.

The Brother Tohrment, who Eddie gathered was the King's right-hand male, was the one who put the lion's-head knocker to use, and the reverberating sound was the kind of thing that could be heard even outside of the grand manse.

It was a while before the summons was answered, and the butler who dragged open the heavy oak door looked worn out.

When he saw who was in the drive and on the stoop, his brows went high and he stumbled his footing.

The Brother Tohrment spoke softly in a language Eddie couldn't translate, but the servant clearly understood what was being communicated. The butler bowed low and motioned for them all to enter the home.

Eddie and Ad were the last inside, and right before he stepped in, Eddie took one last look around. He couldn't sense evil anywhere on the property, but that didn't mean shit couldn't go south at a moment's notice.

When they were all in the receiving area, the servant bowed again and spoke in that language. Tohrment nodded, as did the others, and then the lot of them were taken farther back into the home. As they went along, Eddie checked out the interior. Every mirror was covered with black draping and so were all the hearths—and when he caught sight of a maid, he realized what he'd failed to notice right off the bat: The butler didn't have any white in any component of his uniform, and neither did the female servant who scurried out of sight as soon as she saw what had come into the household.

Eddie wasn't exactly an expert in staff dress, unless it came to what people wore behind the counter at McDonald's or Burger King. But he was pretty sure most butlers wore white button-downs and most maids had white aprons. Like he'd seen on *Downton Abbey*.

Mourning had been made manifest at all levels of the residence.

The room they were shown into was all dark wood and shelves of leather books with gleaming gold lettering on the spines. There were no mirrors to be covered in the masculine space, but the pall that was around the house had nevertheless managed to change the weight of the air somehow.

The Brothers lined up against the far wall, standing shoulder to shoulder, clasping their hands together in front of their hips, and setting their heads to face forward.

Ad wandered over there as well, but Eddie couldn't stay still. He paced down to the partner's desk by the cold hearth. The blotter was marked with fine old accessories made of green stained glass and weathered brass overlays in an ivy pattern. The inkpots, trays, and bowls were part of a set, and he picked one up, even though it was rude.

Turning the box over, he read the tiny inscription on the bottom.

Tiffany & Co.

He was just replacing the thing exactly where it had been when footsteps approached.

Stepping away from the desk, he did not join the others, for a reason he couldn't quite figure out. Maybe it was the need to pace around that had dogged him since the second he'd set foot on the property.

The male who entered the library was accompanied by the butler and was obviously the head of everything, and as soon as he was through the doorway, the latter stepped back and closed the library up.

The master of the household's fine clothes were likewise all black, no color in the tie, the pocket square, even the socks. With his dark hair slicked back, he looked suave. With the dark circles under his eyes, he looked tragic.

"Forgive me," the male said to his guests as he came forward. "But we offer no libation or fortification unto you as we are in mourning."

Tohrment stepped out of the lineup and nodded. "We completely understand."

Good, they're doing this in English, Eddie thought.

The male went around behind the desk. The carved chair had already been pulled out, as if in anticipation of him sitting down, but he did not lower himself, though he got into position like he was going to . . .

On the verge. Similar to the way the guy seemed to be almost ready to break down into tears.

"Your loss is an unimaginable tragedy," Tohrment said. "The King would like to extend his personal sorrow unto you and your *shellan.*"

The male inclined his head. "I thank you for your expression of condolence. And for his majesty's."

Tohrment approached the desk and took out a small envelope. Placing it on the blotter, he slid it forward.

There was writing on the front, in a heavy black script, and the male's hands trembled as he picked up the missive and turned it over. On the back, securing the flap, there was a round red wax seal with a crest on it.

On account of the shaking, it was an effort for the envelope to be opened—

The gasp was so loud, Eddie jumped even as the male himself seemed incapable of movement. And then after what seemed like an eternity, the sire of the vampire who had been killed closed his eyes, put the envelope to his heart, and sagged into his chair.

"The King has a son," Tohrment said roughly. "He wanted to convey to you—"

The Brother had to clear his throat, and it was weird. All of a sudden the others came forward to back up their leader—but not as a show of solidarity for the benefit of the head of house. Rather, it was for Tohrment, who took several deep breaths like he was suffocating.

As the head of the household opened his eyes again, and Vishous placed his hand on Tohrment's shoulder, the Brother's voice was nearly inaudible. "Forgive me my lack of . . . decorum. I, too, lost a son . . . so I find composure at the moment a bit difficult to summon."

The male's face slowly lifted. Then he was getting out of his chair and coming around the desk. The Brothers made room for him.

"You have lost . . ."

"I have lost . . . a son. Yes." Tohrment cleared his throat again. "I am . . . so very sorry . . . I know how you are suffering right now."

With a choked noise, the male stepped in and embraced the Brother—and Tohrment wrapped his arms around what was a stranger by acquaintance, and kin by happenstance. As Eddie watched them stand together, he reflected how you never knew what someone had been through. He'd never have guessed the Brother who appeared to be the most put together had such a fault line in his life.

When they finally parted, Eddie had to wipe his eyes. He wasn't the only one.

"I shall treasure this always," the male said as he held up the envelope. "I . . . it was most unexpected."

"As I said, the King himself has a son," Tohrment murmured.

The male nodded. And then gripped the heavy arm of the fighter in front of him. "And may I say that I am sorry for your loss."

With that, they both composed themselves, the male returning to the far side of the desk to blot his face with a handkerchief, Tohrment looking up at the ceiling, around at the books, down at the floor, as he blinked fiercely. And as the Brothers receded back to where they had been in their lineup, there was this very guy-thing where everybody pulled-it-the-fuck-together.

This time, the head of the household sat down in his chair with control, and he reopened the envelope. Sliding out the contents, Eddie was interested to find that it was a pressed satin bow made up of a pair of red and black lengths, secured by a diamond cluster. The reverence with which the gift was handled was clear, and as he placed it on the blotter and stared, he shook his head.

"Most unexpected, indeed. And my *shellan*, who suffers so, will pin this unto her mourning dress."

"Your mourning is the King's, and he would have come himself, but the times are fraught."

"Yes, indeed they are."

Tohrment glanced back at the others. "And that is why, I am sorry to say, you and your remaining bloodline and all your staff must depart from these premises right now."

The male looked up in alarm. And before he could ask, the Brother Vishous stepped up and took over. "We have reason to believe that the Omega's son was in this neighborhood last evening. We're not entirely sure how or why he was here, but his presence was irrefutable."

Tohrment continued, "There is a very real possibility that he's already aware of your home. He may have even been on your premises. We cannot urge you with any greater gravity to relocate right now. Further, we would request that you allow us to remain on-site."

"The Omega? Here?"

"We think he might have followed the remains of your son," Vishous said. As the male blanched, the Brother shook his head. "We can't be sure, but it's a logical inference. And what we don't want happening is him showing up again, maybe even tonight, with slayers."

"Please," Tohrment said, "take your mate, whatever other family you have, and all the staff under this roof, and dematerialize immediately to your safe location."

"N-n-n-now?" the male stammered.

"Don't take a car, don't take your things, just go," Vishous echoed. "*Now.*"

With a shuddering breath, the male seemed unable to process anything. But then he fumbled his hand toward a phone that sat beside a brass lamp with a green glass shade.

Picking up the receiver, he punched three buttons and rose unsteadily to his feet. When he spoke, his voice was sharp. "We need to leave the house—don't ask any questions. Tell your mistress I am coming the now. Get her ready—then find Marls, Twina, and the other maids and inform them we're departing. I'll gather Charle and the cooks, the chauffeurs, too. We're leaving. Right now."

When he went to end the call, the receiver clattered around its cradle so badly, Vishous stretched out an arm and was the one who put it back where it belonged.

Then his eyes bored into the male's. "We want to stay here. In case they come—and we think they will eventually. If they do, there will be fighting. Do you understand? And though we're not going to worry about what gets damaged if we engage, I will promise that we'll fix whatever gets broken."

The male blinked a couple of times.

And then his fine features darkened into pure vengeance. "I care not about this house or anything under my roof. Just kill the bastards. *Kill them all.*"

CHAPTER FORTY-EIGHT

The night passed very pleasurably indeed for Rahvyn, and 'twas not all exploits of a carnal nature—although much of it was. Lassiter and she very much enjoyed the bathing temple, and several romantic strolls. Further, his private quarters were so cozy that she felt instantly at ease, and the fountain outside of them was enchanting.

"Are you ready to go?" he asked her.

Standing in the marble courtyard, in front of a beautiful blooming fruit tree, she reached up and touched one of the branches. Then she looked over her shoulder. On the far side of the colonnade, the doors to his chamber were open and the messy bed with its white sheets and pillows made her flush.

A smile haunted her lips as she measured the zebra print on the walls. Pink and black. They had laughed that he had put things as such just to get a rise out of the Brother Vishous.

As Lassiter came in behind her, she leaned back against his chest and wished they could stay. The day was soon approaching down below, and she knew he was eager for an update on the night from those who had been out in the field.

"We'll come back as soon as the ceremony's over," he said, as if he were reading her mind. "The humans call it a honeymoon."

"Honeymoon. I like that word."

They were in agreement that the mating ceremony should happen immediately. There was no reason to wait, and every reason to move forward with the official part of it all: Nothing was going to change her mind, and he was likewise settled and resolved—and though he wouldn't put it into words, she could tell he was holding back his worry over the future. The tension was in him whenever she caught him unawares, the moments of unbidden revelation spiking her own anxiety.

They had spoken of none of it, however. Why would they. The threats down below existed whether they were talked of or not, and this time up here was precious and short.

"We need not do anything elaborate in terms of celebration," she said. "The Brotherhood have been so kind and generous as it is—"

"Are you kidding me? That butler loves a good party and it's the kind of challenge Fritz lives for."

"For certain?"

Lassiter stepped around in front of her. "Okay, that *doggen* literally advised the King, when he was trying to pick out a service dog, to get a golden retriever because it meant more vacuuming."

"No. Verily, you jest me."

He put his hand over his heart. "On my immortal life. Rhage told me. So we'll just let them do whatever they're going to."

"Far be it from me to argue with the King and his household."

They laughed some and then kissed a little more . . . and then it truly was time to go. Just before she removed her corporeal form back down unto the training center, she took a last look around—

No, she corrected herself. Not a last time.

"Let us go the now," she said as she closed her eyes.

Traveling between the Sanctuary and the earth was like going between any two planes of existence, and there was a funny reassurance that Lassiter had been doing regularly what she had thought was so unusual and exceptional.

Once they re-formed back in the training center's break room, they grabbed some food in the form of sodas and chips, and following his lead, she snacked her way down the corridor, through the little office she'd spied earlier, and out into a long tunnel that she felt a bit vulnerable in.

"Does this go forever in each direction," she asked as she glanced back and was unable to see any terminus.

"No, there's an escape hatch down that way, and way up here there's the Pit, an outbuilding where V and Butch live with their mates."

"The First Family's house . . . I never pictured myself thusly." She wadded up an empty bag of pretzels. "Are you sure I shall be welcome therein?"

Lassiter brought up her hand and kissed the back of it. "You're going to be my *shellan* and it's where I live. Of course you will."

"So you have a bedroom within the larger home?"

"Better." He stopped in front of a steel door. "I have a couch, a TV, and a remote."

As he put in a code and opened things up to reveal a narrow staircase, she frowned. "And that is enough for you—not that I judge. I shall be happy wherever I am, as long as I am with you."

"When *The Golden Girls* is on and I have orange juice? It's a palace, trust me."

As he indicated the way through the entry, she ducked even though she didn't need to and entered a compartmentalized set of steps. He had to press by her to put in a code at the top, and her hands lingered around his waist as he passed her by.

They were kissing again as he opened the second portal, and as a result of their preoccupation, they all but spilled out into wherever they were.

"Master! Mistress!"

At the exclamation, they jerked apart. The butler who stood before them was one she recognized from her times down in the training center, the elderly, proper male as ebullient and natty as ever.

He cleared his throat and wrung his hands—and she got the impression he had been awaiting their arrival. "Forgive my temerity, but would you, by chance, have news?"

Lassiter put his arm around her and the way he puffed up with pride was positively endearing. "My good male, we have a mating ceremony to prepare for! We're going to need you to take care of everything."

The butler gasped. And then clapped his palms together with the kind of glee one would assume he should reserve for tidings of the greatest joy imaginable— as opposed to a raft of work.

"Indeed?" He clapped again. "For truth?"

Glancing down at her, Lassiter smiled. "And I have even better news." He looked back at the butler. "We must needs be prepared by nightfall this evening."

There was a reverent inhale. And then tears formed in those wrinkled eyes.

Just as Rahvyn was about to protest the incredible rudeness and incomprehensibly bad manners of it all, the butler burst into a cry of triumph.

"Yes! Upon the nightfall! All shall be perfection!" He flushed with joy, as if it were his birthday and he had been presented with a wish list's worth of gifts. "Whatever should you like to serve for your mating meal? Do you prefer beef? Chicken? A mix? Prior to that, we shall need hors d'oeuvres. A French theme perhaps? What is your color scheme, so that I may set upon gathering proper flowers, and what music do you prefer? We shall require a cake choice as well. Are you mating in the foyer? We have done that before and it is quite beautiful when the female comes down the grand staircase. Will we need garments tailored? Do you have a dress in mind? Are there jewels that require cleaning? What special guests are we including?"

The butler paused, and Rahvyn assumed it was to take a breath so that he did not require resuscitation following an event with his heart.

But no, it was worse than an emergency requiring the Brotherhood's very competent healers: The expectant look upon that wrinkled face . . . suggested he actually was looking for answers.

To what some distant, stupid part of her had hoped were rhetorical inquiries.

When only silence came back at him, Fritz looked to Lassiter. Then looked to her once more. "Perhaps my lieges have not considered any of the particulars as of yet?"

The words were spoken very delicately, as if he feared they might faint—and he might join them as he clearly did not like pushing them.

Lassiter glanced at her and shrugged. And then both males seemed to be waiting for her to respond.

Clearing her throat, she said, "You are most gracious, and forgive me—us—our indecision, but given our

utter unfamiliarity with events of this nature"—she
looked at Lassiter, and the relief coming over him gave
her the sense he understood where she was heading—
"perhaps, in light of your considerable faculties and
knowledge of this most beautiful home's staffing and facilities, you would be in the best position to remove
from us the burden and stress of choice?"

Rahvyn glanced at Lassiter once more, all how-did-
I-fare.

As he gave her a discreet thumbs-up, the butler got
teary all over again. Then he bowed so deeply, Lassiter
actually reached forward, as if in concern.

"My lieges, it is the honor of my station to perform
such a service for you both!" He put his hands to his
face in delight as he straightened back up. "Please, permit me my departure. I must needs remove myself this
very moment—there is much to do, much to do! Rest
assured, it shall be the very most perfect ceremony
ever—"

"Wait!" Rahvyn interjected. "Before you go—how
shall we remunerate you for the costs?"

She made the inquiry because a sudden worry was
going through her. She had no funds, and had never
spoken to Lassiter about his financial prospects. There
were always ways, of course, but—

The butler's shock was not the good kind: He had a
horrified look on his face, as if she had just set the First
Family's house on fire.

"I meant no offense," she rushed in. "Please know—I
am a stranger in your midst and it would be unforgiv-

ably rude for me to make any assumptions. My sire and *mahmen* raised me better than that."

"Oh," the butler said, clearly relieved by the explanation. "But of course. And rest assured, my master the King provides for all under his roof, whatever the occasion. So there is no cost to you as an extension of his beneficence and grace to those whom he rules and protects. Now, I must needs attend to the festivities! Blessings unto the new couple!"

At that, the butler all but skipped away.

In his wake, Lassiter turned to her. "You are a miracle worker with him. That could have gone badly."

"I do feel a bit like I have bested a gauntlet."

When he put his arm around her, she followed alongside him as they stepped out from behind some kind of stair—

"*Dearest Virgin Scribe*," she blurted.

The splendor before her was unimaginable and her eyes bounced around the majestic foyer and the grandiose rooms she could see through archways and open doors—and then she realized something.

Turning to Lassiter, she put her hand to her temple. "I must needs stop praying to her—it is just that I feel a bit odd sending entreaties unto you."

Lassiter's lids lowered and he dropped his mouth to her ear. "I can think of plenty of begging you were quite happy to do earlier."

She was laughing and batting at him, when the grand doors of the front entrance opened. All at once, escorted by a gust of cold spring air, the Brotherhood streamed in, their voices filling the space as much as their bodies did. But both the movement and the talk halted when they saw Rahvyn holding hands with Lassiter.

There was a shuffling of the males, and Sahvage stepped through the sea of broad shoulders.

His expression was reserved, and for a split second, she wondered if there was going to be trouble.

"Sahvage," she told her cousin. "I love him. I want to be his *shellan*, properly—"

A sudden cheer exploded all around, and as Sahvage broke out into a smile and came in for a hug that swung her around, she glanced upward.

There were females all along the gold-leafed balcony. Some of them she recognized from when they'd visited Luchas House, others were not known—but as they rushed down the grand staircase, it was as if they were friends of hers: They were all so happy.

Just like the Brothers, who were busy high-fiving Lassiter.

Beth, the Queen, was the first of the females to step off the stairs, and as she reached for Rahvyn, the embrace was spontaneous—and a little overwhelming.

The Queen.

As Rahvyn held on tight and blinked away tears, she thought, *At least I still have your pants on, Your Majesty.*

When Beth pulled back, she took Rahvyn's hands. Her face was so open, so gleeful, her clothing so casual, it was possible to forget who she was. Until that ruby winked.

"Do you have a dress?" the female asked.

"Ah, no?" Rahvyn looked down at the jeans and fleece. "But there need not be any—"

"Let's get you one, come on!"

Immediately, the other females circled, all hugging and laughing and clapping, Sahvage's *shellan*, Mae, chief among them. Before she knew it, Rahvyn was swept up the red-carpeted steps in a wave of friendship.

Unable to fight the ascension—and not inclined to argue, for it had been so very long since she had had friends, perhaps never—she glanced down to the foyer.

Lassiter picked that moment to look up at her through the congestion of powerful males.

For a moment their eyes met, and Rahvyn thought . . . at long last, everything was falling into place. Though the war was beginning again, and there were losses and stress, she knew, deep within herself, that as long as they were together . . .

. . . they could get through anything.

CHAPTER FORTY-NINE

The daylight hours were a blur of pre-celebration, and Lassiter was all for it. He also knew why the buzzing levity was front and center. The Brotherhood was gearing up to go against the enemy for God only knew how many new decades or centuries, and the stress needed to be burned off: The mating ceremony gave them an excuse to laugh and play billiards and eat and drink all day long.

An unexpected shift off, when no one knew when the next one was going to be.

And people thought he wasn't like GE, bringin' good things to life? Come on.

On his side, because he was worried about exactly the same thing they were, he participated in all of it. Meanwhile, Rahvyn got pampered by the females of the house;

and sure, traditional sex roles shouldn't be taken seriously, but as he yukked it up with the guys, it was nice to think she was with a group of females getting her properly ready for the ceremony.

Then it was noon. With the sun at its peak, he broke off from the partying and snuck through the kitchen, ooh'ing and ahh'ing at the *doggen* who were frosting the biggest cake he had ever seen. There were also roasts in the ovens, and the aroma of baking breads, and enough green beans to feed an army—to say nothing of the silver polishing that was going on.

Jeez, his tennis elbow got triggered just walking by the lineup of three servants chatting happily as they worked the Gorham's paste over forks, knives, spoons, candelabra.

You kind of worried that if you interrupted them for too long, you might get buffed like a platter.

Heading through the mudroom, where the boots were lined up and the parkas and windbreakers hung on pegs, Lassiter found the door into the garage and used it. Striding past the mowers, snowplows, and trucks, he exited into the backyard.

As soon as he felt the sun, he closed his eyes. The golden rays penetrated through his clothes and his skin, and replenished strength he hadn't been aware of doing without—and though he'd intended to walk down the house to where the terrace had just been set up with patio furniture, he stayed right where he was, leaning up against the great gray stone wall.

He thought about how Rahvyn touching him was just

like this . . . the feeling of warmth and kindling was the same. In fact, it was almost as if she were with him—

He knew the moment he wasn't alone anymore.

"Go away," he murmured. "Not that I mean to be rude."

Eddie's voice was full of irony. "You? Never."

Turning his head, Lassiter looked at the other angel—and he was about to tell the guy off when it dawned on him. "You don't need to protect me out here. I'm perfectly safe."

"Circling the wagons seems prudent. Don't you think?"

"Where's Adrian?"

"Getting taken for five hundred bucks by that Butch guy."

Lassiter whistled under his breath. "If the angel is smart, he'll pull out now. That former human is a shark at the billiards table."

"And here I thought the bastard was just a Red Sox fan." Eddie leaned back against the rear of the garage, too. "God, it's so nice out here."

"Creator, you mean."

"Amen."

As they both took deep breaths at the same time, Lassiter felt a rare moment of communion with the guy. They were so different. Eddie with his rules and his reserve, him with his no rules and blaring lack of reservation. But here, standing together and drawing in the sunlight, he was reminded of everything they had in common, as opposed to all they did not share.

"So now you know," Lassiter said.

"Know what."

"How hard it is not to help." When there was no response, Lassiter looked over, and he had to blink a couple of times as his eyes focused. "It also feels good. Like you're doing something right with your immortal life."

After a moment, Eddie said, "What can I say—I felt the Omega's son by the Audience House. And I want to fight."

"I'm glad you've come around and joined the team."

Eddie shrugged. "You know what, me, too. We've been on ice for far too long."

They went back to sunning themselves . . .

And as was the way, what felt like no time at all was actually—

"Five o'clock," Eddie exclaimed. "What the hell?"

Lassiter looked over again. The angel was staring at his phone—and then texting madly.

"Nah, it's not late." Except Lassiter checked the angle of the sun and frowned. "Holy crap."

"They're saying it's time for you to go in and get ready." Eddie stood up off the wall. "I'm supposed to tell you that there's a traditional robe for you if you want it? That's what the Butch guy just texted to the loop. But everyone . . . they seem to think you're putting an Elvis suit back on? What the hell?"

"You're on a text loop with them now?" Lassiter put his arms over his head and stretched his back. "Look at you, with your new buddies. And no, I already used that getup for Wrath's marriage ceremony. I don't want to wear it twice."

Eddie's brows lifted. "What are you doing with an Elvis suit in the first place?"

"There are things you don't know about me, angel."

"Yeah, and I'm comfortable with it staying that way. So what do you want to wear?"

"The traditional robe is great."

Besides, he didn't want to be a jackass. Not in front of Rahvyn, not during their mating ceremony. But for sure he wasn't giving up his zebra-print tights altogether.

Eddie opened the side door of the garage. "Are you really going through the whole deal? Like . . . what vampire males do in this kind of thing?"

"Yup." He stepped into the cool interior and smelled the faint mix of oil and gas he hadn't noticed before—proof that the recharge had been necessary. "So yeah, the robe's great."

"Wow. Intense."

"It's her tradition and she's my mate. I want her to know I'm embracing the way things are done for her people—I will say, it's a damn shame I don't have my jesses, though."

They walked across the concrete floor together, sidestepping a John Deere mower the size of a car.

"You never did find them, huh."

He thought of that lovely Indian couple, from the shelter. "No, I didn't."

"Pity."

This time, he got the door for Eddie, standing aside so the other angel could enter the mudroom first. "What am I going to do? They should technically be given, not bought—and anyway, I threw away all my gold."

The kitchen smelled even better now, the roasts out and resting, *doggen* mashing potatoes at the stove, green bean casseroles everywhere.

"Butch says the fighters are all waiting for you in the billiards room," Eddie murmured as he held up his phone.

"Let's do this."

They wandered out through the dining room—and what a spread, crystal and china on everything, arrangements of imported roses and peonies down the center of the highway-long table, a forest of candles ready to be lit. In the foyer, he glanced at the table that had been set up. Draped in black and red cloth, there was a sterling silver pitcher of water and a large sterling silver bowl of salt on it. And there were more candelabras on stanchions set up all around—and other preparations, with music, too.

Someone was playing an acoustic guitar.

Following the gentle strains of notes, he went into the billiards room.

And stopped dead in his tracks.

Lined up on the far side of his favorite couch, the Black Dagger Brotherhood, as well as all of the other fighters and males of the house, were dressed in long black robes. And in front of them, another table, of similar size to the one in the foyer, had been set up and was draped in black cloth.

"Hey," he said, looking toward the music.

Seated on a chair, Zsadist was playing the tune, a

quiet blend of harmonious notes that Lassiter didn't recognize.

Clip. Clip. Clip—

He glanced behind himself to see Wrath and George coming in. The great Blind King was also in a black robe, and the golden had a collar made of flowers.

"Good, you're here," Wrath said briskly. "Come with me."

Lassiter glanced back at Eddie. When the angel just smiled knowingly, he realized he'd been managed by the other guy, purposely monitored and kept out of this room for a while, not that it had been a hard job, what with the recharging.

Walking down to the table with the King, Lassiter looked at the warriors and tried to read their serious faces. "What's going on—"

"We understand that you're missing something. We didn't have time to do it all the way right, but we're making do with what we've got." Wrath put his hand in the pocket of his robe, and when he took something out, Lassiter couldn't see what it was. "This is from my *shellan* to you. Well, from me, too. But it's hers."

The King put something on the table—

A necklace. A gold necklace that was thick as his thumb and as yellow as the sun.

Lassiter frowned sharply. "What is this—"

Rhage was the next one who came forward. "This is the gold Rolex my Mary wears. I took it off my wrist and gave it to her as a present. This is from us."

Qhuinn and Blay stepped up, and the former nodded at his *hellren*. "This was his *mahmen*'s. When Lyric was named after her, she gave it over."

A gold bracelet now, ornate and Victorian.

One by one, the males came forward, adding to a pile that grew and grew. There were gold chains that were as long as an arm, and chunky-linked chokers, signet rings and dainty bands, earrings that were hoops and studs and danglers, bracelets that were braided, or solid, or . . .

When the last male came through, all Lassiter could do was just stand there and stare down at the gleaming load.

"Okay, time to get you robed up," someone said. "Who brought the slacks?"

"I got 'em."

"Here we go."

He stood there as he was stripped and helped into a loose pair of pants that tied at the waist. When they were secure, a black robe was draped on his shoulders and not zipped up.

"I can't . . . accept this all," he choked out helplessly. "It's too much."

"They're loaners," Wrath announced. "Borrowed, blue, old, bought. I don't know what the fuck the human saying is. But what we're clear on is that you're not getting mated without having a boatload of gold on your body. So let's get started putting it on—"

"Wait," someone else said. "We have that other thing."

"Oh, shit. Right." Wrath nodded to the assembled. "We did one other thing."

All of a sudden, the notes Zsadist was playing changed, morphing into . . .

Lassiter recoiled and looked over at the guy. "What are you—"

The entire lineup of males parted to reveal—

Four life-sized cutouts of Rue McClanahan, Estelle Getty, Bea Arthur, and Betty White as Blanche, Sophia, Dorothy . . . and the great Rose Nylund.

"How did you . . ." Lassiter started to laugh.

"Fritz is a genius," the King said. "For real."

"And there's nothing you can't find on the Internet," V tacked on.

Zsadist's incredible voice started to sing, "Thank you for being a friend . . ."

The others instantly picked up on the words. ". . . traveled down the road and back again . . ."

Eddie put his arm around Lassiter's shoulders. ". . . your heart is true . . ."

Even V walked over and muttered along, ". . . you're a pal and a confidant . . ."

Lassiter stared at all the gold, all the pieces of the lives he had endeavored to serve, to protect, to save. And suddenly things got wavy.

But not because he was sad.

As they continued to sing, the voices rising and falling as Zsadist strummed the chords, he picked up the first of the chains with shaking hands . . . and put it around his throat.

CHAPTER FIFTY

I think it's time."

Rahvyn looked away from the reflection in the mirror before her. "I cannot thank you enough for this."

The Queen smiled. "It's my pleasure, trust me. And you look amazing. I mean, you were good in the jeans, but this is next level."

Glancing down at the gleaming, silver dress, with its long skirting and lovely bodice, Rahvyn flushed. "I've never worn a proper ball gown before."

"If that male of yours doesn't cry, I'm the Easter Bunny."

"You would become a rabbit?"

Beth laughed. "It's just a silly expression. Come on—only watch where you step. Fritz is going to be so happy that we've trashed this room with such abandon."

The sitting area on the second floor had become the locus for all the females in the household to get ready, and there were clothes, dresses, crinolines, stockings, shoes, makeup, curling irons . . . everywhere. As she measured the mess, she remembered the fun that had created it, the dressing and undressing, the consultations on hairstyles, the joking.

The other females—including dear Mae, who as Sahvage's *shellan*, had taken an extra special interest in it all—had departed to the foyer, but she could picture them with such clarity, it was as if her memory were the actual experience.

"Rahvyn? You okay?"

She glanced back at the female, who was still the King's beloved *shellan*, but now also a friend. Beth was stunning in her red and black gown, her brunette hair falling down her back, a set of large diamond earrings twinkling on her lobes.

Rahvyn thought of the little cottage she had been raised in, the small, joy-filled life she had led before her parents died . . . and the changes had come unto her. There had been so many years of sorrow and then all that trauma. She had never expected happiness to return.

"This is all so unexpected," she whispered.

"Life can be really amazing, right? I remember when I mated Wrath, I thought the same thing—wait, hold on. Are you . . . you know what Lassiter's going to do, right? During the ceremony."

"About the—oh." Rahvyn put her hand over her mouth. "I, ah, we didn't speak of it? I certainly did not ask. Is he . . ."

"The pitcher and the bowl are on a table down there. So I think it's going to happen." Beth's expression tightened. "When I got mated . . . someone . . . was there for me, supporting me, and she helped a lot. I want to be that person for you when it's time. Unless you want Mae?"

Something about the energy of the Queen told a story that did not need words to resonate: The one who had stood in for Beth was gone now. She hadn't survived the war.

"What was her name," Rahvyn asked roughly. "Your sister who died."

"Wellsie. Wellesandra." Beth sniffled a little. "And she wasn't of my blood, but you're absolutely right, she was my family. She gave me my dress, just as I'm giving you yours. You would have liked her a lot. She was a strong female."

Rahvyn picked up the heavy, beaded skirt, and went over to the Queen. Dropping down into a low curtsy and bowing her head, she said, "I would be most grateful for your kindness during the ceremony. Thank you."

Beth nodded and smiled sadly. "Let's get you mated, Rahvyn."

With a brisk stride, the Queen went over to open the door—and when she turned back around, she was deliberately happy, in the way someone was when they were determined not to ruin somebody else's special moment.

"You know," she said, "silver really is your color. You look like a diamond."

Rahvyn glanced down at herself and then walked across the clutter, deliberately choosing where to put her feet. The gown's fabric, with its subtle pattern of beads, really was extraordinary, a shimmering fall the color of a dove's breast—and she liked its weight and the way it rustled.

"You all worked miracles," she murmured as she drew a hand down her hair, which had been curled and brushed into waves.

Beth reached out and squeezed her hand. "The miracle is you. Everything else is just window dressing."

Rahvyn all but floated out of the sitting room, and on the far side, there was no electrical illumination: Candlelight was everywhere and it was incredible, a soft, dewy glow replacing the artificial source that hadn't seemed harsh until it was replaced by something so much more gentle.

"Here she is."

As Beth spoke up, Sahvage stepped forward, and her cousin was handsome as ever, with his dark hair and deeply set eyes, yet he was also fierce in a floor-length black robe.

"You ready?" When she nodded, he tucked her arm through the crook of his elbow. "Beth, let Z know to start the music."

The Queen gave her one final hug, and then she lifted

the skirt of her own gown and rushed off. A moment later, a guitar started to play some classical music.

Her cousin led Rahvyn to the head of the staircase, and along the way, she found herself glad for his sturdy arm. She was nervous, praying she did not make a fool of herself.

And then she could see down below to the foyer. There were so many people . . . yet only one registered.

Standing next to Wrath, bathed in the candlelight, Lassiter was resplendent in a black gown, his blond-and-black hair split upon his shoulders and flowing down the front of his chest, glints of gold on his ears, around his throat, on his wrists and fingers—but that was not all that gleamed upon him.

Stretching out from his upper back, extending to the sides, a pair of gossamer wings were magically translucent, all the colors of the rainbow shifting along the pattern of feathers—and up over his head . . . a circlet of gold hovered and winked. Indeed, the calling cards of his status were both muted, but very present, and as Rahvyn stumbled in her awe upon the stairs, her cousin caught her.

Lassiter, the fallen angel, with his halo and his wings, was the most beautiful thing she had ever seen, and now that the illumination within him had somehow returned, she could not escape the feeling that all was right in the world.

Verily, this was a night for miracles—especially as he stared up at her, his eyes rapt on her own as if he could not believe what he was seeing, either.

In fact, his mouth actually fell open ... and indeed, halfway through her descent, he brushed at his eyes.

What a relief, that the Queen would not have to turn into a rabbit of Easter.

Down at the bottom, Sahvage stopped, and there was a moment of pause. Trying to catch her breath, she had to look away from her intended, and oh, what a wonderful assembly. The males and females of the house, as well as the young of all ages, and the *doggen*, had formed a semicircle around the foyer's fringes, the mosaic depiction of an apple tree in full bloom upon the floor like a hearth they had gathered about for warmth.

They were all smiling, the goodwill like the candlelight, bathing her and her angel, in peace and love.

"Who giveth this female unto this male?" the King demanded in a loud, booming voice.

"I do," her cousin, and sole surviving member of her bloodline, answered in an equally thunderous voice.

"Join her then with her intended mate that I shall conduct this ceremony in the right and proper way, that their union shall be recognized according to my authority and station."

Sahvage walked her around the table and there was a gloss of tears in his eyes as he put her hand in Lassiter's— and the instant she looked up into the face of her intended, she was transported to another place, everything disappearing ... until there was only him.

This is home, she thought. *He is my home.*

The rest of what Wrath asked, and what she and Lassiter answered, was lost to her, in large part because of the majesty of the proceedings—and also because she kept glancing at the table and the pitcher of water and basin of salt that were upon it.

She marveled about what Fate provided. She truly did.

◆ ◆ ◆

Rahvyn was the most resplendent thing Lassiter had ever seen, and as he answered the great Blind King's prompts and stared into his *shellan*'s silver eyes, he was blown off the earth and sent into the stratosphere: Considering it was his mating ceremony, you'd think he'd pay more attention to the ins and outs of what was being said, but really . . . all he could focus on was Rahvyn and how he was the luckiest male on the planet. On any plane of existence.

And then it was time.

The Black Dagger Brotherhood lined up by the table, and as Lassiter removed his robe, revealing his bare torso draped in all of the gold that had been lent to him, he was aware that both Beth and Mae had stepped in beside Rahvyn and put their arms around his female's waist.

They hadn't talked about this beforehand, and the tense expression on Rahvyn's face made him wonder if she didn't want him to complete this part of the ceremony.

But then she nodded and he nodded back.

Wrath unsheathed a black dagger. "*Kneel,*" he commanded.

After Lassiter retracted his wings and complied at the feet of the King, Wrath said, loudly and clearly, *"What is the name of your shellan?"*

"Rahvyn," he answered with equal strength. *"She is known by the name, Rahvyn."*

He looked across at his mate as Wrath, guided by Tohr, made the first of the carvings, the symbol for the letter *R* cut into the skin on his upper left shoulder, his silver blood flowing, warm and vital, down the side of his ribs. To present himself as worthy, he bore the pain without flinching, without weakness. For his *shellan*, he would be strong in this and all things.

Sahvage, as Rahvyn's next of kin and eldest male relative, was next, accepting the dagger from the King, and then moving over to Lassiter's back.

"What is the name of your shellan," the brother demanded.

"She is Rahvyn, and she is my one and only love."

And so it went, each symbol carved into him by another member of the Brotherhood, the stinging agony something he continued to bear without submission. Beth and Mae stayed by Rahvyn throughout the cutting, and then, though his skin would not scar unless he willed it such—and he did—the salt water was brought to him. Bracing himself, he locked his molars as Wrath spoke.

"The name of your shellan is now upon your skin as in your heart. May you bear her symbols unto the world for your life, that all may know to whom you belong."

The splash was cold, the burning like fire had been poured on him.

And as the Brotherhood's chanting exploded in the foyer, he rose to his feet—and Rahvyn broke free of the Queen and ran to him.

Throwing her arms around him, he winced and she apologized, but he didn't care and neither did she. They were kissing as cheers echoed all throughout the grand foyer.

"We did it," he said against her mouth.

"We most certainly did." She touched the gold that draped down his chest, the various necklaces and bracelets locked together, forming one long chain that he'd wrapped around and around his torso. "Are these your jesses?"

"They're loaners." He put up his jingling wrist. "All of them."

"And earrings. Oh my, they loaned you . . . everything."

"It was a group effort."

And then she reached up to above his head. "Your halo . . . it has returned."

"Has it, then."

"Indeed."

"Ah, well. You found it and brought it back to me, haven't you." He brushed her lips with his own. "I told you, you are the Gift of Light."

She shook her head at that, but he was glad that there was no argument from her as the household converged upon them, everyone hugging and clapping, the *doggen* breaking out from the dining room with silver trays of champagne flutes.

And then Vishous was standing in front of them, the brother's icy white eyes narrowed. As usual. "I still hate your taste in TV."

Lassiter shrugged with a grin. "That's because you're emotionally stunted. It's okay, I love you anyway."

The tic in that eyebrow next to the tattoos at his temple was so dang satisfying. "We'll talk about mental health later. But I will say this, right now. I totally approve of your taste in females." He bowed. "Rahvyn, he's very lucky to have you."

As the brother straightened, Lassiter nodded and looked down at his mate, who was positively glowing. "You know, V. That is one thing that you and I are always going to agree on."

Other people came by, a receiving line forming, and some kind of toast was made. And then another. And then came passed trays of little bits of food and more champagne as the meal was getting ready to be presented in the dining room.

Over the course of so many centuries, Lassiter had heard the expression "such-and-such was a blur," and he hadn't truly understood what they meant. He did now. He knew that Rahvyn was with him, and everyone in the household was happy, and the champagne was cold, the hors d'oeuvres involved melted cheese and almonds on crackers as well as other things, and everybody was celebrating.

But like the details of the ceremony, so much of what was going on around him was lost.

Maybe the nuances would come back. And even if

they didn't, the night was . . . utterly unforgettable, even if only parts of it sunk in.

Just before they went in to take their seats at the table, Rahvyn tapped him on the arm. "Lassiter," she whispered.

He bent down. "Yes?"

"Um . . . who are they?"

As his mate discreetly pointed to the corner of the foyer by the billiards room, he started laughing at the lineup of cardboard cutouts.

"They're friends," he said as he tucked her against his side. "And I'll show you all about them later, I promise. You're going to *love* them."

CHAPTER FIFTY-ONE

The festivities went on for hours, and Rahvyn absorbed it all, learning names and faces, and eating and drinking in an outrageously luxurious dining room, and listening to the guitar player with the scarred face who was certainly a master of his instrument. But eventually, she could not hide her yawns, no matter how much she tried. Not wishing for Lassiter to have to leave their own party, she went into the room with all of the green felt tabletops, and found a leather couch with the perfect contours to curl up in.

Her borrowed gown, though formal and certainly the most beautiful thing she had ever worn, was surprisingly comfortable, the long, loose skirting allowing her to tuck her knees up, as her head turned to the side and became cradled in the sofa's arm.

In the background, there was the curiously enchanting sound of billiard balls knocking and falling into pockets, and males and females talking, and she was aware of feeling so at peace—which was a surprise, given this was the First Family's mansion—

"Come here," Lassiter said, "let me pick you up."

Her eyes fluttered open. "Oh, I did not mean to fall asleep—"

"I've got you." His arms shifted under her, and then she was being lifted. "And I'm going to take us home."

"I can wake up—"

"No, it's the perfect time to go." He raised his voice a little as he spoke with someone she did not track as her lids somehow weighed more than she could lift. "What? . . . Yes—oh, come on, you're the ones we need to thank. Can you make our goodbyes? And we'll be up in the Sanctuary . . . honeymoon, yup."

She intended to tell him that she would be able to make her way around and express her gratitude to all and sundry—but every time she tried to open her eyes, things got even heavier.

The next thing she was aware of . . . was a whirling sensation, as if the world were spinning—and then came a tinkling sound. The fountain. In the white marble courtyard . . . with the fruit tree and the colonnade.

Forcing herself to rouse, she said, "We're back."

"Mm-hmm."

Lassiter carried her into his private quarters and she smiled at the zebra-print accents. "Your decor . . . is so original."

The double doors closed behind them, and the strange ambient light, which had no discernible source of which she was aware, dimmed.

"You know, it's been called worse." He laid her upon the bedding platform. "And I spared you a pink and black suit for the reception."

"Pink and black?" She arranged herself against the pillows, her body languid. "How vivid."

"Again, that's a kind word." He sat down on the mattress beside her and stroked her leg. "You okay? The ceremony is a little intense at the end and I know we didn't talk about it."

She nodded and returned unto the moment when his silver blood had flowed and he had borne the carving with utter bravery. "I am so honored. Although I am not sure I could have stood up on my own. Thankfully, Mae and Beth were there beside me."

"Good. I wanted everything to be done right."

When there was a pause, she smiled as she recognized what he wanted but would not ask for. "I am not *that* tired, you know."

All at once, her *hellren* pounced on her, finding her mouth and kissing her deeply, his body settling on top of hers, pressing her down.

"I've wanted to do this all night," he moaned as he nuzzled his way down her throat. "And this dress is fantastic—but it's got to go."

The zipper was on the side, and he zeroed in on it with such confidence, she knew he had been eyeing it and strategizing what it would take to get the thing down its track. As the bodice loosened, she sat up, but the skirt trapped things, so she had to lie back down. But then they couldn't get the top off.

"Be of care," she said. "This is the Queen's—"

"How do we get this—"

"Here, I shall stand," she suggested with a laugh.

Up on her feet, the dress flowed off her body and formed a pool that shimmered at her feet, and after she stepped out of its splendor, she was careful to pick it up and fold the shimmering weight. There was a white table in the corner and she laid the gown upon the top, so that it was not wrinkled.

"The females were so kind to me, and—"

The words froze in her throat. From across the way, Lassiter was staring at her with such intensity, he arrested her where she stood.

"Come to me," he said in a guttural voice. "*Shellan mine.*"

She had worn a sleeveless shift beneath the gown, and nothing under that, and as she complied with his order, she was aware that the fabric was so fine, her body was visible unto him.

As soon as she was in range, his hands reached out and pulled her in, and he went right for her breasts, sucking on them through the silk's fragile layer. The sensation was exquisite, especially as he switched to her other nipple and the wetness cooled and tightened her tip even further.

Sweeping her off her feet, he laid her down again, and between one blink and the next, all the gold upon him disappeared and reappeared beside the Queen's beautiful gown.

"Will you turn about," she whispered. "That I may see properly my name upon you?"

He pivoted, just as she had asked, and her breath caught. Stretching across his upper shoulders, in a subtle arc, were the symbols of her name, the scars already healing and leaving a clear imprint on his skin.

Lassiter looked back at her. "Is it good? It feels good. I mean, I don't even care what it looks like."

"It's . . . the most beautiful thing I have e'er seen."

The smile of his satisfaction was masculine pride made manifest, and he came at her anew, although this time he did not mount her. He went unto her feet and started kissing her ankle, and then her calf, just below the knee—and thus he continued upward, his hands moving the shift up as his mouth brushed over her skin.

She had a thought about where he might be heading.

And he did not disappoint. Spreading her legs, he stared at her sex. "I want to taste you."

As she moaned in anticipation, he went in to her core, his lips sealing on her, the wet-on-wet caresses sending her into a release that surely shattered her corporeal form—except no. She remained whole.

She knew this because after he worshipped her most intimately, he repositioned her limp, hungry body, and stretched out as if he were making himself comfortable for the duration.

He did not stop.

The pleasure was . . . unparalleled.

♦ ♦ ♦

Talk about heaven.

As Lassiter sucked his female off with his mouth, making it all about her, he was very aware of not wanting to do anything else or be anywhere else. Nuzzling into her sex, he savored her, and after her first couple of orgasms, he licked two fingers and slipped them inside of her. Paying all kinds of attention to the top of her slit, he penetrated her with a rhythm that he knew was going to—

"*Lassiter . . .*"

The sound of his name leaving her mouth like that was more than he could handle. And he made his own need even worse by looking up as he ate at her. On the far side of her taut breasts, all he could see was the column of her throat and the tip of her chin as she arched back in ecstasy.

Fucking hell, his cock had its own heartbeat, and the damn thing was running a sprint between his thighs.

Rearing up, he shoved the loose pants down, grabbed his shaft—and plowed into her. As she cried out again, he propped his weight on one palm, stretched her leg up, and went in deep. He had marked her before, during the hours they'd spent in the cave, but now was different. It felt so . . . very different.

He started to come, ejaculating inside her, and as soon as the release passed, he pulled out and started pumping himself off.

He covered her core with his essence, and he knew

she loved it by the way she spread her legs as wide as she could, her open folds receiving everything he had to give her, his releases gleaming on her sex, her lower abdomen—now her breasts.

The bonded male in him, which he hadn't known he had to offer, was taking over, marking her, claiming her as his own.

And when it was all over, his energy spent, his come drained, his body loose as water, his collapse was so abrupt, he literally fell on her as his arm gave out. Panting together, he rolled onto his side and took her with him. Fitting her into his chest, he closed his eyes as her breathing regulated into the steady rise and fall of deep sleep.

He could not join her.

The evening had been perfect, and he wouldn't have changed a thing. But time was passing, the uncomplicated joy of those joyous hours receding as an island departed from. And the sea of destiny was getting rocky.

It was time for him to go see the Creator.

There was no putting it off any longer. Eddie and Adrian had joined the fight, which was great—and also wrong. But they were going to have to deal with the fallout from their situation, just like he was going to have to deal with his.

He had to make things right with the Creator. Whatever that looked like, whatever he had to do.

"Rahvyn," he whispered, though he hated to wake her.

"Mmmmmm?"

He smiled at the way his cock, as exhausted as it

was, sprang back to life at the sound of that one, drawn-out syllable, coming off her lips.

"I've got to return the gold to the brothers." He hated lying to her, but he didn't want her to know where he was headed—and at least there was no reason to worry about her safety here. "Listen, these quarters are totally secure. I've willed it so no one can enter them right now, not even Wrath himself. If you do decide to explore, just stick to the library and the Temple of the Sequestered Scribes, okay? I'll be back soon, and will go with you if you want a stroll."

"I doubt very much I shall go anywhere else but this bed," she mumbled. "Love you."

"I love you, too." He kissed her on the top of her head, and when she lifted her mouth, he kissed her there as well. "You're safe, I promise."

Moving away from her was like peeling the skin off his corporeal form, and after he pulled a soft blanket over her naked body, he swung by the bathroom he'd created for himself so he could stand beneath the waterfall there for a minute. After he donned a white robe in a show of respect, he went back and watched Rahvyn sleep.

He and the Creator had never particularly gotten along.

But there was no way he was leaving the female who rested so peacefully in his bed.

He was prepared to go up against the greatest force in the universe just to stay by her side.

The last thing he said to her, before he left . . .

"I love you."

CHAPTER FIFTY-TWO

Sometime later—it felt like hours, mayhap it was merely a solitary single—Rahvyn woke up. Stretching her arms over her head, she arched her body and curled her spine back, releasing tension that had been created by muscles sore for the very best reason. Indeed, Lassiter's scent was all over and around her, and she patted the bedding platform beside herself in the dim glow, convinced for a moment he was still with her.

Alas, no. She was alone—and remembered him telling her he was going back down to the mansion.

Refreshed in a way that belied her earlier exhaustion, she got up and walked about the room. In the far corner, there was the sound of falling water, and she was transfixed by the sight of a cascade pouring into a basin the size of three proper tubs.

Stepping under the rush, she washed herself, and then used a white robe that smelled like her mate to dry and cover herself. As the garment was clearly meant for Lassiter's size, she had to roll up the sleeves, and there was a train behind her as she promenaded, but she rather felt as though he were with her and that was a lovely comfort.

Mindful that he'd said things were safe only within this complex, she went to the door and opened it outward. The fountain drew her once again, and she went down the colonnade and over to it in her bare feet, sitting down on its lip and trailing her hand through the crystalline water. After spending time there, she proceeded over to visit the tree.

It occurred to her why she did not sleep. She was so happy to be in her new reality that she wanted to be consciously aware to enjoy it, the quiet, satisfying knowledge of what had transpired, and been blessed by the great Blind King and so many others, a meal of great sustenance to her soul.

After a further passage of time, she approached the connected entry unto the library. Stepping inside, she glanced around with wonder, and the freedom to go where she chose within its confines struck her as a liberty well worth savoring. It had been so long since she had explored a place. Back in the Old Country, she had always stayed hidden when she went out, and after coming to Caldwell, she had only ventured out that one night.

Whereupon Nate had been killed.

Well, and then she had gone out a second time ... and that civilian had been killed.

So no, she had not explored Caldwell.

Continuing forth, she was in awe as she contemplated all the volumes upon all the shelves. So many lives. So many fates. It made her think of how fortunate she was to have found Lassiter—needle in a haystack, indeed. At the far corner, she made the turn and came back down the opposite side. She repeated this march over and over, marveling at the effort required of the sacred scribes and the uniformity of the collection, how all of the volumes were so perfectly fitted unto their positions—

Abruptly, she stopped and frowned. There had to be, what, a hundred thousand tomes? And here was one, the only one, it seemed, that was not set properly in its place.

Feeling as though she were doing a duty to help, she put her forefinger on the spine and went to push it in. Except then she saw the name.

It was her own.

As a sense of unreality came over her, she reread the Old Language symbols, just to make sure. And then she smiled as she recalled that the precise pattern was borne now with pride by her *hellren*.

Pulling the volume out, she remembered standing right in this place, with Lassiter. He had drawn this book and put it back as a random example. Funny how, at the time, neither of them had recognized the identity of the individual.

"You must have wanted us to read my story," she murmured as she opened the cover. "In some secret place of your heart."

The script was beautiful, the symbols precisely drawn, like art, the flow of meaning at first lost to her—but then the events of her life were presented, in a narration that was both objective and kind. The early years, when she had been such a happy pretrans, were difficult to relive, and she tried not to become emotional. She often avoided thinking of her parents as the loss of them was something she had not recovered from, yet now as she skimmed specific events, there was warmth, too. That had been such a lovely time in her life, when her "gifts" had not been so difficult to conceal—and she had not yet attracted attention she had not wanted. She recalled, too, how Sahvage had been off with the Brotherhood, a warrior spoken of with pride and awe in and among the family's bloodline.

And then . . . the terrible period thereafter. When she had been alone, even though Sahvage had come home unto her.

She read it all, even up to when she had met Lassiter at the garage of Luchas House. She had known then, as their eyes met, that he would change her immortal life forever . . .

Surely that had been after the Scribe Virgin had departed? During one of their quiet talks after mating, Lassiter had told her what that moment had been like, when the *mahmen* of the race had asked of him to take over from her.

514 J. R. WARD

Yes, it had been afterward.

She glanced up and around at the shelvings. So the books were writing themselves now, for he had told her the Chosen were released of their service before he had taken over. What magic was that? And would her mating ceremony be represented thus—

Dropping her eyes back to the script, she read on . . . until she got to a passage that made no sense. Thus she backed up and reread it.

Then she read the lines of symbols a third time.

The Book. It was about . . . the Book.

And a demon. And a spell that required the evil that was called Devina to break up love in order to find it herself.

Lassiter's name appeared next . . . and then the meadow of flowers was described. The wonder and heartbreak of the moment was perfectly captured, a beginning and an ending detailed in a poignancy of sadness—and yet it had worked out. He had come back unto her with a complete reversal of his previous intention, and ever since then, they had been together.

Anticipating a revisit of all their joy, she continued on—

The symbols that arrived next in her field of vision were such that her heart slowed . . . and then stopped in her chest. The now she reread, and a sickening dread formed in the pit of her stomach.

As she weaved on her feet, she had to throw a hand out and catch herself. Surely, she was misconstruing all of this.

And yet she remembered a statement Lassiter had made in reference to all vampires: *I will do anything to help them.*

Backtracking a page, she returned to the description of a demon and a spell whereupon love must be lost for the evil to find its own mate.

Lifting her eyes out of the tome, she stared ahead and saw nothing of the library. In the back of her mind, she heard Lassiter telling her . . . that he had done a bad thing for the right reason.

At the time, she had felt such a communion with him, for she had done the same and knew well the guilt and self-loathing that had radiated from him.

But what if he had felt as such not because of an event he had been recalling . . . but because of an event the angel was living in the moment.

He had brushed her off at the McDonald's, as they had stood before the golden arches. But then, after he had been injured, he had professed his desire to return unto her. The about-face had been something she had been so grateful for that she had not questioned it— and thereafter, she had reveled in his change of mind.

The image of him standing before her during their ceremony, with his wings and his halo resplendently visible, burst into her mind. She had been so touched, so enthralled.

Turning the page back to what had frozen her heart, her eyes went to the passage . . . that read loud and clear what she sought to deny: *Whereupon the angel resumed with the female Rahvyn, such that the race and the*

Brotherhood were protected from the demon Devina finding her own mate, for the love within the female Rahvyn must be kindled for the future to be best assured.

Her vision grew indistinct as tears marshaled.

Which was fine, was it not. There was naught else that she needed to read.

As she closed the book and slid it back into its proper place, she revisited the image the Book had shown her, of Lassiter in the cave, the firelight upon his face.

She had assumed it had been a beacon to draw her forth.

Now . . . she knew it had more likely been a warning that whate'er else she had endured in her lifetime, what the angel was going to wrought upon her was going to be a far, far worse devastation.

CHAPTER FIFTY-THREE

When Lassiter returned to the Sanctuary, he was wrung out. An accord had been reached with the Creator, but it had been a long, harrowing conversation, steeped in tension that, considering the stakes, had nearly collapsed his head. Or blown it apart.

But in the end, the Creator had allowed him to stay on the earth. The other two angels as well.

It appeared that Lassiter, and all the chaos he brought with him, was part of the balance in the universe, just as Devina, in her own way, and Lash, in his, and the Brotherhood and the King, in theirs, were part of the equilibrium.

Good to know that tormenting Vishous was part of the grand plan.

And then, as he was leaving, the entity that had brought all life and light into existence had winked at him. As if all along, He had been resolved of this outcome and had just wanted Lassiter to work for it.

Fine, dandy. Do you, big guy, Lassiter thought to himself as he re-formed by the courtyard's fountain.

All he cared about was that he was sticking with his mate and the Brotherhood, and he couldn't wait to tell Rahvyn the good news.

With a spring in his step, he hit the colonnade, although he was careful not to make a lot of noise as he entered his private quarters—

"Oh! You're up—and I see you found the bathroom and my robe." He frowned and stopped. "Rahvyn?"

When she didn't look up at him—but just sat on the corner of the bedding platform, staring at her hands that were twisting in her lap—he felt an alarm start to ring at the base of his skull.

"What's going on?"

She took a deep breath and reached to the side. "I found my book. In the library."

He glanced around. "All right. You're allowed to read it, if you're worried about—"

"It was an interesting biography." She finally stared over at him, and her silver eyes were dark as pewter. "Naturally, you are in my book."

"I would hope so." He motioned her to continue. When she didn't, he shook his head. "What's wrong?"

Placing her palm on the front cover, she cleared her throat. "I need you to be very truthful with me right now because there is a lot riding on what I am going to ask you."

"Okay," he said slowly. "Let's have it."

"You have stated all along there is nothing that you would not do for those under your care."

"You know I have."

"Yes, I heard you." Now she touched the side of her head, tapping her temple. "I have been replaying everything you told me, actually. All along. And there is this one thing that I cannot get out of my mind."

"What's that."

"'I can build on that.'" She shrugged. "It's such a throwaway line, really. You spoke it unto me after I attended the King's dog. At that time, I was so . . . happy at your decision to return unto me, I did not question it a'toll. But after reading my book, I have to ask myself, what is he amplifying? Why would you say that."

"Because I wanted you to fall in love with me properly."

"Yes, that is exactly right," she said in a choked voice. "And why was that." She put her palm forward. "And this is where I need you to be very honest with me. Why did you want me to fall in love with you?"

"Why the hell are you asking this?"

"Do you know about a spell in the Book, one that provided Devina could fall in love as long as she separated us?" As he ever so subtly stiffened, she nodded as if she could read his mind. "You do know about it, do you not. And when did you know. Was it when you left me in the field of flowers? You must be honest with me now."

A choking sensation made it difficult for him to breathe, sure as if a hand had locked on the front of his throat. "No, I didn't know then."

"No, you did not, that is correct. But you knew after you were attacked and had recovered, when you stated that you were coming back to me and staying. Then, you knew about the spell—you knew if you and I were together, the demon, Devina, who has been tormenting your vampires, those whom you would sacrifice all for, those for whom you would do, in your own words, a bad thing for the right reason, would be denied a union with her desired mate."

There was a pause. And a lancing pain went through his chest.

"So I am not wrong," she said. "You came unto me, you spoke all the right things, did all the right things, to engineer a very specific result."

"Rahvyn . . . you're wrong about this."

"Well, you see, I went and found another book." She took a second tome out from behind her. "I had to figure out the cataloguing system to locate it, and that required a good deal of time. The object of the demon's love. Do you know who that is?"

The way he closed his eyes probably made him look worse, but goddamn it, this couldn't be happening—

"It is the son of the Omega. Devina is in love with him, and if they were to form a union, both would be more powerful and dangerous than they are the now." Her eyes were luminous with pain. "I complete the spell. You and I do. If we are together, the pair of them cannot unite forces and redouble their energy—and you knew this when you seduced me."

"I didn't seduce you—"

"Oh no? You did not tell me everything I wanted to hear, knowing that if we're together, your vampires are safer?" She put her hand up again. "I believe that you feel bad about this. When I think about those moments, especially in the beginning when you were kissing me, there was tension in you. I know now that it was because you were aware you were doing a job and you are not completely cruel."

Frustration, fury, terror . . . a toxic swill invaded his body, as he knew she was both right . . . and totally wrong.

"I have your name in my back," he snapped.

"Just more proof of what you have said all along. There is nothing you won't do for your vampires."

He shook his head. Over and over again. "You were there with me in the meadow that night with the flowers, you know how hard that was for me, to leave you."

"The issue is not why you left me. The problem is why you came back."

Lassiter leveled his eyes on hers. "So there's nothing you'll let me say to you in my own defense."

"You are not evil. You're actually . . . the best kind of savior there is, willing to sacrifice himself on any and all levels." She got to her feet. "I expected our forever to last a little longer than it did. But I should rather know the truth than live a lie, even if it is a noble one. And I shall say this the now, for having arrived at your truth, I have found my own. If what was between us was just duty to you . . . then that is all it was for me, too."

At the end, her voice failed, but she cleared her throat again. "Goodbye, Lassiter."

And with that, she up and disappeared.

CHAPTER FIFTY-FOUR

They were back at it and on post the following nightfall.

As Eddie walked through the Tudor mansion's front door, he immediately fell into his routine. Well, okay, fine, he'd done this when he'd been on-site the one other time, but it was a good practice and he was an angel who liked repeated processes. Striding through to the back of the house, he went straight into the kitchen, and started a loop that took him around all the rooms on the first floor. And hey, the architect had made good choices. The place had obviously been built with efficient servants in mind—because there was an unobstructed circle of access.

Which meant he could have started anywhere, but the kitchen was first because, coffee.

Ad stuck right with him as the Brothers fanned out, some heading to the second and third floors, others sweeping the basement. Command central was manned by Vishous and set up in the very center of the house, at a console table tucked in behind the stairs in a males' bathroom. The location was the perfect spot because there were no windows, but two ingress/egresses. So yup, that was where the backpacks of extra ammo, the flamethrowers, and the bombs were dropped.

Following his caffeine grab, he proceeded into the library, where they'd had that meeting with that poor sire who'd lost his son. Then it was out into the ballroom. Into a ladies' parlor. Off on a sidetrack to the conservatory.

All around the mansion, he could hear the footsteps of the Brothers doing the same thing he was. Maybe they had their own prescribed routes, too.

Eventually, there was a reconnoitering in the front foyer. Nobody said anything because it was clear nothing was out of place. With that, the shutters were raised by V. The pattern of lights that had been left on was similar, but not identical, to the evening they'd been on-site delivering the bad news—you know, so if the slayers were watching already, it would seem like there was nothing odd going on, as if the family of aristocrats were inside moving on—or trying to—with their lives.

Come on in, boys, nothing but a bunch of rich folks mourning the son they've lost. You slayers really need to breach the house and finish the job.

In the lull that followed, a bunch of the Brothers

took up res in the darkened dining room, and the library that was likewise kept lights-out, and the ladies' parlor. Eddie and Ad were the ones who moved around, and now when they did, they traveled by air—and they did not stick to the ground level. They went upstairs, even out onto the roof.

It was like pacing on a grand scale.

As the hours crawled at a snail's pace.

And meanwhile, not a slayer or essence of evil was to be seen.

The sense that something was coming was undeniable, however, as tangible a presence as any physical attacker, and it was fucking with Eddie's head. Fucking with everybody else's, including Adrian's.

Even the angel was being quiet.

For the most part.

During one of their transitions from the upper levels back to square one on the ground, just as Eddie returned to his physical form, his best friend lost it.

"I can't *fucking* stand the waiting."

This happy little missive was sent out into the airwaves at the very moment Vishous started cursing over in command central.

Hustling around the base of the staircase, the pair of them screeched to a proverbial halt.

"Please tell me I can hit something," Ad begged.

The Brother looked up from his phone. "Fucking aristocrats."

"Oh, so there's a list." Ad cracked his knuckles. "Even better."

Tohrment stalked around from the back. "What's going on?"

"The *glymera* are organizing again." Diamond eyes, narrowed and nasty, went back down to the glowing screen. "They've sent a letter to Wrath about the death of that young male, about the resurgence of *lessers*. They're questioning his leadership at the same time we're cooling our jets in this fucking house, waiting to fight."

"Strongly worded memos have always been their primary offense," Tohrment muttered.

"They're conflating the death of this family's son and the fact that the Audience House is on pause as evidence that Wrath is unresponsive. For crissakes, we're working on setting up another location—and like any of those fuckers come to see their King?"

Eddie thought about what had been in that envelope the other night. And how much Wrath clearly cared about his people.

"We made it clear that there's just been a delay in audiences," Tohrment said as he curled a fist around one of the black daggers that were holstered to his chest— like it was an unconscious tic. "It'll be a week, tops. We communicated that in our announcement—"

"They're calling the Council back into existence."

"*What*," someone else bit out.

As the other Brothers on the first floor pulled in and closed ranks, Vishous showed his screen, not that anybody could see the email or the text or whatever it was. Then he went back to reading aloud.

"Yup, and they are challenging Wrath to try to disband it."

"There's no critical mass of them anymore," another Brother pointed out. "This is bullshit. After the raids, there are what, five families left?"

"Ah, but here's the kicker." The laughter that came out of Vishous was as aggressive as a right hook. "They're going egalitarian. They're . . ."

As the words drifted, everyone leaned in—except for Adrian.

The angel abruptly went in the opposite direction, wandering off instead of closing in. Then again, he was known for his short attention span—and really, he was looking to fight, not wallow in the social posturing of vampires.

"They're opening up their ranks," V stated.

"I'm sorry, what?" Tohrment asked.

Eddie looked over his shoulder and frowned. Where the hell was Adrian?

"They're reestablishing their criteria based on net worth. They literally have a financial cutoff—if a bloodline has over that amount, they're on the Council."

"Oh, that'll be fun for them," Tohrment shot back. "One self-made guy who doesn't know which fork to use and they'll throw an embolism. Besides, Wrath might be democratically elected now, but he has all the powers he ever had. He can just disband it again, so the fuck what."

Vishous frowned and shook his head, falling silent as he continued to read. Then he looked up. "They're filing a vote of no confidence and going to pass it at their first meeting."

"There is no such thing—"

"According to them, the very fact that there was an election and Wrath won means that they can dethrone him. And there's some twenty families involved in this already, going by this list of signatures. It's a classic power grab with, at least in their view, the resources to back the shit up."

"Jesus," somebody muttered. "It never rains but it pours—"

"We have company," Adrian announced grimly from the library. "Out here on the side lawn, and it's not FedEx looking for the front door."

Instantly, guns were in hand, conversation ended, and everybody got ready to fight.

Be careful what you wish for, Eddie thought as he jogged over to his best friend.

CHAPTER FIFTY-FIVE

I t all started with the cat.

Or rather . . . the end began with the cat.

Wrath was standing in the doorway to the second story playroom, talking to Beth as L.W. stacked his emotional support blocks, when he heard the first of the meows. The sound was off in the distance, somewhere out in the Hall of Statues, and he didn't pay much attention at first.

But then it came again.

And again.

Out of habit, he glanced over his shoulder, which was, from a sensory perception perspective, incredibly inefficient. Unsighted, he gained nothing from his eyes pointed in that direction, and he'd turned his ear, which functioned very well indeed, toward the *doggen* wing, which was where the sound was not coming from.

But old habits dying hard and all that.

"Something wrong?" his *shellan* asked.

Other than the fact that the vast majority of the brothers and the fighters were out in the field, waiting to fight, while he was stuck in this house like a veal?

"No, it's just Boo talking," he murmured.

"That cat. I love him so much."

Wrath thought back to the first time he'd gone to see his Beth. Darius, her father, had enlisted him to ensure she made it through her transition. As a half-breed, she was in danger of dying when the change hit, and with Wrath's pure blood, she had a much better chance of surviving. The kicker? She'd had no idea what she was. There'd been a hope she wouldn't flip over to her sire's side, but want in one hand, shit in the other, as the saying went.

He'd showed up at her little apartment, in that backyard where the picnic table was, and watched her through a sliding glass door.

Boo had known instantly he was there, and had started pacing in front of the exit—

Meooooow.

"I'm going to go check on him," Wrath said as he once again turned his useless eyes in the direction of the noise. "I'll be right back, *leelan.*"

"We'll be here," Beth countered happily. "Taking care of business with these blocks."

As he strode off, George followed, the golden padding along, ready for any new adventure.

"Helluva mission," he bitched. "Feline patrol."

It was as he punched through the doors and left the staff part of the house that awareness coalesced in his mind.

An odd sense of urgency made him walk faster. "Boo?"

But the sudden surge of paranoia wasn't about the cat. None of this was about . . . the cat.

The next meow was out by his study. And then there was one halfway down the staircase.

As Wrath descended, a sense of unreality came to him, and when he got to the bottom, he pivoted to the left without the sound guiding him.

Progressing through the dining room, he was aware of feeling like he was being swept by a tide, carried through the spaces, though technically his feet were walking. At the flap door in the back corner, he pushed through, the scent of silver polish thick in his nose—

"—insisted on going," a female *doggen* was saying.

"That shouldnae be, though. Why'd you tell him ought?"

"I did not. He o'erheard me saying that I had left my young's blanket therein, and that the wee male was distraught and wouldnae sleep. What was I 'ta do—"

"Sire!"

There was a gasp, and then a silence, and he pictured two uniformed maids bowing at their waists.

"Where did he go," Wrath said. "Where did Fritz . . . go."

Even though he knew.

Jesus fucking Christ, the dream that had woken him up that day in a cold sweat was coming true.

+ + +

Far from earth's toil and trouble, in the alternate plane she had created for the Book's safety and her own sequester, Rahvyn sat upon grass that was no longer colored. In fact, all was shades of gray about her. Prior, she had lackadaisically amused herself with changing chromatics. Now her suffering was such that she had no interest in such wasteful pursuits.

As the Book flapped its pages again, she thought . . . this was where it had all started, had it not.

"I'm not talking about him." She shot a glare over. "Why didn't you tell me about the spell? About my role in all this? You let me walk into heartbreak."

The Book made some sort of response, but she did not track it. Why the hell did she care—

Another flapping. And more.

She would have left the thing, but she had no idea where to go. Certainly not down to earth, ever again—

Flappingflappingflappingflapping—

Aware that the ancient tome was giving itself a heart attack apologizing, she glanced over. But it was not an apology.

The second her eyes shifted in its direction, the open folio stopped its agitation and an image began to appear, summoned once again by symbols swirling—and of course, that reminded her of what Lassiter had gotten carved in his back.

Rahvyn shook her head and looked away. "I am done with all that. I am sorry."

FLAPPINGFLAPPINGFLAPPING—

She twisted back around and ignored that image of Wrath and the black tide of symbols swamping his portrait. "No, I am taking care of myself from the now on! I am sorry if there is a bad destiny awaiting the King—or whate'er you are attempting to tell me! But it is not my problem!"

The Book jumped up and down on the ground, its covers popping it up off the dingy gray grass over and over and over—while that portrait, so lifelike, so real, got inundated with the black tide again and again.

Indeed, the swamping was on repeat: The moment Wrath's face was eaten by the tide, it repaired, just to be consumed again.

Through her own pain, she had a memory that caused even more agony: She was standing on wobbly legs, witnessing her name getting carved, symbol by symbol, across Lassiter's upper back. He had not wavered for even a moment as what surely had hurt terribly continued. He had just stared at her with what had appeared at the time to be love, his silver blood running down off his torso, those gold chains that had been loaned by members of the household hanging loose and touching the mosaic depiction of an apple tree in full bloom.

Beside her on the left . . . had been Beth.

Holding her up, keeping her steady.

The Queen had been so helpful, so necessary, in that

moment, and yet she had been apart from it because she had not been staring at Lassiter and what was being done unto him.

The female had been looking at her *hellren*, the King, who was standing so proud, so true . . . staring back at her even though he was sightless.

Rahvyn watched as the portrait was once more covered by the symbols, and she thought of the young on the Queen's hip.

Closing her eyes, she shook her head as she started to weep. "I cannot stop what is destiny," she said aloud. "Whatever it is . . . I cannot interfere."

It was a statement she had made many times recently. But as she spoke it now, it was not from some duty to maintain balance.

She was just too consumed by her own pain to prevent anyone else's.

And her powerlessness increased her mourning tenfold, for the Queen would surely feel as she did the now if aught were to happen to her beloved.

"I am so sorry," Rahvyn said unto the great gray landscape that existed . . . only in her own mind.

CHAPTER FIFTY-SIX

L ash stood outside the Tudor mansion with a detonator in his hands. Just before he triggered the charge, he had a thought that he had learned all about explosives from the Brotherhood. Kind of ironic, really. As a result of having been in their training center program, he had been taught about bombs—how to make them, how to buy them, how to set them, how to release their power.

Zsadist had conducted many of those classes, and he could picture the Brother even now, perched with one hip on the corner of a desk, an IED next to him, his scarred face a thing of nightmares as he described exactly how a Crock-Pot and some nails could be deadly. How C-4 could be used.

How you could set up explosives in . . . say, just randomly . . . cars. Windows.

Doors.

Lash had given himself quite the refresher course the night before. Real hands-on, *in vivo* sort of stuff. Fun. And now he was here—at one of the two sites he had rigged.

The Brotherhood hadn't been around the evening before for some reason—which had given him plenty of space to work. But he knew they'd be back, and sure enough, they were.

Glancing to the left, he saw that his new crop of slayers were at the ready. He'd charged two of the women recruits to raid a black market arms dealer they knew, and they'd performed brilliantly. Courtesy of their little foray into Caldwell's commercial underground, the rest of the Lessening Society had firepower and ammo that was worth talking about, as opposed to a couple of shotguns that had been boosted from Dick's Sporting Goods.

Looking to the right, he saw his second and third classes of male slayers lined up with more of the women.

None of them seemed to care one way or the other about the equal-opportunity thing with the sexes. They were all just ready to fight because it was in their nature. As humans, they hadn't cared about vampires—hell, they hadn't known that the species existed. But it was a case of right person for the job. Each was on a hair trigger, in the best sense of the word. At least from his vantage point.

They hadn't cared one way or another about what the target was.

As he turned back to the fragile glass expanse of the mansion's conservatory, he fucking hated that the demon had been correct.

Except Devina had been. Thanks to her advice and efforts, he was so much further ahead than he had any right to be. But he couldn't think about that right now. As a huge shadow passed by in a darkened parlor, he thought that the Brotherhood were so fucking stupid. Like anybody would be fooled into thinking what was currently inside the mansion were the aristocrats who owned the place?

Come on.

Nope, the Brothers had taken over the site, as if they'd known that Lash had intended to use the family who was supposed to be there as a training ground for slaughter techniques.

Alas, no time to develop skills.

The war restarted properly . . . *now*.

As he triggered the charges, the explosions went off all around the mansion, brilliant fireballs and loud sounds breaking through the night.

And talk about kicking a bees' nest. What came out of the house was vengeance personified.

The Brothers streamed out onto the lawn, not from the doors that had been blown apart but from all around the roof, the second floor, the first floor.

As his slayers started shooting and there were shouts, he shoved his phone into his pocket, palmed his own gun—

And joined the fray with a bloodthirsty war cry.

✦ ✦ ✦

In the wake of the explosions, Eddie broke out onto the grass, took a bullet to the shoulder, and kept right on steaming. Pile-driving into one of the dozens of slayers that were shooting, he fell immediately into a hands-on ground game, the undead possessing incredible strength—

As he felt himself get flipped over, he looked up and lost his concentration.

It was . . . a woman . . . on top of him, her long dark hair braided in rows on her skull and flowing down the back of her leather jacket, her face, though full of rage, set with very definite feminine contours.

And yet, she was clearly a *lesser*, the stench of baby powder rolling off of her—

A gun shoved in his face cured him of the momentary check-out. He was immortal, sure, but damage was damage and his utility was in continuing to fight. Getting a bullet up his nose and into his frontal lobe was not the kind of mental health evaluation he was looking for.

With a quick slap, he put his palms on either side of the barrel, but she was ready for him. She brought out another gun as he redirected the first off to the side.

Sonofabitch—

A quick duck and twist, and he was out from under, slipping a bar-hold around her neck and hauling back. She immediately started choking, and through the pungent smoke that was drifting all around from the explosions, he caught a quick glimpse of Ad engaging with a male with a bald head. And Vishous with a woman who had dyed-red hair. And Tohrment with a guy who had tattoos on his face.

Gagging sounds came out of the woman—*slayer*—and one of her guns was lost as she clawed at his forearm. If he could get her to lose consciousness for even a split second, he had a steel hunting knife on his belt and he could—

The grip on his braid was sudden and powerful, and the jerk brought his head so far back, it nearly popped off his spine.

A massive male with blond hair stood over him.

As Eddie looked into a pair of eyes that were all wrong, a pall went through him. This was not a mere *lesser*. This was the master of them all.

The born son of the Omega.

The scourge upon the earth.

As recognition landed with a terrible pall, the evil put out his palm, and in the center of it, a black swirling smoke coalesced and began to build in size. As he lifted his arm over his head, and the angle of impact was directed at Eddie, his smile was cold as first sin.

This is where I end, Eddie thought as the sights, sounds, and smells of the battle around him began to recede.

Whatever was in that hand was the kind of thing that took the *im-* away from *mortal*.

Death had appeared, unexpected and dispositive, when he had least expected it, but wasn't that the way with fate sometimes. You were living . . . and then you were gone—

The yell was so loud, so furious, that even the evil paused and looked over toward the source of the sound.

Well, what do you know, Eddie was suddenly transfixed, too.

From out of nowhere, appearing right in front of them both, Lassiter was larger than life, his wings outstretched, his powerful body tensed for an attack, his face drawn with such rage that he was nearly unrecognizable.

The angel surged forward before the evil could react, and the impact was so great, he blew the blond entity off his feet and through what was left of the conservatory's glass wall.

The shattering was yet another explosion, sending shards into the air where they fell back to the earth in a shimmer, like diamonds.

But there was no time to watch the fight, or more importantly, help.

Another gun, from another slayer on the right, was pressed directly onto Eddie's temple.

"Oh, for *fuck's* sake," he spat as he got back into the fight.

CHAPTER FIFTY-SEVEN

The why didn't matter.

Who gave a fuck about the why.

And Wrath didn't even ask about the when. The who . . . that was obvious, and all that mattered really: Fritz had left the mansion and gone down to town, and was making a stop, for a valid reason given the way the old male thought, at the Audience House.

Where he was going to die.

Wheeling away from the two maids at the sink, Wrath didn't think. There was no time. He ran to the vestibule door, punched his way out, and dematerialized off the mansion's front steps. As fast as traveling through thin air was for him, it wasn't nearly fast enough, and he told himself he had to calm the fuck down.

The last thing he needed was to have his concentration broken to such a degree that he snapped back into being corporeal, re-formed in midair, and plummeted to his death over a mountain.

Navigating by memory and practice, he went directly to the Audience House's backyard. He had been to the property plenty of times when he'd been sighted, so as he returned to a solid, he knew he was at the rear, facing the entry into the kitchen.

Fritz's scent was obvious.

So was the click of the handle on the back door as the loyal butler went to turn the—

"Nooooooo!" Wrath screamed.

With a powerful lunge, triangulated by instinct and a spatial awareness that never let him down, he shot forward and shoved the *doggen* out of the way.

Right as the explosion went off.

In the split second between making sure Fritz was free of the impact and hearing the click of the detonation's ignition, he braced himself for the blast of heat— but when it came, it was so overwhelming, it didn't even hit as any kind of warmth. Like the pain was so great, his body literally could not register it.

And funnily enough, there was no sound. At all.

Just a weird, sickening swirl as he was carried up, up, and away.

His final thought was . . .

Oh, shit. Beth, I'm so fucking sorry.

CHAPTER FIFTY-EIGHT

Lassiter held nothing back as he and Lash went at it, two immortals throwing each other around the inside of a conservatory. Bouncing off furniture and miniature fruit trees. Getting scraped up, silver blood mixing with black. Glass breaking, sculptures knocked over, vases shattered.

After one particularly violent kick, Lassiter went into a tap-dancing retreat he did not intend—and when he hit something very hard on the small of his back, a ripple of discordant music played out.

Piano. A Steinway had caught his fall.

Across the ruined space, Lash was gearing up for a running offensive, the evil sinking down into his thighs and wiping the black blood off his mouth with the back of his hand. Malicious eyes stared forward with maniacal glee, and as he opened his mouth to hiss, his fangs were a pair of enameled daggers, long as elephant tusks.

The Omega's son started across the black-and-white marble floor, and Lassiter, who'd managed to get one hell of a thigh wound, needed to find his breath before he could keep going with the goddamn arm wrestling.

So he picked up the motherfucking grand piano and slung that bitch right at the piece of shit with the bright ideas.

Talk about your sonata in the key of ouch.

The ringing cacophony was satisfying, even if rough on the ear, and the force sent Lash pinballing into the next room.

Lassiter glanced over his shoulder. Out on the side lawn, battles were ongoing in the smoke and the shadows, the Brotherhood and fighters engaging with what seemed to be an army of slayers. He could hear guns discharging, and saw a good news pop-and-flash as someone managed to stab one of the enemy. But there were so many *lessers*.

No rest for the weary.

And really, given what had happened up in the Sanctuary with Rahvyn, he didn't give a shit—he was so in his feels, fighting was the only release that could distract him for even a moment from his pain.

Bleeding, limping, pissed off and violent, Lassiter went in search of his prey—

Without warning, he was tackled from behind, Lash's attack so competent that he was on the ground and sliding like a floor mop down some kind of hallway before he knew what hit him.

The rest of it was a blur of ruined furniture, paintings that were shredded, carved doorjambs that were cracked, and walls punched through with bodies. They were so equally matched as they hand-to-hand'd it through the first floor of the house that they might as well have been a pair of wrecking balls. And then he picked up Lash by the scruff of the neck and the seat of the pants, and threw him, headfirst like a battering ram, at the front fucking door.

The evil opened the way out nicely.

Well, not nicely at all, really. The evil blew the heavy oak panels right off their fucking hinges.

The shot of fresh air was reviving, and Lassiter dragged himself across the foyer, sidestepping a crystal chandelier that had fallen in a crash, lagging a leg because one of his ankles was probably broken.

The last thing he did before he stepped out was glance up, for no particular reason. Well, what do you know. His own blood was smeared across the ceiling. Guess the ground game had taken to the roof for a bit.

As he stepped outside, he looked at the sky and took a deep breath to try to ease his panting, sawing respiration. The pain that shot through his sternum was intense, but not because he was physically wounded. No, that was his broken heart, fuck him very much.

How was he going to go on without his female . . .

That was the thought that went through his head as

Lash pulled his own sorry, wounded ass off the ground and faced off, again.

Lassiter didn't know how much more he had in him—or what exactly was going to happen if he stopped, or more likely couldn't go on. He had seen what the evil had conjured up in his hand when he'd been about to do in Eddie.

That black void shit was lights-out time, whatever the hell it was.

And maybe he wanted that, he reflected as he gave the enemy time to get back on its—

The explosion that went off was distant, not on the property, but close enough that the noise gathered attention.

As he and Lash both looked to the horizon, in the back of Lassiter's mind, he had a thought that they really needed to take this whole business elsewhere. The estates were big in this neighborhood, but a couple of acres was not going to insulate this kind of light and sound show from the neighbors completely.

Sooner or later, cops were going to show up. Or security guards. And he was familiar with the only rule the Lessening Society shared with the vampires.

No human involvement—

The strangest ripple went through Lassiter's chest.

And what was weirder was that Lash also glanced down at himself . . . and put a hand on his own sternum.

Time slowed. Then stopped. And all the fighting ceased, like some siren call that could be heard by both sides of the war had registered, the smoke from the fires that were kindling all around the house billowing about on the cold spring breeze, making ghostly figures out of those on the battlefield.

Overhead, a shooting star traveled across the night sky.

Then the evil threw its head back and started laughing. The sound was so rich and triumphant, so unexpected, that all eyes turned in his direction.

Lash re-leveled his malevolent stare, whistled—

And the entire army disappeared.

In the utterly bizarre vacuum of presence and movement, the chiming of cell phones going off all over the property was as loud and obvious as a marching band.

With a frown, Lassiter glanced over his shoulder. Vishous happened to be standing in the busted-ass doorway of the mansion as he checked his phone.

And there was no forgetting, ever, the expression on his face as he looked up in numb shock.

"Oh . . . my God," he breathed.

CHAPTER FIFTY-NINE

Where's Daddy?" Beth said as she handed another block to her son. "Hm? Where'd he go?"

L.W. didn't pay any attention to her. He was like that when he was focused on something, those dark brows down over those now pale green eyes. She thought back to the early months after his birth, the whole first year really. They had been blue, then, and that had been a source of relief for Wrath. He'd wanted his son to not take after him with the blindness, like the so-called defect was a curse he hoped not to pass on.

They had changed, though. And now they were just like his father's.

Who knew whether he would end up blind, however—and if he did? It was not something that could not be embraced and integrated into a full, vibrant life. Wrath was proof of that.

"You're just like your dad," she murmured as she smoothed his cap of black hair and checked her watch. "Jeez, it's been well over a half hour. Where has he gone?"

Then again, Wrath was like that, always getting pulled into things as King. She wished they had more time together, and remembered what he'd said. Yup, they definitely needed a little private time down in Manhattan in that bolt hole of theirs. A good two whole nights of nothing but them naked in that bed—

Initially, the footfalls did not really register. She just assumed someone, probably Rhage given how heavy they were, was going next door to the movie theater because he was off rotation and bored out of his mind. But then the sheer number of them made an impression.

"Like a frickin' army is coming, huh, L.W."

She handed him another block. The construction he was working on was a tower that was way over his head, the levels stretching up from the ground a good four feet. He needed his little step stool with the railing to keep building, and she'd brought it over for him, but they were reaching critical mass. He was smart, and he'd built a solid base, but things were getting tippy and the fall from that height was going to do some damage if the whole thing toppled onto his head.

"I think we gotta be done with this one, my guy."

L.W. looked up.

At first, she assumed he was meeting her in the eye to argue even though he was essentially nonverbal. Because he was like that. In spite of the fact that he had yet to speak—because vampire young mature differently than human kids—he seemed to understand things way before his time, and he certainly communicated his thoughts with her through that stare of his—

Abruptly, she realized her son was not focused in her direction.

He was looking over her shoulder. To the door.

Through the glass inset, she saw Vishous's face, pale and hollow, and a ripple of unease made her fumble the block she'd been about to give to her son.

The door opened, and when she saw what was on the other side, she started to shake her head slowly. "No . . ."

One by one, the Black Dagger Brotherhood funneled into the children's playroom. That they were dressed for war would have been bad enough against the innocence of the toys and the colorful murals. That they were injured and bleeding, stinking of *lesser*, made their presence downright horrific.

And there was one, and only one, reason, for all of them to come to her at once.

"No, no, no—" She put her hands up to stop them and closed her eyes. "No! Fucking *no!*"

Next to her, the tower fell in a clatter.

"Don't you say it, don't you say it, don't you say—"

She popped open her lids on the chance that maybe—*maybe*—she wasn't seeing anything right. But the Brothers were crowding in, and behind them, out in the hall, the other fighters were clustered around: All of them, the Band of Bastards, those two angels ... Lassiter, who was bleeding silver from a head wound.

There was a milling of the big bodies, a breaking of the crush, as someone came through them.

It was Tohr. And George was mincing with stress at his side, the golden panting hard.

That was not what she noticed most, however. What registered in her mind, with all the impact of a blow to the head ... was Tohr's dagger hand on George's harness grip, the one thing, for all the petting the dog received from everybody, no one ever, *ever*, touched.

Beth fell forward onto all fours.

And screamed.

CHAPTER SIXTY

Three nights later . . .

The Tomb was the Black Dagger Brotherhood's *sanctum sanctorum*, a place deep within the earth on the mansion's mountain, a secret location where the ancient rituals and traditions of the membership could be carried out in private.

As Lassiter walked through the forest, he was part of an immense lineup of people.

Watching those ahead, and feeling the presence of those behind, he noted that the black robes were out again, and marveled at the swing of destiny. Happiness one moment . . . paralyzing grief and shocking loss the next.

Although he'd led the way in the topple, hadn't he.

And people thought *Dhunhd* was bad? The loss of the *shellan* that he'd barely felt like he'd had was, for him, the first death ... the harbinger of the second that laid waste to all of the lives in the Brotherhood's extended family.

And now they were here, everyone, servants and young as well, traipsing through the forest of the mountain, the scents of pine and mourning intertwining such that he doubted he would ever smell a conifer again and not think of this procession of black robes.

Then again, he was going to spend the rest of his interminable nights and days grieving. So what was one more association, really.

The foot travel ended at the camouflaged opening of a cave system, and there was a slow-up as the mourners waited to pass through the constriction. Everyone took their hood off as they entered— because it had been decided that anonymity didn't set the right tone—and he did the same, pulling the cloth off his head as he stepped into a winding passageway that culminated in a meshed gate bolted into the rock.

No one was talking, and he was aware that rules were being broken here. In the past, no one but members of the Black Dagger Brotherhood were allowed in the Tomb. Tonight, though, it certainly felt as though the whole of the household had joined those hallowed ranks.

Grief had inducted them all.

After he stepped through the gate, which was being held open by Rhage, there was a long hall of empty, new-built shelves. He remembered when they had been filled with the jars of *lessers*, those trophies collected by members of the Brotherhood over centuries, the earliest ones imported on ships under sail from the Old Country.

The Omega had broken into them all on its last-gasp attempt to stay alive, consuming the bloodied hearts that had contained the dregs of his essence. After the infiltration, V and Butch had cleaned up the mess and rebuilt the setup.

Fresh start. For an old war.

Eventually, the great hall opened up to a tremendous, nearly arena-sized chamber that was lit by black candles and torches, and had a gradual descent to a stage-like platform with an altar on it. Behind the locus of worship and ceremony, a wall that was twenty feet tall and God only knew how long owned the focal point of the cave.

Countless names were carved in the stone.

Every one of the Brotherhood was listed, right up to the most recent addition to the membership, John Matthew.

As the solemn crowd filed in, instead of going to the front with them, Lassiter hung back, taking his place against the rear of the cave. In a way, all this sorrow fit his mood, and although he didn't want the suffering for anyone, it did make things easier as he didn't have to pretend to anybody that he was fine.

And no one had questioned Rahvyn's absence, so consumed were they by the absolute tragedy.

Which was the only relief to be had for him.

As he wondered where she was, and prayed she was safe, he stared all the way down to the ancient skull that sat on the center of the altar. It was the first brother.

The first warrior.

How was this happening, he thought as he watched the crowd gather below the stage in a semicircle—just like it had been at his and Rahvyn's ceremony.

As a fresh wave of agony swamped him, the last of the mourners trickled in, and then there was a dense silence broken only by sniffling and the occasional cough.

When he heard a soft shuffling sound, he glanced over and closed his eyes briefly.

It was Beth, dressed in a white robe. L.W. was in her arms, George by her side.

She was positively gray, her eyes sunken in her head, her aura one of such profound anguish, she was a dark shadow that lived and breathed.

Tohr followed her, holding a bundle of something with reverence.

The pair of them walked down together, and when they mounted the stage, the brothers joined them, lining up with the widow and the young. With his head lowered, Tohr stepped forward to the altar.

Next to the skull, he placed a leather jacket and a pair of wraparounds.

And then beneath, he set a pair of black boots that had been shined so perfectly, they might as well have been floodlights.

Tohr stepped back and began chanting. On his cue,

the brothers picked up the mourning cadence, swaying from side to side. And when Beth looked like she was about to faint, Zsadist stepped up and put his arm around her to hold her steady.

Lassiter could only stand in the back and try to breathe. As he attempted to contain his emotions, he had the thought that he'd finally gotten the job description right: He wasn't getting involved in this. He was going to stay back.

For the moment, at least. There was no way in hell he wasn't fighting that goddamn Lash again. No way—

Down in front, as the cadence rose to a deafening level, the King's dog broke out of the lineup and slinked forward, its head lowered, its ears drooping.

George went right to the boots his master had worn and lay down beside them, placing his boxy blond head across the steel toes.

Lassiter lowered his eyes, and decided he had to leave. He just couldn't take any more pain.

Just as he was about to turn away, he heard another soft sound of folds of cloth next to him, and he wondered who the straggler was—

As he looked over, he froze.

And it was clearly the same for Rahvyn, as the hooded black robe she was wearing did a double take.

Staring across at the female, he tried to see her face, but there was nothing showing because she had not revealed herself as everyone else had. She was looking at him, though. He could feel her eyes, even though he couldn't see them.

And he had a thought. Over the past couple of nights, the loss of her had solidified in his chest, in his mind, in his life, the absence of her like a construction that was built in a hardy fashion because it was going to be permanent.

He had to accept the god-awful reality because he had no choice, as there was nothing to fight for, no opportunity to argue. Over. Done with. His fate sealed because Rahvyn had gotten half the story right, and been disinclined to listen to the rest of the truth.

Glancing back down to the altar, he stared at that leather jacket. Then shifted his eyes to Beth.

Abruptly, he decided, fuck it. Life was short and violent, and destiny was a cunt, and he was very sure, if Wrath had been in his shoes, the King would have busted out of a funeral to try to save his relationship with his Queen.

Or, at the very least, explain himself.

Lassiter leaned over to her and said in a low voice, "I need to talk to you. Right now."

CHAPTER SIXTY-ONE

I t was all so overwhelming. All of it.

Everything.

So in a way, as Rahvyn showed up late to the great Blind King's funeral, she really should not have been surprised that Lassiter happened to be standing way in the back, right at the entry to the cave's torchlit amphitheater.

And naturally, he was now demanding to be heard. In a way that suggested he was prepared to start the conversation right here.

With a shout, if he had to.

For so many reasons, she was not up to any kind of talking with anyone. But she also did not have the strength to argue with him at a whisper about how not only was it inappropriate for them to deal with their personal issues at a time like this, she was truly not interested in hearing anything he had to say.

In the end, she merely shrugged and backed out through the archway she had just put to good use.

Lassiter marched off, going all the way back to the start of the hall of empty shelves, and when he finally halted, and she tilted her hood up to regard him, she felt like she was looking at a stranger in the light of the torches that hissed and seethed from the mountings.

"You're right," he said in a harsh tone. "I did come back to you because of the spell. It was to keep Devina and Lash apart because if they joined forces, the Brotherhood and the vampires would surely not survive. I did learn about the Book's provision about breaking up true love, I knew that you and I were the couple involved, and I pursued you because I wanted to affect an outcome."

Rahvyn pushed her hood off her head and crossed her arms over her chest. "That is a fine recitation of facts. I am not certain why it bears repeating, especially at this particular moment in time—"

"What you got *wrong*," he interjected sharply, "was why I left you in the first place."

At this, he broke off from her, pacing up and back, his footfalls over the bare stones of the floor louder than even his voice, it seemed. When he stopped again in front of her, she tilted to the side and eyed the length of the corridor, estimating how far it was to the exit—

"That night in the meadow, I knew I was turning

myself over to Devina. So she could use me. Use my body."

Rahvyn blinked. And slowly righted herself.

"I made a bargain with the demon that she could"—he cleared his throat—"that she could do with me what she pleased . . . if she would leave Balthazar and Erika alone. She'd wanted me. From the beginning. I didn't want her. I never . . . wanted her. But she was contaminating Balthazar's soul and she was going to kill him. When I met you in the field and conjured those flowers, it was right before I left to turn myself over to her, and I said goodbye to you because I knew that, on the other side, I was going to be a different male. I'd saved myself, you see. I'd . . . saved myself. *That* was the bad thing that I did for the right reason. It was *not* going back to you and manipulating you into a relationship."

As a dawning horror swept through Rahvyn's marrow, she brought her hands up to her mouth.

"After it was over," he continued, "I was broken. I was ashamed. I felt dirty . . . in this body. I couldn't bear to think of being in your presence, much less touching you. But then again, after you revived me, I was talking to the brothers about the *lesser* induction in that basement downtown, and how Lash and Devina were together . . . and I figured it out. That was why she wanted to fuck me. She knew I wouldn't be able to go back to you in good conscience. The more I thought about it all, I knew there had to have been a spell because it was the only explanation—and it was clear that we had to do everything to keep the demon apart from the Omega's son. So yeah, I went back to you because of the spell—but it was the only thing that could possibly have gotten me over the way I felt about myself after what the demon put me through. When I was with you, kissing you, making love to you, I put what had been done to me aside so that I could make it good for you. You had been hurt much worse than I had, and I . . ." He paused and cursed. "When you said you were grateful for what happened to you because it made you stronger, I really get it. I was grateful for the spell. It gave me the strength I needed to shove it all down underneath and keep going, instead of wallowing in that cave on the mountain, a hollow husk because I was ruined for the female I loved."

There was a stretch of silence. And then she choked back a sob.

"Lassiter," she said with horror, "why didn't you tell me?"

He laughed harshly. "Really? You're asking me that? After everything that had been done to you, you think I was in any kind of hurry to tell you my story? You were carrying enough, and I didn't want you to worry about me."

As he got wavy in front of her, she realized she was tearing up, the implications of all that she had accused him of pounding her like blows to her body.

"Anyway, that's the why of it," he said baldly. "I know it doesn't make a difference, but if I'm going to lose the female I love, I'll be damned if I lose my integrity along with her."

At that, he spun around and headed for the gate at the far end of the hall.

◆ ◆ ◆

In all the TV talk shows he'd ever watched, Lassiter had heard hosts and experts preach the confession-is-good-for-the-soul rhetoric. And during his brief period of self-improvement a little while ago, he'd also listened to the TED Talks. Read the inspirational posts on FB and Insta. Watched the TikToks.

But you know what? He didn't feel any fucking better for having bared his truth.

Then again, he was still walking out of this cave alone—

"Lassiter!"

At the sound of his name, he pivoted around—and he had a soul-searing visual of Rahvyn standing there in the midst of all the empty shelving, her silver hair catching the torchlight as waves escaped from the neckline of the black robe she wore.

The female was still, and ever would remain, the most beautiful thing he'd ever seen—

With a hoarse cry, she lunged forward and ran toward him, hitting him so hard she nearly knocked him off his feet—and his arms shot around her by reflex.

But also because, in a pathetic part of his soul, he had missed her so much that he'd use any excuse to hold her one last time.

He wasn't surprised as she pushed him back.

The tears streaming down her face were a shocker, however.

"Oh, my angel," she said, "how could you have not told me? I would have been there for you—I *want* to be there for you. I am so sorry I misinterpreted everything—I think I questioned, in ways I could not acknowledge, that it was all too good to be true, that you would want me, and need me. That you would choose me. Oh, verily, I am so sorry . . ."

She was talking fast, tripping over words, snuffling. Then her hands were on his face, his shoulders, his chest.

He watched the goings-on for a moment, as if from a vast distance. Then he tentatively—reaaaaaaally tentatively—touched a strand of her hair. You know, just to make sure this was real.

"I did not know your truth," she said in a broken voice. "And I never would have guessed."

He shook his head slowly. "It wasn't duty for me. Just so you and I are perfectly clear . . . you were never a duty. You were only ever a gift. The spell just got me over my fears and my self-loathing. That was all it did."

Now her hands were back on her face, her expression so appalled she looked as though she was going to faint. "Lassiter, how can you ever forgive me . . ."

Reaching out, he eased her arms down. Then he searched her panicked face.

"What can I do to help it," she whispered. "Tell me how I can make it up to you, tell me . . . if it is not too late, please, I love you, and I wish to make this right between us, if I am able."

A warm, fuzzy pool of relief started to flush into the cold vault he had become, and he found himself weaving on his feet.

Then he said softly, "For you and me, it is never, ever too late. If I've told you once, I'll tell you a thousand more times. You are my Gift of Light. Without you by my side, I am forever in darkness."

As he spoke, her eyes shifted over his head. "Your halo . . . I love that it is with you."

He smiled a little. "That's because you bring it to me."

With a muffled sob, she threw her arms around him and kissed him.

As the funeral wore on and grief found expression deep within the recess of the earth, outside, closer to the surface, love rebloomed in the midst of the early spring.

Like wild flowers in a meadow of April snow.

CHAPTER SIXTY-TWO

One hundred million years after Beth donned a white robe and left the royal suite, she returned to the third floor of the Brotherhood mansion, aching and tired. Worn out. Cried out. Hollowed out.

As she closed herself in, she forced herself to look around. The jeweled walls still gleamed, the furniture remained in the same places, the layout with the bath beyond and the nook with the crib was identical.

A wrecking ball had busted through the place, however. Everything was ruined. But that wasn't the worst part of it all.

The worst part was that Wrath's clothes were still hanging in their closet, and the pillow beside her own still smelled like him, and there was his cell phone, right by his side of the bed.

566   J. R. WARD

The worst part of coming back here was all the evidence of the life interrupted, the personal possessions that no longer had an owner.

On that note, George walked by her, passing by his bed and his water bowl, going straight over and hopping up on the mattress. He curled into a ball where Wrath had always slept, tucking his tail in and putting his head on his front paws. His brown eyes watched her as if he were waiting for her to fall apart again.

And as if his heart was broken, too.

Glancing down into L.W.'s face, she found the young staring at her in exactly the same way—and looking into those pale green eyes, she nearly started weeping again.

Not for the last time, she couldn't decide whether the fact that those were his father's eyes was bad or good.

Maybe later on, when the grief wasn't so fresh, it would be a solace to look into them. Right now, it was a dagger straight into her heart.

Going across the grand and glorious space, she had a thought that she should eat something.

A thought that she should change out of the robe.

A thought . . . about something else, something practical, that likewise went right out of her head.

Lying down next to George, she put L.W. to her chest and let the tears fall. Then again, she couldn't have stopped them if she'd tried.

Shifting her stare over to Wrath's pillow, she moved the thing out of the way. There, under where he had put his head for all those days, a black dagger was pressed into the mattress.

She remembered back to their beginning, when he had come to her at her old apartment and told her that he was what she needed. He had been terrifying and beautiful—and also the explanation, finally, as to why she had always felt so apart from everyone around her.

He'd been the trailhead to her true identity, to the father she had always wanted to know, to her community.

How was he gone.

Even after the first night and day alone, and now after the funeral, she still could not get a part of her brain to comprehend that he was dead, that she would never hold him, or smell him, or hear his voice or laugh again. No more heavy shitkickers pounding the way into this suite. No more masculine beauty arching back under the shower to wash his long hair.

No more a whole.

Only a lonely half.

She supposed the fact that she didn't want to go on was typical. But just because things happened to other people, that others had shared some or all of what you were feeling, did not lessen the impact when you were the one going through the experience.

Collective grief was not subject to the law of diminishing returns.

As she lay alone and contemplated the years ahead, she didn't know how she was going to do it. She had thought a lot in the last twenty-four hours about how she had to live for L.W., and she liked to think she would embrace the only purpose she had, but she really could have used a sign—

The knock was soft and she closed her eyes, debating whether she could pretend she was not in. But like the entire household hadn't watched her go up the stairs?

"Yes," she croaked out.

The door slowly opened, and she thought it was probably Fritz. The *doggen* was having a terrible time of it. From the moment Wrath had pushed him out of the way of that bomb at the back door of the Audience House to the text he'd sent out to the Brotherhood as soon as he had come around on the ground . . . to the funeral preparations and the ceremony itself . . . the butler was suffering almost more than anyone else, for he blamed himself.

Even though it was absolutely not his fault—

Beth frowned and lifted her head. "Rahvyn?"

As the mysterious, silver-haired female stood in the doorway to the bejeweled suite, there was the strangest energy pouring off of her in invisible waves, the effect buffering across the space, distorting the air or perhaps the room itself.

I need you to trust me, she said in a deep voice.

Even though she did not move her lips.

A feeling of complete disassociation unplugged Beth from her body. Which wasn't hard to do given how numb she was.

Trust me, the female said without speaking. *When you are of despair, and even though you do not know me, you must trust me.*

With a sudden surge of motivation, Beth found herself nodding. "All right. I will."

CHAPTER SIXTY-THREE

Well, the demon Devina thought, she was almost packed up.

As she looked around her lair, she regarded all the empty racks and the occasional empty hanger that had fallen on the floor. She had done the work herself, needing something to occupy her hands and mind.

Jesus, movers were not fucking paid enough.

Walking over to the kitchen area, she double-checked that the cabinets were empty—not that she'd had much in them, because outside of that stretch when she'd been on the human heart diet, she didn't cook a lot. Fridge was empty, again, not that she ate here much. The tub and toilet areas were good to go, the drawers of the little storage compartments cleaned out.

Everything was carefully set in U-Haul boxes. Now, those she'd conjured, because who the fuck needed to lug back all that cardboard physically? Likewise, the truck waiting at the loading dock was an out-of-her-ass manifestation because she had not been in the mood to deal with the reservation process, even if she could do it online.

Staring over at the lineup of those boxes—there had to be fifty or sixty of them—she thought about the hours it had taken to get all her haute couture sorted and packaged. In a way, it had been nice, the handling of everything she loved. It felt . . . grounding in the midst of her pain.

And oddly, she'd thought a lot about Lassiter, the fallen angel.

She was still evil, it was true. Down to her marrow. But as she listlessly contemplated the future ahead, she was coming to the heretical conclusion that she'd had no right to rob him of what had been his due.

There had been a moment, when she'd been fucking him and enjoying the idea she was taking away what mattered most to him because she had been cheated of what had mattered most to her, that his mask of composure had slipped . . . and the pain in him had shown in his face.

At the time, she'd been so damned satisfied by his show of weakness. So triumphant, the angel's ruination part of the prize, in addition to her getting her true love.

And now she was here, stewing in an agony that was eternal for her: Because the reality was . . . no one wanted her. Not really.

'Cuz she was a demon.

Yeah, yeah, boo-hoo and all that bullshit. But the truth was, she hadn't been asked to be born as she had been, made as she had been . . . created as she had been. There'd been no consent even contemplated by the Creator when He'd conjured her out of space and time.

And the thing that she was coming to realize was that if He had asked her? She would have begged to be different.

Everything that had gone down with Lassiter was letting her see that now, and that meant, in so many ways, he was as important to her immortal life as Lash was. Kind of ironic, really. That angel was probably living his best life with his female, not thinking of Devina even a little—and dismissing her if she did cross his mind for a brief second. Meanwhile, he was a ghost that constantly stalked her in the shadows, a reminder that her nature was immutable . . . and what do you know, she didn't want to be alone with herself any more than anybody else did.

"It's me . . . hi, I'm the problem, it's me," she sang under her breath.

Thanks, T. Swift.

Fucking hell, no wonder she liked retail therapy so much.

On that note, there was just one collection left to deal with.

Throwing off all her damned introspection, she pivoted and regarded her Birkins. Of all the things she owned, the bags were her absolute favorite, her most prized, and she went over to the display of Lucite stands. The boxy purses with their perky handles and their little buckles were in all kinds of colors and different types of leathers, the most exclusive handbags in the world, made by the very best artisans in the world.

And she had so many that she loved so much.

Ultimately, though, it was the ruined one at the top that she loved most. Man, it had been her true pride and joy, that Himalayan. And though it had been burned beyond utility, she still loved it best anyway.

Which was why she had used it for that stupid fucking spell.

But again, there was no reason to retread all that. And no, she wasn't making yet another promise to move on, get over herself, be independent. She was just going to go along, putting one Louboutin after another, and see what happened.

What *wasn't* happening next? She wasn't bribing anyone to love her. She wasn't engineering any destiny for herself. And she wasn't making herself indispensable in the hopes that reliance could take the place of true regard. After Lash had inducted all those women she'd found him?

He'd just waltzed on out with them and left her behind. He hadn't even looked back.

So yup, she was just packing up her clothes and moving on. Maybe she'd find something to do, or maybe, like so many mortal souls, she'd just wander her days and nights in the shadows of dreams that had never manifested—

The knuckle rap on her door was loud, and she rolled her eyes. Stupid fucking security guards. This was a goddamn storage space as far as they knew. Who the fuck did they think was going to answer.

When the knocking came again, she marched across and yanked open . . .

. . . the . . .

. . . door.

Out in the hall, dressed in the dark gray suit she'd picked out for him, Lash was standing in the low light of the commercial hallway.

He of course looked beautiful and pathological. Which made her hate him—and in a way, the return to her normal state of rage felt good in a nostalgic sort of fashion. Like a friend had come back for a nice meal.

"What do you want," she said.

His eyes went down her body and he cocked a brow.

Yes, I'm wearing blue jeans and a fucking sweater, she thought. *I'm packing, you asshole.*

"*What,*" she snapped.

As he arched his other aristocratic brow, yes, she did entertain a brief fantasy of shaving both of them off. With a chain saw.

"I have a table for two reserved in twenty minutes at L'Orangerie," he announced. "I want to know if you want to go on a date."

Devina opened her mouth. Closed it.

"I also got you a present. Here."

He held out an enormous orange bag, the thing swinging gently between them.

The demon looked at him. Looked at the bag.

And when she just stood there, frozen, he bounced the weight a little—like maybe she hadn't seen it.

As if she could have missed the thing, especially given the logo in the center, of a jaunty little man in front of a horse and carriage.

With a shaking hand, Devina reached out and took the handles. Stepping back, she wondered where to open it—and decided her coffee table, over where her white leather chairs and love seat still were.

As she padded across the concrete floor, Lash said, "Where are you moving to? You got a new place?"

Sitting down on her little sofa, she took out an orange box the size of a microwave, and boy, it was heavy. Undoing the brown ribbon, she lifted the top and saw layers of carefully folded tissue paper.

She was gentle with the revealing, peeling back the fine sheets until she exposed a pale herringbone-patterned bag with the Hermès crest once again on it, the little horseman and his trotter a perfect visual vignette to remind the customer that saddlery was where it had all started.

As she pushed the box aside, she opened the neck of the giant fabric pouch, and the instant she saw the handles, her heart stopped.

With careful tugs, she pulled out . . . a pristine Himalayan Birkin 35 with the diamond hardware.

"Yours got wrecked," Lash said remotely. "So I bought you a new one."

Putting her hand to her mouth, she had to blink away tears.

"There are matching bangles. I bought them for you, too. They're in the bag itself."

When she could compose herself, she looked up at him. The Omega's son was staring down at her, his evil eyes guarded, but unwavering.

"So," he said. "You want to get dressed and head out? I've got a limo waiting for us."

It was an eternity before Devina could find her voice to answer him.

Clearing her throat, the demon replied, "I do."

CHAPTER SIXTY-FOUR

The night after the funeral, the Brotherhood and the other fighters convened in Wrath's study, and Lassiter made sure that he was down from the Sanctuary for the meeting. Unsurprisingly, no one spoke as they filed in and found their regular spots, like they were visiting hallowed ground and didn't want to be disrespectful.

On his side, Lassiter felt conflicted. He and Rahvyn had spent the daylight hours up in his private quarters. They had made love, yes, in a reconnecting, reverent way—and when they hadn't been joined in that special fashion, they had both lain awake. Until she had gone to check on Beth just now.

And he had come here.

It was hard to balance their joy with all the suffering.

But life was like that, an equilibrium that was sustained, by the good . . . and the bad, both parts required.

By design.

As the doors were shut by Tohr, Lassiter glanced across the way. Eddie and Adrian were in their spot in the corner and the angels lifted their hands in greeting to him. They were going to be a great addition, especially as things got rougher. Which they were going to.

When everybody was present and it was time to get started, Tohr went over to the desk and the throne, and stood there for a moment, looking like he was lost. Then the brother who had seen more grief than anybody else slowly pivoted around.

Taking a deep breath, his voice was low and strained. "We need to, ah, discuss the memo that was circulated by the newly established Council." He cleared his throat and went around to stand beside the throne and face out into the room. "There is the meeting of them tonight, and I've asked Saxton to check the legality of what they're doing, see if there's some way of stopping them . . . He doubts there is, but, yeah, he's going to look."

There was a grumble from a couple of males. Halfhearted, at best.

"Um, so we are going to have to get an announcement out about what . . . happened." Tohr took another deep breath. "Civilians have a right to know. Of course, this couldn't be a worse time . . . not that it would ever be a good time."

The brother looked around the room. "As for succession, Wrath was democratically elected so ... there is none. Not in the traditional bloodline sense. I imagine that, with the Council re-forming, they'll put up somebody. I don't know if any of you want to step forward for consideration? I won't be putting my name into the ring. I have no interest in ... anyway, we're going to end up being ruled by some dandy in a suit. And I ... well ..."

He let the sentence drift. Then there was a silence that no one filled.

It was within the dense quiet that the implications of the tragedy clawed into them all anew, it seemed: A private guard with no King to protect. Brothers who had lost one of their own. A family ... without a patriarch.

A *shellan* without her mate.

A young without his father.

A species without a leader.

All those levels of loss, private and public, intersecting into one void the size and shape of a grave ... that would never be filled because the explosion had left no remains to bury.

"Anyway ..." Tohr sighed. "That's where we are, which is nowhere, actually. The King's power was extensive, but he was the one who abolished the monarchy. So, yeah ... of course, the irony is, the civilians he's been meeting with all wanted his lineage to continue. They told us so, every time they showed up."

Grumbles of agreement percolated around.

"But yeah, nothing to be done."

More silence. To the point where Lassiter realized, it

was all over. The Brotherhood. The mansion. This community. There were many parts to what had made the whole, but Wrath had been the binding. Without him, all was going to scatter, and Lassiter had the strangest sense that this was the last time they were going to be together at once—

The double doors to the study burst open with such force they banged against the walls.

Filling the void of the archway, a dark-haired female in a red and black gown stood proud and tall. In her arms, a young dressed in a black robe. By her side, the dead King's dog.

Beth, the Queen, marched through the room, and as she went along, she looked at every single one of the males, her stare full of vengeance and purpose.

At the desk, she went around, faced them all . . .

And sat upon her *hellren's* throne.

There was no weakness in her voice, no stammer or stutter, and there was no forgiveness, no quarter, no compromise:

"I will not allow the Lessening Society to rob my son of his father's legacy." Then, with even more power, she said, "Rahvyn."

As ripples of confusion shot around the room, Lassiter recoiled and wheeled toward the door.

His beloved entered, and immediately looked at him.

I love you, she mouthed.

What the hell is going on, he wanted to ask. But instead, he just mouthed back, *I love you, too*.

With a nod, as if she needed his support and had gotten it—and thus was ready to move forward with something—his *shellan* started walking across the study, in the path cut by the Queen.

The transformation was sequential, the stages coming with each step his female took: First, her hair changed from platinum to black. Second, her body began to lengthen its limbs and fill out. Third, her robe altered shape and color.

Taller. Broader. No longer feminine, but masculine.

No longer Rahvyn . . .

. . . but Wrath.

By the time she reached the throne and turned around, she was the very image of their lost ruler, the one who had been killed saving his most trusted and loyal servant.

The eyes were pale green and had tiny pupils. The midnight hair fell from a widow's peak down to the waist. Heavily muscled arms with tattoos of the great Blind King's lineage along the insides were on display.

The black muscle shirt. The leathers.

The shitkickers.

One of the brothers started to faint; someone caught him. Vishous looked like he was going through a mental splintering. Even Eddie and Adrian had thrown out arms and were using one another as crutches to stay upright.

The last thing Rahvyn did was reach forward to the blotter.

And pick up a pair of black wraparound sunglasses that had been left behind.

Just before she slipped them onto the image of Wrath's face, she mouthed those three words again to Lassiter.

Then it was complete. The transformation . . . done.

Beth spoke up in that new voice of hers. "We continue as if nothing happened. No one will know outside of this household. The civilians will continue to be heard, their concerns and problems sorted. The Lessening Society and Lash will believe they failed to kill my mate. And my son will have the opportunity to grow into maturity."

She looked around. "First thing tonight, my husband Wrath will reinstate the monarchy. Though during his lifetime, it was his wish for democratic elections, in this current situation, the Council will take control of ruling the population, and they will abuse their power because they always have. Families without means will suffer, the slayers will get the upper hand, and the species will die off. That is what will happen. Therefore, we will reverse his decision. Sometime in the future, my son can reinstate the election process in honor of his father. But it is too dangerous for all of us right now, and I'm not just talking about the people in this house."

With that, she stood L.W. up on her lap. "That is how we are going to handle this. It is not only what my *hellren* would wish us to do, it is the best thing for those he served and his father served and his father before that."

Lassiter swallowed through a tight throat. *Holy fuck*, he thought. *These two females just saved the whole fucking vampire race—*

It was hard to know which of the fighters unhol-stered his dagger first. But soon enough, those who were sitting were up on their feet, and every warrior, whether they were a member of the Black Dagger Brotherhood, or of the Band of Bastards, or one who had fought alongside the others . . . they were all raising their blades overhead.

As Lassiter caught an image of all those daggers, black and steel alike, a chill went through his entire body.

And then came the war cry, so loud that it surely blew the mansion's roof off.

So loud . . . that surely Wrath heard it in the Fade.

Moving as one, with a coordination that was as if practiced, the whole of them dropped to one knee before the Queen and the image of her beloved *hellren*—

And buried those blades through the fancy rug, and into the solid floor beneath it.

The sound, like the sight of all those proud heads bent in supplication, was something, for all his immortal life, he was never, ever going to forget.

The Black Dagger Brotherhood and their allies, unified, once again.

Serving Wrath's bloodline, as always.

Ready to fight for the survival of their kind.

Forever.

EPILOGUE

Thirty-three years, nine months, three days . . .

. . . and nine hours in the future.

I.

The pair of black shitkickers tromped through the snow, leaving treads that were unseen, and not only because of the strong wind that almost immediately covered them with drifts. For the male who had arrived, the change in season was a shock, and confusion was the name of the game—and neither had anything to do with his blindness.

Where the fuck had spring gone? Wrath wondered.

The last thing he had felt was a blast of heat, and then an elemental turbulence. After that . . . nothing.

And now he was here and it was winter?

Stopping, he moved his head left to right, his hair whirling around his face, lashing at him. There was a strange smell under the familiar currents of pine up on the mountain . . . burning dirt and something like soggy firewood?

He kept going, without panicking. Then again, he knew where he was—

Clonk.

The steel toe of his shitkicker hit something hard, and his shin followed along for the ride, the cracking impact turning his body into a tuning fork for *ow*. As he dropped another f-bomb and jacked over to rub away the pain, he put his hand out. More snow—yeah, no shit—but the curve and scale of the marble feature that had done him in was unmistakable: The fountain in the mansion's courtyard.

Navigating with his fingertips, he continued around to the far side and knew the distance and direction to the first of the grand entrance's stone steps. As he walked straight ahead, the whistling sounds in the mansion's eaves confirmed his rock-solid instincts, and in a way, it was as if he could see. In his mind, he conjured from memory the variegated roofline and the diamond-paned windows, the gray stone walls and the gargoyles.

A piercing longing went through his chest, the emotion so vast, so fundamental, he faltered. For some reason, he felt as if he hadn't been home for a very, very long time, and he didn't get the sentiment. Where the hell had he been?

He was halfway up the steps when his bullshit meter started firing. Nope, this wasn't right. Nothing about what was going on with him made sense, not the weather, the way his mind was working, or that fucked-up smell.

And then he was at the carved cathedral-worthy door that opened into the vestibule.

Just as his hand reached forward, he heard a voice right beside him . . . an old, familiar voice that he hadn't had in his ears for a long time.

The King returns.

He looked to the right. "Analise, what the fuck is going on here."

The Scribe Virgin had never allowed questioning of her, and her name was something that he had only used once before in his life, but he didn't give a shit about all that right now. And anyway, that was a demand, not an inquiry, he'd put out there.

As always, your charm precedes you, the *mahmen* of the race communicated dryly.

"Look, I don't . . . understand what's happening."

All at once, she appeared in the dense void of his blindness, and not because he'd conjured her out of memory. The diminutive entity draped entirely in black robing, with a brilliant white glow emanating from under the hem of what covered her from head to foot, appeared sure as if she was standing before him. As ever, she was floating just off the ground—

And that was when he realized . . .

The architectural details of the mansion were

emerging, sure as if an artist's hand was penciling in its entrance. He saw the aged brass handle he had been reaching for, and the carvings in the panels . . . the hinges that were big as a male's forearm, and the molding that was so deep that snow collected in the curls of the acanthus leaves.

Stepping back, he looked up . . . waaaaaay up.

The roofline he'd just imagined was now really visual before him, as were those diamond-paned windows— and also the mythical creatures that were poised in stone, rearing their ugly heads forward to frighten the unwise who were not welcome.

Fumbling with his wraparounds, ripping them off, Wrath twisted on his hips and looked out to the fountain and the Pit, the snowflakes biting into his eyes.

That was when he saw the steaming crater in the earth, like something from outer space had landed on the front lawn.

Now he felt terror as he turned back.

I don't belong here, he thought.

"Why are all the windows dark," he said roughly as a growing awareness clawed into his chest, conclusions striking through him like bullets.

He turned to the Scribe Virgin. "*Why.*"

Allow me to help you with the doors.

As all the portals, both the exterior ones and those on the far side of the vestibule, ceded to her will, he looked into the darkness on the far side.

"Turning over a new leaf, are you," he muttered because he was shitting himself. "So helpful."

Do not o'erstep.

She timed the words perfectly as he extended his shitkicker and stepped over the threshold into the vestibule. The security monitoring systems were still in place, but they were darkened, too, as if there was no one around to receive the information—or no expectation that anyone would show up, wanted or otherwise.

"Where are they all," he said roughly.

Emerging into the foyer, he looked around and wondered if she hadn't taken his vision from him again. The darkness was so dense, it was like a solid he'd have to cut through, and just as he was getting desperate for a light, a single candle flared over on a carved marble bench.

He went across the mosaic floor and picked up the antique holder, locking his forefinger through the curving hook, lifting the slight weight of the dish with its soldier of wax and tiny glowing flame. The circle of illumination was a portable aura, and he walked forward without realizing where he was headed.

The dining room.

And what he saw did nothing to reassure him: Everything was covered with custom-made sheeting, all of the chairs, the sideboards, the long table itself. Moving the candle around, he heard ghostly echoes of the clinking of silverware on china, and the ripples of talk and laughter that had always filled the space. He smelled the roasts and the bread, the wine and the flowers. He sensed the movement of *doggen* bringing in food, clearing plates, refilling water glasses—

Wrath wheeled around. "*Where are they.*"

In the darkness beyond the candle's anemic reach, there was no glow down by the floor, and as he strode back out to the foyer, he knew the Scribe Virgin was gone.

It was as he halted that he caught the scent.

Faint, but clear now that his senses were tuned in to it.

Blood.

Holding out the candle, he flared his nostrils, tracking the copper tendrils that hung in the still, cold air.

The runner that came down the grand staircase was red, and he had to lower what light he had to the carpet's thick pile. There, in the fibers, soaked in as if a meal for the wool nap . . . a drop of fresh blood. He extended his arm. Swung the glow around. Three steps up, he found another. Seven steps up . . . another.

He was halfway to the top when he saw the firelight.

Like a rising sun, the glow was seated at the horizon of the second story's floorboards, and as he marched toward it, he remembered the days when he had been able to see the sun, when he'd been a pretrans and his parents had still been alive, the start of his journey which now he recognized had always meant to take him here, to this night, to this ascension . . .

To whatever horror was awaiting him.

Cresting the great staircase, he stood before the open doors of his study, and it was then that he scented much more blood as well as the acrid smoke of a fire.

For a moment, as the subtle cracking of burning logs registered in his ears, he felt a strange immobility, and he thought . . . *Could this be the Fade? Is this the door?*

If so, it was already open, and he felt a sweep carry him forward, as if there was a void sucking him in, no chance of escape from the powerful undertow.

As he moved toward the firelight, he felt like he was hovering above the carpet instead of walking and he had a vague, peripheral awareness of ghostly furniture, the gold-leafed benches and console tables against the gold-leafed balustrade, the ornamental chairs dotting the open area of this second-story foyer, all of it protected from dust destruction with those eerie jackets made of pale cloth.

He arrived at the threshold of his study an eternity later. Or maybe it was just a heartbeat.

The first thing he saw, across the pale blue room, was the throne that was, for some reason, uncovered, on the far side of the desk. The next was the first aid kit on the coffee table in front of the fireplace, the thing poptopped and surrounded by bloody gauze, surgical instruments, and a spool of black thread—as well as a stained black muscle shirt.

But it was the male sitting on the covered sofa, facing away from him, who commanded all his attention.

Walking silently forward, he could not have looked away for anything in the world. And as utter disbelief clogged both rational thoughts and crazy conclusions, he moved into position so that he could see the profile against the firelight's restless glow.

The male's body was corded with muscle—and covered with tattoos. From the cut of his hard jaw, down his chest and arms and hands, disappearing into the waistband of his leathers, a pattern of black ink carved out a design that was not readily apparent. Injuries—some new, some in the process of healing, and one clearly just dealt with, going by the bright white bandage—marked his ribs, his biceps, his back.

The sides of his head were shaved, and the black hair on top had been pulled back and tied in a knot.

The face was . . . a mirror of Wrath's own.

And the eyes, which he could not see from his angle, were trained on the throne. Like he was staring at someone even though there was no one sitting on it—

The attack was so fast, so vicious, that there was no preparing for it in advance. One moment, the male was by the fire; the next, he was bursting forward with a steel dagger above his shoulder, his green eyes spitting fury, his upper lip peeled off enormous fangs, the hatred in his face a physical presence that was one hell of a co-pilot.

For a heartbeat, Wrath couldn't move, but then instincts, training, and experience took over, and he caught the thick wrist controlling the dagger and deflected all that momentum by shoving out his other hand to the throat, stiff-arming his elbow, and spinning them around so they traded places. The energy in the attack was redirected like a pool cue into an eight ball, and he stuck with the male as he stumbled backwards, staying engaged, because it was going to be only a split second before there was a recovery and a second wave of aggression.

The impact of the male's back against the wall was so violent, there was a crack like thunder.

And, as followed a lightning strike, there was an abrupt cessation in the storm as Wrath pinned his attacker.

The face that was in front of his own slowly transformed, the fury draining out of the features, the brows easing and then rising in shock, the mouth falling open . . . the dagger not lowering, but getting dropped entirely.

As it clattered to the hardwood floor at the edge of the fine antique carpet, all of the fight went out of the male, and those green eyes, eyes that were the color of Wrath's own, grew luminous with pain.

In a small voice, the voice of a young, a single word was uttered: "Father?"

Wrath went from holding off the big body to dragging it against his own, his arms shooting around what made no sense, pulling the heavy muscularity into him.

He couldn't breathe.

And then abruptly he couldn't see, his vision starting to dim back into the darkness he was well used to.

In a panic, he pulled back and memorized that face, from the widow's peak that was just like his own, to those jade eyes with the pupils that were way too small, to the tide of tattoos that crested at the jut of the jaw.

Wrath looked down at the ink pattern across the mountain of a bare chest.

It was a depiction of a skull with a dagger through the top of the cranium at an angle, the fangs viciously tipped, the empty eye sockets pits of hell, warnings in the Old Language emanating out in rows to cover all the skin there was.

He is just like I was, Wrath thought with the kind of sorrow that carved through the soul.

But then he let that go for the moment as the dots were crudely connected in his shell-shocked mind: The only thing that could explain how he had last held his son in his arms as an infant, but now L.W. was a fully transitioned male . . .

Was the passage of time.

"*Where is your* mahmen," he choked out.

II.

Sitting at her modest kitchen table, Beth looked across to the sink. "Nalla. That pot is clean, I promise you."

The female stopped with her scrubbing routine, her head lowering in defeat, her shoulders lifting and relenting as she took a deep breath.

"What's going on, my girl. Talk to your favorite auntie."

Nalla as an adult was a combination of both her parents, her long, multicolored hair and yellow eyes clearly her father Zsadist's, her steady nature absolutely Bella all over. She was such a good person, working at Luchas House, loyal to her friends and extended family of Brotherhood cousins, a devoted daughter.

But she wasn't happy tonight. Hadn't been happy for a while, come to think of it.

Muttering under her breath, the female rinsed out the pot using the nozzle and put it aside on the drying rack—where it couldn't stay. If Fritz came in and saw it there, he was going to worry that he hadn't cleaned the thing fast enough, even though he hadn't been at home when Beth had boiled up the potatoes about an hour ago.

She was going to have to put it away before he returned to argue in a desperate, respectful way about who was preparing Last Meal.

Nalla dried her hands on a dish towel and turned around. "You know Cellia? At the House?"

"Oh, sure." Beth took a sip from her mug of coffee. "Mary trained her."

"She got engaged."

"Oh, how nice—"

"She asked me to be her maid of honor."

"That's great." Beth lifted an eyebrow as the girl looked away. "Wait, is it not great? So this is bad. Okay, I hate it, it's terrible."

Nalla's stare drifted around, and for a second, Beth measured her own spaces, the ones she had been living in for three decades. The ground-up floors of the house were modest, just a regular-looking Colonial in a street packed with other, regular-looking houses. It was the underground that was extensive. The house had been built specifically for her, after she'd insisted she was fine in something far less . . . vault-like, for lack of a better word. But the Brotherhood had prevailed, and construction had started in what had been vacant farmland just outside the ring of Caldwell's suburbia.

There were well over a dozen houses in the neighborhood, and they were all connected by a tunnel system. Rhage and Mary were on her left. Tohr and Autumn were on her right. Across the street were Z and Bella, and all the others filled out the street. Fritz and the *doggen* took care of everyone, staying in underground quarters themselves.

On the surface, it all looked perfectly human, perfectly normal, just as V had designed it to be. Underneath was where the truth lived.

She just hadn't been able to stay in the mansion, with memories everywhere haunting her. Frankly, neither had the others. But the Brotherhood had refused to scatter, and besides, they were right. The Lessening Society had come back in full force, and the demon Devina was a permanent fixture in Caldwell . . . so circling the wagons was a safety-first move.

"It's never going to happen for me," Nalla said. "The marriage thing."

Funny, Beth thought, how assimilation had happened over time. Sure, people still used "mating" to refer to tying the knot, but now "wedding" and "husband and wife" were equally common in speech.

So was "widow."

"Don't say that." She looked at the girl and swallowed through a tight throat. "You never know what destiny has in store."

For good, and for bad.

As she took a sip to clear the block in her throat, an old, familiar pain flared in her chest. Immediately after Wrath's death, her grief had been white-hot and paralyzing, capable of leveling her for days. Over time, the acute phase had eased into a chronic, low-level hum that was always with her. She'd come to think of her mourning like the weather, something that ebbed and flowed, and sometimes stormed, and rarely, but on occasion, destroyed her anew.

Like it was flexing just to prove it was still in charge.

And what had she learned? After all this time? Well, it was that all she could do was walk through the rain and wind, and the cold, cold climate of her grief. Wrath's absence had brought a nuclear winter to her life, and for her, there was no ultimate recovery. She remained the earth, lashed and set upon, hurtling through an icy void, even as other people's stars continued to shine.

And it was what it was.

Nalla crossed her arms over her chest. "They won't even talk to me."

Plugging back into the conversation, Beth shook herself to attention. "Who won't?"

"Males. Of any description."

"I'm sure that's not true—"

"They're afraid of my father. Terrified. One of the

groomsmen told Cellia that if I was in the wedding, he didn't want to get paired with me to walk down the aisle during the ceremony. He said he was afraid he'd wind up in a ditch in pieces."

Beth opened her mouth to deny it. But then had to close things up. Hmm, how to put this. "Zsadist is . . . a little protective of you, maybe."

"He's going to have to let me go. I'm not a child anymore, Auntie Beth. I want my own life, my own family, and I can't . . . I want to move out."

"Oh. Boy."

Okay, she could just imagine how *that* conversation was going to go.

"Can you talk to him?" The girl pressed her palms together in prayer. "Please? He'll listen to you. They *all* listen to you."

Thinking back to the moment she had walked into her *hellren's* study and told the Black Dagger Brotherhood exactly how it was going to go, she remembered the males down on their knees in deference to her, their daggers buried in the antique rug.

Nalla wasn't wrong that she could stand up to them, and that they gave her special clout, but there were limits—and she was very sure that such boundaries started and ended with interfering with their children. Especially the girls and anything sexual.

Sure, things had evolved in so many necessary ways, but fathers were still fathers, especially if they were warriors.

That groomsman had a point about ending up in pieces.

"I think you need to speak to your father yourself, honey."

"He doesn't listen to me."

Or worse, does and just doesn't agree, Beth thought.

"What about your *mahmen*?" she asked.

Tension tightened the female's features. "She's always been more worried about him. But it's fine, I can stand up for myself. I don't need her."

"Your mother loves you."

"My mother loves my father. I'm just what came along when I did."

Beth shook her head sadly, thinking of her own struggles with L.W. "Families are complicated."

"Well, I'd like to start my own someday and find out. But at this point, that's not going to happen because my sire will slice the throat of anybody who wants to take me out for a coffee."

"I'm sorry," Beth said. "I really am."

"Me, too."

Nalla stayed for a little longer, then left to clock in for her shift at Luchas House. As Beth listened to the back door shut, she looked across at the pan in the drying rack, and the silence closed in. Loneliness, her ever familiar, least favorite roommate, pulled up a chair and sat too close beside her, radiating a coldness that made her zip up the collar of her fleece.

A noise down below in the basement quarters, quiet though it was, reminded her she wasn't actually alone, and a moment later the cellar door opened. Excellent timing. She'd found the best thing for composure was the requirement for her to find some.

"So are you and Lassiter staying in tonight—" Beth straightened as she saw Rahvyn's face. "What's wrong?"

After the tragedy, the quiet, mysterious female had been such a source of strength, and when Beth had moved out of the mansion, it had seemed only natural to have her and her mate move in with her. They hadn't had anywhere else in mind to live in the physical world, and over the years, Lassiter had proven to be as loyal a friend as he was a protector of the race. And you know, *The Golden Girls* wasn't so bad as TV went, after all.

Abruptly, she realized what time it was. "Rahvyn, aren't you going to the Audience House? The civilians will be arriving soon."

The female came over and sank down onto her haunches. If the strange expression on her face wasn't alarming enough, the way she took Beth's hands sealed the deal on OMG.

"Do you remember," Rahvyn said softly, "a long, long time ago, when I told you to trust me."

Beth nodded numbly. Yes, she recalled everything about that white-hot-painful time when the female had come upstairs to the bejeweled suite—and she especially remembered the first moment she had seen her *hellren*'s face emerge from the features of the female.

"Yes," Beth breathed. "I do."

"I want you to believe what you are about to see the now. Know it is not a dream. This is everything you've been waiting for, everything I haven't been able to tell you."

"What are you talking about—"

"The fallow time is through." The female reached up and brushed Beth's face. "You have been so very brave."

"I don't understand—"

"Do not try. Just feel." Rahvyn rose to her feet. Then she bent at the waist and pressed a kiss to Beth's forehead. "You have done well—"

The security system let off a beep as a door was opened, the front one. And justlikethat, Rahvyn up and disappeared.

"L.W.?" she called out in a shaky way. "Is that . . . you?"

Probably not. He didn't come around much at all, anymore.

Except then she heard the footfalls, heavy ones. "L.W.?"

She was in the process of standing up and turning around when a figure appeared in the doorway that led to the living room. It was a tall . . . male . . . with long black hair that fell to his waist from a widow's peak and shoulders that were as big as the whole world and a muscle shirt that showed off . . . forearms that were tattooed with lines and lines of Old Language symbols.

The trembling started at her legs and worked its way up to her chest and throat. Rahvyn was gone. Who was this.

And yet, as she stared into those pale green eyes with their pinpoint pupils, she *knew*.

"Wrath?" she choked out.

"*Leelan.*"

He charged forward, and lucky for that. She couldn't feel her body anymore, and she was falling.

Her *hellren*'s strong arms wrapped around her, and though her mind was paralyzed, some kind of muscle memory snapped back and she fitted herself to him as she always had . . . and had known she never would again.

Except he was *here*.

She pushed back and touched his face, running her shaking hands over his features. "Where have you been."

"I don't know," he said hoarsely. "I don't know."

He kissed her, then. Kissed her like he once had. Kissed her like she had ached for him to do, just one more time.

An eternity, a bottomless pit of time, suddenly opened up in the little kitchen, the love between two true hearts an immortality that could not be touched by any force in the universe, even the dark void of death.

"I don't understand," she whispered against his mouth.

Do I have to? she wondered. *Did I ever?*

A half-bred human who didn't know her other side, being found by the last purebred vampire on earth, because the father who had always protected her from afar sent her a savior so she could live . . . and love.

And be loved.

As she blinked her eyes clear, she saw her son—their son—looming in the periphery, and as L.W. stared back at her, she thought . . . at least he was still alive, although a quick catalogue of his bandages made her stomach roll—

A scratching and whimpering drew her attention over her own shoulder, but before she could react, Lassiter opened the cellar door from the far side and let George, who was known for liking a cuddle with the fallen angel, bound forward.

The golden's paws paddled on the tile for purchase, and then he shot himself toward his master in a scramble of blond fur and whimpering.

"George!" Wrath crouched down and opened his arms. "My boy!"

Wrath's blind eyes stared straight ahead as he waited in the unfamiliar environment for his dog to come to him—and George tackled him and then went shimmy-all-over as he cried and yodeled his joy, the contortions of his body a physical release of his devotion and his own mourning because he had no words.

Beth looked up at her son. L.W.'s face was showing a rare moment of emotion, the hard features as soft as she had ever seen them, the vulnerability showing and making him appear far younger.

Maybe things would be better now.

Wrath rose back up to his full height and took George with him. Then again, it wasn't like he had a choice. The golden had curled both front paws around his master's shoulders like he was afraid another separation was coming and was holding on for dear life.

She knew how that felt.

What the hell is going on? she thought as she glanced back at Lassiter. Given the shock on his face, the angel wasn't going to be much help with that. He looked like someone had just pummeled him over the head with a bag of bricks.

As Wrath extended his free arm, Beth went to him and wrapped herself around his chest and hips. Closing her eyes, she breathed in. And breathed in. And . . . breathed in.

The scent of him had been torture in the beginning. On the pillow beside her. On the sheets. On his clothes in their closet, the last towel he'd used in the bathroom, the rocker he'd sat in as he eased L.W. off to sleep.

Now it was back, and she squeezed him harder.

Like he would go away again, like this was a dream.

"I love you, *leelan*," he said against her hair.

The tears that fell from her eyes soaked his black muscle shirt, and the source of them was not complex. Gratitude overwhelmed her. That and the confusion as to why was she so lucky? What had she done to deserve this? So many females of worth had lost their mates in the last thirty years.

Had it only been that long? It felt like eternity.

"I love you, too," she croaked to her husband. "There has never been anyone but you for me . . . ever."

III.

As Lassiter stood in the open doorway at the top of the basement stairs, his hand stayed locked on the handle he'd turned to let George out.

He'd been lying on the sofa in the common area, the

dog snoozing on his chest as he often did, the last episode of the first season of *The Golden Girls* playing in
the background, when he'd heard the footsteps overhead. And it was weird. The sounds that were transmitted down to him had seemed like what he'd been
waiting for: For the previous three days, he'd been un-
settled and twitchy, especially when Rahvyn had gone in
to be Wrath for the civilians.

Driven by some kind of paranoia, he'd stuck with her
for every moment of every hour, the sense that something was coming making him extra protective. She, on
the other hand, had seemed perfectly calm, and out-
wardly speaking, there had been nothing unusual to
anything, the *glymera* a constant simmering threat, Lash
and the Lessening Society all over Caldwell, the demon
fucking shit up, the normal stresses of the Brotherhood
and their grown families ever present.

When Rahvyn had announced she wasn't going in
tonight to the Audience House and had canceled the
session, it had been a relief just to chill.

Sensing his mate's presence beside him, he shook his
head.

"You knew about this," he whispered as he stared
across the kitchen at a reunion that seemed as shocking
as the tragic loss of Wrath had been all those years ago.
"Didn't you."

He glanced over at his mate as the King pulled his
son into the clinch as well, the family made whole once
again.

Rahvyn was invisible to everybody but him, and she

was wiping tears from her eyes, her silver stare worried. "I wanted to tell you. It's been eating me up for all this time. But I had to be the only one who knew. The demon Devina has the ability to travel through time as well, and though Wrath experienced the time jump as but a moment, his soul has been in the in-between for thirty years. If anyone had known, there was a risk that it would get out to her somehow and she could have gotten to him. If we'd lost him at that point? There was no coming back, and he would have ended up in a place that was worse than *Dhunhd*."

"You hid him in time," Lassiter whispered with awe. "That night . . . when I saw the meteor in the sky, that was Wrath."

"And me. I swept him up the second before the explosion went off." She reached for him. "Please . . . forgive me—"

Lassiter opened his arms, and as she became corporeal, he drew her in close to him. "Oh, my God, there's nothing to forgive. You're fucking brilliant!"

As she snuggled in to his chest, she said, "The Book let me know what was going to happen, and I fought going down and getting involved. But then I thought of Beth. It all happened so quickly, and this was the solution that came to me."

"Genius. Absolute genius."

She pulled back. "I hated lying to her. To you."

The torment was in her face, her eyes luminous with the conflict she'd kept to herself.

He shook his head and turned her so she could see

the clutch of the First Family. "That is all that matters to me. Whatever sacrifices we had to make, known and unknown, don't matter—as long as we can have *that*."

Lassiter wiped his face, and as he brought his hand down, he regarded the shimmer of silver on the pads of his fingertips.

And then Wrath looked up. "Rahvyn! Lassiter!"

There was more hugging at that point, and then the King wanted to go find Fritz. As the First Family, and the golden, descended down into the basement, Lassiter glanced around and marveled at how the house seemed full again. Even though it technically hadn't been empty.

He looked into his *shellan*'s silver eyes. "You're a miracle, you know that?"

"I'm not an angel, though." Rahvyn reached up above his head. "I don't have a halo like you do."

"You don't need one, you're my Gift of Light." He smiled. "Like I always tell you, you brought it back for me. Forever."

As he stared into her eyes, he felt the future before them all, stretching out into time. He could see no details, none of the grand events or nightly minutiae, neither the sunshine nor the rain. He knew there would be both, of course. That was the way life worked—and because you couldn't predict any of it, and could control only some of it . . . the most important thing was who you were with, who you surrounded yourself with.

Who your friends were.

Maybe that was why *The Golden Girls* was his favorite show.

And why he knew the great Betty White got it right when she'd spoken his favorite quote of hers: *Replay the good times. Be grateful for the years you had.*

That was everybody's immortality right there.

"Hey, you want to go down and watch some TV while Wrath shocks the shit out of everybody we know and love?" Then he murmured, "And maybe a little somethin' more, you know, if you're interested in a religious experience?"

Rahvyn smiled and linked her arm around his waist. "You bet, angel mine. It's a date."

ACKNOWLEDGMENTS

With so many thanks to the readers of the Black Dagger Brotherhood books! This has been a long, marvelous, exciting journey, and I can't wait to see what happens next in this world we all love. I'd also like to thank Meg Ruley, Rebecca Scherer and everyone at JRA, and Hannah Braaten, Jamie Selzer, Sarah Schlick, Jennifer Bergstrom, Jennifer Long, and the entire family at Gallery Books and Simon & Schuster.

To Team Waud, I love you all. Truly. And as always, everything I do is with love to and adoration for both my family of origin and of adoption.

Oh, and thank you to Naamah, my Writer Dog II, and Obie, Writer Dog-in-Training, who work as hard as I do on my books!

Turn the page for an exclusive excerpt from:

MINE

The final installment in the Lair of the Wolven series
by J. R. Ward!

CHAPTER ONE

Exit 38S, The Northway (I-87)
Plattsburgh, New York

His doctor, the one who'd been keeping him alive, was dead.

As Daniel Joseph threw his Harley onto the Northway's exit ramp, he cranked the accelerator and worried about how much gas they had left. And he had other problems. The snow that had started to fall halfway through the rocket ship ride was only a little late November squall, but when the flakes hit his face, they were shards of glass, on his cheeks, in his eyes, up his nose.

Fuck the stop sign at the top. He didn't slow down

before merging onto NY 22S, and as he and the bike leaned into the turn, the love of his life, Lydia Susi, tightened her arms around his waist and ducked her head into his back. During the twenty-minute, breakneck roar from that apple orchard in Walters to this road leading into Plattsburgh, he had taken the brunt of the cold air, and he was feeling it. She was warmer, though.

He hoped she was warmer.

Goddamn it, he wished she weren't with him.

"We need Route Twenty-Six," Lydia said in his ear. "Toward the bay."

"Roger that." He had to shout over the wind. "You okay?"

She gave him a squeeze. "Yes."

There was a pause, and all he could think of was, *Don't do it. Don't ask back.*

She didn't.

Lydia was a master navigator, not that finding the condo development was all that hard, and once they were inside the property's confines, the whitewashed, black-shuttered unit they were gunning for was an easy-to-find on the far side of the central core. Pulling into the driveway, he opened his mouth to tell her they had to stick together—

His woman ejected herself off the back of the bike, landed on a lithe run, and raced up the front walk.

"Wait! Stop—" He tried to catch his breath. "Lydia—"

She all but attacked the door, twisting the knob, jerking, yanking. "Gus!"

"Around back," he wheezed as she pounded on the panels. "Go 'round . . ."

She took off again, jumping through some short-stack bushes, and the idea that she might find some bad news in the rear was a shot of terror that got his leg up-and-over the seat. As he stumbled after her, he couldn't feel the asphalt under his boots, and in the recesses of his mind, he knew he was out of energy. It was not because he was tired in the conventional sense. The shit he had going on was nothing that good sleep hygiene or a nap would do anything about.

"Why don't I have a gun," he muttered as he shambled his way down the side of the single-car garage, batting away the gnat-like flakes. "Why am I unarmed . . ."

At the far corner, he answered himself: "Because you were about to pop the question. And who brings a— wait for me! Christ!"

Lydia was already at the back sliding glass door and in the process of opening things. "The slider is un-locked—"

No shit. "Hold on."

He grabbed the railing and hauled himself up onto the shallow porch. He wanted to stop to breathe, but he knew her halt had a timer on it—

Bingo. She launched herself into the condo without him.

"Sonofa*bitch*."

On his own entry, Daniel caught the tip of his boot on the lip of the slider, and as he pitched forward, he got a quick impression of an anonymous, middle-of-the-road kitchen: clutter on the granite counter, generic GE appliances, one chair, one small IKEA-ish table.

He caught himself on the four-top, and the thing screeched over the tiled floor, his forward momentum transferring to the inanimate object and making it live for a good yard or so. After the bumpy little ride, he stayed where he was, draped as a human doily, gasping through his open mouth. Out in the front of the condo, Lydia was moving from room to room, and he pictured her, so coordinated, so strong, bouncing on the balls of her feet as she went around.

God, he loved her. With everything that he was, all that he had . . . and what time he had left.

"He's not here," she said off in the distance. "But oh, God, there's blood on the carpet, where all this mail is . . . I'm going to go check upstairs."

He opened his mouth to throw another wait-stop-slow-down onto the bonfire of good advice she was ignoring. But she was already halfway to the second floor.

With the drumbeat of her footfalls ascending, he followed her example, pushing his chest up. Getting to the full vertical was a process, and to give himself something to focus on other than how dizzy he was, he assessed the empty take-out containers and packets of sauce on the counter, the bin that was overflowing with crumpled restaurant bags, the empty Coke cans that were everywhere.

As if Gus St. Claire had a breeding program for the damn things.

It was normal living chaos, not ransacked shit.

He looked out toward the living room. On the far side of the counter's drop-off, he measured the no-furniture and the big-screen TV over the electric fireplace and the closed blinds across a bay window—

Frowning, he motored around the partition. A wedge of paperwork was on the carpet, fanned out around its staple, as if it had been dropped or thrown.

And he would have ignored whatever it was except for the fact that he recognized one of the signatures on the page with all the notary stuff.

His own.

While Lydia strode through the upper level, he pushed a Pizza Hut box out of the way, locked a hold on the counter's lip, and lowered himself to his knees. His hand was shaking, and he made a mess of the pickup, papers flip-flopping, flapping, justifying their need for that staple.

As he started to go through the document, he had to go back and try again. Because surely this wasn't what it looked like.

"What the *fuck* . . ." His eyes continued to sift through the words, the operant meaning stunning him. "Well, there ya go."

Was this what Gus had been abducted for?

As if the condo itself could answer that question, he limped out into the front of the mostly empty space, and yup, Lydia was right. In the midst of a messy pile of unopened mail below the slot in the door, there was a pattern of dig-deeps in the wall-to-wall and some bloodstains that were turning brown.

"He's not here," Lydia announced.

Daniel was careful as he pivoted around. Halfway down the stairs she finally stalled out, her eyes wide, her cheeks windburned and bright red against a base of pasty white panic, her blond-streaked dark hair blown straight from the no-helmets ride in. With her gray trail pants and her black turtleneck and heavy fleece, she was wearing what he thought of as her uniform, yet she might as well have been in a wedding gown: For a split second, silhouetted on that staircase, she was all he could see, all he could think about—even with the urgency of what certainly appeared to be a kidnapping at best, a beatdown-and-disappear-forever at worst.

Everybody probably thought their love was a mysterious gift from the universe from time to time. In Daniel's case, his was that a hundred thousand times over.

A wolven. A beautiful, shocking, evolutionary miracle, who could appear as human as anybody else, but was oh-so-much more.

"Are you okay?" she asked in a voice that was as weak as he felt.

Remember this moment, he told himself. *Imprint this and store it with the hoard.*

At the end, when things got really bad and he was just a flicker of consciousness trapped inside the husk of his body, he was going to need images like this.

"Daniel . . . ?"

I love you, he thought at her.

During the frantic ride in, with all his focus on getting them here and gathering information, he'd slipped back into the operative he'd once been—and the return to his old self had landed him in such a familiar place that amnesia had wiped out reality. Everything was back now, though, from the rolling nausea to the god-awful wobble that dogged him . . . to the goodbye that was coming for them, sure as if they were stalked in the shadows, his killer closing in.

Fuck it, his killer was already here, inside of him.

He put up his hand as more alarm hit her face. "I'm fine."

Liar. And yet it was a truth. He was no worse off than he had been, and when you were in his situation, no change was the new getting-better.

"What do we do?" she asked.

For a brief moment, a flare of intention reignited his body, purpose and sharp thinking tingling through him. But the energy didn't last, nothing more than a pilot light that flared and faded—

The sound of a vehicle screeching to a halt brought both their heads to the front door, and through a part in the blinds, the blacked-out Suburban gave the impression that a presidential detail had rolled up.

He looked back at Lydia and waved the document. "You're never going to believe what—"

That was as far as he got. The blackout came with no warning. One moment, he was up on his granted-they-were-loose legs. The next, the carpet was coming at him like a rugby player who felt its welcome-mat momma had been insulted.

The last thing Daniel was aware of was the graceful

wings of the paperwork as the legal pages that transferred ownership of a billion-dollar pharmaceutical compound fluttered to the floor ahead of him.

Goddamn it, he needed Gus more than ever right now.

And someone had gone and killed his fucking cancer doctor.

♦ ♦ ♦

Lydia Susi knew that Daniel was going down a split second before the collapse happened. Over the last few months, she'd developed a sixth sense about it—or maybe the change in his scent was the tip-off, her super-sensitive nose a barometer for the subtle shifts in his hormones.

With a lunge and a swing of her legs, she vaulted over the half-wall balustrade of the staircase and rushed for him. She didn't make it in time. Gravity was quicker than she was, and Daniel's fragile body landed in a heap on the carpet, his arms flopping when he didn't even try to brace himself against the impact, his head bouncing in an alarming way thanks to the face-first.

As she threw herself down beside him, the tile in the kitchen registered out of the corner of her eye. At least he hadn't been in there when he'd passed out.

"Daniel," she said hoarsely. "*Daniel . . .*"

With gentle hands, she rolled him over, and the way his head lolled to the side made her send up a plea to her dead grandfather. But like that ghost who showed up from time to time but never said a damn thing could help?

Why hadn't she thought more about Daniel on the

ride over here? She should have known that he didn't have the strength for that trip, much less for what was waiting for them here at this . . . crime scene.

Cursing her all-too-familiar panic, she tried to calm down. "We need Gus—"

Except there was no Gus. Anywhere. That was why they'd come here to his home.

With a fresh stab of horror, she tried to imagine going back to the underground lab and turning Daniel's care over to one of the other clinicians. Like that white coat who had given her the latest round of bad-result PET scans like he was reading stereo instructions.

"Daniel, can you hear me?"

Waiting for a response, she pictured the love of her life as she had first seen him, coming into her office at the Wolf Study Project, knocking her off her feet even though she'd been sitting down. Candy, the receptionist, had given her a heads-up, but she hadn't been prepared. Daniel's face had barged into her brain before his features had even registered, and from across the room, the sheer size of him, his big shoulders, his strong legs, his muscled arms, had made her aware of her own body in ways that should have gotten her written up for an HR violation.

"Daniel?"

Six months later, he was a fragile echo of that man. He was down fifty pounds, maybe sixty. His hair was nothing but a shadow of new growth on his bald skull. His skin was sallow, and his eyes, which were an unfocused half-mast at the moment, had sunk into his cheekbones.

"Daniel—"

The door in from the garage flew open, and the woman who burst into the kitchen was another past-present compare-and-contrast. C.P. Phalen, the corporate battle-ax, as Daniel called her, had downshifted from her black suits, stilettos, and precisely waved cap of blond hair to sweatpants, sneakers, and a flyaway pinned down by a cheap barrette.

Oh, and Gus St. Claire's favorite fleece.

The woman hadn't taken it off since . . . well, whenever she'd put it on.

"Oh, shit," C.P.—or Cathy, as she was going by now, not that Lydia could get used to it—said. "I'll call Gus—"

The intention was stopped short, and as those blue eyes shot out to the bloodstains on the carpet, Lydia nodded.

"He's not here. I've checked the house."

C.P.'s face tightened into a mask as she took out her phone. "I'll call Lipsitz. He's the number two at the lab."

Men in black uniforms without any state, local, or military insignia strode in from the garage. With guns in their hands and hard eyes scanning the condo, they wasted no time fanning out and going through the rooms. Lydia wasn't going to bother informing the private guards that she'd already looked around. They wouldn't take her word for it.

And Daniel was her primary concern. "I need help getting him back—we came on the bike—"

"We'll put him in the Suburban—"

"I'm *not* leaving my Harley."

Both of them looked down at Daniel. His lids were

more open, but nothing much else had improved. His body was still in an awkward tangle and he didn't seem to have the energy to straighten himself out of the crumple he'd landed in.

"We're not going to worry about that." Lydia smoothed what little hair he had back. It was so fine and sparse, it was like that of a newborn. "Let's take care of you."

As C.P. started barking orders into her phone—proving that the exterior wardrobe changes hadn't shifted the nature of the inner core—Daniel tried to sit up, and he fought the help that was offered, pushing aside Lydia's hands. When he successfully braced his upper body against his palms and took some deep breaths, Lydia sat back and tried not to stare at him like she was searching for evidence that he was about to die. Right in front of her. With there being nothing she could do to stop it.

A familiar helplessness settled on her shoulders like a pair of heavy claws, the crushing sense of inevitability causing her to collapse on the inside.

"I'm not leaving that bike," he repeated with exhaustion.

"We have other problems—"

"Well, *I* have that problem. And it's going to be solved before I go anywhere."

His voice was sharp, and she opened her mouth to argue. Then she shook her head. He didn't have the strength for a heated exchange, and frankly, neither did she.

"We'll come back for it."

"No." He swallowed like he was trying not to throw up. "I want you to take it back. They can load me into the SUV like luggage. You'll be on my bike. That's how it's going to go."

Who gives a shit about the Harley, she thought. But then she put herself in his position. When easy options were impossible, you thought in different ways. You put out demands because you had no choice about so much in your life. You dug your heels in on things that felt arbitrary and insignificant to other people because that's all you had.

"All right."

"They're waiting for us back at the lab." C.P. hung up. "Let's get you moving. My men will process this scene—"

"What the hell did you do to him," Daniel cut in.

The other woman's eyes narrowed. "Excuse me."

"You gave him Vita-12b." Daniel pulled over the paperwork he'd been holding and had dropped. As he lifted up the pages, they shook as if they were in a breeze. "That's what I signed in your office. You gave him the rights to the compound and you made him a target. What the fuck, Phalen."

A bored filter came down over the woman's features. "Can you stand? Or are we carrying you out of here—"

"You put him in the crosshairs. You live with an entire platoon of those rent-a-guns—and you give Gus the drug that necessitates all that security with no thought for his safety."

"Okay, we're moving you." C.P. motioned at the men

who were coming down the stairs. "Pick him up and put him in my car. He's going back—"

"Fuck off."

Daniel grunted and heaved himself up to his feet. As he weaved, he reached out and Lydia steadied him by instinct. Realizing what she'd done, she braced herself for pushback from him—and as none came, she started to really worry about how bad he was feeling.

"It's all going to be okay," she said roughly.

Who was she talking to, she wondered. Or rather . . . who was she lying to?

As they went toward the garage door, he did lean on her strength, but his back was straight and he seemed determined to go out on his own two feet. He hadn't been using his cane for the last week, his immuno-therapy's side effects winding down after it had been stopped because it hadn't worked against his disease.

It was nice to see something, anything, improve with him.

See, this was the problem with smoking, she thought for the thousandth time. Some people got away with it—and some did not. And you didn't know which group you were in until it was too late. Meanwhile, his terminal cancer was a detonated bomb in her own life, laying ruin to her present and her future, but also taking her past, the beautiful memories from the spring they'd shared buried in a toxic swill of more recent flashbacks featuring crash carts, and treatments that hadn't worked, and scans that had spelled out more and more bad news.

"Here, let me get the—"

"No, I'll get the door," Daniel said firmly.

She stopped and waited for him to slowly move ahead of her, open things, and hold the panel wide. Standing there, off to the side, his eyes were down on the tile, his dignity ravaged by the physical infirmities that had robbed him of so much.

"Thank you," she whispered as she passed by him.

Emerging into the garage, she glanced at Gus's Tesla and thought of the gas-guzzling Harley—and then remembered being in the apple orchard just before the breakneck trip here in search of the doctor who had been trying to save Daniel's life.

In that moment in and among the rows of gnarled, charming trees, she had felt, as her one true love looked into her eyes, that they had briefly stepped away from the cancer grind and been what they had been before.

Two people without a terminal disease.

But like all vacations, you had to return to your real life. Even if it was a nightmare.

"Can you make it to the SUV," she asked softly as she looked out the open panels and measured the distance to the vehicles parked outside in the drive and on the street.

"Yes," he answered roughly. "I can."

Lydia took a deep breath and straightened her shoulders. "Let's go, then . . ."